C000089249

Peter Preston

PENGUIN BOOKS

PENGUIN BOOKS

Published by the Penguin Group
Penguin Books Ltd, 27 Wrights Lane, London W8 5TZ, England
Penguin Putnam Inc., 375 Hudson Street, New York, New York 10014, USA
Penguin Books Australia Ltd, Ringwood, Victoria, Australia
Penguin Books Canada Ltd, 10 Alcorn Avenue, Toronto, Ontario, Canada M4V 3B2
Penguin Books (NZ) Ltd, Private Bag 102902, NSMC, Auckland, New Zealand

Penguin Books Ltd, Registered Offices: Harmondsworth, Middlesex, England

First published by Viking 1999
Published in Penguin Books 2000
1 3 5 7 9 10 8 6 4 2

Copyright © Peter Preston, 1999
All rights reserved

The moral right of the author has been asserted

Set in 11/13 pt Monotype Sabon
Typeset by Rowland Phototypesetting Ltd, Bury St Edmunds, Suffolk
Printed in England by Clays Ltd, St Ives plc

Except in the United States of America, this book is sold subject
to the condition that it shall not, by way of trade or otherwise, be lent,
re-sold, hired out, or otherwise circulated without the publisher's
prior consent in any form of binding or cover other than that in
which it is published and without a similar condition including this
condition being imposed on the subsequent purchaser

For Ben, Rupert, Kate and Alex

I am the daughter of Earth and Water,
And the nursling of the Sky;
I pass through the pores of the ocean and shores;
I change, but I cannot die.
For after the rain when with never a stain
The pavilion of Heaven is bare,
And the winds and the sunbeams with their convex gleams
Build up the blue dome of the air,
I silently laugh at my own cenotaph,
And out of the caverns of rain,
Like a child from the womb, like a ghost from the tomb,
I arise and unbuild it again.

Shelley, *The Daemon of the World*

Chapter One

Every night, on his travels, he would write to her. Occasionally, if time pressed, there could be only a few sentences on the tiny computer he kept in his breast pocket: no more than a reassurance that he was still there, somewhere at the ends of the earth. But at heart he hated the bleeps and flashes and the stumbles of his thick fingers on the keys. The screen in the corner of her room rang a hollow, imperious bell when such messages arrived – just as, long ago, the bell in the servants' quarters at Balmoral had sounded when his great-great-grandmother demanded tea with lemon, or something rather stronger. There was no warmth to such communication. Upstairs: downstairs. Love, as in 'I'd love a gin and tonic.'

Instead he kept a pad of cream vellum in the old leather briefcase his equerry carried. He would ask for a desk and sit there for a few moments, adjusting the light and fiddling with his gold fountain pen, practising to make sure that the ink flowed smoothly from the nib. Then the words would come as he wanted them. 'Dear Lilibet . . .'

He knew she hated the name. 'It's just wet nursery stuff,' she'd say. 'But I'm grown up now. I don't care about what your great-great-grandpa used to call great-grandma. They were them a long time ago. I'm me, now.'

He would shrug and take no notice. It was too late to change. He had been writing the Lilibet letters for thirteen years, ever since she had first learned to read. Usually three pages in his jagged hand, dried with the curved Moroccan blotter before they were fed into the fax; and always, after transmission, folded into the parcel of originals that he would post on to her so that they could be tied, year by year, with red ribbon and stored in the tea chest by her bed.

'Why do you do it?' she'd asked him last summer at the school open day, as they had stretched on the bank of long grass at the end of the hockey pitch and eaten potato crisps from a big yellow bag. 'I mean, I love it. It makes me feel remembered. But it's also a bit strange. I know the other girls laugh at me when I dash out of play rehearsals to check the fax. They think I'm running some kind of dodgy business. One third-former came up to me last week in the gym and asked if she could buy a couple of joints.'

He smiled and then grimaced. 'Honestly,' he said, 'I don't quite know. It just seemed natural when I started. There I was, flying around, taking salutes on every parade ground under the sun, never in one spot for more than five minutes. And there were you two kids when your mother walked out, my little girl and little boy lost and hurried off to boarding school. Out of sight, out of mind. It was all too much like when I was growing up. My brother and I weren't human beings, we were royal objects. We were the parcels

Mum and Dad passed between them. This way, at least, you know where I am every day; and you know I think about you and Nicholas and that I care what you're doing. Sorry, does that sound soppy?'

She'd squeezed his hand and brushed the hair back from her eyes. They had watered for a moment. 'No, not at all. Maybe Nicky doesn't like it much. He's such a spotty idiot at the moment. But it sounds just fine to me. Have some more crisps before I change for the match. It's three sets, so tea may be a little late this year.'

Dear Lilibet,
They tell me it's cold and wet in Sussex. Poor you!
I'm sitting on the 24th Floor of the Park Tower in
Rio, watching the sun go down. There are brown
girls in unbelievable scraps of costumes coming out
of the sea for the last time today, shaking their hair
and everything else dry; and men in raggedy shorts
selling coconuts along the promenade. When I open
the window, you can hear the sound of drums and
saxophones. Good evening Ipanema. It feels like
carnival every day.

In a few minutes, I think, it will be totally dark.
The sun is vanishing like one of those golden balls
that float when conjurors cover them with a cloth.
Sugar Loaf is etched against the sky and there's a
warm blackness spreading, where the lights from
the hotels and clubs seem to sparkle more brightly.
I've bought myself a disgusting flower shirt from the
lobby shop and a straw hat wide enough to pull
over my face. Can I get a couple of hours out on the

town without the photo hounds by the front door picking up the scent? We shall see. Or rather, you'll see, my love, when you open your paper.

Don't be too jealous, though. This is still the tour from hell. Brother King is confined to barracks on the 25th Floor with some Curse of the Amazon he picked up at the Belem chamber of commerce dinner, and the Viking Queen is staging all her usual strops. Why is the air conditioning too hot or too cold? Who says the ice cubes are safe? Why can't the Little Emperor have fish fingers and beans?

Our Foreign Secretary has gone AWOL again, predictably enough. Locked himself in with a couple of secretaries and enough red boxes to last the night. Affairs of State! The final refuge of politicians who've fouled up. I mean, anyone with their head screwed on could see that carting the entire Royal caravan round Brazil for a week in the sacred name of Commerce wasn't the brightest FCO notion of the century.

'We didn't realize what a big country it was, sir,' they said when they called me. 'We think we've scheduled too much and we'd be awfully grateful if you could fly down and, you know, share the burden a bit.' So I drew a sardine-canning factory in Porto Alegre and a fashion show in São Paulo before lunch while the Top Crowns were getting the squits up north. And tomorrow, after a delightful working breakfast with the Minister for Industry, plus a mandatory flip round the Palace museum in Petropolis, we've got to be in Salvador for tea with the engineering employers' federation.

*Solid grind, my love: though they say I can zip
back to Guyana by myself at the end of the week
and maybe mix a spot of fishing with the usual
base-inspection stuff.*

*Anyway, that's business and pleasure pending –
and you'll want to get on with your revision. I can't
say how proud of you I am. Oxford in the autumn
(cross fingers!) and you've done it for yourself
because you're bloody bright, not just plodders like
the rest of us. I don't know where you get it from.
Not your darling mother, for sure. And it can't be
from me, second-hand Dukey doing second-tier
jobs. But I light a candle every time I think of you.*

Muchest love,
Your devoted D.

She had sat up too late the night before, hunched over
her history notes and drinking mugs of coffee as she
tried to get the dates and names straight in her head.
There was bound to be a question about prime ministers and their chancellors. It came up every three years
on average, and this was year three. Mrs Bowler had
been as positive as ever. 'Of course we can't be certain
sure – but there are themes, strong strands of interest,
which are always resonant. If I were you, I'd make
sure that I was specially up on Macmillan and Selwyn
Lloyd, and Major and Lamont, and Blair and Brown.'

But was that enough? What about Brown and Balls?
She could do the fault lines and the structural bits.
But that was no use if you mixed the details wrong.
Somehow everything was getting too close and too
oppressive. She needed air.

It was a morning of free periods. Indeed, nobody kept much track of them in the last couple of weeks before the exams. They were eighteen, for heaven's sake. Old enough to be married with kids and curlers in their hair, trooping down to the launderette. Too old to be models or swimmers in their dreams. In three months, they'd be far away at universities around the world, with nobody to raise an eyebrow over drugs or sex, or even a cigarette end thrown through an open study window.

The rain had cleared. There was a shimmer of heat to come behind the thinning clouds.

She walked along the cliffs at Rottingdean and looked down to the expanse of Brighton Marina, already beginning to bustle as summer arrived. Doctors sprucing their boats for the weekends away from persistent patients, pausing to answer mobile phones between strokes of paint; estate agents hauling crates of cheap Spanish bubbly aboard their motor yachts for the client cruises yet to come.

No one turned to look at her as she strode right along the cliff path, then down towards Brighton. She was an ordinary girl in a raincoat with a sensible maroon sweater and a sensible charcoal skirt. Her hair needed washing, she knew. One of the many things there wasn't time for last night. So it was pulled back in a tight band, a greasy tug of blonde which left her ears exposed: less obtrusive now than before the plastic surgery her father had insisted on, but still large, still dominant.

She was tall, with wide shoulders which helped to diminish the bosom – the sodding family bosom – but she did not move in the family's way. She was not stiff or tense. She was loose, with an easy, athletic grace. She loved tennis and cricket. She had opened the bowling now for two seasons in the Roedean first eleven. The best action of anyone for the last ten years, they said: real nip off the pitch. Her eyes were green, and sometimes almost seemed gold in the glare of the sun. Her skin was pale, translucent, needing a touch of blood in the cheeks. Her nose, she thought when she looked in the mirror, was too – how would they put it? – too assertive. Hooked, a trifle imperious: a Spencer nose, not the knobbly ski-lift of the Windsor women. She did not think of herself as beautiful.

In twenty minutes she was walking The Lanes, looking in antique dealers' windows, sifting through the tourist bric-à-brac, pausing to watch the coach parties of Japanese chatter their way through the narrow streets and to smile a secret smile. She was lost in her own world.

The postman emptying the box on the sea front felt a twinge in his back and stretched upright for a moment just as the girl in the mac wandered by. 'Good morning,' he said automatically. 'Yes,' she said; and her eyes caught his.

It was an effort to bend back to the open box of packets and brown envelopes. They were wonderful eyes: frank, clear, piercing. And something else. He tied up the neck of the sack. Something memorable. Deep, humorous; with an intelligence which unsettled him and made him turn – haplessly, without choice – to watch her walk away.

*

7

'I am not travelling in this plane,' said the Queen. 'It is so old and so disgusting.'

Her jaw, always too square, always heavy with imminent fury, had swelled to an ominous jut, so that her whole face seemed to balance precariously on her thin neck. One more indignity and it would fall of its own volition to the tarmac.

She had never been, nor could ever be, remotely pretty. But she was the available third daughter of the Danish King; and His Majesty's advisers had never doubted what must be done. 'No more commoners, Sir,' they'd said. 'No more horsey girls or simpering virgins from broken homes. No more actresses or television weather presenters. You are royal in a Europe where royalty still means something and there are a few royal princesses who know about duty. You have played on the machines in the gymnasium of life, probably for too long. Now there has to be an alliance and an heir: and this marriage is serious. It cannot afford to fail. Indeed, failure must not be countenanced. We have searched most widely and, we believe, found someone suitable. You may or may not grow to love her. Who can say? If not, then there will always be other pursuits to be followed discreetly. But she is necessary, Sir. This alliance is necessary.'

They had not, of course, mentioned her scrawny buttocks or her dark, contracted eyebrows; they had not mentioned her sour breath or temper.

'See,' she said, bending forward and pointing. 'The seats are filthy and the carpet is old and frayed, and it smells of tobacco. How can a King travel in such squalor? How can a young Prince with a delicate stomach endure such an ordeal?'

The King, as usual, had moved a few yards downwind and, hands clasped behind back, appeared deep in meditation. Do not disturb; do not embroil or consult or appeal to. The little Prince stood by his mother's side, grinning more broadly as her anger grew and giggling with each explosion. No wonder the tabloids were calling him Hamlet already. The Foreign Secretary hugged a red box to his chest as though in protection. The equerries and ladies-in-waiting stood in a defensive ring like the wagons of a train camped for the night.

'Look, Ma'am,' said Emery, bag carrier extraordinary, white-faced beneath the livid insect bite on his forehead. 'Look, we know this is less than ideal and we apologize as profusely as we can. But there are circumstances here . . .' He hesitated. Ah, circumstances! 'You were due to travel everywhere by scheduled Varig services. It is what the taxpayer demands these days. But we had not been told that there are no first-class sections on some of their flights – to Salvador, for instance. And the taxpayer would not, I'm sure, want to see such a distinguished party crammed into economy cabins with Indians and mulattos and their plastic packages and parrots in cages. That would be an economy too far.

'We're all very grateful that the Duke managed to intervene with the MoD and get the Governor's Boeing flown up from the Falklands. I know it isn't exactly palatial and it breaks all the old protocol rules. We specifically asked for two 777s, but one's stuck in the

Azores – and London were at their wits' end. Even their emergency budget's bust, and the Expenditure Committee are going up the wall. But please, Ma'am, the flight is only ninety minutes and Captain Cox and his crew will do everything to make you comfortable.'

Her lips set into a thin slit of discontent. Emery swung round in desperation, searching for an ally. The Duke was wearing his RAF uniform, the full Squadron Leader kit. A smear of higher authority.

'Isn't that right, Sir?' Emery implored.

'I believe so,' said the superior officer reluctantly. 'I think we must all make do. Christina, please be so good as to fasten your safety belt. Make sure that the Prince has a paper bag ready. We can't spend the afternoon arguing on a runway in Rio. The press in the terminal will be getting curious. And our engineer hosts are waiting. They will not understand a spanner in the works.'

'That was awfully well done, Sir, if I might be so bold.'

Cox had a puppyish air to him, eager, youthful, wide-eyed.

The Duke shut the flying deck behind him with a firm swing, as though in protection. 'I wouldn't say that. But she can be a bit fierce when roused.'

'Would you like a turn at the controls, Sir?' asked the puppy. 'Flight Lieutenant Crabb here is pretty flaked out. He'd only just got back from Northolt with the Governor when the call came. And it would be a real honour to sit beside an officer of your distinction.'

The young man was trying too hard, he thought. Still, it wasn't a bad idea. Anything to avoid sitting back there with the cowed and the baleful. 'Thank you, Captain. That's a kind notion.'

They were taking the Atlantic route north, heading a score or so miles off the coast, then hugging its outline past Campos and Vitória and Belmonte. There was a light breeze from the east which had cleared the clouds from the sea so that, far below, it glistened and danced. He saw a tuna fleet set in relentless hunt; an oil tanker lumbering south towards Florianopólis; a white cruise liner steaming east with a swimming pool cut into its deck so that, at first glance, there seemed to be a giant blue hole in its heart.

'Coming up to Salvador now, Sir,' said Cox.

It was a sight to remember: a flurry of islands and bold green hummocks rearing out of the water, and then a rocky stretch of coast flanking great bays and wide beaches, with valleys of skyscrapers running back, like veins, up the hillsides.

'Nice-looking spot,' said the Duke.

'Oh rather, Sir. Absolutely. Though they say the low cloud has banked up a bit at the airport.'

'Landing on Automatic?'

'Don't think so, Sir, if that's all right. Crabb said it came down a touch heavy in Stanley. May need a bit of fine tuning. I don't want to give the ladies more of a bump than necessary.'

They swung left in a wide arc and began the final descent. 'Seatbelts please,' said Cox. 'Crew, five minutes to landing.'

The wind was stiffer than they'd been told, piling

cloud against the mountain range, hiding the single stretch of black runway and the acres of red earth where another was being built. They were coming in low, roaring over the palm trees and the fields of sugar cane and the desolate townships of shanties and open drains. He could see the faces of children raised upwards.

'I'll take it,' said the Duke suddenly. 'This looks like an easy one.'

Air traffic was burbling away in a thick Portuguese accent, harsh and rising shrilly. 'Airport. Airport.'

'I know it's the bloody airport. What else do you think it is?'

'No, Sir,' Cox cried. 'Not Airport. Abort. ABORT.'

There was a damned little Piper Cheyenne coming in due west, touching down on the earth track and heading slap in front of them. Fucking amateur, the Duke thought. Some bloody playboy taking a spin and zonked out of his brain on coke.

'Climb, Sir, CLIMB.'

The door swung open and he could hear the Queen shouting at the Foreign Secretary. 'So rough. Intolerable. I shall complain to the Prime Minister.'

But the Piper had climbed too and now it clipped the Boeing's starboard wing, spinning it almost lazily on to one side as it hit the runway. The explosion and the burst of fire came five seconds later. On the beach, the brown girls in bikinis clutched their towels and turned, eyes wide, to watch the smoke billowing into the sky.

*

She was lying on her bed in a track suit re-reading Nigel Lawson's biography, marking the paragraphs that mattered with a blue pencil. Could a Chancellor pursue a policy irrespective of a Prime Minister's wishes? Only if she didn't know he was doing it. But surely that wasn't possible, at least for more than a few months? There was a shuffle and a knock on the door.

'Come in if you've brought a bottle. It's open.'

Christ, it wasn't Emma or Caroline. It was Mrs Granger and she looked impossibly grim.

'Gosh,' the girl said, sitting upright, then scrambling to attention. 'I'm very sorry. I was only joking, Mrs Granger.'

Still utter grimness. The headmistress's face was somehow rigid and her arms were clasped across her stomach. 'No, it's I who am sorry, my dear. And there is no easy way to say it. I've just had a call from the Palace. They can't be quite certain yet. There is awful confusion. But they think the plane your father was travelling in crashed a couple of hours ago at Salvador airport, and they think there are no survivors. Not the King or the Queen or the little Prince. Not your father. They've tried for a temporary news black-out, but they do not expect it to hold. I can't tell you how shocked we all are.'

She moved towards the bed and, awkwardly, put an arm round the girl's shoulders. 'Would you like to phone your mother?'

The girl pulled herself straight. 'It's not worth it,' she said, the words careful and clipped. 'She's on some yacht somewhere off Antibes. She didn't leave a number. She'll find out long before we could reach her. And then I suppose she will phone me if she wants.'

She stood up and turned to look at the Head. Her face was set, her eyes dry. 'Do you know if they're telling my brother?'

'No. They didn't say and I'm sorry, I forgot to ask.'

'I'll call him myself,' the girl said. 'He's at such an awful school they'll be sure to make a muck of it.'

The office at the south-east corner of the Palace was long and low and panelled in a light walnut from the Dordogne. He had ordered it on the spot at the Riberac timber merchants who'd refitted the library at the Château Coumin when his friends, the Foxley-Woods, bought it. No mahogany; no heavy flock; and absolutely none of that plaster and gilt crap left over from Edward VII's Café Royal phase. The carpet was beige and lushly piled to put a spring in his step. The desk – a banana-shaped swirl of matching walnut – had won a Design Centre award five years ago. A single picture hung to the right of his chair, a pleasant enough Canaletto of St Mark's Square he had recently intercepted on the way back from the restorers. He wasn't sure about the gold frame – too obtrusively ornate, perhaps? – but the vividness of the blues gave the room an infusion of colour which his visitors always praised. 'Ancient and modern, Sir Edgar. Such a refreshing contrast.' He was a man of taste.

Edgar Peniston Rowley Fountain, Chief Executive of the Royal Household, welcomed such admiration. He deserved it, he felt, because he had earned it. The last two CEOs, frankly, had been handed the job on a silver platter. They'd been insiders, bit players on the Windsor circuit by marriage, tumbled out of convenient merchant banks after the usual 'soundings' and plonked on the edifice like icing on a wedding cake. But Fountain broke that mould. His father, it was true, had been Lord Lieutenant of Northamptonshire, but only in the last years of his life when the first Blair reforms had tried to spread such appointments amongst what were called 'the ordinary people who are the lifeblood of Britain'. Basically, Dad had made bathroom fittings: top-of-the-range taps and toilet seats. The young Fountain had been to Rugby and Trinity Hall, Cambridge, and Harvard Business School. Decent enough staging posts in their way, but hardly inner circle. He didn't talk much about his twelve years in Shanghai and Harare running British American Tobacco's cigarette distribution networks there. Low tar and lower prestige. He encouraged only cautious remembrance of his term as Administrative Director at the South Bank Centre. Committees under his chairmanship had warned repeatedly of the dangers of flood damage unless Government – or 'those responsible', as he'd said in that unfortunate TV interview on Waterloo Bridge – provided adequate funds. It was not his fault. Nevertheless, he had been distinctly amazed when the ad in the *Sunday Times* – 'Old established family company seeks Senior Exec for Ambitious Modernization Programme' – had turned out to be a front for Whitehall headhunters on the Windsor prowl. 'Must have good grounding in management control systems.'

And he had, hadn't he? Could anyone complain about the profit record of Regal Enterprises 2000 (Malibu) Inc., or the cash flow from Amalgamated Crown Properties plc, or the European sales figures for Saxe-Coburg Franchise Developments SA, or the prospects for the Diadem Experience Hotel and Theme Parks Division? His Clinton Lecture at Harvard last year on Resource Maximization had been specifically praised in the *Wall Street Journal* – 'an object lesson in family corporation expansion without direct family involvement from the new business king at the court of olde England'.

Fountain had been preparing a second address on Royal Risk Management for Yale next semester. But some risks were beyond management. He licked his wet lips. He wiped a distraught hand through the crinkles of white hair which paraded back from his forehead. His head was throbbing and he could hear the constant ringing of phones at his secretary's desk outside. God rot it, the family had fucked up again – as they always did. Killed themselves off this time and left him to pick up the pieces, as usual. He flicked the switch on the intercom.

'Get Chetwode-Belcher to call me the minute he's made contact,' Fountain said.

Emma brought the bottle and Caroline the corkscrew. They sat with her for an hour, chatting and hugging and crying in turns. She kept staring at the fax, silent on the desk.

'I can't take it in. I just can't believe it.'

There was another shuffle outside the door. This

time there was a young man in a grey suit beside the headmistress: pink cheeks, brown hair scraped back across a curiously flat head, a pimple of a nose. He did not seem to know where to put his hands. Behind him in the corridor, two more men in suits shuffled in the shadows.

'I apologize for intruding,' said the man in grey. 'We have never met, I think. I am Captain Rodney Chetwode-Belcher, an equerry here on behalf of Sir Edgar Fountain. The Chief Executive of the Royal Household, of course. This is one of those moments when words seem insufficient – but it is my duty, on behalf of us all in the Household and allied enterprises, to record our deepest sympathy for your loss.'

'Of course,' said Caroline sharply. 'But you're talking to the wrong person. She's over there.'

'No, that's all right,' the girl said, walking towards him, pulling the top of her track suit straight, shaking his hand solemnly. 'I haven't been much on Palace show for years. My father wanted to keep me out of it. "She isn't core royal by the rules," he said. "She'll have to make her own way. Let her live her life."'

Chetwode-Belcher licked his lips nervously. 'I'm terribly afraid that's one more aspect of this tragedy that your father was mistaken about,' he said. 'We all face the most awful series of upheavals. We at the Palace find the situation quite terrifying. Press queries have jammed the switchboard. Sir Edgar has cancelled all holidays indefinitely. Just when I'd got a week in Antigua fixed.'

He seemed, for a second, to be about to stamp his feet. The hand flapped petulantly. Mrs Granger coughed. He paused, cheeks flushed, and screwed his hands into tight balls. 'But, by tradition tonight,' he said, 'before anything else can be decided, I am required to ask you one question. What title would Your Majesty be taking?'

She wiped her swollen eyelids and laughed. It was the only thing to do. 'Why, Elizabeth the Third,' she said. 'What other choice is there? But I hope my friends can still call me Bess.'

Chapter Two

They left for London at seven the next morning, a fleet of deep-maroon cars and police outriders speeding through the crowd of photographers at the school gates and heading towards the A23. She turned for a second to look at the mêlée of cameras; hunched solemn and still on the back seat, a coat draped over her shoulders, its high collar turned up. Her gaze was level. Her pale face seemed to frame her eyes. 'I'll travel alone,' she'd said. Occasionally, when the car was speeding, when no one could see inside, she would turn to the empty seat beside her and seem, for an instant, to see him sitting there, as he had always been when she needed him. Her hand ran across the leather, looking for the touch of his hand.

Heavy showers beat on the windscreen. Dark banks of cloud rolled across the sky. As they slowed in the commuting swell of Purley, a handful of men and women stood silently by the side of the road, umbrellas pushed back as she passed. Suddenly there was a thin cheer. Two schoolgirls in navy coats with heavy brown satchels unwrapped the red scarves from their necks and twirled them in excitement. A policeman at a panda crossing looked round bemusedly then, helmet tipping to one side, gave an incongruous salute.

She found herself leaning forward towards the window. Her eyes were red and her cheeks felt stained and blotchy: but somehow she had to show herself. She found her hand, as though of its own volition, rising limply, moving two inches to the left and then two inches to the right, cautiously acknowledging the existence of the world outside. Is that it? she wondered. My first royal wave.

The crowds in the Mall were denser and, through the hours of waiting, had decided what was expected of them. There were no cheers. Men and women, mostly elderly in shapeless coats, lined the pavement. As the cars approached they took their hats off and stood still, eyes down. A busload of Japanese tourists, clutching little paper Union Jacks and Rising Suns on thin sticks, looked around them, then began stuffing the flags into their pockets. A phalanx of television scanners, camera hoists mustered in leering congress, waited by the Palace gates, scouring a thousand faces. 'There's a great one two up on the right, Harry,' called a BBC producer. 'The old dear in green weeping into her handbag. And then pan to the Chelsea pensioners. No, wait. Stop. They're coming now.'

She drew back into the recesses of the leather and, in a moment, the jaws of the Palace forecourt seemed to swallow her up.

Fountain was standing at the top of the steps. The man young Belcher calls the Chief, she thought. Like me, he can't have slept. There were violet bags under his eyes and he shifted restlessly from foot to foot. But there was also an authority to him. Frock coat, striped trousers, black tie, the full aura of mourning. And he had his lieutenants with him here, two anonymous men in black: one balding, with a sandy moustache; one with a clipped crop of yellow hair and an absence of chin.

'Your Majesty,' he said, and the three swayed forward together from the neck, chins stroking chests, eyes somehow fixed on her sensible school shoes, 'may we offer our deepest condolences? I can only apologize that the pressures here made it impossible to come to you in person last night.'

She felt her bottom lip tremble again. Her shoulders were rounded to hide her bosom as they had been at her first dance with some boys from Lancing three years before. The vast bulk of the Palace walls seemed to tip towards her as Fountain straightened, and she stepped back to steady herself.

'Can I introduce your Majesty to two of my – and now your – closest colleagues? The Honourable Nigel Montgomery, Deputy Chief Executive and Financial Director.' The yellow-top bowed again. 'And Sir Richard Baron, our Director of Public Relations.' Baldy scraped. She thought she remembered his ruddy, plumpening face from the tabloids a couple of years ago. Hadn't he been editor of the *Daily Express* or something? Hadn't there been a bit of row – something about poachers and gamekeepers – when he was appointed?

'It is a pleasure to meet you, gentlemen,' she said. 'I'm obviously in your hands. I shall depend on your advice and counsel.' Somewhere inside her head she could hear a shrill voice screaming. 'You're making this up from the TV,' it said. 'You're just parroting what you think kings and queens are supposed to say – but you don't know anything.' She hesitated, uncertain what to do next.

'Naturally,' said Fountain, 'there are decisions to be taken. We have a list to complete by noon. But I suppose that first Your Majesty will want to pause in your private apartments before the briefings.' He beckoned a slim finger and a fat woman in a dark taffeta suit puffed on to the steps.

'Lady Clementine Cross was one of the Queen's most respected ladies-in-waiting. Unhappily, health problems prevented her taking her place on the Brazilian visit.' Unhappily? Fountain pattered on without pause. 'But, happily, she is fully recovered and I'm sure she'll take good care of you while other arrangements are set in place.'

The fat woman put one leg behind the other with great deliberation and began to subside, teetering on the brink of collapse into a cellulitic heap. Is it a heart attack? Bess thought. Is it a stroke? No: the heels came unsteadily together again. It was a curtsy.

Her jowls were shaking and her untidy white hair had fallen across her face. There was a puffing and a flurry of tidyings and tuttings. 'My dear, my dear girl . . .' she began.

Gosh, thought Bess, she's trying to be motherly: a great beached whale stuck with a role she hasn't played for thirty years. But it reminded her of the question she most needed to ask. 'When is Nicholas coming? I talked to him last night, but he didn't say much. I said I'd see him here today.'

It was Baron who answered. 'Your brother won't be here till this afternoon, Ma'am. Your mother is flying back from France on a chartered aircraft. She will pick him up in Bath and be with you by around three.'

The voice in her head began to squeal again. Mother? What bloody mother? Who asked her? What had that bitch with the curls and the greedy mouth and the pumping thighs got to do with any of this?

'Oh', she said. 'I see.'

'It's only a guest set of rooms, I'm afraid, Ma'am. Ever since they opened the main Palace round the year, we've been awfully short of space. You'd think 690 rooms would be enough, but it's amazing how they get eaten up. And of course nobody's had a second to do anything about the poor King and Queen's apartments yet. We thought, if you wouldn't mind camping for a bit – then we can get you and the rest of your family close together. This is a family time, isn't it?' Fat Clemmy bustled round primping cushions on the green brocade sofa and running her fingers along the edge of the oak dresser as though she feared a sudden dust storm might bring fresh tragedy. Behind her, a slim young man in a black jacket and grey trousers stood languidly to attention, wrists pressed elegantly to his sides. 'Forster, this bed is damp.'

'Oh no, your ladyship!' he lisped. 'Oh no, surely not? I got the sheets fresh from the laundry and made it up myself.'

'Well, get some more and do it again. We can't have Her Majesty catching a cold on her first night, can we?'

Bess's head was beginning to throb. 'Could I please just have a few minutes by myself before the meetings start? Could you please worry about all this . . . all this stuff later?' It was the first time she had spoken inside the Palace. The pair froze at the sound of her and began to move towards the door, shuffling backwards. 'You'll be all right, Ma'am?'

'I shall be quite all right, Lady Clementine. You may call me at eleven.'

The door closed. She could still hear the clatter of their feet on the parquet flooring, fading as the great river of red carpeting swallowed them up. She was not really alone. Perhaps she would never be alone again.

Bess stood at the window for a while, looking east towards Green Park, a spread of trees and tarmac starved of sun. No wonder it was all so chill. They'd chosen to live in permanent shade. She sat on the bed and pulled her knees up under her chin. Forget the sheets; the room itself felt dank and musty. Perhaps no one had opened a window for years. Faded green chair-coverings, thick green wallpaper with a spread of damp in the corner by the sideboard. In a month or two it would begin to peel away. Two pictures in incongruously glistening gold frames hung on either side of the marble fireplace. One watercolour, one oil: both showing a parade of open carriages along some racecourse, presumably Ascot. It felt for all the world like one of those down-at-heel country-house hotels her father had taken her and Nicky to on quiet February weekends long ago, when Selene was still living in The Beeches, refusing to admit that the marriage was over, that she had gone one random fornication too far.

'Oh, Dad,' she said to herself out loud. 'Oh, Dad, you hated all of this. And now see where you have left me?'

At three in the morning, after her tears ran dry, she hunted for the old letter she needed amidst the packets tossed higgledy-piggledy in the canvas games bag from school. Cream vellum: flowing hand.

Dear Lilibet,
Garden party time again! More lawns, more
military bands playing Souza, more asparagus rolls
for ravenous mayoresses – and more rain. I've
shaken 435 hands and made 246 brief attempts at
small talk. Only the loos offer peace. Thank God,
my love, that you're outside this loop; thank God
this is none of your Duty. Duty is a killer, my love.
I remember your great-grandfather, when I was a
boy, patrolling down the endless lines of matrons in
pink-and-white hats, always two steps behind the
Queen, and I remember his face when he turned
into the tea tent. Pure exhaustion, spiritual as well
as physical. Once he'd been a man. You could hear
it when he talked of Germany and Greece and
growing up. He believed he could amount to
something. He had been a sailor, and he could have
been a soldier. But Duty made him a cypher, Duty
made him the Prince of Two Steps Behind, the
Consort of No Account feigning interest and

*happiness when inside you could feel the furies. He
was an Admiral of the Fleet and a Field Marshal
and an Air Marshal and a Captain General of the
Royal Marines: but really no more than Servicer of
the Royal Bedchamber, Retired. Take pity on those
for whom Duty calls, Lilibet. And rejoice that you
will never be one of them.*

She could feel a fresh tear running down her cheek.
She wiped it angrily away.

'Now,' said Fountain as they sat down around the
mahogany table in the Old Library, Bess and the
members of the board, 'we would all wish that there
was some proper break for reflection and adjustment,
but sadly there is no such opportunity. We have no
option but to move on, to remain open for business,
and we think it critical to construct a proper framework for the rest of your day. People understand that
you will need some time to come to terms with events,
Your Majesty. They take your age and inexperience
into account, and I'm certain they recognize your
sorrow. But the Archbishop of Canterbury and the
Prime Minister will both require audiences at an early
juncture to offer their formal condolences – and Baron
is anxious that there should be the briefest of photo-
calls for the press, for you alone before the rest of the
family arrive. Thirty seconds' availability now will
save a deal of difficulty later. Not surprisingly, there
are very few contemporary pictures of you available
in newspaper computers, and your people will wish
to make the acquaintance of their new Queen as

swiftly as possible. I don't need, I'm sure, to tell you how such thoughtful gestures help.'

'On the contrary,' said Bess, 'you really need to tell me everything. Father never talked to me about how this world works. I don't know how it's run or who runs it.'

Fountain permitted himself the thinnest of smiles. 'It is we who run it, Your Majesty – in, we hope, a modern and efficient fashion. You must, with respect, be aware of the changes of the last forty years, of the first Way Forward group and the necessary reform programme which averted the dangers to the Crown at the turn of the century, before your great-grandmother's untimely demise.'

'Yes,' she said, 'my father sometimes talked about that. He called it the Kensington Palace Clearances, all those useless old relatives losing their titles and allowances and moving into the servants' flats while we negotiated mortgages for them. He said it was the beginning of our liberty.'

Fountain frowned and licked his lips, the pink tip of his tongue signalling disapproval. 'Here, Your Majesty, we see it as the beginning of a rolling programme of reform which lies at the heart of the survival of the modern, streamlined regime your people can be expected to accept – and, if I may say so, we treat the subject with the utmost seriousness. As Queen you are now automatically Life President of the Continuing Way Forward group which, under your late uncle, did so much to advance the process of acceptability . . . not merely the completion of limiting the use of titles such as His or Her Royal Highness to the most tightly drawn circle of the Sovereign and immediate heirs, but the joint development of designated palaces and estates with the Kyoto Monarch hotel group, the opening of this great Palace as a permanent year-round attraction, the creation of an accessible business model with satellite income streams. There is so much you will need to master quickly.'

He pressed a button in the arm of his chair and a small screen dropped from the top of the bookcase behind him. One more press and it was covered in hieroglyphics. Almost without thinking she picked up a pencil and pad. Back to school.

Fountain began tracing lines across the screen with a clear plastic ruler. 'You may or may not be familiar with what we call the Blair-2 reform structure – more commonly referred to as the McAusland framework of governance, instituted as a result of that committee's recommendations in 2005.'

'He was Sainsbury's?' she said, feeling foolishly eager to please.

'No, Tesco.' He sucked a wet lip in irritation. 'Sir Gregor McAusland advocated the development of a hierarchy with names your ordinary subjects could relate to. After extensive market research he proposed a light-touch pattern of what we call enhanced comprehensibility. No more Earl Marshals or Masters of the Horse to begin with, then no more Keepers of the Privy Purse – or even Lord Chamberlains. No more private secretaries and the like who were not secretaries at all, but a structure for the Firm which has direct parallels with commercial enterprises outside these walls.'

'The Firm?' she said hesitantly. 'That's what my father always used to call it, but I thought we were just part of government now.'

Why was he screwing his face in irritation? She felt desolate, bereft. And he was snapping at her.

'No, Ma'am,' he said with an immense effort. 'Well, yes and no. There was a brief time, in the third New Labour administration, when the Monarchy was, after a fashion, nationalized. The Secretary of State for Culture, Media and Sport became the Secretary of State for Culture, Media, Sport and Regal Affairs. Your grandfather, in short, became a sort of civil servant. But he insisted on delivering speeches attacking the policies for Culture, the Media and Sport, so it was not deemed a great success. And the management of the finances was frankly shambolic, somewhere between the Royal Opera House and the Football League.

'That led to a form of re-privatization which drew much inspiration from the evolving form of the BBC. The organization itself was secured for the public by what we call a golden share and the Prime Minister of the day became chairman of the board. But the other enterprises under that umbrella of control were deemed break-even-oriented and we have a parliamentary responsibility to "strive for profit" wherever possible. That is why I am Chief Executive Officer. That is why Nigel and Sir Richard can go into any City boardroom and instantly have their functions recognized. We know, of course, that a girl of your tender years cannot be expected to grasp such nuances swiftly – but I trust that you will find the formulations more simple to come to grips with as you gain experience.'

She felt her face freezing. God, he was such a humourless twerp! He lectured as if she'd just walked in from kindergarten. Did he resent her especially? Had she done something wrong? Was he like this with everyone? 'They've really got a handle on Brother King,' her father had said to her a couple of years ago. 'Wild oats are off the menu. The machine has clapped him in irons.' Perhaps that was why Fountain seemed so weary and so oppressive. He'd got control of one set of freaks, and now he had to do it all over again. Her instinct, everything she felt and knew, was to fight back somehow, to show him that she was independent. But that was ridiculous. Her hands were clenched into tight fists. She had lost her father, she was adrift on seas she could not possibly know. 'I need help,' she told herself. 'I need to find my bearings. I have to understand and then think, and then be sure.' The fingers broke from their clench and flexed, seeking freedom.

'Thank you, Sir Edgar,' Bess said quietly. 'I shall try to make you a good pupil.' Out of the corner of her eye, she saw Baron stroke his moustache.

'Darling! My poor darling!'

Bess flinched. She had not seen her mother for six months – not since the Roedean Players had done *The Lark* in the school hall and she had been Saint Joan. Her parents, of course, had come on separate nights. Her father had sat at the back and, after it was over, after the applause had died away, come shyly forward and told her she was a star. Her mother had arrived as the curtain rose and clattered to the front row on teetering heels.

'Darling, you were wonderful.' It was as though, at the end, her mother was the star, clapping noisily in that tight lime suit with the shoulder pads, shouting so that those around looked at her and not at the line of smiling girls on the stage.

Mother. The Duchess of Muck. In repose, she was still beautiful, the face a delicate heart, the bright blonde hair shimmering in the familiar bob. Those old covers of *Tatler* and *Vogue* and *Elle* had not lied. Selene Woodruff deserved her cameras and her contracts. She was innocence and knowingness, ice and warmth, mystery and approachability. Until, that is, she moved and opened her mouth. Then the voice seemed oddly dissonant. It was loud; it boomed in the lower registers and squeaked on the higher notes of excitement. 'Oooh fantastique!' She had picked up a few French words through the Paris seasons with Givenchy, and they dotted the burble of her conversation like pirouettes of cream on some expensive gâteau. 'Oooh merveilleuse! Oooh absolument superbe!' She was the daughter of a Guildford car dealer – Woodruff's for Good Stuff – who had moved, with him, into society after the tenth million was stowed safely in banks across Europe. He bought her ponies, which she rode with fair grace round the Home Counties gymkhanas. She never won, but she always got her picture in the papers – and in the thick, glossy magazines where celebrity and aristocracy mingle. 'The Earl of Hexham and Miss Selene Woodruff enjoying a joke at the Badminton ball.' 'The Right

Hon. Roderick Lascelles and Miss Selene Woodruff together again at Burleigh.' Getting closer. 'Helping hand: the Prince of Wales holds her horse steady as Miss Selene Woodruff mounts Guildford Rover at Gatcombe Park.' She was society now, because she moved in society. The photographers and the couturiers pursued her. She became a staple of the gossip columns – but favouring them with her presence, not clawing her way up through them. Famous, because she already seemed famous.

It was a wonderful trick. Had the young Prince offered her more than a helping hand? Who could tell? There was the tiniest ripple of speculation before HRH moved on to the daughter of a Bolivian tin magnate. But Selene was a natural part of the set by then – a concert or dinner date for his smaller, shyer brother. She was the catch, not him. Nobody mentioned dear daddy's beginnings in the second-hand motor emporiums along the Old Kent Road, or dear mumsy's time as second receptionist at the Posthouse, Croydon. They were deemed irrelevant. She was not Cinderella. And nobody, either, saw fit to mention the stream of men – or to hear the constant banging of the bedroom door.

Bess looked at her as she trotted down the corridor. She wore a black silk dress with a tiny twist of blue velvet around her neck. A little heftier at the hips, more cushioned, more prone to totter on her heels than ever; the face, as she drew nearer, a dense cake of peach and raspberry, an elf drowning in artifice. But of course she could still draw the men she needed: Swiss supermarket tycoons, Romanian counts, Greek bankers. As long as they had money, she had the energy. Oh poor, poor father! She shrivelled him and threw him away. Had he hated her at the end? Worse than that. He had never got her crudities and her flirtations and her rasping laugh out of his system.

Behind her trailed a thin, disconsolate schoolboy in a blazer. Nicky was blotchy and hunched. The spot on the bridge of his nose seemed almost bigger than the nose itself; the little, baleful eyes seemed to shrink into his skull, glowering out of the darkness at the passing show. There was no Windsor and no Spencer to him, nor any trace of the Woodruff bones. Some said quietly that he looked curiously like Rudy Timmins, a British racing driver who'd gone splat at Silverstone fifteen years before – but nobody said it out loud. Nicholas, poor Nicholas, belonged to no one and came from nowhere. He was a runt, and he seemed to know it.

'Darling, are you all right?' Selene embraced Bess and kissed the air a millimetre from her cheeks, the fine bow of pink lipstick puckering away from physical contact, mouthing refined distaste. 'My love, you look so tired. It must have been simply awful for you. Absolument horrible. I mean, what an appalling blow. I just couldn't believe it. Everybody in Antibes was totally stunned. Now, are they looking after you? What can I do?'

Bess had known the question was coming. She had been thinking about it for hours. She did not hate her mother. How could you hate something so pathetic? But she hated what her mother had done to her father – and to her solitary, stammering brother. Were Queens

33

supposed to hate, though? Surely not. They had to be polite: regal, serene, above emotion.

'Of course it's good to see you both,' she said carefully. 'There is so much to plan and so much to get organized. There's the Accession Council tomorrow and the Lying in State, and they want the funeral a week on Friday. I'm sure I'll need a lot of help with that . . .' She paused for a second. 'If, that is, you haven't got to go rushing back to France for something?'

'Good God, no,' said Selene. 'I think I know where my duty lies now. Close to you and Nicky. Perhaps you could tell them to let me use Clarence House.' She reached out and took Bess's right hand, kneading it like a lump of dough. 'After all, I am the Queen's Mother.'

She had not been to church for three years – unless assembly prayers counted, which they didn't really since so many Arabs had started to send their daughters to Roedean. Enlightenment was a properly educated daughter without a veil; but it was also a mullah from Regent's Park standing side by side with the chaplain, taking turns at the incantations. They couldn't be serious. She remembered a few desultory mornings long ago in Sandringham, togged out in a velvet and lytch-buttoned little coat, trailing along to morning service with the Family and pausing at the church gates for the photographers. 'Don't smile,' her father had told her. 'This is religion, not fun.' He wasn't serious.

The Archbishop was a small, rabbity man with lank

strands of grey hair arranged across his pate. His teeth nibbled at the air as he came towards her in a running crouch. 'Your Majesty,' he said, the teeth first expelling the words then retrieving them, gnawing at the vowels like wilted lettuce leaves, 'on behalf of all your people, or at least those who count themselves followers of a Faith, howsoever defined in this liberal age, I bring you our thoughts and our prayers at this dark hour. Insofar as it is possible to stand beside you, metaphorically and spiritually, we are there.'

Bess found her eyes wandering to the left, and pulled them sharply back to the spectre of Archbishop's overbite. 'I appreciate that, Your Grace,' she said. 'That's right, isn't it? Your Grace? I'm afraid this is all very new to me.'

'There is no need to worry, my child,' said the lead incisor, moving ever closer to her neck. 'Your Grace, Archbishop, Robert, Bobby to my friends . . . God has no time for the formalities of life. God speaks for the humanity which blesses us all and tells us that the wilderness is forever peopled by Good Samaritans pausing to lend a hand to the highest and lowest in the land. I may no longer be part of the Established Church, but I am still the vicar of tradition for you and your family, and indeed Chairperson of the Inter-Faith Council. I want you to feel that you have a friend in me, Ma'am, a shepherd through the rocky terrain ahead.'

She found herself edging backwards as he advanced. His breath, whistling through the teeth, had a smell of mulligatawny which hung on the air.

'Thank you,' she said. 'That is very comforting.'

'Bless you, Ma'am. We shall always be with you. Unless, of course, you prefer to be left alone.'

The Right Honourable Simon Millward had been Prime Minister for two years now, and looked forward to remaining so for another ten at least. Even then, he'd only be fifty-five. Plenty of time to make a pile from a grateful City, which had long since adjusted to life under the stretching permutation of Labour leaders the PR system from the beginning of the century had provided. Sometimes Labour – or Democratic Social Labour, as the dominant faction called itself – needed the Liberals or the Progressive Tories to keep things rolling sweetly along: but that was easily contrived, and lent a blush of freshness to a world of continuing power, where the knives came out only in the darkness of closed committee rooms.

Millward was a little left rather than a little right and relied particularly on the Traditional Liberals (as opposed to the Reform Liberals) for his majority. Yet it was not really weakness, he told himself. If the minority parties tried to shoot him down, they'd shoot themselves out of office – and right out of the action. There was no advantage for them in that, at least not yet. He would only hit trouble if events contrived to weaken him personally, if his DSL brothers saw a better hole to run to. And there was no chance of that. Simon was young and almost handsome. He was a fine, though slightly florid orator, with a profile which sometimes made middle-aged matrons lose restraint at party functions. He was extremely clever. He believed in himself, and thus in his sincerity. 'I promise you a Britain rich in tradition, yet a Britain dynamic and thrusting; a Britain for the young and for the old; a Britain which believes in enterprise yet has compassion written on its heart; a Britain of springtime and hope, yet a Britain for all seasons. I promise a Britain for the individual and for society, a Britain which puts Britain first but plays its full part in the world. My Britain, your Britain, our Britain.'

But here was one of those tedious crises which required choices. 'To choose is to take the risk of making the wrong choice.' Millward hadn't cared for the dead King, and thought even less of his bacon rind of a wife. They had been beginning to make waves again.

His Majesty seemed, late in life, to have inherited his father's penchant for brooding lectures on the moral sickness of the nation. Yatter first, think later; then cancel his last announcement and sack some hapless press adviser. They weren't sufficiently aware to be let out on their own. The old Blair concordat – secured over decades – was starting to look a touch rocky. Through the years, to be sure, those Royals who ought to be diminished – the dross and hangers-on – had been diminished, put out to grass or to obscure gainful employment. McAusland had done his duty. The Government had had the lead role in appointing Palace CEOs (one from a shortlist of two, just as they'd once done with big bishops). The Prime Minister, or his special nominee, was the automatic non-executive chairman at all Household board meetings, sitting at the end of the long, baize-covered table immediately below the great portrait of Lord Irvine.

Blair's memoirs – *If I May Say . . . : the Early Years* – had not been strong on revelations. Indeed, his American publisher had publicly requested 50 per cent of the advance back. But the chapter on the monarchy – modestly entitled 'Rebuilding a Royal Community' – was now a standard text for Millward. He had re-read it last night. 'Premiers of whatever political hue have a duty to preserve our most valued institution. They must intervene constantly to safeguard its relevance and proper profile. They must ensure that those who speak to the country are always on message, part of the fundamental coherence public life requires. At times of crisis for such institutions, the Premier has the duty to lead and to harness the public mood.'

Millward, in the hours after the crash, had moved rapidly to gauge that mood. Who was at fault? The Foreign Secretary. But he was dead: indeed, he could be blamed because he was dead. But what of the living? Three telephone and Internet polls had confirmed it. There was shock and some grief – though around five points less than the relevant computer model had predicted. There was a flood of sympathy for the girl Queen. Her recognition factor, however, was low: no more than 15 per cent said they 'might' recognize her in the street and 67 per cent 'feared she could be too young and inexperienced to rule effectively'. Damn it all to hell! She'd need nursing for years, and every stumble, every foul-up, would beat a path straight to Downing Street. He would have to make sure she was under control.

'Your Majesty,' he said, and the pale wraith on the

green sofa looked up at him. 'Your Majesty, you must let me take care of everything.'

'It's the mother who concerns me,' said Fountain over tea in his walnut-lined office. 'The girl doesn't know whether she's coming or going. She may be difficult, but we can squeeze that out of her. But can we do without the mother?'

'Not according to the polls,' said Millward, helping himself to a second slice of Duchy Traditional chocolate cake. 'They're a total nightmare. Fifty-four per cent think the Duchess is a Hopeless Spendthrift and a Poor Example. But 67 per cent agree that "at times like this, a daughter needs the presence of a mother". We can't ease her out of the action. That means we'll have to do a deal. You are the one on the spot, Sir Edgar. Why don't we consider the outline of an approach?'

Dear Lilibet,
Bro King called me round last night for a snifter.
Hugely depressed and knocking back the Famous
Grouse as though there was no tomorrow (which,
since it was already 12.25, there wasn't). He'd
wanted to make a speech on family values. Vetoed
on high: offensive to single parents and the gay
community. Well then, how about Christianity in
modern society? Vetoed: offensive to other religions
and atheists. The value of inter-faith dialogue?
Leave that to the C of E. 'I'm so boring I bore
myself,' he said. 'They've wrapped me up in total
tedium and thrown me in the cellar. I said I'd make

a speech about how wonderful the PM was, just for a lark. No, they said, that would be getting involved in politics.' He called it Cancer of the Livery.

She put the last cream sheet away and reached, wearily, for the light switch. In the blackness she stared, eyes wide, at the ceiling. She thought, yet again, that he was up there somewhere, looking down at her, his own eyes troubled and clouded with love. He could speak to her. The letters gave him voice. But she longed for the sound of him and the fusty smell of his hugs, all engine oil and boot polish. Whenever she was left by herself, she grieved; but they did not leave her for long in her cocoon of misery. She was required to move on.

'I, Elizabeth the Third, by the Grace of God made Queen of this Realm and of Her other Dependencies, and Chairperson of the residual Commonwealth Association, Defender of the Faith as variously specified and amended, do solemnly proclaim . . .'

What was she solemnly proclaiming? She held the typed script high in front of her, as though to mask her face, peering over the top at the choking crimsons of the Throne Room and the massed bellies of her Privy Counsellors, thinking of lunch, and the residual High Commissioners, fingering their medals.

'It's just a necessary formality,' Fountain had said, casting around for some analogy he thought she might understand, 'like signing a mortgage. The point of the occasion used to be saying that you would preserve the Church of Scotland – but that went out of the window after devolution when the Presbyterians had their nationalist seizure. But you cannot succeed, in logic, unless there is some quick accession ceremony, so they kept the St James's Palace meeting on the schedule. It has its uses. It allows the politicians who matter to see you in action. We are not, though, allowing any television cameras near. There is, we consider, no benefit in drawing attention away from the funeral, or indeed from your Coronation. Just read the script, Ma'am.'

'Do solemnly proclaim . . .' To keep the law of the brownie pack, to do my duty to God and the Queen. Dib, dib, dib. She lowered the text so they could see her, cleared her throat, and ploughed forward. There was nothing else to do.

The grey balloon was anchored to a pontoon by the bridge. 'No helicopters,' the Chairman of the BBC Governors had ordered. 'The nation will want to mourn in peace.' From three hundred feet, there were panning shots of the line shuffling into Westminster Hall. 'Great pictures,' said the producer in Wood Lane. 'We're up to a mile and a half now. You can say the Churchill benchmark's gone, if you like – but make it tasteful.'

She sat on the green sofa in the green room with the green curtains drawn, watching the flickering screen on the sideboard. 'And now,' said the young man in the balloon – Jolyon from the fifth generation of Dimblebys – 'a true moment of history. The queue you see, this vast ribbon of grieving humanity, is destined for the *Guinness Book of Records*. Never in history have so many queued for so long to express so vast a message of condolence.'

Bess raised her hand and turned off the set. She had been watching for an hour. They had not mentioned her father once. So cold, so formal, so instantly forgetful. Symbols come, symbols go. She shivered with an apprehension she could not define. There were endings. But were there beginnings?

Chapter Three

Montgomery had wanted hearses all the way from the Palace. 'Four for the Royal coffins going two by two down the Mall. The King and Queen up front, the Prince and Duke behind. Then pause. Maybe fifty yards' gap. Then the hearses for the two ladies-in-waiting and the two equerries. When we get to the Abbey the cheaper hearses at the back can simply peel off and disappear down Horseferry Road, letting HM and the rest of the cortège cut through by Central Hall and get there a couple of minutes early. We calculate fifteen hearses and Rolls in all that way; there's a 20 per cent discount on every vehicle over eight – and 30 per cent over ten.'

Baron disagreed. 'Hearses are fine for ordinary funerals,' he said. 'But we have to realize that this is an extraordinary opportunity. Simply the chance of a lifetime. When will we ever be able to put on another pageant of Royalty which sets calamity at the heart of a nation united, which reaffirms the centrality of the monarchy in such a huge outpouring of grief, which anyone who sees it will always remember? The BBC reckons four billion viewers in 231 countries minimum. That's gold dust image-wise. And don't forget the point of the exercise. We have to get the new Queen's recognition ratings up, and you don't do that if she's diving in and out of cars. No, it has to be gun carriages from the Palace and an utter break with tradition. I want her out there, walking alone ten yards back: then the mum and the brother, then what's left of the rest of the Family footing it on behind. Anyone who's too decrepit can have a motor, but I want them assembled outside the gates so that we get the basic contrast. You know, the milling love of a dynasty bereaved in absolute contrast to the solitary girl who carries a nation's hopes on her frail shoulders. The script writes itself.'

Fountain sniffed. 'Aren't you staking too much on her there? Suppose she faints or starts snivelling. We don't know she's up to it.' And, he almost added under his breath, we don't know how she'll make out when the job gets going properly. Teenagers were always iffy. They'd been a real pain in the Shanghai cigarette factory. And teenage girls particularly. Christ, when you looked back through Family history, the perils jumped out and bopped you on the nose.

Impasse. They turned to the great umpire by the window. Millward looked out over the lawns for a few seconds, then swung on his heels. 'Gun carriages,' he said. 'It's a risk but it has to be taken. We can always dose her with something if she starts to crumble. And perhaps I could walk with her mother and brother in case I'm needed? A sort of father figure, if you get my drift.'

Dear Lilibet,
I remember when I was a boy and walked the mile
to the Abbey. One step in front of another, head up,
act like a man. I could hear grandpa hissing at me
as we turned into the Mall. 'Shoulders back, lad,
shoulders back. You're royal and strong. Only the
hoi-polloi wallow in emotion when people can see
them. Don't blub, lad, don't blub.'

It was another chill day, an east wind stripping the
blossom from the trees in St James's Park, the crowd
twenty deep along the Mall hunched together for
warmth.

They had tried to make a velvet coat with a high
collar that would frame her face, but she hated the
tight fit around her shoulders and breasts. 'It makes
me feel like a guardsman,' she said. 'I want to be
the way he'd remember me.' She had picked out the
straight, sensible, school skirt and the white linen shirt
she had worn over the leather breeches for Joan's
trial. There was a simple lambswool sweater he'd
bought for her in Hove last year. 'And I'll wear the
mac I came in.'

Lady Clementine had shaken her chins and called
for Fountain. He had called for Selene and Baron.

'Darling, you can't ... You're the Queen,' said
Selene. 'I've spent thousands on a coat and hat because
it's what people expect, and you'll just look so
scruffy.'

'No,' said Baron suddenly. 'If that's what Her Majesty wants, that's what should happen.' He had turned
and whispered urgently to Fountain. 'There's often

45

something quite touching about simplicity, and the tabloids will love the tale about the pullover from M&S. One up for the heartstrings, I think.'

And so, in the forecourt of the Palace, she tugged at the belt of her raincoat and looked at the rest of the Family as they peered at their instruction cards and cowered as the young equerries barked orders at them; then, shivering, fell into line. Plump aunts from Gloucester and Swindon; plump uncles from Sandwich and Threadneedle Street; dowagers from Dorset and Hampshire; second cousins from York and Chelmsford and Barbados. She barely knew any of them. Faces glimpsed fleetingly years ago at funerals and Christmases in the prison called Sandringham. The Harewoods and the Linleys and the Mountbattens and the plain old Windsors, the Earl of Obscurity, the Marquess of Early Bath, the Duke of Dereliction – the gang who'd drifted away in search of an honest crust when the House of Lords shut its doors against them and the dwindling rivulet of the Civil List had finally sunk into the sands. Earning a living meant fending for yourself, running boutiques or caterers or fronting for City PR dinners. One by one, in the coffee room, they'd come up to her and muttered the same stale words of sorrow. After today's free lunch they would be gone again until a wedding or christening issued its ritual photo call.

'Ten seconds please, Ma'am.'

The great horses with their gun carriages lumbered into place. There was a murmur of anticipation outside. Millward adjusted his tie. Selene put a delicate gloved hand on the crown of her billowing hat and pushed it down once more over the blonde bob. Nicky blew his nose.

She walked out alone, eyes set into the distance of Admiralty Arch, teeth chewing gently at her bottom lip. Don't blub, girl, don't blub. Overhead a TV helicopter dipped closer, the roar of its engine drowning the whisperings and the shufflings as the crowd craned forward to look.

'Dignity,' Fountain had said. 'Dignity is the key. No pop songs, and as small a showbusiness contingent as possible. I don't want to see any of the King's old flames within a mile of the Abbey. No sunglasses, no legs, no actresses. The Danish connection makes this a pan-European occasion beyond individual personalities. I want every crowned head there and I want them built up with proper solemnity. We can strike a general blow for all monarchy if we get this right.'

'Monaco?' asked Baron laconically.

'They've been asked but they won't come, thank God. The Princess is pregnant again by some nightclub bouncer.'

Bess took her seat with head bowed, still trying to find a fixed point to concentrate on. The Elgar and the psalms washed over her. The Archbishop talked of the Agony of Adversity and the Joy of Redemption. Crown Prince Harald said his sister had been a 'kind, quiet and loving woman whom all who met her would remember with warmth and affection' and paused to glare as an ITN man knocked over his microphone. Millward recalled a king who was like a brother to him, and a king's brother who was like another brother, and a tiny boy who might one day have grown into a fine man. 'But looking back is not what this country does best. We must only look back in order to look forward. We must burnish their memories by creating memories of our own.'

Bess felt sick. The emotion she must not show was piled high within her, straining at the dam of self-discipline she had built. And it was her time of the month again.

There was a green hill far away.

Did she summon Fountain, or did he summon her? Either way, there was no escaping a meeting. The crowned heads had departed; her mother had gone shopping; outside in the Mall a posse of cleaners was sweeping away the rubbish. She sat with a book open by the window, pencil in hand.

'Now, your Majesty,' said Fountain, entering with only the most fleeting and feeble of knocks, 'it is time to begin taking a few decisions. You have a personal staff to appoint and a diary to familiarize yourself with.'

He paused. Bess said nothing.

'We have discussed the situation most thoroughly amongst ourselves, and with the Prime Minister.' He pulled a sheet of paper from his breast pocket. 'We suggest that Lady Clementine, who is already most attached to you, becomes your lady-in-waiting, and that her dear friend Lady Margaret Swayne, the second daughter of the Earl of Ventnor, be invited to serve with her. That would also be convenient because Rodney Chetwode-Belcher, who you know already, is her nephew and the Foreign Office's choice to be your personal equerry. He's a Captain with the Black Watch on secondment. He was due for a tour in Dubai next month, but we've ascertained that he can be made available. Suitable and available.

'We see no benefit at this stage in appointing a separate diary secretary. Your uncle and his wife had one each, which was always a trifle excessive in my view, quite beyond established productivity ratios. There would be useful headcount savings if, at least for the time being, I took charge of that myself.'

He moved to her side and began stabbing a finger at the paper. 'See, Ma'am. Once the mourning period is over, it is a question of which standing engagements should fall with the death of the King and which may suitably be transferred. Speeches at the Household Cavalry dining-in night, for instance, are not within your perceptual compass, and some alternative may have to be found. But the week beginning the twelfth has opening an extension to the Henley Conference Centre, visiting primary schools in the Stepney area and attending a bring-and-buy sale at the Commonwealth Institute. All that raises no objection in our minds.'

Bess took the paper and ran her eye slowly down the dates column. 'I am so sorry, Sir Edgar,' she said, 'it's just very awkward. Henley clashes with my History A-level, and I can't be in Stepney because the Economics paper is 9.30 to 12.30 on the Thursday. Of course I can do the Commonwealth on the Saturday but, with Physical Geography first thing on Monday morning, I'll really need the maximum time for revision. Not that it counts for anything, but the last few days have ruined my schedule.'

Was he rolling his eyes?

'A-levels, Your Majesty?'

'Of course. I thought you knew I've a place at Oxford this autumn if I can get two As and a B. History and Economics are fine if I can just keep on top of them, but the Geography is a real sweat. All facts and no scope for the imagination.'

'Oxford?' He was sweating again, she thought. 'Oxford?' The second syllable rose querulously.

She stood up and looked at him squarely. 'Surely you realized that it was all arranged? At least it used to be. But I thought . . . if princes can go to Cambridge, why shouldn't queens go to Oxford?'

He was recovering his poise, beginning to speak slowly and loudly as though to a small, recalcitrant child. 'With the greatest respect, Ma'am, there is all the difference in the world between a young prince, many decades from the throne, attending to the final years of his education, and a queen whose duties and obligations present no such opportunity. Can a student deal with affairs of State? Can a student tour abroad or move among her people at home if she also wears a crown? Can a queen afford the time to study? Can she play the part of an ordinary undergraduate in a city teeming with tabloid journalists and police guards? With respect, Ma'am, the proposition, when you have time to reflect upon it, is simply ridiculous.'

'You always say "with respect" when you mean I don't deserve any,' said Bess. 'And of course I've thought about it. Of course I know there'll be problems. But turn your own questions on their head. Do you want a queen whose education was cut short by protocol and terrorists and reporters? Do you want a queen whose intellect is turned off like a light switch because the Palace can't adapt to modern ways? Do you want a queen who met no ordinary people and had no ordinary friends after she was eighteen? Why is it fine for kings to have been to university, but not queens? What will the Equal Opportunities inspectorate make of that?'

He was growing angry. She knew the signs already. The tiny, twitching muscle at the left side of his mouth; the puce flush at the temples.

'I shall have to consult, Ma'am. I shall have to see what the other members of the board say, what the Prime Minister himself feels about the risks entailed. With respect . . .' He paused, and flushed deeper. 'I must be frank. Had you been born a few months later you would have been a child and been treated like a child. Others, wiser in the ways of the world, would have made your decisions for you. Perhaps, technically, that is not the situation now – but emotionally it still applies. If you have the maturity you claim, then you know that the respect in which the Royal Family is held – indeed, its very continuance – has hung by a thread for nearly half a century. There have been too many headstrong young people who put self-gratification before reputation . . .'

'Like my mother?' she asked sharply.

'Like . . . I name no names. The late King inherited a throne tarnished by lust and selfishness. He, too, knew those impulses. But with our help, with the aid of myself and my devoted staff, he was able to come to terms with a role which needs sobriety and prudence. You cannot put that slender legacy at risk, Ma'am. You must conform to our best model of behaviour.'

Bess bit her lip and clenched her hands again. 'I don't want to be difficult,' she said, 'but please think about this carefully. Please consult with the others, by all means, and tell them that, without Oxford, I shall become a cypher. Tell them that, by denying me, they put my happiness and my fulfilment at risk.'

'Very well, Your Majesty. As you wish . . .'

He began to retreat, then stopped by the yellow chaise longue and gripped it tight, bending towards her. 'And what shall I tell Lady Clementine and Lady Margaret?'

'I'd rather you told them nothing. Whether I study or fret here, I'm bound to need some friends of my own age with my own interests. Caroline Northcott and Emma Lacey – you remember? the girls Belcher told you about from Roedean – are both going to Oxford, as it happens. If I go too, I'm sure they would be happy to help me. On – what do you call it? – a short-term contract.'

Dear Lilibet,
Great news about the John's interview and the offer. You'll do it, and you'll be there because of your mind, not because of who you are and where you come from. The old family's never been any great shakes in the brainbox stakes. Turn on the telly, go for a walk, pass the bottle, we used to say.

But never read a book – unless, of course, it's one about you. The boys could go shooting, the girls could stay at home and paint their nails. I remember one August day yonks ago in Balmoral when I was sitting in my room listening to the radio. Desert Island Discs, probably: anyway some opera singer had chosen a spot of Mahler and Grandpa came in. 'What's this muck?' he said. 'A boy your age ought to be out in the open air catching fish.' So he bundled me into waders and twenty seconds later I was three feet in water. And I looked over at the bank. There were the cousins from the cottage where they and their mum were sometimes allowed to stay as long as she didn't come up to the big house with them. They were all decked out in frilly dresses as usual, watching and obviously wishing they could come and have a splash too. And Grandpa turned to them and shouted, 'Surely you gels have got some knitting to do?'

That's why I'm so excited for you, my love. Poor Nicky will probably never amount to anything. Can't learn, can't ride, can't carry a conversation. In the bad old days they'd probably have had him put down. We all have to look after him and make sure he's all right. But you have the gift of being able to make your own future. It is the most precious gift I can think of.

He had believed in her so utterly, she thought: almost as though he worshipped her. If he'd been here at the start of term, he'd have filled one of the estate wagons from the garage with her stuff, the discs, the books, the stupid collection of soft toys that made her grimace when she saw them, and carried her away to the promised land of learning and opportunity. Letting it go, letting his belief in her future slip away, would be letting him down. She was not going to do that. Oxford was a commitment she had made to him. Her life, now, was not letting him down. She remembered him constantly, always with a wince of pain and stiffening of her lips. He was still with her. She could not betray him.

Bess squatted on the hearthrug in her Palace room going over the ecology of rain forests one more time. Her board was meeting quietly in Downing Street. 'Easier here,' Millward had said. 'Fewer hacks to avoid.' He brought his new press secretary, Robin Leckie, along. A nice, quiet young man with a flop of black hair and a gift for doe-eyed sincerity. Warwick University, three years' training on the *Sheffield Star*, two years at the *Mirror*, then the usual think tanks and Millbank. The Prime Minister had had enough of rowdy press factotums who bullied him as much as they bullied his ministers and the lobby. After all, Millward told himself, I'm the story. When the last incumbent had thrown a steak and kidney pie at the junior minister for higher education in the Members' Dining Room, it had been time to lower the safety curtain. 'You're a conduit,' he told Leckie as he shifted on the carpet in front of him and grinned anxiously. 'You are your master's modest, effacing, gentle, honest voice. At least while memories fade. Right?'

Fountain, Baron and Montgomery sat together at the round oak table. Millward kept a distance. Leckie's chair was eighteen inches back, so that he seemed half there, half not.

'First, the finances,' Montgomery said, tipping a sheaf of papers out of his briefcase. 'We always reckoned it would be nasty, and we were right. The King left the Queen an allowance, but everything else to the Prince. As they're all dead, though, it's just a bloody shambles, a total field day for the lawyers and the Revenue. Say 800 million euros in death duties before you start on the small change. I tell you frankly: we can't put our hands on it. Oh, if we could sell some pictures and furniture, plus the stables, we could make a start. But we'd have to establish ownership to do that, and best estimates make that three years minimum, even supposing we win.'

There was a heavy silence.

'The obvious thing', said Fountain, 'is for the Government to chip in – in the public interest. Is one random act of tragedy to spell bankruptcy for our Royal Family? Does the sacrifice of a Foreign Secretary count for nothing? Isn't a waiver from the Treasury exactly what common humanity, the finest instinct of the British people, demands?'

'But then,' said Baron, fiddling with his moustache, 'that could all get very political. We've a schoolgirl monarch nobody recognizes and her mother, who everybody recognizes and nobody has a good word for. A Gold Card adulteress. Give them the money and she'll blow half of it in an afternoon at Harvey Nicks – and the Government will be heading for Carey Street.'

'You're not up to date on the Virgin Queen, Prime Minister,' said Fountain. 'She's turning out to be a stroppy little madam. She tells me she doesn't want to take our instructions and keep her head down. She's taking her A-levels and going to university – and that's almost an order, if you please. How do we tie her down? It took twenty years to bring her uncle under starter's orders, and we haven't got twenty minutes. Of course, normally you'd rely on the parents. But the wretched Selene is all we've got. The whole thing is just circular. No relevant business applies. We're simply at our wits' end.'

Millward sighed and looked at his watch. The Bulgarian trade mission would be here in a quarter of an hour, vinegar breath and vinegar wine.

Leckie coughed and edged his chair closer. 'If I might say something, Sir, the idea of a student Queen isn't quite as ridiculous as Sir Edgar is making out. It could be a wonderful fairy story. Commoners' gowns and all that stuff. If we could manage her properly, it might be worth going along with.'

'But that', said Millward suddenly, 'is only one track of a policy, where any fool can see we need two. We have to have the mother wrapped up as well. Get me Davidson on the phone at MI 5 and inquire whether he might be free to join the Duchess and me for a drink here tomorrow evening. And tell her to keep her head down and her mouth shut.'

Bess sat in the yellow box they called the music room. The piano was locked. The harp was zipped in a stained beige bag. No music: only work. They had brought in a small card table and a hard, high-backed chair. The clock on the mantelpiece showed two minutes to ten.

'Right, Ma'am,' said Mrs Granger, opening the sealed brown envelope with an unnecessary flourish. 'History One . . . starting in ninety seconds.'

She had always found exams easy. If you hunched in line along the stretch of the Roedean hall and looked at nothing but the narrow desk and the lined paper, then the rest of the world soon faded away; the intakes of breath around you, the squeaks of nibs, the sighs and the grating of chair legs became the essential background to concentration, signals that this was a big one.

But here, in the Palace, the noises were different and annoying. Chink went a tray of coffee down the corridor towards Baron's office. Outside the Guards were marching to and fro. Heels clicked in unison, gun barrels smacked against concrete. She thought she heard an echo of Selene's shrill laugh as another hard day at Harrods began. Mrs Granger had a cold. She sniffed.

'Ready, steady, go.'

Bess turned the paper over and frowned.

Question 1: 'Though God has raised me high, yet this I count the glory of my crown: that I have reigned with your loves.' Assess the role of public opinion as a restraint on the power of the monarchy between 1533 and 1603 and analyse Elizabeth 1's belief that personal popularity was a factor in her success.

She grinned.

Doreen Granger grinned back.

*

'Thank you for coming,' Baron said. The curtains in the office were half drawn so that the light from his desk lamp seemed unnaturally fierce. It was turned towards the chair in front of him. His face and the face of the bulky man beside him lay in an arc of shadow.

'Oh, no bother,' said Selene gaily, putting the shopping bags at the side of the chair. She was still wearing black, but a silken scarlet scarf at the neck signalled the beginning of the end to mourning. The suit was shaped and tight. The end of the scarf drifted over her bosom. 'I'm sorry I wasn't here when you called. There are so many wonderful jewellers in Bond Street these days, one just loses all track of time.'

'Can I introduce my colleague, Duchess?' said Baron impatiently. 'This is Angus Davidson. He works for the authorities in an advisory capacity. He has a special brief for protecting the Royal reputation.'

'Oh, super.'

Davidson shifted a couple of inches forward, then subsided. His flesh seemed marbled with fat, somehow bolted into place so that it moved in solid lumps. His face was curiously large, clamped on to a jaw which fused into a red, thick neck.

'Mr Davidson has one or two things he wishes to share with us.'

The hulk, incongruously, had his own shopping bag. He emptied its contents on the desk.

'See, photographs,' said Baron, sliding the prints one by one into the glare of the lamp. 'You and Teddy Rogerson on the yacht. An object lesson in what may be achieved on a single sun lounger. You and Abdul

Narwaz on the same lounger two days later. He seems not to be – how shall I put it? – so athletic. You and Count Esterhasen in the grounds of the Villa Mimosa. A simple, rather touching embrace. You and Nathan Glass at one of those interminable Hollywood parties. So boring . . . who can blame you for just a snort or two of coke? You and Yves De Clement in Paris after the Spring Collection. And to think they thought he was gay.'

He pulled the bundle together, stacking them neatly. 'Of course there are many more. But some, I fear, would be simply too embarrassing, even in this company – and no family newspaper would dream of printing them.'

Her face had whitened beneath the rouge. Her red lips seemed detached from her, as though quivering on a corpse. 'Everybody knows you can fake photos easily these days,' she said thinly.

'Perhaps. Perhaps not. But not sound tracks, Duchess.'

He pushed the first of three tapes into a tiny recorder.

'*Don't stop Munchikins. Again, again. There, there . . . Yes, yes, yes.*'

The squeal rose and fractured into a frenzy of squeaks.

'*Oh fuck, Munchy. The sodding bedhead's coming loose.*'

Baron grinned affably. 'Now my friend Davidson is a happily married man. We don't want to go out of our way to shock him, do we? The question we all need to discuss is where we go from here. You see, we think the Queen needs a mother we can trust. And so – from a slightly different position, if you get my drift – do we.'

She had pulled the scarlet scarf undone and the sweat on her forehead had begun to cut gulleys through the matt of her make-up. 'It's disgraceful – absolutely disgusting. You've been spying on me?'

'Oh not us, Duchess. We have been protecting you, and now we must protect your daughter together. See? The bag stays in my safe. It won't come out if you stick to the straight and narrow. No more shopping binges, no more movie stars and billionaires and clapped-out counts. You are going into Good Works on a full-time basis – and one of those works will be smartening up that spotty son of yours. We've all learned a lesson from the past few weeks. Davidson's a football fan. West Ham, isn't it?'

The silent mountain nodded.

'He says you need discipline on the pitch, a strong manager in the dug-out – and a good substitute on the bench in case a hamstring goes. It's not bad advice, Duchess. Keep your daughter under control. Keep your knickers out of a twist. And keep young Nicky running up and down the touchline, just in case.'

She pulled a minute gold mirror out of her handbag and began tending to the ravines and the canyon cracks.

'Anyone for tennis?' she asked.

Chapter Four

Tom Bowler was dripping sweat. June had begun, as usual, with ten days of wind and rain, but now all that was history. A sultry High from the Sahara hung over Britain, indeed appeared to be hanging directly over the College gardens. It was 6.30 and the trail of tourists had long since been ushered away. A few undergraduates lay chatting idly under the clump of beech trees. A red-haired boy, naked to the waist, and a girl in a pink cotton dress were stretched together on the lawn beyond the rose bushes. The boy ran the back of his hand along her bare arm then let it fall limply to the grass.

Bowler was wearing jeans and a bomber jacket. They were two days away from the first dress rehearsal and the heavy metalled tunic he would have to wear then. Perhaps, like the others, he could have worn a T-shirt and jeans, but he needed the weight of the jacket on his shoulders and the feel of the sword belt around his waist. The movements had to be exactly right.

'OK,' said Adrian Pryce from his deckchair. 'You're back from the sea fight.'

Bowler wiped his brow and straightened, left profile carefully maintained.

'All is lost!
This foul Egyptian hath betrayed me;
My fleet hath yielded to the foe, and yonder
They cast their caps up and carouse together
Like friends long lost. Trip-turn'd whore! 'tis thou
Hath . . . ttt . . . hast . . . Oh shit!'

Julia Curry broke into one of her familiar peels of laughter. 'Why is my lord enrag'd against his love?' she asked, nose cocked towards him, breasts heaving as he stamped his foot and threw the wooden sword to the ground.

Adrian moved surprisingly quickly from the chair and stood between them. 'Look,' he said, 'I know it's bloody hot and I know we'd all rather be doing some easy little comedy this summer, not Antony and bloody Cleopatra. But that's what the British Council wanted for the Pakistan tour this summer, so that's what they're going to get. Of course it would better if we could bring the thing up to speed in Peshawar in decent obscurity, then haul it back to the gardens and the critics. Chance would be a fine thing! Meanwhile can we all keep our cool and try to be moderately professional.'

Julia wiped her eyes and giggled on.

'O! he is more mad than Telamon for his shield; the
*   boar of Thessaly*
Was never so emboss'd'

Bowler shrugged and smiled. 'Fuck off to the monument,' he said. 'There lock yourself and send me word you are dead.'

He was tall – six two – and muscled, with a barrel of a chest and a thick ripple of thigh. Seeing him running down the Turl in the distance, you might take him for a rugby player: a three-quarter, say, or a wing forward. Closer to, though, that illusion vanished. The nose was aquiline, the chin sculpted and constantly flexing. His eyes were dark and fierce and the brown hair, worn so that it tumbled over his forehead, had the sheen of care to it. He would have been handsome in any age and he knew that – but he bore the burden with a shrug and a rumpled, rehearsed grin.

'Come Dolabella,' said Adrian. 'And so to Rome. That's just enough of all that for the night. I'm calling an early break, and we'll all start at four again tomorrow if our tempers have improved.'

Bowler looked rueful. Maybe a cold beer and a shower would do the trick. He was almost twenty-two – a year or two older than most of the other first-year undergraduates. His year off beach-bumming around Thailand and points east had turned, haplessly, into two. Sometimes he felt a little too grand, a little too mature, for student games. One day, for sure, he would be a professional actor. He'd be noticed on the stage and then find his way into television – and films. *Spartacus*, *Ben Hur*, *The Robe* – all those ancient epics made him tingle. Since he was a tiny lad he'd fancied himself in a toga ravishing a succession of empresses and peasant girls. There'd been TV talk last week about remaking Cleopatra as a musical and he had drawn his breath in sharply. The St John's Mummers, by rights, ought to be doing *Two Gentlemen of Verona* or *As You Like It*. Smiles for a summer evening. Mark Antony didn't make many jokes. But perhaps, somehow, God was working in mysterious ways. Perhaps a talent spotter or an assistant producer would be there in the crowds next week, perched creaking in the wobbly wooden stands on the lawn. Perhaps opportunity would knock far ahead of schedule.

His room was no distance. Left through the first archway, first on the right. Squalid chaos. Dirty jeans and underpants strewn across the unmade bed. A half-bottle of rancid milk on the cheap plastic table. Bloody Reg, his bloody scout. 'If you leave it disgusting, Mr Bowler, you won't expect me to touch a thing. I helps gentlemen who helps themselves.' There was an acrid stench of sick coming from the basin where he had retched the night before.

The mobile phone on his desk was flashing. Bowler pressed Re-call automatically, then cursed when he saw who had called. Mum. Are you all right, dear? Are you too hot? Are you taking enough fluids?

But no: his mother was burbling away about something quite different.

'I shouldn't say anything, of course,' she said. 'But I think you're going to have the most amazing new student next year. Doreen Granger came back with the A-level papers and, though she shouldn't have looked – don't tell a soul, Tom! – she said they were brilliant, a definite A all the way through. Well, I always knew she could do it. A wonderful student, one of my best. What with everything on her mind, though, the poor thing, I never thought she'd make it.'

'Mum,' said Bowler blankly, 'who on earth are you talking about?'

'Why, Bess, of course. My Bess. The Queen of the quads.'

She felt chilly in the heat. She shivered in the glare of the sun. She was isolated again.

Fountain had seemed awash with unexpected concern. 'You've had the most traumatic two months, Your Majesty. There are no engagements that matter for a while. The King never took on much in the summer. We all think that a quiet holiday while you wait for your exam results is completely sensible. I've arranged to have York Cottage at Sandringham set aside for three weeks so that you can relax in peace. I'm afraid you may find it a little restricted. It's not a cottage, of course, indeed rather more like a small hotel. We used to use it for administration before the Japanese offered us a wing in the Congress Centre, but it's really quite comfortable. You realize, I'm sure, that most of the main house is open to visitors as usual, and there's an everlasting run of conferences on top. But the royal compound is totally secure. The tabloids will be lucky to get a glimpse of you.' Was he pitching it too strong? 'We think it should be just what the doctor ordered.'

There was no choice, when she thought about it. She couldn't have the kind of holidays she knew. No trekking in the Alps with her father or lying on a French beach with friends from school. 'We need to find something structured for you, dear,' Lady Clementine had said. The constant photographers were beginning to sap her confidence. Whenever she left the Palace, there were always thirty or more of them in tow; never in hot pursuit, of course not, but always somehow there. A caravan which could never really be left behind. She knew Sandringham a little. She remembered its stretching fields, its feeling of space and openness. It had none of the choking dark pine or clumping statuary of Balmoral. There was a lightness and air to it in summer. Perhaps she could breathe again there. The dankness of the Palace oppressed her and she had swiftly grown to loathe the weight of Windsor.

'Can I have company?'

'You will have your mother and brother anyway, Ma'am. Holidays are a time for family. But if there are suitable friends . . .' – Fountain's voice had grown plummy, so that suitability undulated from his lips – 'then by all means let us be in touch and see what can be arranged.'

But nothing could be arranged quickly. Caroline had two weeks in Greece on an archaeological dig; Emma was on a badminton tour of Belgium. They would both be there at some point. Some time soon, with luck: not now.

Fountain had been right about York Cottage. It was a great grey lump of Victorian stone hiding from the rest of the grounds behind a stream and thickets of trees. The road to the front door curled through walnut trees and oaks. Policemen leaned against the trunks as Bess passed and fingered the hand guns hanging from their belts. The back of the cottage, shielded from the masses, had a new expanse of lawn and a pool cut out of the woodland from the estate. At night, when you walked around the pool, the fat beetles from the wood drifting on its surface, there was a seclusion she loved.

Nicky stayed in his room and watched television. He had a sty on his left eye, which was almost closed. Selene lay by the pool and read thick paperbacks, complaining at ten-minute intervals about their tedium. 'Just so shriekingly boring, darling.' Bess, in an anorak and plaid headscarf borrowed from a housekeeper, walked alone across the park beyond the great house, two policemen ambling never more than fifty yards behind.

I'm a prisoner. I can't choose where I go, or who I can go with. I must always be followed and there will always be people who follow me. The family? I don't have a family. Her Majesty's pleasure? Her Majesty is permitted no pleasure. Oh, I can stamp my foot and insist. I can say that I'm taking the exams and going to university and they must all make the best of it. But will things be different if I get to Oxford? Will I be able to be ordinary, going to movies in jeans and sweaters, drinking in pubs, having coffee between lectures? Will I be able to make new friends? Even – and she paused as a rabbit scuttled for cover under a hedge in front of her – even boys of my own age?

She already knew the questions. And she was beginning to know the answers.

'Ma'am,' shouted one of the policemen, sprinting clumsily towards her across the spongy grass. He was red and puffing as he reached her. 'Call on the mobile, please. One of your guests wanting to talk to you from Sallysomethingorother.'

'Salonika,' she said.

Caroline had fallen off her motor scooter on a mountain road and cut her head open on the metal post of a road sign. 'I was out cold for half an hour. They say it's concussion and they're not sure how long it will last. Maybe a day, maybe a week. At any rate, I'm confined to hospital barracks, all plans cancelled. I'm just so terribly sorry.'

It seemed like the final straw. Bess picked up a shard of flint uncovered by some rooting sheep and threw it hard into the deepest part of the hedge where the rabbit had run.

Dear Lilibet,
Do you remember old Benson, the deputy head gardener from Sandringham? Whiskery fellow with a big behind and bad breath. The chap who fished your brother out of the lake that summer when he stuck his pole through the bottom of the punt, Silly Ass! I went up for his funeral yesterday. Happened to be in Mildenhall and there was Bro on the hotline. Benny's finally copped it, he said. Incinerated somehow, up in smoke. You're nearest: would you mind popping along for the last rites?

No problem! It was a sunny day and I quite enjoyed the ride. There were all the usual suspects at the Church and we sang Rock of Ages and We Plough the Fields and Scatter before zipping him off to Kings Lynn for the cremating bit. But coming out of the gate, doing the condolences for the relatives et al, I saw this wan-looking blonde hanging back by the gate. Smartly turned out, but knocking on when you got close. Potential bus-pass fodder. It was the girl we used to call Aunt Sally – you know, that other P R person who we thought might do for your Great Uncle before he finally popped the question to the double-barrelled one. Sal! I said. Exceedingly long time no see. What are you doing here?

A terrible tale. She's still in the same line of business, churning out little television documentaries about the palaces and stuff which the Japanese pick up for a few yen over a load of sushi. They'd been making a new one about the making of the old one of Sandringham your Great Unc did ages ago for I T V – called A Prince's Progress, or somesuch – and Benson cut right through the cable with his spade. Instant teriyaki.

I've been thinking about her ever since, my love. We don't operate like ordinary mortals, do we? Even now. We draw in the ordinary mortals and give them a taste of the toff life; and then, when it's all over, they can't really ever escape. The once and forever Girlfriend Fridays, always poised for the Big Day and never realizing that there aren't any big days, just more of the same – until the last spade turns the last sod.

Opening night: closing night. It had rained, torrentially, at 7.28 that evening. One minute the heat was unbearable, a weight of inert oppression bearing down on them, the next it was gone as the skies opened.

'"Spout you hurricanoes",' said Adrian, making no attempt to run for cover. 'We should have been doing Lear. It would have been bloody magnificent.'

'As long as the audience didn't get washed away in the flood,' said Tom.

There was nothing to be done. The first warning clatter of rain had cleared the ring of wooden benching in front of them, sending the girls in their summer cottons and the boys in their white shirts and linen jackets racing back towards the college arches, with a handful of proud parents in suits panting behind. Then the monsoon came, so that the wooden planking seemed to roar in constant drum rolls and the lawn turned to a shallow lake. The thin tenting behind the laurel bushes where the cast changed lurched and tottered, then subsided into the mud. Some cursed and ran, the legions of Caesar routed before the first battle. Adrian and Julia and Tom stayed and laughed and rubbed themselves, sloshing back and forth ankle deep in water.

'I'm singing and dancing in the rain,' Julia chanted, hands criss-crossing on knees. Her dress of scarlet silk was plastered, transluscent, to her body. The narrow strip of her panties was etched across her hips.

There was a moment's slackening in the downpour, and they began half-heartedly to gather up the scatter of props; but then a flash of lightning snaked into the beeches a hundred yards away and seemed to skip along the barbed wire on top of the garden wall.

'Abandon ship!' Adrian shouted, and they sprinted, arm in arm, still laughing, towards the quad.

Tom's room was the obvious sanctuary. The other two, both second year, were in digs somewhere in Summertown. 'Have a shower and put on something dry,' he said, rummaging for towels and a pile of shirts in the cupboard.

They sat, dry and giggling, on the carpet by his bed. Adrian wore Tom's denim dungarees, which ballooned around his scrawny body as though he were some second-rate clown in a third-rate circus. Julia wore the candy-striped pyjama top his aunt had given him for Christmas, her short brown legs bare and tucked beneath her. Tom fished a bottle of Sangiovese from under the wash basin and passed plastic cups round.

'It's not really funny,' he said at last. 'It's a total bloody disaster. And on the first night, Moses led his people into the Red Sea . . . and the sea closed over them and the critic from the *Oxford Mail* was turned into a tadpole.'

Adrian drank the last of the plonk and walked over to the leaded window. 'Storm over,' he said. 'No point everybody getting muddy again. I'll go and root out Ted and the rest of the army and see what we can save for tomorrow, if there is a tomorrow.'

There was a hint of depression to his voice.

'Are you sure?' Julia asked.

'Never more . . . If we ever get the show on the road, I don't want Cleopatra dying of pneumonia.'

When he had gone, Tom opened a second bottle and Julia sat on the bed beside him, idly massaging her feet. 'I still feel a bit cold,' she said.

The top two buttons of the pyjamas had come

undone and he could see her breasts shifting and rippling as she rubbed away. He had barely noticed her before the play was cast. He was from Brighton. She was from Nottingham. He was reading English. She was reading Modern Languages. He was tall and broad and angular. She was tiny, no more than five foot one, but with a softness to her body. His hair was long and lank from the drenching; hers was cut short to frame her face.

They had not even liked each other until tonight. He knew he was a good actor, and probably a passable poet; he thought he could be more, much more. She was merely competent, her voice too light, her gestures too bird-like for tragedy. 'She might be fine as some coquette in a light comedy,' he'd said to Adrian, 'but Noel Coward never wrote anything with pyramids in. "I am dying, Egypt, dying for a Daiquiri."'

Adrian smiled his campest smile and duly passed it on. Julia, little mouth curled in contempt, had begun to rile Tom day after day. 'Has my Lord forgot to turn his profile to the stars? Doth vengeful pride chew up his lines and spit them forth in self-regard?'

She had been bloody irritating. But now he was not thinking of that.

'Cold?' he said. 'There are all sorts of interesting ways of dealing with that.'

The quadrangle was black and deserted an hour later. Tom got up and looked through the window of his bedroom into the gardens. They were empty too. There was a moon and a clear sky, and the rows of benching, sagging jaggedly into the mire, looked like vanquished extra-terrestrial hordes from some war of the worlds.

'Your clothes are dry,' he said. 'If I lend you a coat, we could go and see if we can find the others.'

He knew where they'd be. The Welsh Pony, a pub by the bus station which real actors from the Playhouse had turned into their local. Sure enough. Adrian, still in those absurd dungarees, and Ted and the rest were in the public bar with lagers and crisps. They had become melancholy.

'It's a wash-out. A total sodding wash-out,' Adrian said. 'They used cheap dye on the tunics. They've had it. The gardener says the lawn won't be fit for anything for three days, even if it doesn't rain again. The old Garden Theatre is a building site. We'll just have to see whether we can find a rehearsal room somewhere and hope we can get things straight for Pakistan.'

He suddenly looked at Tom and Julia. 'And where have you two been all this time . . . while there's nothing to rehearse?'

'Let me buy you a Scotch,' said Tom, and they retreated to the bar, shoving through the damp crowd to catch the eye of the surly blonde who sometimes poured doubles for you if you winked at her.

'My round, I think. Something strong to cover the actor's retreat.'

Julia nodded warily. She had just seen Sammy Wittman in the crowd. She did not like him. A worm with attitude. He was short and dark in an old leather jacket with tassels at the neck. 'Quite a decent story, anyway,' said Wittman. '"Flash Flood Sinks Bard: Red Alert for Missing Mummers." We're putting it on page one – and I'm seeing whether the nationals would like a sniff. You know, "Royal Choice College Under Water Horror."'

Wittman was the news editor of the university rag, but *Cherwell* was merely the home base for his operations. Sammy's big brother William ran the gossip column on the *Express* – The Wicked World of Will Wittman – and Sammy dined perpetually on the connection. 'Of course,' he said, 'nobody really thinks the Queen will come to John's in the end. Will says the Palace will do everything it can to turn her off, and anyway she's a bit of a thicky. But while the show's running, I'm making a fortune out of it. Five hundred euros last weekend over that spot of food poisoning you had. "Killer Pie Bug in Queen's Buttery". Page Three lead, and all the quotes.'

Tom looked down at him as he waved a 100-euro note over the bar. Why was Julia smiling so intently? Surely she couldn't be impressed by this gabby turd?

'Oh, she'll come all right,' he said suddenly. 'And she's not at all thick. I happen to know she's waltzed through her exams.'

Wittman put one of the blonde's special doubles into his hand.

'As a matter of fact,' Tom said, 'I've met her a few times at fêtes and things. My mother used to teach her economics. She says she's great and that she's passed by miles. I saw her do Joan in *The Lark* a few months ago. I thought she was terrific – the vulnerable waif with steel right down her backbone.' He paused and tossed back the Scotch.

Julia had stopped smiling. 'Always a sucker for blue bloody blood,' she said, with the old edge back in her voice.

Sammy Wittman said nothing, but five minutes later Tom looked round for him in the bar and found that he was gone.

Emma had pulled a hamstring in Ostend. She arrived late and limping, a chunky thigh strapped in bulbous bandages. 'Just our luck,' she said cheerfully. 'A week in the lap of luxury, and Caroline does her head in while I do my leg in. We're a couple of crocks . . .' She began a shambling dance, head bent forward, arms flailing. 'We both take fortune's knocks. But we prefer the city, Far away from the sheepy flocks.'

Bess laughed out loud. Caroline was her real friend, but Em – round, bouncy Em – was always a tonic. Where did all her fun come from? Heaven knows. Her father was a retired Permanent Secretary from Agriculture, her mother wrote rather sombre little children's books about a neurotic mouse called Snodgrass who always got indigestion when he ate cheese. She'd only seen them at Open Days, but they were both thin and disapproving of everything – especially their pneumatic daughter with her floppy mimes and throaty chuckles.

'Carrie's back in London tomorrow,' Bess said. 'I think we should pack up here in the morning and sit by her sick bed with grapes and mags and a bottle of gin. Mistress Nightingale, I presume?'

'Can you just do that? I mean, up and off? Isn't

everything notified to *The Times* three weeks in advance? Don't they have to give the flag people warning so they've someone on shift to pull it up?'

'Perhaps. Selene and Nicky are still here and they'll want the full treatment with all the regal trimmings. But they can stay if they want to. I'm sure I can fix it.' Easier said than done, she thought. They'd probably play the security card if they were truly dead set on keeping her locked up. Oh no you can't, Ma'am, the London detail will need two days' notice. But who was going to take a pot shot at her? She had no enemies; she knew nobody to fall out with.

The noise of a car braking hard on the gravel, spitting stones into the rose bed, brought her to the window. 'Oh, Fountain,' she said. 'Nobody said he was coming.' The only good thing about Sandringham had been Fountain in London. 'And Baron. All my chocolate-box favourites.'

As usual he barely paused to knock. 'Your Majesty . . . and . . .'

There was something of a mother scolding a stupid child in Bess's voice. 'Emma Lacey, Sir Edgar, one of my oldest friends. She was there when Belcher brought the news about father.'

He nodded, the neck constricting by no more than two centimetres, the mouth twisting for a milli-second into acknowledgement. 'Yes, absolutely. Perhaps though, if Miss Lacey could excuse us for a few minutes?'

Emma hauled herself to her feet and hobbled to the door. Bess felt her temper straining again. Always, always, they treated her with elaborate contempt.

'You won't have seen the *Express* this morning, Ma'am,' said Baron, opening his attaché case.

'I haven't seen any papers. I'm supposed to be on holiday.'

'Well, you might call this good news in a way. They've got you with straight As. Brilliant Queen tops the form. Oxford poised to welcome its most illustrious undergraduate. Security headache for university guards. It's not written as speculation. They've had a tip from somewhere.'

Fountain was beginning to splutter. 'You must realize how this puts us under pressure, Ma'am. We haven't decided what is best yet. The Prime Minister is still weighing up all the pros and cons and consulting with Scotland Yard and MI5 and Oxford City police, who of course are after substantial subventions. The Cabinet hasn't even discussed the possibilities. But now, from somewhere, there's a leak and the whole damned thing is simply treated as settled. It's an intolerable development. It forces our hands in the most unfortunate way.'

'I don't know why you seem so cross with me,' she said. 'I've no idea what my grades will be. I just hope the *Express* has got it right for once. But at least, now, we can start to think about things. The results, whatever they are, will be out in three weeks anyway. If I can go to university, I'm as keen on it as ever. Please give my regards to Mr Millward and his colleagues. Please tell them of my wishes. Meanwhile, Sir Richard, are you saying anything to the other papers?'

'Only that it's obviously speculative and that we never comment on speculation.'

'Quite,' she said. 'If you don't object, I'll come back to the Palace in the morning. We'd obviously all feel far easier if this thing was settled.'

Fountain made another minute bow. 'Very well, Ma'am. But remember, this cannot be your decision alone. There are so many others to consider.'

She could see Em out in the garden, hopping on a crutch down by the curve of the lake and sending a gaggle of geese screeching into the water. Emma smiled at her. Bess smiled back. 'Quite. There are others to consider.'

'Do we need to turn straight round?' Baron asked morosely as they retreated down the corridor. 'Up at six to get here, twenty minutes with Her Royal Teenageness, then back for lunch. It isn't much of a life since Millward cancelled the choppers.'

'Actually, I've nothing till four,' Fountain said. 'Why don't you wander over the main house and spend an hour or two with the papers? I haven't checked on the Duchess this week.'

It was eleven when Fountain found her and the sun was already hot. Selene was lying by the pool, moodily stirring a long pink drink with a straw. Her body shimmered with grease. Her mouth, before she looked up and saw him coming, was turned downwards in profound boredom.

'Oh, it's you. Aren't you awfully warm in that terrible suit? Take off your jacket and come and talk to me. I'll talk to anybody these days.'

There was nobody in sight. He felt somehow sheepish, almost clandestine, as he wriggled out of his jacket and pulled a deckchair closer.

'And the tie?'

He flushed, and loosened it.

'I've been thinking . . .' she said.

It seemed unlikely. She was wearing a small green bikini with polka dots of cornflower blue. She had, as everyone said, put on weight, but her body seemed to absorb it so that the pounds filled the skin with flesh rather than drooped from it. Her breasts were full and he could see the beginning of her nipples peeking from the top of the polka dots as she swung round towards him. There was a light crevice across the top of her stomach. Her thighs, flattened on the sun-lounger, were parted so that strands of hair wisped into view from the whiteness at the crux. Her face, beginning to fill and gather at the chin, was still unlined. She looked, he thought, like a debauched fairy.

Fountain felt an abrupt, unwelcome hardness between his legs and reached down hurriedly to drape the grey worsted jacket across his knees, as though a sudden breeze from the Wash had chilled the air. He saw a smile flicker on her lips for a second, and a long, pink tongue leap from between her teeth to lick it away.

'I've been thinking hard. Very hard.'

He pulled the coat closer over his lap.

'If Nicky and I are on the team, honorary minders of the Royal reputation, shouldn't we begin to get a little recognition for services rendered?'

'Services?' He was finding it hard to concentrate.

'And recognition,' she said. 'If I'm core royal now, I need something to tell people so. The old title they left me with seems all right for the moment. Duchess of Albany isn't much, but it has a ring to it: and I'm not thinking of upgrading until something really luscious comes along. But HRH would make a super difference to the way the footmen treated you. And poor Nicky has just got nothing. I mean, he's an absolutely entitled Prince, and he ought to be the Duke of Something Suitable at the very least. You're so influential, dear Edgar. Couldn't you fix it up for us? I would be so terribly grateful.'

He clutched the dignity of the worsted around him, like a matador with a cape, and scrambled to his feet. 'I shall consult as I think best,' he said, feeling pomposity biting at his ankles as he edged away from her. 'I can make no promises, of course. You have to remember that your conversion to propriety is still very recent and that public opinion will need to be prepared for any change in status.'

'But Edgar, I'm a good girl now.'

Her laughter pursued him around the edge of the pool and through the open doors of the conservatory.

Millward merely informed the Cabinet. 'I've decided that the Queen will, after all, be allowed to go to university. She's a strong-willed and difficult girl and I don't pretend the decision is other than awkward, expensive and inconvenient. But the focus groups are clear enough. They see no over-riding reason to cut her education short and we'd take a lot of stick if we tried to prevent her. When you try them with propositions like "In this modern age, monarchs need to be as educated as their subjects" or "Equal opportunities are for everyone in the land, from Palace to Peckham", you can see the trouble ahead. I wish I could get majorities like that. Whether they'll continue to be so sure, of course, only time will tell. There's an interestingly split result on "Kings and Queens must exercise self-sacrifice in the national good" and no contest on "Queens have a duty to work within society's norms". The young lady will have to watch her image – though that, alas, is our responsibility too.'

The Home Secretary groaned about the cost. The Education Secretary complained about Oxford elitism and bad examples. 'Why not Central Lancashire or Tees-side or North Staffs?' The new Foreign Secretary, already growing pompous beneath the weight of office, said that the royal African visit would be almost impossible to re-schedule. 'Once we're into the Kwa-Zulu election run-up we might as well forget it for years.' But there was never the beginning of an argument. When Leckie distributed the research conclusions they all sipped their coffee for a moment, then folded the findings away. The dossiers shut together with a definitive thud.

Chapter Five

Bradshaw, the editor of the *Express*, did not care for his exalted predecessor. Jammy bastard! Three years of circulation falling off a familiar cliff, spending all his time fawning around Downing Street. 'Government Heralds New Dawn for Pensioners'; 'Premier Charts Success Path to Prosperity'. Dickie bleeding Baron had only been in it for the knighthood right from the start. Bradshaw was made of dourer stuff. He came from Barnsley, where the *Express* (to general surprise) still sold particularly strongly to the over-fifties. He believed in brass and clawing your way up the greasy pole and hanging on tight when you reached the top. He did not approve of Baron's pale grey waistcoats or the new line in superciliousness he traded in since the dust of Fleet Street had been wiped from his gleaming brogues.

'Well, Dickie, always an honour to welcome you back. Watch that Dickie, I tell the lads on the floor when they get depressed. You don't have to end up on life's bloody spike. What can we do for you now?'

Baron smiled manfully and fingered his moustache. Braddy had been his Chief Sub ten years ago, always banging into his office demanding decisions. 'First edition's late again, Mr Baron. If you can't make up your mind what we're bloody leading on, could you find us somebody who will? Time and tide and Ulster newsagents wait for no one.' Deference always died in the boiler room.

'I just wanted a quiet word about that story of yours,' he said, with elaborate warmth. 'Good scoop. It really put the cat among the pigeons. There was always going to be a debate about what the Monarch was going to do, but you moved it on too fast for us, I can tell you. Off the record, the whole thing's settled.'

The voice dropped an octave. The smile broadened. He leaned forward across the editor's desk. 'And even further off the record, old son, we're into trading territory. You help me on this, and I can help you. You see, my masters these days are twitchy about leaks they don't control. If you could drop me a hint or two where to look, there'd be a lot of gratitude around. You'd be the natural place to have the official confirmation that she's going, travelling times, interviews with her tutors, the works. We could cut the *Mail* right out of it. You play ball with us, and we'll play ball with you.'

Bradshaw leaned back in his chair and laughed. 'You mean shop a good source and put us Number One on the Palace force-feeding belt, Dickie? Where are the bloody ethics in that? Anyway, you wouldn't stick by the bargain for fifteen seconds once you've got what you want. Anyone with their head screwed on knows that you of all people can't keep chucking sweeties to the *Express*. No, I'm sorry, old mate. No can do. It's a moral issue. I couldn't live with myself, you know.'

When Baron had gone, face flushed, down the back elevator, Bradshaw called Wittman on the phone. 'Get weaving sharpish, lad. The toffs are trying to nobble that brother of yours. They must reckon he's got something they want. And if that's true for them, it's true for us too. Tell young Sammy to keep his head down and keep passing us the mustard. There's a staff job in it for him if he plays his cards right.'

He paused for a moment. 'Oh, and I've a story for you. The Student Queen: Official. There's no point being half unpopular, I always say, when you can go the whole bleeding hog for tuppence on top.'

'So it is with great pleasure today that I name this hall the Prescott Memorial Rooms. May they provide, over the years, a source of community and assembled strength for the people of Humberside and remind them for ever of the devoted public servant who worked for so long to make a better environment for us all.'

She pulled the string and the fig-leaf of blue velvet over the plaque dropped away. There was a measured round of applause. The Mayor stepped gingerly to her left side. 'Wonderfully done, Your Majesty. Most gracious. And now the canteen ladies are offering us tea and scones in the refectory . . .'

He was at least twenty stone, she thought. See what a lifetime of tea and scones did for you? Baron hovered ten yards behind, talking to Chetwode-Belcher, who seemed to be always on hand these days. 'Thirty minutes maximum,' he said. 'We've got to be in Catterick at six for drinks in the mess before the regimental feast. Keep her moving and don't let her get too interested in anything. If she's going to have years enjoying herself, she might as well find out about the graft as well.'

Bess stopped and waved as she clambered into the car. The scones lay solid on her stomach. A couple of hundred people in anoraks raised a chilly cheer. The smoke from the new oil refinery in the port joined with the pall from the motorway and blotted out the last shafts of sunlight.

Mrs Bennett's Boarding House in Rawalpindi had not seen Mrs Bennett – or indeed any of her daughters, the Misses Lizzy, Jane, Mary, Lydia and Kitty – for nearly a century. Nor anything much by way of upkeep either. Said Akbar, only heir and successor to Mrs B, spent most of his time selling carpets to visiting Americans and Japanese in the bazaar. He left old Zulfi to serve the boiled eggs and cornflakes to those who ate breakfast on the peeling verandah, and ferry the thick tea and sodden toast from the greasy tin-roofed kitchen at the back; he left Moni, otherwise known as the Begum Zulfi, to change the grey sheets once a week and sweep the cockroaches under the bed with her straw broom. The spirit of the Bennett frontier lived eternally, untouched by time or tide of humanity. The establishment was cheap, a tenth of the price of the Pindi Hilton with its manicured grounds and turbanned concierges a hundred yards away. The travelling salesmen from Lahore or Karachi who stopped at Mrs B's, hanging shining, threadbare jackets over the chipped baths to ease away the wrinkles, expected nothing else. They were one step up the ladder, a small shuffle from the shanty hotels across town where Afghans looking for work or Biharis still sueing the Government for damages hung their hats.

'I'm sorry,' said the young man from the British Council. 'We got our financial years muddled in April and I'm afraid HMG is rather punishing us on the permissible hospitality front. But the theatre is really quite presentable for this part of the world – though I don't advise using the showers.'

As first nights went, it went nowhere. Adrian counted the audience. Fifty-one . . . fifty-two . . . No, that was a goat. The British High Commissioner had offered them lime juice and little cakes of boiled milk and sugar on the lawn in Islamabad, but not his presence. 'This Shakespeare wallah, alas, has got a trade mission from Doncaster to look after. My wife would have loved to come, I'm sure, but the old Khyber Revenge has rather laid her low again.'

What audience there was appeared to have only the barest acquaintance with the English language. Five brown, solemn little boys in white shirts and neat blue ties sat on the front row with dictionaries, straining to look up words in the dim glow from the footlights. The rest chatted constantly in Punjabi. The goat slept.

They walked disconsolately home to the boarding house, smeared with dust from the battered taxis which always seemed to drive with their wheels in the grime of the gutter. Youths in grubby T-shirts stared at them as they passed and shouted ritual incantations. 'You want souvenirs, Sir/Madam? You want be shown good time?'

Tom was bone tired with the futility of it all when they got back to the darkened slump of the building. The crickets in the garden seemed to be taunting them, exulting in their humiliation.

'Coffee?' asked Adrian wanly.

Tom shrugged and put his arms around Julia. She had seemed, after the second act, to have shrivelled into herself. She was a small, tight ball of misery. 'No. No thanks. There are some days that don't end soon enough. See you for a better tomorrow.'

Her room was next to his. She fiddled with her latch. He opened his door. 'Why not come in for a moment and cheer yourself up?' She shrugged and followed him. There was whisky at the bottom of his suitcase, under the pants and socks. And the Afghan who'd met them at the station had sold him enough joints for a couple of evenings. He tipped the toothbrush out of the mug and poured her a fat finger's worth. She drank it at a gulp. 'It's not good to mix,' he said.

'Sod mixing. Give me a light.'

They opened the window and lay on the floor for a while in silence, smoking and drinking turn and turnabout. 'Last knockings?' he said, with a smile she could not see. She sat upright and peeled the shirt over her head, then wobbled to the narrow, squeaky bed with the rusted iron bedhead. The smile never slid from his face as he stripped and flung himself on top of her.

She was always noisy. The sounds of pleasure seemed to start somewhere deep within her and burst to the surface like bubbles from a diver fifteen fathoms down. 'Oh Christ. Oh Christ, Christ, Christ.'

Suddenly there was a blinding beam from the window, transfixing them so that they broke away from each other and turned in bemusement. 'What the hell?' said Tom.

Feet pattered along the creaking verandah. The bare bulb clicked into life. Zulfi, naked to the waist, clad only in bulging cotton trousers, was looking at them, pointing a finger and beginning to jabber. Beside him was a tall man in a khaki shirt with buttons that gleamed as he brought the torch upwards. Tom reeled off the bed towards him and began, instinctively, to throw a punch.

'No,' Julia howled. She was sitting bolt upright now, her round breasts jutting towards them, her swollen mouth taut with panic. 'He's a bloody policeman.'

'Well,' said the young man from the British Council with a mincing exasperation, 'I hope you've learned one or two necessary things. This is a Muslim country. No sex – at least not as a spectator sport. No drink with the window open. No drugs if you're a foreigner asking to be excused a night in the cells. And No No No punching policemen. I had to call the High Commissioner personally. He is absolutely furious, I can tell you. One or two favours London wanted up their sleeves have been wasted on a bunch of student actors who'd be better sitting in some Soho gutter, if you ask me. If it wasn't for the Council's reputation, we'd have left you to stew.'

Tom, right eye puffed and black where the policeman had hit him with the revolver butt, was flinging his clothes into the suitcase.

'Where's the Scotch?' he said thickly.

'Evidence. Confiscated with the pot. You won't see any of them again, you idiot. It'll be party night at the station.

'I've paid your bills and slipped the wretched manager enough to keep him quiet for a couple of days. The taxis are out on the left under the jacaranda trees. Now please, just get in one, go to the station, catch the six-fifteen train and don't call me when you arrive in Karachi. You're gone, you're out of here. And good riddance. We've got the Torquay Sinfonia arriving next week. I just thank my lucky stars they aren't here to see this.'

Julia had stuffed one of the joints into her bra as they had handcuffed Tom. She lit it as they walked clumsily through the garden, swinging their cases defiantly. She giggled. They climbed into the taxi.

Fountain was carrying a pink file with a purple ribbon hanging loose. He sat down at the table and tied the ribbon carefully back into place, then pulled at the bow and opened the folder so that Bess could see its thickness. Caroline and Emma, sitting behind her, craned forward.

'These are your regulations, Your Majesty,' Fountain said, splaying the papers like playing cards in front of her. 'See, each one carries a Cabinet Office stamp. That means they have been subject to discussion and approval at the highest level in your Government.'

'You mean they are serious, Sir Edgar,' she said. 'But, of course, none of us ever doubted that. We have always expected our marching orders.'

He wondered for the thousandth time whether she was mocking him. He thought so, but not certainly enough to snap back at her. He coughed instead. 'The negotiations with the college are complete. You have been assigned all three rooms on Staircase 7 in the front quadrangle. Here, immediately to the left of the President's Lodgings. The ground room will be unoccupied during the day, though Special Branch will always have an officer on duty in the Porter's Lodge which, as you can see, has an uninterrupted view of the staircase. One of the officers will sleep in that room at night. You will inform him of your movements and not deviate from notified schedules without prior warning.'

'Oh,' she said bleakly, 'and will there be more armed guards on top? What happens if I'm caught in the crossfire?'

'These are trained professionals,' he said. 'It would be quite unthinkable for them to make such an error, as I am sure Your Majesty understands. In any case, the room above yours has been reserved for Miss Northcott. Since she, too, is a student of St John's, it makes sense that she is constantly to hand.'

Caroline ran her fingers through the tight bob of

blonde hair. 'And am I to be guarded as well, Sir Edgar?'

'We do not think that necessary, though you will naturally be required to complete the intensive induction course offered to all ladies-in-waiting before term commences. You and the Queen will both be doing PPE, so the coterminosity makes for simpler planning. If on occasion you wish to undertake engagements of your own, then we suggest that Miss Lacey operates with you on a rota system. She is only a few hundred yards away in Trinity. The logistics do not present insuperable problems.'

'It's rather like a war,' Emma said, bouncing up and down in her chair. 'If the first wave falls on its sword then here I come with my handbag.'

He sniffed. 'We shall of course have communication lines open to the Palace day and night, but for the first year we think it prudent to have an experienced equerry on hand. You know Chetwode-Belcher well. He has rented a service apartment in the Randolph. He will not intrude gratuitously, but he will be able to involve himself in matters of protocol and lend a steadying presence to any social events you may undertake.'

'He's my date?' said Bess incredulously. 'People will talk.'

'On the contrary, Ma'am. It is his role to prevent people from talking.'

Fountain seemed unstoppable that day. His file had pink papers and green papers, yellow papers and blue. It had flow charts and alarm numbers, maps of Oxford with dangerous rooftops ringed in red, photos of

American pickpockets and rapists from Cowley.

'And finally,' he said, reaching the section in palest lemon, unclipping it for rapt display, 'there are what we may term your working hours. These again have been most carefully liaised with the university and college authorities. During term you will spend every weekend from 11.30 p.m. Friday until 8.30 a.m. Monday at home – by which, in normal circumstances, we mean Windsor for convenience of travel. Your mother and brother will be in attendance on these occasions. Should there be any permissible variance, say an invitation to Blenheim or some house of similar standing, your mother will, in the first instance, be invited too. Mondays and Fridays will normally be kept free of lectures and tutorials. Where there are imperative affairs of state, they will normally be targeted at those days. The Prime Minister has signalled his intention to brief you once a fortnight during term: at Windsor whenever possible. You will obviously enter into no arrangements for vacations without due clearance. There is already a heavy burden of work to be organized within those boundaries of availability. The Bath EU summit in early December, the visit of the Cypriot President on 2–4 January inclusive, the Estonian State visit in July . . . They're all here for diary synchronization.'

'When do I have any fun?' Bess asked in her smallest, meekest, mockest mouse of a voice.

'Fun, Ma'am?' said Emma, clapping her on the back and roaring with laughter. 'Fun is an optional extra on this tour of duty.'

Dear Lilibet,

I bumped into third cousin Stavros at Wimbledon this afternoon. You recall? The one who might have been King of Greece if they still had a king and he hadn't got two older brothers. I was sitting at the front of the Royal Box with the American Ambassador (who chews gum) and the Prime Minister's wife (who chews her nails), and he was right at the back, wrapped up in a raincoat the size of Macedonia.

Well, when the latest British Great White Hope had gone down the pan in three sets – 'Unbelievable,' he kept shouting at the umpire, 'frigging unbelievable' – and we'd all tottered off for tea, I thought a touch of politesse seemed indicated. Long time no see, Stavros, and suchlike. What are you doing with yourself these days?

And here's the rub, my love. He'd been earning big bucks in California, working for some chip zillionaire near San Jose, and he'd met this Bulgarian girl on the beach. And she said she'd have been a Bulgarian princess – if they still had them, etc. etc. And he said – well, you can guess what he said.

Anyway, they got spliced and some of the tattier LA rags ran a story and flogged it on the Eurotosh mag circuit – and then, guess what? They jacked it all in and came back to live in Hemel Hempstead to try to break into British society. Prince Stavros and Princess Tatyana, without a sou to rub between them. Available for garden fêtes and car-boot sales. 'We are waiting for the call,' he said. 'We are

schooling ourselves for the moment our people say
they need us.' I lent him the Tube fare home.
    Like the G W H kept saying, my dear: frigging
unbelievable.

Chapter Six

Nobody had spent a euro on Caroline's room. The wallpaper was yellowed and slack, flapping around the door frame until she'd anchored it with chewing gum; the carpet was cheapest hessian in what appeared to be brown until she lifted the bed and saw the dull cream beneath it. The curtains were a faded green, and frayed where they touched the floor. The electric kettle didn't work unless you held the plug into the socket. The pilot light on the old water heater in the kitchenette was feeble, destroyed by any passing draught. The wind howled through the cracks beneath the dark leaded windows.

'Servant's quarters,' said Caroline brightly. Bess loved them. They had been her only escape for the first three days, a haven where she and Carrie could sip a warm Moselle and talk about the old days of tennis-team tours and French-set trips to Toulouse – and the weekends sailing with Caroline's dad in Poole, when the grind of eight open-heart operations a day made him seize up with fatigue and he'd cancel his private list.

Downstairs, the college, with the good fortune of a Lottery grant, had done what it considered seemly.

The walls were lush and detailed, newly decorated with paper kept in store now for the moment when the Lord Chancellor's apartments needed refurbishment; the carpets were thickest Persian. Two Hogarths of David Garrick and wife hung over the bed. The secure telephones – one black for Downing Street, one white for the Palace – seemed to lie in wait. Downstairs she was trapped. Sergeant Crawley or Inspector Finch were always there at dusk. The narrow stairs squeaked whenever she moved on them. They would open the door long before she reached the bottom flight. 'Are you going somewhere, Your Majesty?' 'Just for a stroll in the gardens.' 'I wouldn't advise that, Ma'am. Not till we've had a security sweep. And there's rain coming on, they say.'

But upstairs, squatting on the hessian drinking coffee or lying on the bed listening to her music, feet curled behind her, she felt almost human. And Caroline, after a fearful row, could have visitors once the X-ray in the hallway had been installed. Emma was round every evening with a plastic shopping bag. 'Bath Olivers and Chocolate Chips, by appointment to Her Majesty.' She brought friends to pay court and hover nervously near Caroline's sofa, wondering whether to curtsy or bow or merely scratch their noses in the presence. 'This is Rachel from Wadham. She plays badminton too. This is Clare from Somerville. She's American. This is Johnny from Queen's. Johnny, meet Queen from John's.'

She went out by careful arrangement. The President invited her and Sinclair – 'Your Moral Tutor, Ma'am'

– to breakfast. The President was a white-haired classicist who had once written a book about Herodotus called *Ancient as Modern* which had won the Norman Stone Bursary, ten cases of fine claret, but there had been nothing new for thirty years now and he had retreated, through rolls of pendulous fat, into an eccentricity he found convenient defence. 'See, Your Majesty, I always make the toast freshly for my guests myself. White or brown down into the toaster and watch … See, it pops up … How did Virgil ever manage without a pop-up toaster?'

Sinclair was a desiccated chemistry don nudging fifty with deep lines of disappointment running from his mouth. He wore his oldest tweed jacket with leather patches, as if in defiance, and spoke to her only briefly as they left. 'I imagine Your Majesty is never short of moral tuition. But please leave me a note in the Lodge if I can ever be of assistance.'

She had Mrs Lauder from St Hilda's for philosophy and Morrison from Hertford for politics. They were both strangely cautious when they met her, she thought, in case some unwelcome beam of publicity had flickered across their lives. But Toby Hunter was 'a John's inmate' with a booming voice and a pleasant lope which devoured the flagstones of the quad as he moved cheerfully back and forth. He was always on television prophesying some kind of economic doom. 'Manufacturing can't live with these rates. It'll be desert all the way from Dagenham to Dover.' 'The question isn't why monetary union has survived so long; it's whether it can last until the end of the year if Croatia devalues unilaterally.' He shook Bess by the hand at her first tutorial and grinned. 'I'm a merchant of doom, I know, but I never let it get me down.'

She went out two or three times a day, peering through the open half-gate to watch the security detail raise a hand, glancing behind as the rest of the caravan mustered. There were lectures, of course, but no one seemed to go to them. She had waited, with a couple of dozen others, for half an hour last Tuesday before Hunter finally turned up. 'Ladies and gentlemen, I'm so miserably sorry. I overslept.' She'd be better, she decided, letting the mountains of indolence or indiscipline come to her. When she went out, it would mostly be to the library or the movies or the Union if there was a decent debate. But she was never alone.

Just over St Giles, in front of the Ashmolean, a dozen or so cars were always parked, day and night, with two men sitting in the front seats: one to sleep or read or fetch the coffee, the other to wait for her to move out of the gates.

Sammy Wittman would wander by and watch them – smelly, unshaven, eyes drooping with boredom. Are these Fleet Street's finest? he asked himself. Is this the job of my dreams? Sammy had only filed routine gossip paragraphs since Bess arrived. He was tilling his garden carefully, he told himself. When his moment came, as it would, he wanted it to be a moment to remember.

A blackish Friday. Robin Leckie had a throbbing headache. The Sunday Lobby briefing hadn't been as smooth as he'd hoped. Usually the hacks just sat there, mouths and notebooks open, transcribing the word of their Lord. But today there was trouble. The twelve Traditional Liberals in the coalition had got the wind up after a particularly grisly by-election in Tiverton and had decided to paddle their own canoe for a while. That left Millward with a majority of just two; too close for comfort, especially now the Central Bank was tightening money supply.

'No sweat,' Leckie told them with as much insouciance as he could muster. 'We all know what's happened. The Trads have always been amateurs and mavericks, saying different things on different doorsteps. Ban the motor car if they're in Hampstead; cut petrol taxes if they're in Taunton. They aren't used to the grind and responsibility of governing, and frankly the P M is glad to see the back of them. I can tell you – in confidence, of course – that he was thinking of ditching Baxter at the next reshuffle anyway. There are two sorts of Liberal leader in our experience: those who make jokes; and those who don't make anything at all. Baxter is straight Class B, long on pieties and short on arithmetic. He never balanced the national-insurance budget. He evidently thought it easier to camp outside the Prime Minister's door doing his old Oliver Twist act. More, more, more.'

Not bad if it had ended there. 'Colonel "Twister" Baxter quits to dodge axe. Downing Street cheers as amateur Trads walk out.' But the Lobby were suddenly fractious. Coalition politics bored them and their editors rigid. Parliamentary staffing had fallen every year for the last ten. Even *The Times* had more showbiz reporters than Westminster correspondents now, and the trade press reckoned the *FT* had five extra redundancies in the pipeline for the Christmas recess.

'Come on, Robin,' said the *Mail*, 'don't feed us that bland crap. If Baxter goes over to the Tories in a couple of months, your boss is slap in the mire. The Reform Libs won't touch him while they think Baxter can pull a flanker. The Progressive Cons got burned last time. They hate Millward and all his works. That means there're only the Nats and the True Socialists to think about. The Nats want so much cash they make Baxter look like Scrooge. So if the PM wants to hang on, he's right back where his party started from all those years ago – having to pretend that the people's revolution is just around the corner. Now, tell me I'm wrong.'

But he was right, of course. They all knew it. Millward knew it most clearly of all. Robin did his best, but – an increasingly familiar out-of-body experience – he could hear himself blustering. 'Don't be so bloody stupid. Write that and, I warn you, you'll regret it before your sheets hit the street. You might as well sign on for the dole on Monday.' Cheap shot. They bayed at him, and he turned on his heel.

He worked late in the Cabinet Office, pounding the phones, calling in favours from the dailies. 'Look, my governor and your governor are going on a skiing holiday together in January with a one-item agenda before the fondue. VAT on newsprint is right there on the action list. But I don't need to tell you he has enemies at the moment. He wants a little support in all our interests. Are you reading me? No can do or no can fondue, matey.'

It was almost ten when, as had become his custom, Millward drifted by and perched on Leckie's desk. 'Are we winning?'

'A score draw at the outside. They believe you've got to talk to Cavendish and the Luddites. They can't see you've any cards left.'

'Only a Royal flush,' said Millward under his breath.

Robin heard that. He took the phones off the hook and poured himself a mug of the acrid, burnt coffee which had simmered all evening on the hob. It was the time of night he had quickly learned to relish most: tutorial time, when he played the eager student and a relaxed Millward would unveil the mysteries to him. But first he had to table the question for discussion.

'The one thing I never understand about you is your obsession with royalty,' Robin said casually. 'I mean, what are they? Germans from long ago, washed up on our shores and hugging themselves that the natives are friendly. They're not very bright. They're not very public spirited. They're tight as hell.

'We are supposed to be a government of change and progress. Do you remember that Coventry speech of yours? A country without privilege built on a nation of effort. Good stuff. But if I had a euro for every hour you've spent fussing over that dazed little girl who woke up one morning and found she was Queen, I'd be sitting in Juan-les-Pins right now with my feet up, worrying about sweet nothing ever again.'

'You just haven't got it, have you?' Millward said. 'Is there any Scotch in this rat den?'

'In the wastepaper basket. Under the *Sun*, somewhere.' Two plastic cups; two long shots of Bell's.

Millward had his donnish voice on now: soft, sure and writhing in its own brilliance. 'It's an easy mistake,' he said. 'I used to think that monarchies didn't matter much either. Wholemeal bread and sex circuses for the masses. But the men who built this party were always cute enough to see that they were much more than that. Do you recall all those pictures of the early Blair tooling round the Palace buttering up the old crew? Why did he keep doing it? Why was he so damned anxious to make them seem human? Deference, Robin. Deference: the great British drug.

'If he bowed and scraped to them, then someone would have to bow and scrape to him. Pass the parcel, bend the knee. When you're Prime Minister you need to be able to tell the minions what to do and reckon that they'll bleeding well jump to it most of the time. You don't want endless arguments and conference motions and all that junk. Sure, the people elect you. God bless them every one. But after that you want your own space to operate in. Kings and Queens, just being there, have permanent space. They exist. They have wishes. The trick is to turn them into a higher level of authority so that you are their servant on earth and everybody on down the chain recognizes it – at least until they start thinking, which they don't.'

Robin passed the bottle. 'Another snifter, Cardinal Richelieu?'

'Right track, wrong continent,' Millward said.

'Most of the poncing pundits have never got the point. PR has knocked the jagged edges off British politics. Umpteen parties and factions, not two or three big lumps. So if you keep dodging and weaving, you can spend most of your life in some fat office or other. Italy, they say: the divine right to keep your fingers in the till. But actually we're Japan, when you think about it. The Emperor sits in his Palace pavilioned in deference. The politicians go snuffling round him, letting his light shine on them. Then, when the votes are counted, they carve things up to best advantage to keep the old gold carriage on the road. But take away the Emperor and they'd be stark naked in twenty seconds. The Emperor gives them the clothes.'

One of Leckie's girls – Hillary, the thin one with glasses and shorthand – knocked hesitantly at the door. The first editions. Robin laid them out grimly on the desk. 'Baxter calls time for Millward', said the *Mail*; 'Nowhere to go but Hard Left', said the *Guardian*; 'Cavendish may be the master now', said the *Telegraph*.

'That's all very fine,' Robin said. 'But I don't see what use it is here.'

Millward produced his widest grin of the night. 'Simple. Look in Cavendish's last manifesto. Page 19, paragraph 12. Oh, I know nobody read it. Probably Cavendish didn't read it himself, just let the computer dump in the slurry of ages past. But I read it. I can quote it verbatim. "We shall move with expedition to make Britain a republic in which all the people, irrespective of birth or class, have equal rights to progress by their own toil; we propose an elective presidential system on the Swiss model, rotating annually, to remove cults of personality and inherited authority from the superintendence of the modern State."

'Not many laughs there, my boy. But just think about it. Can I, the custodian of our finest traditions, put them in pawn by doing grubby deals with this radical gang? Of course not. But can the Trads or the Progressive Cons sit idly by, hugging their self-interest, at such a moment of threat? Of course not. Baxter or Bissett will come running back in a second. Even the Tories will start to whimper about grand coalitions.'

Leckie emptied the bottle. 'But where does the emotion get into the act? You'll need total drama to pull off the crisis.'

Millward frowned. 'Slow, boy, slow. A year of tragedy. A slip of a girl finding her way. A Prime Minister bent on guiding and protecting her for the national good. A Coronation which sends a message to the world. Drama? It's a bloody pageant.'

'But the Coronation is ages off yet. Remember, we said eighteen months minimum as a mark of respect to those who died? Her great-grandma had to wait sixteen months; her grandfather took two years to decide, and he was sixty-three . . .'

'The Queen', Millward said, 'is twenty on June 5th. At such a time of trial and uncertainty, I see a natural symmetry in her birthday and the rebirth of commitment and joy which coronations bring. Get me an audience with her in Oxford, tomorrow. Stir up the Archbishop. Tell the BBC they'll get their licence-fee raise if they do a proper job. And make sure the tabloids know there'll be photographs.'

*

There were leaves blowing on the towpath and the wind from the west still had a bite to it, but the autumn sun was bright enough to cast shadows. One or two hired crews rowed back and forth along the Isis, pausing to lift their blades high for the cameras. 'Lovely background,' said the *Star* to the *Standard*. 'We can make her the new Viking Queen.'

Millward had fished an old pair of cords and a yellow sweater he used for yachting out of a bottom drawer. 'My student look,' he said to Leckie, brushing his thinning hair forward then tweaking it into a ingratiating mop.

'But she's the student,' said Robin. 'You're supposed to be the proud father.'

Millward grunted. 'Well, a mature student.'

They had debated Selene for twenty minutes. Should she be invited? On the one hand, a doting mum made it a family occasion. Millward was keen to hint at that. 'Together, we could be her parents. That's right up Middle England's street.' But on the other hand, Selene was Selene. 'On probation,' Leckie said finally. 'Still working her passage.'

So the scenario, as detailed, was set and simple. Youngish PM and Young Monarch together in romantic setting, but without explicit gestures. 'Don't touch her, whatever you do,' Leckie said. 'One handshake and that's it. Eighteen inches between you minimum on the walk. Anything else might look like paedophilia.'

The wind was getting up, blowing Millward's hair back awkwardly, revealing an increasingly tedious expanse of forehead. Bess's hands were thrust deep into a blue duffel coat. The black and red and gold of the college scarf was wrapped twice around her neck so that her small, tense face seemed perched on top of it. She wore no make-up. She looked, perhaps, sixteen.

'But I still don't understand why everything has to be so rushed,' she said.

The cameras were fifteen yards or so back. There was no one to hear.

'If I may put it like this, Ma'am . . . it isn't necessary for you to understand. It is only necessary that you take the advice of your ministers.'

He stopped for a moment and looked over his shoulder to make sure the following pack had stopped too. Then he gazed into her eyes and smiled his widest, most adoring smile, the one he usually saved for party conferences. She pulled the scarf higher over her chin, and glowered into its folds.

Adrian had one more production window open before Finals. He knew he had to use it. The *Antony and Cleopatra* fiasco had ruined his second year: a complete write-off, so nobody remembered his Pirandello from the summer before, which had been decently reviewed, nor the Beckett in the hut by the Cherwell boathouse. No: if he was going to get a job in rep anywhere – Aberdeen, Chester, Luton, never mind Bristol or Leeds – he needed a big one and a pile of cuttings.

But first there had to be opportunity. The Mummers wouldn't provide it; indeed, they would provide nothing until the bills the British Council insisted on for shipping the wreckage of Egypt back from Rawalpindi were paid. Adrian paddled zealously in wider ponds. He directed a handful of sketches for an Experimental Theatre Club cabaret in a drill hall in North Oxford; but there was no heating and the audience, huddled and sneezing, left at the interval. The Spanish Society was holding a sherry evening of Lorca readings. He thought he was in with a chance until he realized they were in Spanish. There was only OUDS left.

The Oxford University Dramatic Society, like so much around it, had seen better days. Long before, in the golden era everybody talked of mournfully in the Welsh Pony, there'd been a grand production every term and the London critics had booked suites at the Randolph to entertain the talents that caught their eye. A glass of champagne, a rave notice and, if you were very good, a night to remember with the indefatigable grandee from the *Sunday Times*. Now, though? Now there was only the money to take the Playhouse twice a year, and the Trinity term had to be Shakespeare: do whatever was set for GCSE Eng. Lit. and the local education authority coughed up 5,000 euros. So it was *Romeo and Juliet*, or nothing.

Adrian saw naught for his comfort there. He was sick of Shakespeare anyway. The gossips in the Pony were still laughing over his last disaster. Salam Gupta at Brasenose had an idea for making the Montagues and Capulets into Hindus and Muslims and turning Verona into Darjeeling, which was bound to wow the selection committee. What was the point of trying to beat that?

'I give up. I just give up,' he told Tom and Julia over coffee in Dunking Delicious. 'They're advertising for stage staff at the New over Christmas. Cinderella, ten euros an hour and all the pumpkin you can eat. At least it would be something to put on the CV.'

'Come on, Ade,' Julia said with a brightness she did not feel. 'Nothing ventured, and all that crap. Cleo wasn't your fault. It was natural forces. In bed and out. And you haven't got to go scratching round for a cast. Put Tom in some of those tight leggings and every spotty fifth-former from here to Banbury will be throwing themselves off balconies.'

Tom flexed his jaw, as he did fifty times each morning in front of the mirror, and pushed the last doughnut to the side of the plate. 'She's right, you know. If we could give them a decent reading, they might go with us. The Gupta thing could turn out to be a tea bag full of shit. What we need is an angle of our own.'

It was Saturday morning and the long, low stretch of the café was barely half full. Two girls were gossiping by the doughnut plates. One chocolate-coated, or two?

Tom thought he recognized the tubby, jolly, shaky one from school. Hadn't she been in the Roedean tug-of-war team which had damned nearly pulled them over the cliffs? But Caroline, tall, slim, hair just touching her shoulders in a golden dance, was unmistakable. She'd been first-team tennis. He could still recall the length of her legs and the flash, on the smash, of her knickers. Tom was living out this second year stuffed in a garret half a mile away at the bottom of the Bardwell Road. He slept three nights a week with Julia and divided the rest between the gym, the Taj Mahal and the Scala Cinema. He didn't go into college much.

'Why don't you pop in and give Bess my love?' his mother had said at the start. 'It will do her good if there're people she can relax with who remember the old days.' But Tom had never felt up to the effort. The photographers mooching outside the college gates and the heavy men in bulging suits who guarded her staircase were hurdles he declined to jump. And anyway, he felt guilty somehow. Well, perhaps not guilty – just uneasy. That drunken evening months ago when he'd been blathering on to Wittman, the smug little rat, about Bess's exam results. There'd been a hell of a stink in the papers. Was it anything he'd said? At any rate, he'd decided to give the whole shooting match a wide berth.

Caroline chose the strawberry doughnut and turned, tray in hand, to look for a table. Her eyes rested for a second on the group in the window: a girl with cropped hair, a spindly youth in a sweater that swamped him – and a rather stunning boy who kept flexing his jaw. Hadn't she met him somewhere? Perhaps in Brighton? She smiled and nodded tentatively in his direction so that the blonde hair fell forward over her face. She tossed her head back.

Suddenly Tom had an idea.

Bess hated Windsor. It was cold and artificial, and noisy without respite as the jets from Heathrow roared overhead. The blocks of grey stone seemed to catch her in the chest and crush her with their weight. The smell of the great fire, decades before, had never quite gone. There was something acrid in the air. Some of the paintings in the big hall caught her in the throat. So many ancestors, so little joy. They were uniformly ugly, with pinched mouths and chilly eyes – like inmates in a prison of the centuries. From time to time, after the gates had shut on the tourist hordes, she would patrol the corridors of state – pausing, from habit swiftly acquired, by the Van Dyck in the Queen's Ballroom where the Second Duke of Buckingham looked out wistfully, as though eye to eye. A blond little boy, but his cheeks were drawn and his chest was concave beneath the red velvet jacket. He seemed about to speak to her over four centuries and say that he, too, was a prisoner – that he, too, would have no life. She would dream of him in the night, and wake up sweating.

The crowds gathered day after day in Engine Court and stared across the Quadrangle to where she sat at her window. No escape. She hated the formality of the private gardens, with their precise pathways and manicured lawns. She would walk, from choice, along the stretch of the North Terrace, seeing the pygmies and the playing fields far below, or in the snug curl of the Governor's Garden, winding with rose bushes around the bulk of the Round Tower; but such things were possible only as evening came and the gates were creaked shut. It was the people who made anything else impossible.

The town looked cheery enough. Tea shops and armadas of buses. But the town was off limits, temptation beyond the walls. They allowed her out from time to time to go through her routine. Last Saturday, a Sikh women's knitting club in Slough and a Gujarati language lab in Southall. 'Please come along now, Your Majesty. The forty minutes are up.' This weekend, though, there was nothing scheduled beyond the Sunday morning plod to St George's Chapel, with Selene and Nicky trailing in her wake – and even they had bailed out for the afternoon. Her mother had 'one or two things' she needed to do in Kensington. Her brother was at the dentist's again, wincing at the slow grind of producing an evenness to the smile he never gave.

She sat silent in her room. The floor was littered with books she did not want to read, instructing her of things she did not want to know for an essay on The British Public School as a Determinant of Victorian Society. 'Report of the Clarendon Commission 1864 . . . The schools, taken as a whole, have been the chief nurseries of our statesmen; in them, and in schools modelled after them, men of all the various classes that make up English society, destined for every profession and career, have been brought up on a feeling of social equality, and have contracted the most enduring of friendships, and some of the ruling habits, of their lives; and they have had perhaps the largest share in moulding the character of an English gentleman.'

The Whole Life of Roedean legend lives! she thought. There was always technology – and the gadgets of amazement, bought one year, broken the next. But nobody had invented a new chip to change the brain of Britain. Where had Millward gone to school? There was an old *Who's Who* somewhere under the bed which she sometimes read when she woke in the night, worrying about the names and waistcoats she would meet the next day. Yes, Millward, Simon Roger; educ. Dulwich College Preparatory S. and Shrewsbury S. Could she get that into the essay somewhere? At least it was almost a joke.

Fountain kept a small service flat on the second floor of the Palace, but he tried not to stay there at weekends. There was the cottage half a mile from Althorp his father had bought long ago when he'd thought that the magnet of the Diana necropolis might inflate property prices. And there was the tiny mews house in a creek of silence just back from the Gloucester Road.

He liked the mews on the deserted afternoons of encroaching winter. He liked the way none of his neighbours, whatever the weather, ever stayed in town. If it was fine they went to Somerset; if it was chill they went to Chichester for the sailing or St Germain for the brasseries. He could always reckon on buying a game pie and tomato chutney in Harrods, picking up a bottle or two of decent claret on the way out, and bank on blank windows and still curtains as he turned the key in the door. Up the steep, narrow staircase. Into the living room of gleaming walnut panelling which reminded him of the cabin of his father's yacht – before the Saudi Arabian bathroom contract went belly-up and certain sacrifices had to be made. Put the pie in the fridge. Check there was champagne still on ice. Then up the second, circular staircase to the great, low loft with its warm, musky walls and the skylight over his king of a bed.

'Oh shit!' Selene said. 'I've lost it. There was a bloody starling sitting on the roof, looking down at me and banging its beak on the glass. Get off and fetch the rest of the bubbly.'

Fountain clambered to his feet, caught a glimpse of his round, white stomach in the mirror and wrapped a towel around his waist. At school he had always preferred boys, and indeed still might – given a free choice. But his dear, departed ex-wife – departed, that is, with a heart surgeon from Pangbourne – had been a resourceful, inventive girl in the earliest days of their marriage. He had learned diligently that there were always two sides to the argument.

The champagne was Lanson N V. Not what, in ideal circumstances, he'd have chosen for himself. But Selene swigged it like pop and he'd found the bills beginning to grate on his current accounting. Still, it was almost over. One more tumbler full and she'd explode as usual, threshing and groaning on top of him, spraying his shoulders with spittle. He, according to custom, came later with a modest sibilance, teeth gritted, stomach carefully constricted. But that was fine. They both, in their various ways, served a common purpose.

She levered herself up on her elbows and looked at him. 'Have you asked her yet?'

'Tomorrow, if you like. After church. It's jumped through all the other hoops. Millward is satisfied with your progress. Baron's latest polls show you two points off an outright lead on Acceptability. The Don't Knows are making up their minds.'

She ran her thumbs gently across the inside of her thighs and broke into the familiar squeak of a laugh. 'So, A for Acceptability,' she said. 'What about T for Titles?'

'Your Royal Highness, the Duchess of Albany, Marchioness of Connaught and Countess of Bonchurch,' he said. 'That's a pretty fair menu.'

'And Prince Nicky?'

'HRH the Duke of Clarence.'

'I don't know,' she said cautiously. 'It's not York or Kent or Norfolk – one of those famous places ordinary people recognize automatically. Not exactement fantastique. I don't call it winning the Lottery.'

'Well it's old and it's free and it's the best I can do.'

She leaned back and tipped the tumbler down her throat messily, so that a trickle of Lanson ran down her chin and into the deep cavity between her breasts. 'Ya, OK then. Let's see what's the best I can do.'

Dear Lilibet,
I had a call from your mother last night. I'm back from Klosters, she said: can I come round? It was 11.35 and, as you well know, love, I hadn't seen her for yonks. But that's fine, I said. I'll put a bottle on ice.

She was wearing a brown headscarf and sunglasses when she knocked, which was jolly odd when you think it's February. But when she came into the light, I could see why. Two lovely black

*eyes and a bruise on her chin the size of a decent
Fabergé.*

*Skiing accident? Ya, she sort of half muttered,
and then started to blub. The sort of skiing accident
where Fritzi, the Austrian downhiller with the pecs
and the Courvoisier habit, cuts loose in the chalet
after dinner over a little harmless flirtation with an
Italian press baron. All a terrible misunderstanding,
of course. It was his papers she thought were
wonderful. But soon she was telling me she'd seen
the light and was sorry she'd ever left me and how I
was the best friend she'd ever had. So I made up the
bed in the spare room and put brandy in her
Horlicks and tucked her up.*

*I had a wretchedly early start this a.m. Working
breakfast at the MoD, so I let her sleep. But I got
home before twelve, and guess what? Gone,
scarpered, vanished, hadn't even picked the sheets
up off the floor or pulled the chain in the loo. No
note, no nothing. I did a phone trace with Telecom.
Thirty-five minutes to Klosters; twenty minutes to
BA at Heathrow.*

*Don't want to sound bitter, Bess: but remember.
Always remember. Always remember what she's
like . . .*

Tom had left a note in Caroline's pigeon hole. 'Saw
you in the doughnut place. Maybe you may remember
me from Roedean, Mrs Bowler's son? Wonder
whether you'd like some pasta one night so we could
catch up on Brighton developments?' Standard, low-
key stuff without a hint of anything beyond. He wasn't

looking for a fling. Julia was quite enough of that to be going on with. He was looking for connections. Her note back was there when he called in the morning. She was at a loose end on Sunday evening. What about a glass of white in her room at seven, then Carlo's just off the Turl?

They kept the X-ray going whether the Queen was there or not, he saw. There was carpet on the first landing, but the man in the blue suit didn't bother to go up with him. So she was still away. *Cherwell*, a few weeks before, had printed a silly little map of her routes back from Windsor and given the times her car normally used them. Nine-thirty Sunday evenings, seven-thirty Monday mornings. There'd been a predictable fuss, and the Proctors were supposed to be considering some kind of sanctions. But what price the freedom of the press?

She shook him rather solemnly by the hand. Soave or Pinot Grigio? The Soave would be fine. Nuts? No thanks. They gossiped aimlessly for a while. How long does a lady-in-waiting have to wait? Oh, it depends. Do you get much of a life of your own? Oh, she's lovely and easy. I'm just there to be a kind of support when she needs me. Still, it must be a tremendous change from school? I suppose so. My mother sends her best regards. Please give her mine too.

It wasn't till they were sitting in the close, white cellar of the trattoria with a bowl of bean soup and a bottle of Barolo that he began to edge the conversation into the areas he planned.

'And you, Tom. What are you up to?'

'Theatre mostly, when the chance comes up. I was Mark Antony last summer for the Mummers in the gardens. We took it to Pakistan with the British Council for the summer.'

'That must have been thrilling.'

'Pretty interesting, yes.'

'What's next, then?'

'We're sort of in a bidding contest for OUDS next term. *Romeo and Juliet*. Adrian, the director, has got some amazing ideas. I'm Romeo. The trouble is, we haven't got the ideal Juliet. The girl who might do it is perfectly capable, but she's sort of brittle. Adrian wants somebody with what he calls "an essential innocence" like . . .'

His face was screwed, as though searching desperately for an example which was always a few yards over the next hill. 'Like, I always think of Bess doing Joan of Arc a year or two back. You know, vulnerable, but resilient with it. Those eyes wide, the shoulders thrown back, that voice steady as a rock. I thought she was tremendous. It's a terrible shame she's out of the running now.'

He emptied the Barolo. Caroline said nothing for a full minute.

'Yes,' she said at last. 'I suppose you're right. But why don't we ask her and see?'

She looked at him and saw the ghost of a smirk flicker across his lips. As expected. He was so bloody obvious, of course, another clumping politician looking after Number One and thinking she was too stupid to notice. Beautiful? He fancied himself too much. But she'd done her homework. He was a decent enough actor, at least on the stage. And why the hell shouldn't she put it to Bess? The girl had a special talent. She couldn't skulk indoors for ever.

The Party council had been over for three hours. Millward had seen the TV pictures of them filing out of the mausoleum they called the National Liberal Club. He thought he remembered a bust of Gladstone in the hall. The old boy was probably looking sourer than ever. Christ, what a useless gang! They hadn't said a word to the press, merely tried to look sombre, statesmanlike, important. 'Pygmies,' he said out loud. Where the hell was Baxter?

He didn't like hanging around his rooms in the Commons for too long. There was only a single outer office and the dragon secretary Minnie between him and the backbenchers he spent his life trying to avoid. They waited every Wednesday to catch him after Question Time, a gaggle of hungry geese breaking into a trot as he ducked out of the Chamber. They would know he was here now. You could hear the squawking in the tea room from here.

The dragon knocked and huffed a little fire. 'He's here at last, Prime Minister. I have told him how inconvenient we've found his lateness.'

Colonel Baxter appeared not to hear. He was ram-rod as usual, the back so rigid that it appeared to transfix his chin at ten to two. 'Well, Simon, good news for the nation I think. We have debated long and hard. It was not easy. But at the close – due in no small measure to my personal appeal – we have resolved not to break from the coalition. You were right to draw our attention to the adverse impact on world opinion of instability in the six months before the Coronation. Our duty is to soldier on.'

'Very wise,' said Millward sardonically.

'And can I assume, as a matter of course, that my old portfolio is still open to me? And that the extra funds we talked about remain available?'

'So sorry, Colonel,' Millward said smoothly. 'Once you start reshuffling, things have their own momentum, and that band, I'm afraid, has left the parade ground. But I have held Culture Secretary open in case you changed your mind.'

He could see the knuckles whiten. Got you, you jumped-up twat! The Colonel's knowledge of culture stopped at Elgar and the video collection of *Dad's Army* he kept on his parlour shelves. Three rounds with the Arts Council and he'd be dead meat by Easter.

Millward was still humming to himself when Leckie came in to check the press briefing.

'Triumph,' said Robin at the end. 'Bloody great. You were spot on playing the Queen. This show could run and run.'

'Maybe, but don't get too cocky. She's a trump because she's young and innocent and people don't have anything against her. Not like the old gang. One slip, though, one fuck up, and she'll be useless to us too. The difference between virgin purity and soiled goods is thirty seconds in the hay. The difference between touching naïvety and a spoiled bitch is thirty seconds stomping on television. Take guard, young Leckie. Uneasy lies the head that wears the Crown. And watchful lies the head beside it.'

Chapter Seven

The dining hall was deserted. The last mounds of fatty bacon and cold sausage had been scraped noisily into plastic bins, the last plates of breakfast washed and stowed away. In an hour or so the kitchens, through the swing doors by the oil painting of Anthony Lynton Blair, Hon. Fellow of this College, would resume their clinking din. Curses over cut fingers. The thud of cabbages dismembered and the scream of mincers stalled on sinew of frozen beef. The gabble of cooks discussing last night's soap operas. But, for now, there was only silence.

Adrian and Tom sat upright on the bench nearest the door, nervous, groomed and shaved and scented. Adrian was wearing a suit. Bess wore jeans and a thick beige sweater which seemed to submerge her. She stood twenty yards from them on the platform where the Fellows assembled for lunch and dinner, raised above the earthlings like Zeus and the gods of greater academe. A small archway on her right led down the new oak stairway to the cellars of wine stocked and cherished over centuries. She stepped under the arch for a second, out of sight, then reappeared. A stray, fleeting beam of sunlight caught her face for an instant. She had made her entrance.

> 'Farewell! God knows when we shall meet again.
> I have a faint cold fear thrills through my veins
> That almost freezes up the heat of life.
> I'll call them back again to comfort me.
> Nurse! – What should she do here?
> My dismal scene I needs must act alone.'

The voice was soft, but clear and crisp. Adrian heard every word, and the rhythm of them carried him along. She had a repose which drew him to her eyes. They seemed to glint and change, now green, now gold, staring at impending death with unvarying emotion.

> 'Come, vial.
> What if this mixture do not work at all?
> Shall I be married then tomorrow morning?
> No, no! This shall forbid it. Lie thou there.'

Out in the quadrangle some loud oaf was bellowing his distress. 'Who's nicked my bloody bike?' She did not pause or blink.

> 'Stay, Tybalt, stay!
> Romeo, Romeo, Romeo.
> Here's drink. I drink to thee.'

She seemed to stagger and fell back into the fat Master's fat chair. Adrian and Tom looked at each other and said nothing. There was nothing to say.

'Is that enough?'

'That was perfect, Your Majesty.'

She jumped lightly from the stage and came and perched on the table in front of them. 'Please, please drop all the titled stuff. If I get the part and we get the commission, I'm Bess. OK? I'll never be able to stop giggling if this turns into another wretched Palace tea party. What matters is what you think and then what the audience thinks. It's the play that counts, not who I am. This is Shakespeare, not my Coronation.'

'Yes,' said Adrian, struggling to his feet. 'And of course you've got the part. You'll be wonderful . . . Bess.'

The President of Cyprus was eighty-two and round and olive green. Bess also found him voluble and deeply tedious. His father, apparently, had been a young blood in EOKA long ago. 'He spat on Britain and everything British. Now I ride with you in carriages and eat off your gold plates. It is the wheel of fortune, turning, turning. In my country we have a saying from the Romans: bury your humble belongings long enough in the red earth and one day they will be antiques and your children's children will rejoice in their prosperity.'

He had, she thought, a protracted maxim for every phase of conversation. In my country we say . . . a watched kebab never burns . . . the Greek walks the mountain crest while the Turk crawls the river bed on his belly . . . the island of Aphrodite has the mind of a goddess but the loins of a woman. She had spent the afternoon with him in Camden Town. The thick yellow curd and gritty mince of the moussaka seemed to cling to her teeth.

'In my country we say . . . to part at last, dear lady, is but to recommence the task of coming again.' Thank heavens he was leaving at last. Was he going to lecture her about marriage now? 'A young womb is a fertile womb, a blessed bed is a fruitful bed.' No, they were almost carrying him out. 'A memorable visit I shall always remember, an unforgettable experience I shall never forget.' Nicky and Selene had drawn the short straw of seeing him off at Gatwick. She breathed a sigh of relief.

'Well done, Ma'am,' said Millward, moving to her side. 'We did our duty. We stayed awake.'

He seemed benign and chatty for a change: almost human.

'Write me a decent part and I'll play it,' she said lightly. 'Which reminds me, Prime Minister, there's another part I have been offered which I would rather like your permission to play. It will be one of our little understandings.'

He scowled when she told him; he talked to Fountain and Baron and Leckie through the next morning; he listened while senior policemen issued all the grave warnings of their querulous trade; but he had seen something in the set of her jaw that gave him pause. In the end, he did not quite say No.

The Christmas message, Your Majesty? Ready now, in your own time.

Her cheeks were too white and her hair had been pinned back and elaborately curled at the edges. It sat uneasily on her head, an ill-fitting saucepan lid. She looked forty-five and frumpish, she thought as she peered into the monitor. Her bottom, encased in a thick and sensible pencil skirt which fell three inches below the knee, squirmed of its own accord on the prickly velvet of the carved gilt chair. The autoscript began to run.

'A Happy Christmas to you all. This is my first opportunity to be with you in your living rooms at our season of festivity and family. But it is not, of course, an opportunity that I either sought or wished for. And Christmas, too, around the dinner table, provides a chance for us to keep chairs empty and to remember those of our loved ones who can no longer sit beside us and enfold us in their warmth. I, like you, have many such memories on this special day. I, like you perhaps, have experienced what my great-grandmother once called "a horrible year, an annus horribilis . . ."'

When it was over, the BBC director, dandruff flecking his black polo-neck sweater, walked towards her and clapped his hands four damp times. 'Wonderful, Ma'am.' The palms barely made contact, she noticed. They brushed against each other as though alarmed that some contagion might pass between them. 'Really excellent for a first attempt. Now, shall we have one more go? And try to take a breath after the "horrible year". Ho-rri-ble. Pause. An an-nus horreebeeliss. You need to signal that this is a different language. Something people of your education will understand, of course – but not all of your audience sitting out there with the beer cans and Brazil nuts are so fortunate, Ma'am. One is afraid these days that Latin is a language of the past.'

The lights were dazzling her. She looked round into the shadows of the room to find Baron.

'Are you sure this is the script you want, Sir Richard? It isn't at all me, if you know what I mean.'

'We all think it hits exactly the correct note, Your Majesty. Familiar, at a time of flux. Reassuring, in the echoes of history it evokes. And, crucially, non-controversial. It marks our loss but charts the possibility of future gain.'

'That's fine, then,' Bess said meekly. 'Just so long as I know it's supposed to be boring.'

After the message, the Christmas. 'But I don't want to go to Sandringham,' she'd said. 'It's freezing and all my friends are here in London.'

'But the family always goes to Sandringham,' Fountain said unblinkingly. 'It is a tradition, Ma'am, not a question of what one wants.'

And so they had had cocktails in the white chill of the Drawing Room, the snow on the lawns outside seeming to reflect from the gloss of its walls as though they were trapped in a giant refrigeration plant. And so they had eaten lobster pancakes and roast pheasant with game chips in the eau-de-Nil of the Dining Room, pulling crackers and pausing in silence when Nicky, four glasses in, had knocked his Copeland Mecklenberg-Strelitz plate to the floor, a splatter of dead bird and broken china. And so, now, they stretched in the heavy panelling of the Saloon, her brother snoring, mouth open, his mother giggling and crossing her knees, the cousins and the aunts around the room stiff with tedium or stiff with drink. And soon they would walk, through the corridors of guns and breastplates and helmets and carved horses kicking their hooves, to the Ballroom where the wooden folding chairs were already arranged in lines and the film projector on the balcony was poised to run its ritual course.

'One old, one new, Ma'am,' said Fordice, the catering manager from the Convention Cafeteria. 'That's the way we always try to arrange it. This year we have *The Sound of Music*, then *Corpse Collector 3* to get the adult timbers shivering.'

Outside, night began to descend on the tops of the spruce trees, wrapping them in a mist of obscurity. A swan skated unsteadily across the frozen lake. An owl settled morosely on the bare branch of a copper beech. And a solitary policeman, etched against the whiteness of the lawn, pursued a solitary photographer towards the rhododendron bushes.

Far away, in the last days of school before the Duke died, she and Emma and Caroline had sat in her room one night sipping some sweet leftover sherry and talking, as they sometimes did, about sex.

Emma, predictably, was all boisterous enthusiasm. 'It's not complicated. You don't have to fall in love or anything difficult. You just find a man who can make it last, drink enough to feel a bit blotto and let him get on with it until you start to come. It's like badminton and horses: just a super way to relax.'

Caroline was quieter and more intense. There had been a boy at home a couple of years ago who had gone to college in South Africa and never, after the first two postcards, picked up pen again. She'd camped in Italy last summer with an archaeology undergraduate from Sussex who was writing a dissertation on the Etruscans: but he'd been in Syria on a dig for six months now. 'I don't miss it much,' she said. 'I need somebody special to make me feel special. But I'm not going to sit in a nunnery at Oxford. I shall be on the prowl for sure.'

And Bess? She was silent, wrestling the top from a tin of stuffed olives and doling out the last of the sherry. 'I still haven't made it,' she said, her voice straining after nonchalance.

They looked at her.

'But what about Terry, that Marquess of something or other Irish who took you to the Hunt Ball at Easter?' Emma asked. 'He looked totally dishy in the mags.'

She shrugged. 'Oh, he pawed me around in the car home, rolling on top and getting excited. But he'd had so much to drink it didn't seem right.'

She tossed an olive in the air and caught it in her open mouth with a grin and the flourish of a curtsy. 'There you go. Still intacto for my A-levels and unashamed. She can't help it, the girl can't help it.'

And now, eight months on, there was even less help on the horizon, she thought. Who'd come near her in college or coffee bars or walking to lectures with a posse of pressmen hovering behind? Who would brave the security checks and the gruff questionings? It was funny really. She didn't seem to mind or care: she didn't lie awake at night worrying. Perhaps, after all, she was frigid? She still thought of that hot afternoon twelve years ago in Newmarket when they'd gone to stay at the hotel with the swimming pool to be close to Daddy at one of his Mildenhall inspection things and he'd been on the base somewhere and Nicky had fallen on the diving board and grazed his leg.

'I want Mummy,' he'd said, yowling and snuffling.

'But Mummy's resting, Mummy said she mustn't be disturbed.' Bess could still hear the words in her head. 'Mummy's got a headache. Be brave and I'll buy you an ice cream.' But Nicky was never brave and, at last, she had led him inside, down the empty corridor on the second floor, and slipped the plastic key quietly into the lock. 'Don't wail. We'll just sneak in and wash the blood off and you'll see there's nothing wrong. Now shush! Mummy's asleep.'

But Selene was not asleep. She seemed, to the two children in the darkness of the hallway outside the bathroom door, to be in some kind of terrible pain, crying out shrilly again and again. Bess held Nicky's hand tightly and, wide-eyed together, they had turned into the bedroom. Mummy had no clothes on. She was kneeling on the bed and there was a naked man underneath her. And his hands were tied up to the bedpost. And he was Christopher . . . Daddy's friend. The accountant Daddy said looked after all the difficult bits for him.

Mummy shrieked and Nicky ran over to her and started hitting Christopher. 'Stop, you're hurting my mother.' And they had both looked round at Bess together. 'Oh shit,' Selene said.

Was that a trauma? she wondered, looking out over the January quad with frost tufting the grass and kitchen lads sliding across a pool of ice. Was she somehow scarred? Nicky had never been the same again, but perhaps he had never been the same before it anyway. And she? Would she find sex disgusting? Or was it just the smell and the memory and the sight of her mother that disgusted her?

She put on her thickest cashmere coat and went downstairs. 'I'm going for a long walk, Sergeant,' she said. 'I need to feel the wind on my face.'

Sammy Wittman was buying one vodka and tonic after another; and Salam Gupta was drinking them. Wittman had never seen him touch anything but orange juice before, but four double vodkas had vanished down his slender throat in – what? – thirty minutes. He was beginning to sway and slop, leaning back on the bar of the Pony and sweeping his right arm in lugubrious arcs.

'Racism,' he said. 'Bloody racism and bloody feudalism and bloody nepotism and a bloody, bloody, bloody disgrace.'

Sammy put his last ten euros back in his pocket and began to shuffle towards the door. Gupta's *Romeo and Juliet* had been a nice little story in the making and he'd nursed it along with a para or two. 'Row grows over Muslim Shakespeare: mullahs demand Verona with Veils.' If Gupta had got the OUDS nod, there'd have been three or four days of page leads in the *Express*. A decent enough earner while he waited for the Crown Jewels to fall into his lap. But Gupta was out of it now. The announcement, just after Christmas, had merely said the John's men – Adrian and Tom – were the winners. There hadn't even been a paragraph of explanation for him to build into a snub or a storm.

'I don't see where racism or anything else comes into it,' Sammy said, turning for the door. 'Even the Equal Opportunities lot won't get fired up about Tybalt in a loin cloth.'

Gupta lurched after him and thrust his thin brown face towards Wittman's. 'But who's the Juliet?' he said. 'Who's the sodding Juliet? Oh, they're not saying anything yet. They're keeping it quiet until the last minute. But I damned well know their little secret. Here, look for yourself.'

The crumple of paper he tossed was a typed cast list. Sammy smoothed it and moved over to the light. Romeo: Thomas Bowler. Juliet: Elizabeth Windsor.

'What about one last one for the road?' Sammy said. 'I think I could do with a few quotes.'

Tom knocked on Julia's door. No answer, nobody home. He turned the handle idly and pushed. It was open after all. Darkness at noon! he thought. The curtains were drawn tight. Where had she gone to so early, leaving such a mess? He tugged at one of the stiff yellow drapes and looked round at the squalor he'd grown to expect whenever he stayed with her. Coffee mugs with a crust of soured milk. Old slices of toast dropped on the lino near the waste bin. Unusually for her – she wasn't much of a solitary drinker – there was a half bottle of mountain rum on its side on the carpet. She hadn't screwed the cap on properly. There was a small puddle spread across the edge of the cheap Turkish rug and a sweet smell which caught him in the throat.

Jesus, what a tip! He'd been away in London with Adrian for the night sounding out a couple of guys from Bromley about lending them a caseload of costumes they'd seen advertised in *The Stage*. He hadn't remembered until they got to Paddington that he was due at Julia's as per rota.

There was a sudden stirring from the battered old sofa in the darkest corner of the room and the pile of newspapers littered across it fell to the floor.

'What's the time?' Julia said. He pulled the other curtain back so that the light fell on her grey, bleary face.

'You look like shit,' he said, then wondered whether that was the best opening for a mercy mission. 'Are you ill or something?'

She staggered upright. Her short hair was matted to her scalp. The make-up of twenty-four hours was smeared under her eyes. She was wearing the creased pink track suit with the coffee stain over her left breast. She scowled. 'I must have just fallen asleep,' she said dully. 'Where the hell were you?'

He lit the stove, filled the kettle and began a light patter about the Bromley Theatre and the hamper of props.

She sluiced her head under the cold tap in the sink and wiped herself dry with a tea cloth. Then she turned four square to look at him. 'It was all crap, wasn't it?' she said. 'All that soft, smiley stuff about how the Queen might or might not be able to do Juliet every night or even at all? All those promises that

I'd get the chance? That if we got a schools tour afterwards, this could be my big break? Adrian and you were stringing me along. When the *Express* ran the story yesterday, I went to see her, and I was prattling away about our being partners somehow – and she didn't know what the hell I was talking about.'

He put the coffee on the draining board and rummaged elaborately for the sugar bag. It was ripped underneath and a trail of granules ran, like ants, over the saucepans stacked on the side. 'You've got the wrong end of the stick again,' he said evenly. 'We were talking about understudies – which, because Bess is always on call if anything happens, is much more important than normal. And of course we can't see her flogging round new model high schools in Cowley in the vac, so you're bound to win a few there.'

Her mouth had set in a trap and her eyes were baleful.

'And the good thing is,' he said, sweeping up the sugar, 'at this point in your career, you really ought to be developing your repertoire, showing you can do character parts and different things.'

'You mean hang on to Nurse for fear of something worse?' she said.

Fountain had a bad back. It ached when he sat down; and, when he got up, he seemed to stagger in stiffness for a few paces like an old man hobbling to the lavatory. The back had gone three afternoons before, just as Selene began to writhe beneath him and scar her scarlet nails across his slack white rump.

'Why are you yelping too?' she'd said, sitting suddenly upright and glowering.

'I think I may have pulled something.'

She'd laughed at him sourly. 'Well, that would make a change.'

He made no attempt to stand when Baron came in and dumped the press cuttings on his desk. 'For once,' he said, leafing through them with his lip curling ever more precipitately, 'I think the Wizard Millward has fallen into error. Not that he'll admit it, of course. You and I will be left, as ever, to pick up the pieces.'

The headlines were rumbling on and turning thunderous. 'Bishop warns on Queen's stage passion: public kiss could threaten Monarchy'; '€500 tout tickets for Bess bonanza leave school kids in the cold'; 'Race-Mad Romeo Threatens to Sue'; 'Top Cop Fears a Killer in the Stalls'; 'Backbench Critics Ask: Who'll Pay for HM's Curtain Call?'

And the comment pieces had begun to get up steam too. 'The bonds that bind the public to our continuing royalty are woven of a mysterious thread,' said the *Telegraph* leader writer. 'When they are exposed too openly to scrutiny – whether in the distasteful cavortions of minor royalty on the television game shows which brought the twentieth century to such an unseemly close, or soon, perhaps, amid the hype of show business which seems certain to enfold our new Queen herself – their silken touch may swiftly be exposed as old rope.' The reigning bitch goddess of the *Mail* was blessedly terser. 'She got the part because she's She. If She's good, we shall all rejoice. But what if She's horrid?'

Baron shrugged. 'I could have written this bloody script,' he said. 'Belcher's at his wits' end. There are 500 foreign hacks parked in Oxford, never mind our finest. If he leaves the Randolph, he says, the management put up camp beds in his living room. I'm going down myself again after lunch, but I don't see why we're stuck with all this. Where are Downing Street's supermen of spin, now that we need them?'

Fountain reached for the phone too swiftly and grimaced.

'That must be the first time your back's stabbed you.' Baron had worked in newspapers too long to resist the cheap shot. He gave a gallows grin.

'Then move not while my prayer's effect I take.
Thus from my lips, by thine my sin is purged.'

Adrian watched for ten seconds then clambered noisily to his feet. 'Excuse me,' he said, 'this is supposed to be the kiss of all kisses. Rapturous, chaste, passion-filled, ecstatic. You look as though you've lost the mistletoe, Tom. Hold her, bend her backwards from the waist. Give me something to swoon over, for God's sake.'

'Oh, right,' Tom said. 'Is that OK by you, Ma'am?' She took him in her arms.

'Then have my lips the sin that they have took.'

He was a bear of a man. She seemed to lighten and wilt in his arms.

'Sin from my lips? O trespass sweetly urged!
Give me my sin again.'

They were both out of breath. Adrian had forgotten to sit down on his stool. He stood transfixed. The chilly yellow of the lecture room had a fleeting feel of Mediterranean warmth.

'You kiss by th' book,' Bess said.

They moved apart and waited.

Adrian's trance was gone. 'Julia,' he bawled at the huddle on the benches at the back. 'Come on! Get a move on, for God's sake!'

The huddle crawled into life and pulled the scarf back from her head. 'Sorry . . .' she said. '"Madam, your mother craves a word with you."'

Robin Leckie let himself in by the door at the side and found a lone chair in the shadows by a tall bookcase.

'But soft! What light through yonder window breaks?'

He was soon lost in his own thoughts.

'I'll be mother,' Emma said. She poured the tea in the general direction of three cups on the floor and wrenched the top off the biscuit tin so abruptly that a shower of crumbs covered the hearth rug. Unconcerned, she broke the nearest stick of shortcake and wiped the slop from her saucer with it, sucking noisily. 'Now, Glenda, give us the lowdown. How's it going? And is he as dreamy as he looks?'

Bess flushed. Em had been calling her Sarah – after Bernhardt – for years, ever since the first Roedean nativity when she'd played Mary and Emma had been the back legs of the donkey. Glenda was a newer, more mystic coinage – probably derived, she thought, from a bony British actress who, half a century ago, had played Lady Macbeth then gone into politics.

'You mean Tom?' she said. 'It's difficult to say, really. He doesn't have much small talk. He actually asked me if I'd ever been to see Brighton and Hove Albion. I don't think he's physically right for the part. Just too big and intimidating. His chest is all muscles and it sort of gets in your face when he comes near you. And his legs are like tree trunks. I think he probably fancies himself too much as well. Always glancing in mirrors and running his fingers through his hair.'

'Cupid seems to have gone a bit bow-legged there then,' said Caroline. 'Thank God you haven't turned as gooey over him as he is over himself.'

Bess rowed back a little towards the shore. 'Oh, maybe he's not that bad. He's got the most wonderful speaking voice. It seems to come from miles down inside him. And his skin is incredibly smooth. We spent most of the afternoon pecking away at each other and I didn't feel a touch of stubble.'

Had she over-compensated? She could have talked about the way that his lips brushed lightly across hers, barely seeming to touch yet leaving a trail of tenderness; about the moment at the end of Act One where, perhaps by accident, he'd kissed her in the right eye and lingered there; about his tongue which tried perpetually to break through the bars of her teeth; about the squeeze of his body in feigned death as he had cradled her close to him.

She could have said these, and many other things. But what was the point winding Em up? Or sending

Caroline into one of her ratty moods? She had not been within miles of a man for months. Of course Tom – or anybody else – would turn a few taps after the drought of desolation.

Dear Lilibet,
Did I ever talk to you about Love? Not the end of it, the beginning of it. How something reaches out Across a Crowded Room and all that jazz. How I met your mother: a cautionary tale.

You know about the horse trials and the gymkhanas and the riding boots, I'm sure. Remember how we'd look at the photos at Christmas? And you know Bro King had one of his roving eyes on her for a time. But I hadn't really registered her till Pa came back from Aviemore or Aberdeen or one of those places one week in May when I was on leave from Montserrat and announced he'd got two tickets for the Wembley Arena. 'It's a Spice Girls anniversary concert,' he said. 'Your stepmother has a headache. Your brother is off rutting in Cornwall with his gang of freaks and nutters. I thought you always liked them so you might come along with me, for old time's sake.'

Well, what was I to say? That I'd really preferred Tori Amos all along? That heading for Wembley with an OAP was not my idea of a night out of the mess? That the show, when we got there, was bound to be pathetic? He'd have been sure to have one of his hurt glooms. So I said yes, great, let's go, Dad. Let's see twelve-stone Baby S looking like the

137

new landlady at the Queen Vic, Ginger back for the reunion tour in a green wig, Posh not even pretending to sing and complaining about her arthritic hip. I mean, ghoulish. But just at the interval, after the Tribute to Scary, when the lights went up, I saw this flash of blonde hair on the front row that I thought I recognized. And she turned to look at me. And she smiled. So I just went over, drawn by the proverbial magnet, and she introduced me to some fat old suit. And then she said, 'This is a grotesque evening. Why don't we just go somewhere and enjoy ourselves.'

That was that, my love. I left Dad in the box with two equerries and a box of Roses. It was roses, roses all the way. For about fifteen months, anyway.

Leckie took Baron back with him to Downing Street. 'The boss won't like it,' he said. 'We'd better make it unanimous.'

Millward had had a stinking day: ambushed in the tea room by a squad of Ulster Unionists banging on about beef subsidies, done over at Question Time by the bloody Tories asking him to confirm or deny Baxter's first disaster of a Granada Culture Lecture. Was the Government really concerned about television's lack of investment in new soap operas? Could a Treasury grant to *Coronation Street* be expected imminently? He made a lame joke – 'I've already got enough Coronations to worry about' – but he knew the Baxter gambit was looking too clever by three-quarters. The Colonel was such a clod that nobody thought it worth going after him. But the idiot who appointed him in the first place . . . there was plumper game.

'Well?' Millward said brusquely as they trooped in. 'I've been tied to the bloody mast while you've been dreaming with the spires, Robin. I hope it was worth it.'

Leckie sensed there was no point in pussy-footing around. When the PM got uptight, you told him where to get off. When bullied, bully back. 'Glad to know I was missed,' he said. 'Three conclusions in short order. One: we can all stop fretting about whether HM is an actress or not. Been there, seen her; she's great. Two: the press scrum is totally out of hand. It's clogging the university and the dons are getting restless. Somebody will get hurt in the stampede if we don't call a halt. If that happens, we'll inevitably get it in the neck. Those who could do something did nothing – that kind of pissy leader-column wind. And three: Sir Richard and I can't see any way out but letting the dogs meet the rabbit. Get the editors in, field the Queen – and plead with the bastards, appeal to their better natures.'

'Jeesuss, we must be desperate,' Millward said, cracking into a hollow guffaw. 'But if you both think it's the way to go, let's lay on a party.'

Robin wanted to register one more thing for the tape that always ran in the marble light-fitting on Millward's desk. 'Oh, and last, least, just for noting. We'll need to keep the key of our beloved Bess's bedroom door locked away. She was snogging her Romeo as though it had just been invented.'

Chapter Eight

Adrian had thrown a tantrum when she'd told him. 'But we need this weekend, absolutely need every damned minute of it. I know you and Tom are OK. You've done nothing but rehearse for weeks. But Edwin hasn't got Mercutio straight in his head yet, Tybalt is as stiff as two planks, and Julia? Well, really! I mean, she's just lost it somehow. I can't think what's got into her.'

He was getting more of a pro day by day, she thought. 'Oh look. Please stop complaining. The reason why the rest of the cast is all over the place is because they keep moaning about press harassment. My people at the Palace say I can help with that, but I'll need to spend Sunday doing it. And Ade, it's just one extra day. I told you all about the ambulance-control centre and the rehabilitation unit for parking-meter attendants ages ago. I've got so many balls to keep in the air.' She had fluttered her eyelids at him. 'Honestly . . . darling . . .'

But now she was feeling apprehensive. Saturday in Croydon had verged on humiliation. 'It gives me great pleasure to press the button which will link ambulances throughout the south-east for the rapid, caring response which patients in distress need' – and the computer went down for two hours. 'What happened to you?' she'd asked the meter maid with the fractured pelvis when they got to Surbiton. 'Got run down by an ambulance, Mum.'

Pray heaven Sunday was better than that. The editors' Daimlers and Mercs were parked on the nethermost corner of the yard where their chauffeurs, in peaked caps and blazers with shiny buttons, played guardsmen. A thin young man in a brown mac wobbled his bicycle down the Mall and was whisked away to the servants' racks in the Royal Mews. 'He's from the *Guardian*,' Baron whispered to her.

They did not swagger into the great east drawing room. They swam in unction. Charmed, Your Majesty. Honoured, Your Majesty. Where is your dear mother, Ma'am? Millward was doing his father act, again. 'There's Otley from the *Telegraph*, an influential chap,' he said in her ear. 'Tell him his is the first paper you turn to.'

'But I've already said that to the man from *The Times*,' she said.

'Doesn't matter. They never talk to each other.'

Fountain had laid on a buffet of deceptive frugality. 'Coronation chicken,' he had said without a glimmer of a smile. 'Economical and, in the circumstances, beyond editorial criticism. You can't afford to give them an opening.' But the wine – the best Gewurtztraminer the Palace cellars had left – was Baron's choice. 'Reckon a bottle per person, and three over for luck. You'll want them mellow when you make your speech; mellow, not rowdy.'

She had memorized the script in Croydon while they'd tried to fix the computer.

'Gentlemen . . .' (There'd been one woman on the list, but Fountain had murmured something about a drug overdose) – 'Pleased to have this rare chance of meeting you all together. So grateful for the coverage and sympathy since my tragic accession. My father always taught me that the press was the bastion of freedom. Think it was bastions he said. (Risky joke, but they smiled politely enough). Wanted to have a small, private talk about my university choice and the things I'm doing there. Seeking to complete a rounded education. First Queen to do that. In this day and age, must be way forward. Also, as you know, wanting to participate in university life to the full. Have always loved the theatre. One of our great British heritages. And Shakespeare. Ditto. Fully recognize public interest in what I'm doing. No law, no code to protect me. Almost twenty, not even a minor. But please realize what the weight of your coverage is doing to me and those who want to work with me.'

There was, for the first time, a tremor in her voice.

'Gentlemen, and I mean that in the purest sense. Be gentle. Please call off your reporters at the gates and your photographers on the stairs. Please let me breathe. There will be tickets for all of you on the opening night. I hope very much to see you there.'

Afterwards, Leckie called it her greatest performance. 'Told you she's a natural.' Baron complained about what she'd done to his text. 'Too many bloody pleases and thank-yous. Monarchs don't beg.' Millward reckoned the mission had been provisionally accomplished. But he wasn't hanging out the flags yet, he told Fountain. 'One minute they're poodles – but give them a bone and they're wolves again. I don't trust that seedy Yorkshireman Bradshaw in particular. He didn't need to ask the question he did.'

Ah! That question. 'Surely you understand, Marm, that your ordinary citizens have had it up to here with all the gallivanting in high places over the years? Surely you know that in Barnsley we don't think actors and actresses usually turn out any better than they ought to? Surely you've heard of the Last Chance Saloon?'

'Yet should I kill thee with much cherishing.
Good night, good night! Parting is such sweet sorrow
That I shall say goodnight till it be morrow.'

She was line perfect, standing in the twilight of her room, repeating and repeating until the words came automatically. She knew now, absolutely, what Juliet would say. She was becoming her own Juliet. Thinking, moving inside that reality donned as easily as slipping on a cloak. It was the greatest of escapes. She could, for a while, be someone else. She could leave the cameramen and the security men and the men in suits behind on the planet of Protocol.

Bess looked in the mirror. The down on her cheeks had gone. The jaw was more tautly defined. The months had honed and etched her. She lived in four worlds: the world of the Court where she must fight constantly to survive, to hang on to what passed for sanity; the world of Oxford and friends and laughter; the world of a sorrow that would never completely leave her; and this, the world of the theatre, where all the other worlds could be forgotten.

> *'Hang up philosophy!*
> *Unless philosophy can make a Juliet.'*

Opening night. They had been trapped in the Play-house for five hours, playing cards, snoozing, polishing the last rough bits. 'Don't go outside,' Adrian said. 'It looks like the last night of the Proms.' She could not resist one lingering peek through the curtain. 'I hadn't realized so many people were doing Eng. Lit.,' she said. Millward and half the Cabinet were on the front row. There was a film director with a grey beard who kept offering the Prime Minister's mouse of a wife chocolates. The Archbishop of Canterbury sat two seats from the loud lady from Leeds who intro-duced *Honeymoon Hotel* on Saturday night prime time. The editor of the *Sunday Times* brought a blonde who kept stroking his knee. Two celebrity chefs signed programmes by the fire exit. Mrs Bowler and Mrs Granger, with selected girls from the Roedean Players, waved from the back stalls. And then, of course, there was one mother, wearing a dress of whipped cream and gold clips; and one brother, wearing a scowl.

Two minutes please . . . one minute. She felt Tom's arms round her shoulders and a hug that took her breath away.

> *'Gregory, on my word, we'll not carry coals.'*
> *'No. For then we should be colliers.'*

Gosh, what a woozy start, she thought. But it was the start. They were running.

Millward was first into the foyer, hunting for the TV cameras. 'A memorable evening,' he said loudly. 'Our finest playwright and some of our finest young people, doing him great justice.' And how was the Queen, Sir? 'I believe everybody who saw her tonight saw a remarkable talent – one that, over time, must be the theatre's loss but the nation's gain.' Wonderful, said the Archbishop. Unbelievably wonderful, said the Lord of Film. Another night to remember, said the *Honeymoon* hostess, with a bleary wink. Enter Selene, from the bar, waving a bottle of Moët.

Bess felt shrunken and drained. She closed the door of her tiny dressing room and slowly, as though on auto pilot, sponged the paint from her face. She looked in the mirror and saw the pale girl with the tired eyes emerging.

Was I good, really good? I think so. There's always been a moment for me when things start to flow. I stop being me, plonking along with the lines and the gestures, and change into something I don't recognize. My father used to talk about 'the old creative juices flowing', but that's only a bit of it. When I'm me, there's only carrying on and trying to make a new life and remembering, but the stage and the play take me beyond that. It's what I can do, and it's wonderful. I have the power. My tears can make others weep. My happiness is infectious.

For three hours she had seemed someone different, somewhere far away. There would be a few more nights like that. But then? She had come to know the answer to that. Then it would all be over for ever. They had let her off the leash once, but they would hardly do it again. She was a Queen, after all, not an actress grubbing for parts. She could have her fun, within reason; but she could not have a life.

'Party, party!' That was Adrian, ecstatic that at last something had gone right.

Her door opened quietly and then was pushed shut. 'And how', asked Tom, 'is the light of my life? Call me but love, and I'll be new baptised.'

She felt so puny and so vulnerable. *This is one of those moments of insanity that I'm not allowed.* He filled the room. There was nowhere to hide; and, with a sigh, she let him gather her up again. If it was all to end soon, then there would at least be memories.

The *Cherwell* offices were three whitewashed rooms in a terrace behind the Union. They housed a half-dozen old terminals, a dark-green filing cabinet, five trestle tables and a peeling montage of posters. The single electric fire had fused. It was still only nine in the morning. No one else would be in for an hour. Sammy Wittman kept his woollen gloves on and typed lugubriously, one frozen finger after another. The *Express* news desk had rung him last night and asked for a piece on 'ordinary student reaction to your new star, old man – you know, the human angle . . . pride, envy, anything you like. But give it us early. There's so much on this, we may want to mix and match a bit, eh?' He knew what that meant. Eight hundred words boiled down to a couple of unrecognizable paragraphs by close of play. But he'd bloody well make sure he got paid for what they'd ordered. You want quotes, sunshine? I've got a bundle of them waiting: some even with names attached.

There was a light knock on the door behind him. 'Sorry,' he shouted, 'we're closed. I'm on deadline. Come back at ten.' But the knocking came again and he swung impatiently to his feet. 'Oh bloody hell. Are you deaf or something?'

She was standing on the step in a flimsy yellow mac with the collar turned high around her face. She wore a blue Paisley headscarf and sunglasses. It was a brutally cold March morning. Her hands were thrust deep into the mac pockets. She was shivering violently.

'Welcome, Miss Garbo.' Sammy made a mocking bow. Julia took off the glasses and sat on the wooden folding chair across the table from his terminal. She was still shivering. 'Coffee?' 'Tea if you've got it.' He draped his own cord jacket round her shoulders and went, humming, into the kitchen.

'Congratulations on last night,' he said, dropping four lumps into her cup. 'The crits this morning are out of this world.'

She held the cup to her lips and sipped it slowly. Her face was haggard and there were green smudges of fatigue under her eyes.

'For her, yes of course,' she said. 'For him too. But I don't think you'll have seen me anywhere in the honours list – unless the *Mail* got me into that last para. The one about "Some of the supporting cast, alas, cannot match the fire of the principals."'

147

'Come on, Jools,' Sammy said. 'Too heavy on the bile. It isn't like you.'

'Christ, you don't think this has got anything to do with the show?' she said. 'I don't care a damn about that – well, only a tiny damn. No, this is much more serious. Tom said he loved me, that one day we might even set up house together. We've been together for nine months. I've got letters that would make your hair curl.'

'We don't run a lonely hearts column,' Sammy said. 'This is university. You're supposed to fall in and out of love.'

She put the cup down and looked at him with the twist of a grin. 'Sure. I am. You are. But she's not. She's Little Miss Goody Two Shoes hanging on to her cherry, waiting for Prince Charming to jet in from Luxembourg. She's the Queen of Hearts, not the Queen of Tarts.'

Sammy's eyes were beginning to bulge. 'How do you know anything for sure?' he said. 'This is great.'

'I know because a woman knows. I've seen him slobbering over her, feeling her, for weeks. I've seen the way he never looks at me now.'

'But that's acting, in public. It isn't evidence.'

'And I saw them last night, coming out of her dressing room after the show. He had his hands on her breasts and she was panting. She was all over him. She couldn't get enough.'

'Would you be quoted yourself? Have your picture on page one? Do the full woman-scorned bit?'

She had stopped shivering. She pulled herself

straight, shoulders thrown back. 'I can do better than that. I can tell you how Tom Bloody Bowler got arrested in Pakistan last year for outraging public decency – with me – and being drunk out of his skull and stoned on pot. I got a copy of the police report before the British Council sat on it. I'll sign anything and prove anything. He's a crud, and she's a silly little fool.'

And I, thought Sammy, can feel a job offer coming on at last.

He called big brother Will when she'd left. 'Can you get down here quick? I've found a fantastic story.' He needed Will. If there was going to be a deal, Will was the deal-maker. He also bought lavish out-of-town lunches.

Sammy had made some notes of Julia's story. She'd signed them, though they'd want that for the lawyers to turn into a proper affidavit. There were photocopies of the Pakistan police forms, pictures of Julia showing a load of B-cup for Cleopatra last year and – best yet – some of Tom's old love letters to her. 'I am pining, Egypt, pining for the cool of your skin, the heat within you, the swelling of my member into an asp which penetrates . . .'

'This isn't quite family-audience stuff,' said Will, ordering an extra half-dozen oysters. 'My *Express* readers don't mind filth, but they can't stand it too arty-farty. Still, we can easily extract some bits and black out the rest. An obsession too hot to handle. Queen's Romeo was a Two-timing Love Rat. Bradshaw will drool when he sees it.' They finished lunch at 3.30 and slept in a lay-by for half an hour before Will drove slowly back to London.

She was as happy as she'd been for years. No, perhaps in her life. The Playhouse had been packed all week and the applause seemed to echo in her head for hours afterwards. It couldn't last, could it? There were moments, when the curtain went up, when she felt a new reality. Perhaps, perhaps. If only . . .

Tom came to her in the dressing room each night and began to send bunches of roses to her room each morning. 'Another delivery from this Mr Montague, Ma'am,' said the porter from Special Branch dubiously. 'There isn't anything you should tell me, is there?'

'Only that it's a lovely day.'

She did not talk to Emma and Caroline. Em would squeal and blab – and Caroline would disapprove. Already her eyes were full of suspicion, wary as they watched her. But who cares? Bess thought. I may not be able to act the things that I love, but there's a man that I love. And perhaps, just perhaps, we shall find a way.

'I just want to see that fucker Baron's stuck-up mouth fall open when he reads this. Two a.m. bomb drops on Palace. Five hundred ruddy nobs feared dead. A nation rejoices.'

The editor wasn't easily carried away, but tonight he felt adrift on an ocean of adrenalin. The stringer in Pakistan had talked to the cops and slipped them a satchel full of dollars. And yes, the arrest form was genuine; and yes, the British Council had called in the High Commissioner to get the charges dropped. 'Clunk click,' said Bradshaw. They'd hit it on Monday morning, with a full week for MPs to chunter over the juicy bits and put down early day motions. 'I want some constitutional experts lined up ready. Is there any precedent for a royal crisis like this since . . . since the last one? I want telephone polls and agony aunts and the Archdeacon of Batley going apeshit. I want the works.'

They came for her in the middle of the night and flung a coat over her head and carried her away. Nobody told her what was wrong. She was torn from sleep and bundled into the back of a Jaguar; she was pushed low into the anonymity of the leather and held there out of sight. Caroline heard the clatter below and ran to her window. She saw the dark shapes run in the moonlit quad. She heard a car engine roar. 'Oh Bess,' she said out loud. 'Oh Bess, what are they doing to you?'

The heating in Fountain's office had failed again. He was wearing a heavy black coat. Like an undertaker, she thought. Baron had a newspaper laid out on the table. The Prime Minister – in a green bomber jacket and polo neck, chin stubbled, teeth clenched – sat on the arm of the sofa.

'So,' said Fountain coldly, no Ma'ams, no courtesies, 'what can you tell us about this?'

She laid her hands on the table to steady herself and read, eyes wide. I mustn't break. I must keep calm.

'You will see there are some questions we have to have answers to. Truthful answers. Are you in love with this man?'

She straightened and looked at him. 'I think so. I thought so.'

'Have you slept with him?'

'Not yet, at least not properly. There was no opportunity. But I think it was only a matter of time.'

'Did you know about this other woman?'

'In a way. He said they'd been friends, but that it was over.'

'And what about his past? The drugs, the drink, the open sex?'

'If all this is true, Sir Edgar, it is as much news to me as it is to you. He told me nothing. But I asked nothing of him either.'

She looked at the pages of photographs. The balcony, with him below. The one where he held her in his arms. Julia, smiling, in a tight black sweater. The Windsor family album of mothers and grannies and great-aunts called 'Other Loves that Rocked the Royal Boat'. If she cried now, she would weep from humiliation.

'Can I talk to him?' she asked.

Millward unzipped his jacket and took centre stage. There was a flash of candy stripe beneath his sweater. He's wearing pyjamas, she thought incongruously. He didn't even have time to put a shirt on.

'We think it best if you talk to no one for the moment, Your Majesty,' he said. Her title was back, but he seemed to spit the words. 'You are an intelligent girl, but you have behaved like an imbecile. Surely you realized the dangers? Surely everything you've been taught through the last months must have made some impression? It took my Party and my Government years of effort to try to make our Monarchy safe again. Too many silly people indulging their lusts and their emotions had brought it to the brink of extinction. We brought the King to realize that. We gave him a wife beyond reproach, a wife who knew her duty, and she gave him a son we thought we could train to behave under our tutelage. But it was not to be. Instead, we got you. We tried to teach you. We admired your resilience. We allowed ourselves, idiotically, to believe that you could move into a different environment and keep control of your senses.

'Apparently not. The old genies have escaped from the bottle. Within hours, we'll be back where we started – and you will be seen for what you are: a headstrong, arrogant young woman who can't tell one rotten man from another and doesn't seem to care.

'It is all over, Your Majesty. I'm sorry, but there's no escaping that conclusion. The risks of giving you your head are simply too great. The institution can't take such strains. There can be no more university, no more acting, no more unsuitable boyfriends to give the tabloids their kicks. We must draw a final line under this little adventure. For if we don't, others will.'

He glanced at Baron. 'Sir Richard and I have some ideas for damage limitation. We shall say that you were foolish and misled, and are now distraught. That you realize your folly and that you have decided to leave Oxford to devote yourself wholeheartedly to the service of your people. You must go somewhere for a month of complete seclusion. Balmoral, we think: without comment or access. It must be as though you have ceased to exist whilst the press exhausts itself. And then, I suppose, we can try again.'

'A re-launch,' said Baron, snarling.

Caroline had tried phoning the Palace. Futility. 'I'm afraid we can be of no assistance to you, Miss.' None of Bess's private numbers seemed to be working. There was only the shriek of the headlines and the incessant chatter of radio and television: otherwise her friend had ceased to exist. She walked, as a matter of routine, not expectation, up the Woodstock Road; then right to Tom's digs behind a timber yard. A dozen reporters sat on the red brick wall outside his house. The door was tightly shut, the curtains drawn. She swung on her heel and hurried on. Some day soon, perhaps, there would be a call. Some day friends would be back on the agenda. But, for the moment, her world had turned.

Chapter Nine

It was almost Easter, yet a thin, brown coating of old snow still lay beneath the pine woods of Balmoral. The clouds were grey and low. The wind seemed to blow straight from Iceland. She strode in the darkness of the trees, wrapped in forgetfulness. The outcast, waiting for the days of exile to end. Thursday, Friday, Saturday. Perhaps tomorrow the pressure would subside and she could think of living again?

But Sunday brought the most savage dawn yet. 'The papers, Ma'am,' said the glum little man from Special Branch. 'The Prime Minister thought you should see them. Tell her to look at the *Mail* first, he said.'

' "My Love, My Juliet." Romeo Bowler talks exclusively about the Queen he loved and left behind. "I never meant to hurt her," the handsome young man told me, eyes blazing with passion. "She was the light of my life, so young and alive when our bodies met and I could feel her throbbing in ecstasy." The other girls were just also-rans, with their spite and petty jealousies.

'Had he intended to tell her about Pakistan and an episode he describes as "grossly overblown"? Perhaps, in time. "But it was long ago and all a bizarre misunderstanding." He realizes, he says, the damage he has caused the Monarchy. "I wish Her Majesty nothing but happiness." But he knows that they have no future together. "I am an actor first and always. It is one stroke of fortune now that others have seen my potential." He will be leaving Oxford immediately for Hollywood where MGM have offered him a starring role in a new TV mini-series, *The Princess and the Pauper*. "I pray each night for those who have suffered. I pray that we may both move on and find inner peace."' That interview in full: pages 17–24.

The *News of the World*, she saw, had a still more predictable angle. 'Love Rat Romeo shops dirt on Queen Juliet for 100,000 euros. So sorry, he says, and flees country.'

Bess locked her door and sat on the bed. She could still feel the strength of his fingers on her waist, and the scent of him as they kissed. She had believed he loved her. Why else would he keep saying it? She didn't believe that he'd lied, only that he was weak. When the winds blew, he'd blown with them. I picked the wrong man, but how was I to know? I know so little, and I have no opportunity to learn. Will all my life be like this, finding ordinary men who can't manage extraordinary pressures? Or is the trouble somewhere buried inside me? That I want to be myself and don't understand that's impossible.

It was not the betrayal alone. It was the isolation which consumed her. Finally, she began to cry without restraint.

'My pauvre petit poppet,' said Selene when she called. 'Let this be a lesson to you. Men are such absolute creeps. If only we could do without them . . .'

Dear Lilibet,
I went to lunch with Bro King and he was very down, barely touched a mouthful of his hake. What's up? I said. Had the Curse of the Vikings been staging one of her raiding parties again? And he smiled. Always, every moment, he said. When I bust up with Tamara and Naomi and Justine and all the rest, I reckoned it was partly my fault and that made it better in a way. But Christina isn't my fault. It's the price of entry to the job, and that just makes it so much harder to bear.

Two days later, walking through the pines, she turned left down the hill to the cottage in the valley the locals called the Refuge of the Damned – where duchesses who had fallen from grace were sent to holiday in obscurity while their children spent Christmas or the summer holidays within the walls. Selene, she knew, had passed that way before. And there was still a giant heart scrawled on the back of the garden shed, with S LOVES A in faded red lettering. Someone had written D HATES C in a small black hand near its left ventricle.

She wandered round to the back and pushed idly at the door behind the water butt. It creaked open. The gillie and the hound who followed her everywhere at a distance had paused at the top of the slope, uncertain whether to come closer. She peered through the dirty window of the cottage. They had stopped.

They were waiting. After all, she thought, looking round, what was there here to worry about? The rooms were empty and chill to the bone: dereliction. But there was a pile of something in the corner of the living room. She kicked at it gingerly. A clatter of metal and wire. Traps. A box of cartridges spilled on to the floor. A packet of cheese sandwiches, covered in green slime. A leather coat.

She picked it up. The poacher had obviously been hiding here through the day and, somehow, been discovered. He'd fled leaving everything behind. Was there a name? No, only in the right pocket something far more precious. She pressed the button on the mobile phone and it flickered tentatively to life. The gillie had not moved. He was still and brooding on the skyline.

'Caroline? Thank God you're there. It's – well you know who it is ... Don't ask me how. I'm a sort of prisoner – for my own good, and so on ... Yes, I know. Brutal. I just feel so betrayed. But you warned me, you warned me. They're using it to cut me off from everybody I care about. They say I must come to terms with it, or the consequences will be incalculable ... Who's they? Millward. Fountain when he's not there. They've got minders on me day and night ... I can't eat, I can't think. Please, please talk to me ...'

The battery only lasted for ten minutes but, even as it died, she felt somehow restored. She thrust the phone down a sweater arm so that it lay unseen against her side and waved to the man on the hillside. He did not respond. She was humming as she walked back towards the Castle, even as it began to snow once more.

Millward, as he liked best, made a short statement to camera outside Downing Street. That way there was a decent background of interesting people doing interesting things and no bloody backbenchers hopping around with their tedious points of order trying to blow him off course. 'I have encouraging news of the Queen,' he said. 'Her doctors inform me that three weeks in the quietness of the country with the time for reflection that Scotland traditionally provides have seen a marked recovery in her health. She will need to take matters gently for a period of months, but it has been decided that the care she needs now may be most conveniently provided in London. The Queen will therefore be returning to Buckingham Palace on Tuesday afternoon. It is, by chance, one of my normal days for an audience with her. I shall, I'm sure, speak for the whole country if I wish her a complete and speedy renewal of health and spirits; and I know, for her part, that she wishes to embark on a new and more dedicated period of public service to you all. The Coronation will take place on schedule. Thank you.'

And goodnight, Bess thought when she watched him on ITN. Care, concern, crap. He'd not been near her through the weeks of solitary confinement. There hadn't been a bleep since the night with the pink pyjamas and bomber jacket. Now he was making her out to be some kind of basket case, teetering on the brink of breakdown. She was thin and she was melancholy: she felt let down, of course, but, worse than that, a bit of an idiot. But somehow she had to fight back. If they all rolled over her now, there'd be nothing left to hang on to.

He came with an ingratiating grin, the boy-next-door look that many women seemed to find so charming. 'Gosh,' he said, 'you're looking well, Ma'am.' A blur of words began to engulf her. 'Constant monitoring for your own good . . . a New Palace for a New Start . . . Staff on duty twenty-four hours a day . . . No opportunity for further slips . . . You must, as I'm sure you realize, conform.'

It was now or never, she felt. 'I hear what you say, Prime Minister. Of course I do. But what you suggest is just impossible. I know I've made a hash of it, and I've learned from that. Really. But somewhere in all this, somehow, I have to be a person with a life of my own. I can't conform utterly, as you put it. I have to be me.'

The grin had gone long before her first sentence ended. She was a naughty child again, but one this time who could be punished. 'Very well. I didn't want to go along this path. I thought you might be susceptible to reason. But you ought to know, Ma'am, that we have sanctions at our disposal.'

'Not abdication?' she said, too lightly. 'That might get us all off the hook.'

'We could only consider that if the evidence of instability was overwhelming. Not a prospect to be relished, as I'm sure you realize. No, I'm talking about something much easier for us, and more potent. In my safe at Downing Street I have the Brazilian Civil

Aviation Authority's report on the Salvador tragedy . . .'

'But I thought that was all over,' she said. 'The other pilot was taking off without any clearance. He was on drugs and his licence was out of date.'

Millward was suddenly feline, seeming to caress his words as he uttered them. 'That is true, Your Majesty. But like most truth, true only up to a point. The official report – which I have taken great pains to see is not published – shows that your father, your beloved father, was at the controls when the collision occurred. That he deliberately ignored clear warnings from Air Traffic Control. That he reacted too little and too late. It finds him, if I quote directly, culpable of a negligence which contributed in substantial measure to the accident and consequent loss of life.

'Now, naturally, we didn't want all that muddying the waters at the time, did we? It would have been most unfortunate; and happily the Brazilian President agreed. But I hear constantly of the Authority's wish to publish its full findings. If I feel that there is some-thing here worth protecting, then it would be my duty to seek to protect the status quo, and your father's memory. I am sure you'd agree, Your Majesty, that it would be quite insupportable for me to act in that way unless you were able to provide – how shall I put it? – the cooperation I consider essential.'

Her head was bowed. She did not look up as he left.

'Don't forget about plenty of early nights,' he said. 'Your doctors think sleep a great healer.'

*

The Palace gardens closed at 6.30. Bess looked out of the window. It was nearly seven and the last of the litter collectors in their brown felt hats and their sweaty brown trousers had cleared and departed. She had been cooped inside all day, sitting mute whilst Fountain paraded ostentatiously through her diary for the month, issuing orders. Now she sat alone in the closed stillness of her high, dark room, the tea things untouched on the table. Fat Clemmy came in and clucked over the tray. 'You haven't drunk a thing.' She picked up the plate of small, white sandwiches smeared with strawberry compote. 'And you haven't touched your jammy dodgers. You aren't being sensible, you know. I shall have to get Lady Margaret to talk to you.' Lady M, the Chief Warder with the steel face. The door banged closed and she could hear the pantings echoing along the hall.

The nights were drawing out fast and there was a spring warmth to the evening. Bess pulled a cardigan round her shoulders and walked out to the steps which ran down to the lawns.

She did not see Nicky until she reached the bottom. He was squatting on the ground behind the great Waterloo Vase a few yards from the white outline of the Admiralty Temple. While she'd been in Scotland, he and Selene had finally moved to Clarence House. They visited her together, as though she were in hospital. She never really saw him alone. He was Selene's appendage.

'Oh, I didn't realize you were here,' she said. 'Is our beloved mother inside?'

'No. She said she was going shopping or something.

There's not much of a garden where we are. I asked to be driven over.' He paused and fingered a livid red spot on the bridge of his nose. 'If that's all right?'

'Of course. How could it not be? What's mine is yours and always will be.'

His eyes seemed to cross for a second and he spat on the stones by his feet. 'Right,' he said thickly. 'Bloody right. You get the grace and I get the favours. You're the Queen, but you hate it and everybody knows you hate it. Mother says you're unbalanced about it, positively unhinged. She says, by rights, it ought to have been me when they all died. And fifty years ago it would have been and you'd have been free to push off and marry any randy bastard who asked you. But now we all have to prop you up and cluck round and pretend it's fair. But it's not. I hate you, I hate you. You've stolen what I ought to be – and you don't even want it.'

She had seen these tantrums before. He somehow sucked rage from the air into his sunken, blotchy cheeks, and grew red with the furies that consumed him.

From habit and instinct she asked the question she had asked a thousand times over the years. 'Have you been taking your pills?'

He rose and swung a fist towards her. She could have stepped backwards, but instead she took the blow to the side of the head without flinching.

'Does that make you feel better?'

'Only if I could do it again and again, you selfish cow. You've ruined my life and one day I'll ruin yours. One day we'll all dance on your grave.'

She turned up the stairs and left him, raging in the dying light. She left her room in darkness and sat alone on her bed, watching the street lamps flicker on down the Mall.

As she had done too often since she had left Oxford and the debris of her life, she wept.

Chapter Ten

Of all the committees in the world – or at least of all those he sat on, which sometimes seemed much the same thing – Millward hated Crown Planning Group D (Special Events) most. It was his own fault, of course: as he might, under pressure, admit. He could have abandoned the whole CPG structure after Brazil. A new Queen, a new challenge, a new approach . . . that sort of thing. The sodding groups, after all, had been hanging around for decades, mutating into ever more bureaucratic monsters since the millennium turned. The 'D' in CPGD had stood, originally, for Dome; it had been the sub-committee of the Opening Ceremony Sub-Committee (02) which had been responsible for Palace liaison the day the old Queen arrived in Greenwich. It ought to have been rolled up with the red carpet. But the innovatory Mr Blair had rather liked the way it brought 'his circle' – the showbusiness stars and media owners – together with 'them' – the crowd from the Palace – as soon as he found that 'they' would take orders: on the little things first, like car waiting times, and then (glory be!) on the whole shooting match. What She said; what She wore; when Her features were supposed to crack into a smile and when She was supposed to look serious. He'd been particularly entranced by the tributes they'd agreed to 'the vision and energy of our young Prime Minister'. CPGD was much, much too useful to be scrapped with the last of the fireworks.

But that was then, Millward thought sourly, and this is now. Twenty-seven 'special events' later, including two coronations, and the arteries have hardened. The man from the Treasury always arrived with the historic accounting costs on his palm-top computer and punctuated every phase of every discussion with his familiar, tedious descant. 'That represents a 19.7 per cent rise in underlying spending on core items: 3.7 per cent more than the agreed norm.' And the Director of the Royal Opera always rose to him like a fat salmon jumping straight into the freezer. 'Well really, how are we to talk art and pageantry and memories ordinary people can cherish with this accounting going on?' The weeks were ticking by ominously. They'd got the routes and the times fixed, of course, but they were still uselessly stuck on the things Millward knew were important.

'Look,' he said heavily, picking up the thick file in front of him and dropping it on the table with a thud that brought a sudden silence, 'let's get back to basics. Style. Tone. Effect. I don't care a damn whether the ermine is real or fake fur. I don't care a damn whether the Archbishop enters right or left or bloody well at all. We're drowning in details. Can we just talk quietly for two minutes about what we want to achieve? Is this going to be another of those human coronations where we try to downplay the majesty stuff? Shy smiles and lounge suits? Or are we going to upload with pomp and circumstance again?

'The last time, as we know, there wasn't a question. The focus groups wanted so much informality the King had to practically bicycle down to the Abbey. We even encouraged the BBC commentary team to make jokes – at least until we heard them. But this time there's a real choice. Queen Elizabeth the Third, gentlemen. Do we want her playing everyone's favourite daughter just dropping in from Sloane Square? Or do we pile on the history and try to get the old echoes going? The third Elizabethan Age. The fire of our nationhood rekindled. A girl with the weight of centuries on her shoulders. Do we, in sum, want a course correction?'

The Opera clapped his hands in excitement. 'Oh, absolutely, Prime Minister. We want *Aida*. . . We do not want *Peter Grimes*. In these difficult times, we have a responsibility to preserve our pageantry.'

The Treasury sighed. 'The budget, if I may remind you all, is not some figure plucked out of the air. It's there in the red book. Fifteen per cent up, inflation adjusted. The Public Accounts Committee will roast us if we start playing fast and loose with what's been set. How many gold coaches make a hospital, Prime Minister? How many banquets equal Crisis at Christmas? I'd have thought, after everything that's happened, that the Palace ought to be paying us for the publicity.'

Montgomery had run his fingers through his yellow hair distractedly. He was a flustered haystack. 'I must say that's a bit rich. I mean, everyone knows we're hanging by a thread while the Revenue makes up its mind. We've done everything the man from Tesco recommended. Multi-skilled the footmen and the cooks. Sold off all the grace and favours so that we pay for everything – houses, travel, electricity, our own toilet rolls. Non-replacement of inessential staff is in its fifteenth year. Sir Edgar practically has to empty his own wastepaper baskets. This is now an efficient, normal business which compares favourably with any of the service companies in the FTSE 500. But we are desperately short of our capital requirements. We need the inheritance tax situation addressing, for heaven's sake, not more demands which betray no understanding of our plight. What does the Treasury want us to do? Sell the Crown Jewels?'

Millward smiled.

'Well. It's an idea,' said the Treasury. And then fell silent.

Fountain leaned forward. 'I know there are no easy answers, Prime Minister,' he said. 'But there is one hard question. Basically, we need bailing out. If that doesn't happen, then the Palace will, quite simply, go broke. It is not our fault. The taxpayers may not love us – and, given the last forty years, we can all understand why. But there are no options. Either we are saved, or we go bankrupt like some Korean car company. We must be saved. The problem is whether, at this pass, we are best saved by a little grandeur or by more parsimony? This Coronation, when you think about it, is really a definition of our own self-worth.'

Millward got to his feet. 'That's that, then,' he said. 'We'll find a grant in aid from somewhere. Nick a bit from Defence – or a standstill on Treasury salaries. And then put on a show. I want the Grenadier Guards back from Belize. I want the day's holiday turned into a long weekend. Let's go for it, gentlemen. Let's give the punters something to remember.'

Robin Leckie had been taking notes. He drew a line on his pad and scribbled a few words beneath. 'Bess needs bread. Call for the circuses.'

She did not go out these days, except when it was required. The day before she had gone to a flower show at Blakeney, wide-eyed over the dahlias, absorbed by a red rose with a pink heart that a pensioner in a cap had called 'Monarch Modesty'. She had eaten rock cakes in a tent, been shown a marrow a metre long and discussed the weather with ladies in cotton dresses. 'Yes, they say it'll clear by Sunday. But, you know, they're usually wrong, whatever they say.'

Chuckle chuckle; cringe cringe. Mrs Beamish, who was ninety-nine, and thirty years retired from service, they said, had a picture of the last time the old Queen Mum had come to the show. 'Choked on a seed cake, she did. We had to sit her down and slap her on the back and pour tea down her.'

Tomorrow she would go to Swindon to open a works canteen, then on to Bristol, where the new docks extension road lay silent, shielded by a single ribbon. There was a public library in Cheltenham along the wide arc home.

Tomorrow and tomorrow and tomorrow. She saw no friends. Caroline would call from Oxford and, occasionally, find her way through the maze of the

Palace switchboard. Emma would write. But they were both sweating it out through the last weeks of term; both planning trips to places – Cambodia, Argentina – that made her stand for a while when she thought of them and wander over to her window, seeking somehow to see the world beyond.

'Letters,' said Fat Clemmy, bustling in. 'We've tried to keep it down, but there are still forty or so you ought to sign yourself. And then there's the speech for Swindon to read and the order of play for Bristol.'

Bess said nothing. She sat at the desk in the study, glancing up as usual at the marble bust of Edward VII which stood on the plinth beside it, square, bearded jaw fixed, neck bulging against collar, eyes blank. God save the Kaiser.

She began signing, page by page. Elizabeth R. Elizabeth R.

'And don't forget you've got the Prime Minister in twenty minutes. Did you do your boxes last night?'

They had ceased, at least in private, to defer to her. Lady Margaret Swayne, she'd discovered, leafing through *Who's Who* one morning in the library at Windsor, had been an Assistant Secretary in the Home Office before her marriage. Prisons department? Perhaps, but Bess rather wondered about MI5. She'd found a couple of old entries on the Net where a Margaret Mansfield was shown as attending conferences in Amsterdam and Frankfurt on drug-enforcement policies. There was a thin-lipped imperiousness to her. She did not ask; she ordered. And Clemmy, jowls trembling, had taken the hint. Deference was dead.

'Ladies and gentlemen. It is four decades now since the first managers from your proud company chose Swindon as the new centre for the enterprises of Mitsubishi here in Britain. And through that span, their contribution not merely to the town, but to all of Wiltshire, has set an example which we have greatly admired. They have shown, time and again, that the pace of progress depends on the will for progress and that the interests of their workforce stand at the heart of all they do. As I look, this morning, around this magnificent canteen, I can see . . .'

Millward coughed. 'Good afternoon. Did Your Majesty read her boxes?'

She found herself thinking constantly about him; sometimes waking in the night, sitting bolt upright in the dark, sweat pouring – with his face floating mockingly from the ceiling.

Was this love? There had been nights when she had dreamed of Tom like this. There were nights when he still returned to her, lips curled in a muttered apology. But where was the space between love and hate? She had loved Tom Bowler. Now she thought she hated him. She surely could not love Simon Millward, with his thinning flop of hair and his twist of a grin which seemed to wheedle and pick at the corners of her mind. He made her skin crawl. So she must hate him, too. Was that right?

'Good afternoon to you, Prime Minister. I read them last night until two, but I'm afraid I couldn't find anything very interesting. You must find politics awfully tedious these days. So much talk with all the partners of this and that, and so little action. I'm afraid that, after Palmerston, I rather lost the swing of things.'

She was pleased to see him scowl. She was surprised, and then alarmed, as he reached towards her, arms outstretched stiff, fingers holding her by the shoulder.

'Enough chat,' he said. 'I know you don't realize it, but you and I are important to each other. I have staked a lot, maybe my career, on making something of you. And, without me, you would already be history yourself – the last, disgraced fling of a broken line.

'You say you loved your father. Now prove it. I know you're a considerable actress. Remember, I saw you and that slimy Romeo falling off balconies on to each other. Today I got you another part. This won't be any old Coronation. I'm bankrolling it and I'm depending on you to be a star. Can I trust you to perform? For your father, if not for me?'

He shook her for a second. She took a step backwards.

The banter had gone, and so had the simmer of hostility.

'Yes,' she said with a shrug. 'Yes, I suppose you can trust me.'

The Director of the Royal Opera had reached Covent Garden via the Royal National Theatre and, indeed, the Royal Exchange, Manchester. 'But, believe it or not, I've never had a proper royal front of house for anything I've done,' Sir Marcus Binstock complained as he circled the Palace ballroom checking camera angles. 'Your grandfather, God bless him, was wonderful before he got inside the auditorium. Very bright and interested. "What this theatre needs is some white Palladian columns, Marcus," he'd say. Or "The gilt frames in the crush bar really need an element of refurbishment." But put him down in a nice stalls seat any night, and he'd be fast asleep within five minutes. It was the outside he cared about, not the inside. A cultured man, Ma'am, but very tired, so very tired, towards the end. Always looking for love and exhausting himself when he found it. But a gentleman of taste, sure enough. Not my taste, I grant you. Not really anybody's taste but his own, perhaps. But certainly a taste.

'Now, wait. Pause there. We'll have the spotlight from the vestry catch you in mid-sentence. "I solemnly promise and swear to serve the people . . ." No emphasis on promising or swearing, Your Majesty, but wait for just a moment after that and turn your face up. Eyes somewhere in the distance. Yes, lovely – "serve the people". Equal stress, please. Suurve. Peeepul. Wonderful. Just one more time.'

I'm the young Queen, she thought. Is this the old queen? But hadn't he had five wives? She looked at the tubby little body slotted into the orange sweater like a torpedo into a tube, and the sparrow legs protruding beneath it. 'Ma'am, Ma'am! Back here, please. Wakey wakey. Take it from the top again, and then we'll do the Robes of Righteousness and the Diamonds of Salvation.'

Fountain lay naked and face down on the bed. The sun was high and directly over the loft window, so that the light was full and the crimson weals on his pale, flabby back had a livid glow.

'I'll get the TCP,' Selene said, disappearing into the bathroom. 'Too much coke. And I should have done my nails this morning. Sorry . . .'

He dabbed at the wound on his hip with a Kleenex and pursed his lips. There was blood all over the sheets. He'd have to take them to the launderette himself. You couldn't leave them like this for Mrs Barker to see and wonder over and chat about with her friends in the café opposite the mews. He could hear her voice now, raised over the chink of the tea cups. 'Lord knows what he was doing there. It was like an abbatoir. Perversion, I calls it. The pervert from the Palace.'

Selene dabbed at him with cotton wool and the breath hissed between his teeth at the sting of it.

'Ouch,' he said. 'Easy. It hurts.'

'You are the most incredible coward,' she said. 'I bet if I hurt you enough you'd give me exactly what I want.'

She ran the sharp edge of her nail down his spine and he shivered with apprehension.

'What do you want then?'

'A coach of my own, of course. Bess in her gold pumpkin. Then Nicky, because that's his right. And then me, in that nifty lacquered number at the back of the stable yard. I don't want to share. I want the coach and the crown with the Kohinoor diamond. I want my moment of gloire.'

She poured the rest of the bottle over his shoulders, and he yelped with pain.

*

Dear Lilibet,
Do you remember when they crowned Bro King?
Hardly, I expect. You were only five at the time.
But you'll remember the rain. Everybody remembers
the rain. And the jeers and the placards in the Mall.
'Here's to the Last Time' and 'Goodnight Sweet
Prince'. It seemed to knock all the stuffing out of
him. 'I thought I was loved,' he said to me
afterwards, 'and now I know we're all just
tolerated.' I don't think he's ever been the same
since. No more blondes and nights out, just sitting
in the Palace watching his hair fall out and that
Copenhagen harpy tearing lumps out of the
servants. It's a terrible blow when you find that
words don't matter, that what the papers and BBC
say about respect and love and all that guff is just
flam – and the people stand there, dripping wet,
letting you know they don't care. Don't put your
trust in what folk say, my love. Always wait and see
what they do . . .

The coach was oddly cramped on the inside, a small
capsule of velvet buried beneath the bulbous curves
and curlicues. It reminded her of the old Buick in the
garage at Windsor, a bloat of chrome and panelling
with nowhere to tuck your knees which Edward VIII
had had made in Canada because it was more 'British'.
They said he'd had Mrs Simpson on the back seat,
but she couldn't for the life of her see how that was
anatomically possible. She shook her head from side
to side, clutching the crown, and concentrated. She
had to concentrate every minute.

Take the Orb of the Cross in the right hand. Right? And the Royal Sceptre. Left? And the Rod of Equity and Mercy. Don't, for God's sake, drop the rod. The Imperial State Crown going in. King Edward's Crown going out. Make sure you don't trip on the Cloth of Gold. Remember not to let the anointing oil drip on anything precious. Look young at the Knowledge and Wisdom bit. Look strong, shoulders back, when the Archbishop says 'Your undoubted Queen'. No, no, no smiling in the Abbey. But try to relax a bit while they all shout about salvation. Gracious, noble: but still a human being in spite of it all.

She looked out of the coach window. The crowds were not tremendous. No more than five deep by the Admiralty Arch. This wasn't the World Cup. But there were no placards and the cheering seemed loud enough. As the coaches behind passed under the Arch she thought she heard a chorus of booing. But who cared? Mother was probably too stoned to notice. She waved again.

A pikeman on the left tripped over his pike and fell headlong as they turned into Trafalgar Square. The crowd cheered and laughed. She grinned for a second and a hundred cameras caught her. That was the front page taken care of. It was going to be all right.

Sir Marcus was not merely pleased. Little chest puffed, little legs pumping, little hands clapping, he was ecstatic. 'Ma'am, you were so, so wonderful.' Mill-ward was terse in private – 'Well, we did it' – and glowing at the Downing Street press conference. 'I think today that the whole nation found a daughter it can be proud of.' Montgomery complained about the police claims for overtime. Nicky had three sherries before anyone noticed, and went to bed early. Selene did not take her crown off all night.

When they came off the balcony for the final time – clutching the bouquets that Sir Marcus had added as his final touch – Fountain clutched at her arm for a second and drew her aside, in the shadow of the great Saxe-Coburg clock. He had a flush and a vigour to him she could not remember seeing before.

'We have had our problems, Your Majesty, but I think I should say that was splendid. Quite splendid. It gives us the financial breathing space we need and time to plan what comes next really properly. Really properly.'

Blow vigour, she suddenly realized: the flush was real, but the flush was drink. The champagne flute he was clutching was empty, but it had been empty several times.

'And what does come next, Sir Edgar?' Bess asked.

'Why, the engagement of course. And the marriage. It's all in my forward-planning dossier.'

'Have you anyone particular in mind?' she said.

The clock over their heads struck six, rather noisily. It seemed as though he had woken from sleep. The flush at the neck grew pinker and then, in a trice, was gone. His face was white and his hands were flustered.

'I'm so sorry, Ma'am. I'm gabbling. It has been a most exhausting day for all of us – and I'm sure any details for the future can be looked at as appropriate. And again: many, many congratulations.'

A butler with a gold tray offered her a small hillock of caviare on a star of browned toast. When she turned back, Sir Edgar was nowhere to be seen.

Chapter Eleven

Bradshaw had sat in his office for eight hours with the door shut. In the morning they had brought him coffee and biscuits with caramel icing. At lunch he called for a sausage sandwich and a can of Strong Yorkshire Bitter. The demand for tea and brownies came at four, the buzz for Scotch and soda at 5.46. Then, as it did on these long days of brooding, the door opened.

'Get me Will Wittman sharp.'

There was enough whisky left for a couple of rounds. Bradshaw had pulled his grimy white shirt out of his trousers, but without bothering to undo his braces. He looked like a half-packed parachute. His feet – black shoes, yellow socks – were parked on the desk by the in-tray.

Will poured himself a double.

'I reckon she's fair game again,' Bradshaw said suddenly.

'She?'

'Her. Her we must all obey. The She Queen from Roedean. That was a cracking show yesterday, and it draws a line under what went before. The lass is twenty. A little girl – a foolish little girl – no longer. Is she saint or sinner? Is she angel or witch?'

Wittman could not quite see where this conversation was going. But there was a pause, and Bradshaw was looking at him.

'Good questions, boss,' he said lamely.

The editor glowered. 'Bloody good questions. And you haven't been doing your bloody homework, son.'

He reached down into the great plastic bin at the left of his desk, searching for something with one hand, spilling biscuit wrappers and the empty beer can on to the floor, until he found what he was looking for.

'Bloody *Daily Mail* page seven. Bloody leader column, last paragraph. "She played a saint in a school play, and perhaps we expected too much from her, too soon. But now, growing in the role, she may be the angel Britain needs for a gentler, more inspirational future."'

He sniffed. 'Bloody rubbish. But that's the *Mail* all packaged up. Endorsing bloody Millward and the gang again. Endorsing that wide-eyed floozy and her poncing Palace guards. You know what that means?'

Wittman had sprinted the first lap from a standing start, but now he was cruising. 'It means we have a duty to monitor the girl every minute of every day, boss. It means that the readers need our vigilance in the public interest, that we must ask the questions others shrink from, turn over the stones that others would prefer us to leave in place.' Bradshaw sat back and pulled a yellow sock deliberately up his hairy calf. 'You sound like a bloody brief for the Press Complaints Commission, son. But I think you've got the hang of it. Nobody wants to run the girl down unnecessarily. Forty years back, you could always rely on the *Express* to be loyal to the Royals. That was our heritage when others of dubious patriotism sniped and carped. But now times have changed, and so has our duty. Praise where praise is due. Criticism, fair and frank, where it's not. I'm giving Hendrick her cards tomorrow. I'm telling Coburn he's to take over your column on Monday.'

Wittman was trembling. Phoebe Hendrick had been Royal Correspondent for twenty years. She was the Earl of Budleigh's third daughter. They called her the Marchioness of Gush on the subs' desk. And Miles Coburn was the new young rat in the reporters' room, teeth gnawing at the backside of any incumbent who happened to flag.

'Where does that leave me, then?' Wittman said nervously.

Bradshaw picked up the beer can and hurled it back in the bin.

'Where do you bloody think? It leaves you Chief Royal Editor with a staff of two and all the expenses you can eat. Give that brother of yours a call and tell him he's on the team. I want stories, son. I want every bloody story that's going.'

It was as though she was out of intensive care, she thought. Visitors permitted. There was a cottage in Leicestershire, in the Wolds where they rolled towards Rutland, that the Duke of Windsor had bought for his caddies when he developed a passing passion for golf. Rose Cottage, Wymeswold. Two hundred years old, set back in three acres of woods and ponds, and briefly offered, in the faraway fifties, to a Princess with a cough and a penchant for gin. But it had been too far from her friends, she said, and too cold in winter when the wind beat in across the Fens. She had found an island in the Caribbean and younger men to keep her warm at nights. They had called it Rose Cottage after her, and pinned the name on the gate, but Margaret Rose was gone, and the cottage had fallen off the map, let to the RAF as officers' quarters until the air strip closed, then rented to the university in the valley below for entertaining visiting professors. But there had been a nasty episode last spring where a waitress from the village told the *News of the World* about her orgy ordeal with a lecturer in anatomical studies in which the pond featured rather too prominently. Nothing, it seemed, could cool his mad lust. And so the very existence of the cottage had been reasserted, through forests of paperwork, until it reached Montgomery's desk.

'Maybe this would do for the Queen,' he said to Fountain. 'We own it. The cost looks negligible. The university renovated it a couple of years ago on the back of some American grant. We need to throw her a bone and we need to put down a marker. At least it's cheap.'

Fountain grunted. 'I don't like the history bit,' he said. 'Look at the cuttings. "Dr Nasty's Nooky Nest". It's not what you'd call ideal. We'd better talk to Baron.'

It took four days and two briefings to get the story right. 'She's a serious young girl with serious young friends,' Baron finally said at dictation speed. 'She wants somewhere quiet and unpretentious to study. There are indications that she is becoming interested in archaeology. Our advisers tell us that the Leicestershire Wolds, so close to the old Fosse Way, may yet contain a number of unexcavated Roman camps. We think this, then, a natural and cost-effective conjunction of availability and opportunity.'

'No nooky then?' said the fat man from the *Star*.

Baron frowned. 'Her Majesty is devoted to her people and her duties,' he said in a pious monotone. But the older hands on the Royal circuit saw the back of his left hand brush for a second against his moustache, as though wiping away a grin. It was a sign language they understood. Romance wasn't back on the agenda. But it was moving up the pending file.

'They want to get her married off and out of harm's way, breeding happily,' Will said to Sammy as they strolled into Victoria looking for a taxi. 'This is the first sign. She has a hideaway of her own, even if half of Special Branch are sitting in the pub car park over the road. Just watch. In a month or two there'll be some very suitable young man dredged out of the European back catalogue. He'll go with her to a show or a supper. Then he'll get invited to Windsor for some boring family carnival. And then, dear Sammy, we shall be given the cottage treatment with roses round the door and the full production number.'

'But she's not even twenty-one yet,' said the junior Wittman dubiously. 'I don't see the hurry.'

Big brother sighed. 'That's precisely why there's a hurry. They can't allow her to rack up a long list of wannabees and might-be-suitables. Oxford was the writing on the wall of that disaster. Has she lost her cherry? Did Romeo do more than grope her? Is she damaged goods in the regal supermarket? They've got to get her off the park and, somehow, they've got to arrange something that works. Nobody can afford another bloody Windsor fiasco. They can't play that one again, Sam. Keep your ears flapping. I can feel a double-page spread on the Men Most Eligible coming on.'

It was still summer in its warmth, but the winds of mid-September were sudden and vehement, stripping the first leaves from the beech trees and strewing them across the surface of the pond. Bess lay in a deckchair sleeping gently. She wore a thin white cotton tunic, and her bare left arm lay trailing on the grass, occasionally fingering the leather-bound copy of *War and Peace*, open where it fell. Emma was stretched face down on a rug, skirt wrapped high around the top of her thighs, the back of her legs beginning to turn a menacing pink where the sun caught the flesh. She was snoring loudly.

Caroline carried the tea tray from the kitchen herself. It was heavy, and she propped it against her stomach for safety. The great silver teapot itself – the only one, for some reason, they had – was big enough for ten. It slithered and clunked against the cups as she approached. Bess stirred and peered into the light and smiled. 'This is bliss,' she said.

They sat cross-legged at the edge of the water, sipping Earl Grey and nibbling at sticks of fruit cake from the blue tin on the pantry shelf. She began to feel human again. There had been no holidays since the Coronation. They were, as Fountain said, lips pursed over the slim computer of a diary he kept in his briefcase, 'not apposite at this juncture'. She had been to Scotland twice, to Aberdeen's new fish cannery and to an old folk's home in Galashiels. She had toured mid-Wales for three days, shaking hands and waving at trees. The flight back from Belfast last night had not touched down at Castle Donington until eleven-thirty. The visit to Stockholm and St Petersburg began on Thursday. She was beginning to ache.

Emma had spent August in Tuscany with Rashid, a cook from Sylhet she'd met on the way to the loo at the Reign of Ranchipur just down Banbury Road. She carried a wad of pictures of him in her bag, standing on the thick grey walls of the Italian countryside, profile etched against the blue of the sky. He was slight and delicate and his eyes were wide with surprise. 'My toy boy,' she said, giggling. 'Only nineteen. He knows nothing, but he learns in a second. He doesn't look very strong, but he has the most incredible stamina.'

'Is this it, then?' Caroline asked sardonically.

'Gosh, no. He smells like a tandoori chicken when he gets off work. That's OK for a while. I sometimes smear yogurt on his chest and lick it off to get the tastebuds going. But you couldn't eat that for more than a few weeks without getting a big pash for a slice of beef and Yorkshire. He's just another of my great dishes of the world.'

They collapsed into fresh laughter. Bess laughed longest, then put her arms around her knees and bent her head forward out of sight. There was a moment's silence.

'Sorry,' she said finally, looking up. 'Sorry. But when we do this routine where you ask me what I've been doing, I always say nothing. I'm off limits. I might as well be locked in a monastery. Mother Superior Swayne has me under constant surveillance.

'From what they say, from the little hints they drop, I think they've got plans for me soon. But they will be their plans, not mine. I can't meet anyone for myself so I can't have plans.'

She glanced round, as though by instinct, towards the gate out into the lane. It clicked open and Lady Margaret came through. She walked by them along the path, acknowledging them with the barest flick of the head, mouth set, eyes down. The day was warm, but she wore her grey raincoat buttoned tight.

The wind made her clutch her throat. It had a wicked edge that did not merely chill but seemed to stab through the stupid silk coat they'd insisted she wear. The autumn skies over the Neva River were blue, untouched by cloud. The waters, despite the wind, were calm. But the cold was visceral.

The Ambassador, God rot him, had come prepared, swathed in a coat of blue wool so thick that it barely rippled when he moved. He stood on the open deck of the motor yacht and prattled on with his guided tour.

'See the Trubetskoy Bastion on the left, Ma'am. And the Naryshkin Bastion to its right. We'll be docking at the Commandant's Pier just to the side there.'

'It's not a fortress I'd like the SAS to have to take on, Sir Michael,' she said. She had to say something. She had to smile and show interest. The Russians clustered behind our man up from Moscow expected it.

'Nearly three-and-a-half centuries gone and never seen a whiff of action yet,' he said. 'A prison, yes; but nothing to set the pulses racing. Their scrubs without the Wormwood. They just had their wars elsewhere.'

The great slabs of red wall grew closer. Four trumpeters on the pier began their tootings. She tried to pull her arms around her against the wind for a second as the gangplank came down. This was not the kind of sightseeing she liked. In the years before – before it all happened – she had loved the discovering of Europe: in jeans and a T-shirt and sunglasses, wandering the Uffizi with her friends or strolling through the Ramblas. Her father had taken her to Vienna one Easter. She could still taste the schnitzels beaten wafer thin and the sacher torte. He had promised her a trip to Venice the week he died.

Would they have done St Petersburg too? Not, she guessed, if there'd been a British trade week to open in the Astoria Hotel and a routine accumulation of ball-bearings and raspberry jams to be sampled for the cameras. Too starchily oppressive on the one hand, too rushed and exhausting on the other. Twenty-five hours start to finish, then on to Stockholm for the night and a little more getting to know you. Wham, bang, thank you, Ma'am.

Inside, the fortress walls cut away the swirl of the

wind. It was unexpectedly calm and random: old houses and offices dotted around a vast cobbled square, with stretches of garden and trees at the end where the officers, long ago, had lived: a sleepy little town within a big city. And there, towering at its heart, the Cathedral of Peter and Paul.

'Prepare to have your breath taken away.' The voice was deep and rounded. English, but with an alien precision.

She turned for a moment and saw that one of the Russians had broken ranks and walked now at her side, hands buried in a coat of grey mohair, head bent a little towards her as though to begin conversation. He smiled. He was neither young nor old. Perhaps late thirties: a thick head of deep brown hair and clear skin and the sheepish eyes of a boy. He was tall and he looked strong, heavy shoulders straining at the coat. He moved, though, in loose, long strides.

'It isn't that this is the greatest cathedral here,' he said, as they reached the steps. 'St Isaac's is grander and I love the colonnades at the Kazan. But here the history just blows your mind.'

They walked through the doors side by side, and he paused to look upwards. She saw the whiteness of the walls, and the swirls of blue and gold stretching as though towards the sky, and she gasped. 'I see what you mean.'

'And so,' he said, still smiling, 'it is time for you to meet the Romanovs, Your Majesty. The Tsars in their tombs await, the spiritual gathering of the royalest clans. It will be quite like Christmas.'

*

'Thank you for that,' she said as they walked back to the boat. 'You brought it to life for me. So much blood and so much passion. There isn't much of that in the library at Windsor. You're a guide to remember.'

He made a graceful little bow. 'It has been an honour. Perhaps one day we may encounter each other again when we return to London.'

'Oh. But I thought you were here. That this is where you did your tours.'

He was laughing again. 'I am sorry, Ma'am. My fault. I thought you knew who I was. Let me try again from the beginning. My name is Yevgeny Roman Alexandrovich. Prince Roman Alexandrovich. Possibly your twelfth cousin three times removed – but the computer blew up trying to figure it out. Of course I know and love Russia. This is my home. But I have lived and worked in England ever since Winchester. Import, export. That was my jam you spread on your toast at the fair, and my packets of borscht in the soup tureen. The ones we make in Swindon. Imperial Bear Brand, the food of the gods and the tsars, we call it. Foolish, but fun. And my old countrymen seem to enjoy it.'

She was laughing too. 'Well then, yes,' she said. 'I'm always in Swindon, opening something or other. You must come to the Palace one evening. I'll take you on a tour of the soup kitchens.'

The valley was green and curiously deserted. One minute the car was winding past the stucco villas and low, white blocks of flats with their shuttered windows, and then, swinging right at the top of the hill, down the dust road through the pines and cork oaks, there was seclusion.

The house, long and low with a swimming pool curling beneath its terrace, stood near the bottom of the slope, shielded by the trees and the dense box hedges. From the terrace, stepping forward, hands gripping the top of the walling, Bess could see a kilometre or so of meadow and streams enfolded by more hills. A vineyard, empty now, hacked back to its stumps, cut a hole in the woodland to the west.

She stretched for a moment. The Catalan sun, even in early November, retained residual heat, the feeling of an English day in late spring. 'Well, this is pretty OK,' she said.

Elena, the Princess Elena, pulled her cotton sweater up over her head and knotted it like a scarf around her neck. 'What do you want to do?' she asked. 'Swimming, tennis, riding? Go for a walk? Have a little siesta? This is your weekend. We are at your command. One royal family supporting another, like a trade union.'

Bess giggled. 'I suppose it ought to be the healthy option. Walk first, snooze later.' They strolled together into the fields.

Fountain had seemed blandly enthusiastic when he had broken the news. 'A thoughtful gesture from the Zarzuela Palace, Your Majesty. The King has a daughter more or less your age and a hunting lodge she likes near the sea north of Barcelona. He wonders whether you would like to spend a few days with her there before winter comes. It's guarded and very private. And the Princess speaks wonderful English.

His Majesty promises to look after you as though you were part of his family.'

Well, why not? It was that or another grey Saturday in Windsor. Elena had called herself to cement the deal. 'Maybe we drink a little and have a few friends round. Maybe we go out and eat. There is no one around at this time of year. The villages are deserted and the tourists are gone. But there are quiet restaurants along the coast and even discos in Girona if you want a trip. We can be girls together, I think. We get to know each other.'

She was tiny. Her hair was black and long and her smile could seem suddenly to split her face in two. On the ride back from the airport she had chatted away with the chauffeur in what sounded like two different languages. 'Castilian and Catalan,' she said when Bess asked. 'One full of music, the other full of harshness. But now I study in Barcelona, both are necessary. And if I get bored, I can always do French or English. That is one part of our royal tradition here which is good for us. They educate us to survive and then they let us go out to work. When I finish university I want a job in marketing, you know. Probably something sporting like motor racing or football, with lots and lots of travel. Who wants to be cooped up in palaces with babies and servants when that is no longer the way in our world?'

Bess grimaced. 'Your world, not mine. The curse of the throne blows all that away in twenty seconds. You can be anything you like as long as you don't have a crown.'

'Well, maybe we talk about all this when my brother

comes for lunch tomorrow. That may be his life too, one day.'

Brother? Surely not Crown Prince Santos of Bourbon and Greece (and the Asturias and Girona and Viana and Castile and Aragón and Navarre). He never dropped in anywhere without a three-ring circus. She must mean the younger one. What was his name in the briefing papers? Jamie. No, Jaime. But why was he calling so casually, without a word of warning. She looked at Elena sharply. The smile splitting her face was almost too wide. On the hillside among the cork oaks she saw a hint of movement and a man standing in the deepest shadow. Security, security. They were always watched. There was always a plan.

'Another plate of the prawns from Palamos? They are the finest we have and there are so few of them left. Even in the best places in Madrid they serve Chinese prawns because there is nothing else. All very well in a chop suey or covered in peppers, I say, but not if you know the real taste straight from the sea.'

He was tall and blond, with a hook of a nose which reminded her of somebody from the old photographs in the Saloon at Sandringham. The hair beginning to recede as thirty approached. When he'd walked over to meet her he had clasped his hands behind his back and his eyes had roved restlessly, only making contact at the end. There, she had it. He was like the great-grandfather she had never met. He was a Greek, not a Spaniard.

She sucked at a fat prawn and wriggled her fingers

in the small, silver bowl of lemon water. Elena was suddenly absorbed by a sea slug, prising it out and then swallowing with a great gulp so that you could see the rubbery bulk of it slip down her narrow throat.

How was she supposed to respond to that? 'Yes, they're delicious.' Where would that get her? He was like a superior elder brother, making statements that led nowhere and made her feel a silly little girl.

'Tell me about your job,' she said. 'I know you're in banking, but I don't know what that involves. And I'm very, very interested in how you can be royal and earn a proper living.'

'Coffee?' he said. 'No. In that case, why don't we sit by the swimming pool while I tell you. It seems a pity to waste the sun.'

They swam first. She looked at the thick mat of curled black hair which covered his chest, an incongruously different colour from the thin yellow streaks stretching back from his forehead. She thought she felt his eyes on her and tugged defensively at the straps on her bathing costume, seeking somehow to diminish and hide the swell of her breasts. He splashed her as they clambered out, and laughed. Elena was nowhere to be seen.

'Spain is full of banks,' he began, speaking artificially slowly. She was the child at the front of the class. 'After Harvard I worked for the Bank of Sabadell as a general trainee and for the Bank of Santander, concentrating on investment policy. But the Bank of the Baix Emporda is much more interesting. I specialize in entertainment financing. Mostly films, but some theatre and television programming too.

Even restaurants, if they're part of the complex. We are the main conduit between the Culture Ministry and the industry. Currently we handle 12 per cent of all Euro-based cinematic funds.'

She slapped her calves against the top of the pool and splashed her feet gently in the water. The long journey of the day before was beginning to tell. She ached. She wanted to curl up on one of the red sunbeds by the pool, cover herself in a thick white towel, and sleep. But that was not – not, not, not – possible.

'There are two main finance channels from Brussels,' he was going on. 'One via Frankfurt and one, curiously enough, through the Gibraltar tax haven . . .'

She splashed again and turned to seek the elusive eye contact. 'Tell me one step at a time. Say I want to direct the new *Don Quixote* and you're my producer. Now. How do we get started?'

It was Christmas at Sandringham again. The pheasant and the Château Beau Séjour and the minutes watching her own message were over. 'A family united and a nation united are the rock on which we all depend.' Selene had gone to bed after lunch and not returned. Nicky lay in a pink-and-green armchair overlooking the lawns, snoring loudly. The servants had scattered into the deepest recesses of the house. And she was restless. She walked the corridors of bronze horses and polished guns. She squatted on the carpet in front of the heavy bookcases stuffed with heavy, leather-bound books. The complete Dryden and the complete Fielding. The complete decline and fall of interest in what happened to the Roman Empire. There was nobody in the Ballroom next door.

She bowed to the stuffed bison transfixed on the wall. She curtsied to the grim bust of Queen Victoria. She begun to hum to herself. Shall we dance? Shall we dance? Shall we dance? As she stopped there was the sound of applause from the gallery, from the box which housed the old film projector.

'Perhaps', said Rodney Chetwode-Belcher, 'you might care to dance with me, Ma'am?' She had never really looked at him before. He was always there and always invisible. The fair young man with the vanishing chin. But now, as he ran down the steps, she was aware of him in a new way. He had left the antique gramophone going in the gallery, and suddenly the room was filled with the skirl of bagpipes.

'Ah, the Gay Gordons,' said Belcher with a grin. 'I think this may be our one, Your Majesty.'

Dear Lilibet,
I met one of those strapping women US Airforce pilots at the base yesterday: long red hair, a gash of a mouth, a figure to make any uniform look great. Are girls good flyers? Anyway, this was one to fly with – if I'd been younger and fitter and free. Why do I tell you this? Because sometimes you meet a person and there's a chemistry from the first touch – and it's so damned hard to keep control of your senses. I know. I lost control. Maybe I got some of that from my mother. But try to remember from one who knows, my love: don't just look before you leap, count to a hundred with your eyes closed . . .

There would be an April election. Probably Thursday 21st. Millward had starred it in his diary. He could, of course, go on for a couple of months, far into June. But what was the point? The polls had been buoyant ever since the Coronation. Not because of the Coronation in any simple sense, to be sure: the economy was much more important than that, and the economy continued to expand robustly. On the other hand, it had been growing for several months before Bess's big day without giving him the least lift. People had just started to feel better about themselves, and his Government, as she came out of the Abbey with the bells ringing. They had started to feel much better about him when he'd talked, man to man, on the Con Conakry show about his relationship with the young Queen. 'She knows she has much to learn, and she acknowledges that openly. Our weekly meetings are more seminars, meetings of minds, than the business of State. I learn from her about the impulses of her generation. They're good, generous impulses, Con. We can be proud of them. And she, I think, learns a little from me about the broader picture – Britain's role in the world, our hopes for the future, the path we must tread together. I like – very humbly – to think we're a team, and that it is my job to build the kind of country that she will reign over long after I'm dead and the baton of responsibility has been passed along.'

Millward was humming as he went through the briefings with Leckie. 'Social Security reform? We're right behind it, but we're still waiting for the Linton Royal Commission's interim report. It would be irresponsible to act without the full facts at our disposal.

The five-year rolling plan? We think it prudent to wait until next year when things, politically, may be a little clearer. Turkish membership of the EU? We have always been committed four-square to a feasibility study, provided all our partners agree. It would be irresponsible to change that principled position.'

Leckie looked at him quizzically. 'You're very cheery this morning. Got into bed on the right side or something?'

'Nope. Just the same old marital four-poster. But the news on the regal front is much more encouraging. Our tame Romanov has been round again and threatens to take her to the opera. Our tame Spanish Prince is coming on bank business and wants a quiet supper. And little Belcher is filling in the dancing lessons in between. Three into one will go, I think.'

'I never quite understood why you went to so much trouble to give her a choice,' Leckie said. 'Choosing takes such a long time.'

Millward gave an exaggerated sigh. 'You're slowing up, Robin. Dizzy from too much spinning and losing the psychology of the thing. Fountain was useless, inevitably, but Baron got the tune in a second. Look, we may have her under our thumb, but she's still bloody difficult. We've got to get her married off – preferably with an engagement just before the election so the populace is knee deep in daffodils and love. But she won't go near a man she thinks is our lad in the royal slips. She has to think she's in control. Any card you like, Ma'am, so long as it's our Ace of Hearts.'

Chapter Twelve

'How does she move when you come near? Do her eyes catch yours? Does she smile?' The Queen's Mother dabbed her face with a small, scented towel.

'She smiles, but I have to search for the eyes. I am, after all, the older man. She hides herself from me. She is demure.' He gave a great Russian shrug.

'And have you kissed her? Have you pulled her down and pressed that lovely darting tongue of yours into her mouth and run your fingers up and down the young skin and waited to hear her panting?'

'Not yet. She takes care that we are not alone for more than a moment. Even at the opera she had her security people checking every ten minutes, and at the interval one of her girlfriends joined us. A blonde girl with a thin face and a mouth which curls in distrust. I did not like her. So, no. I have kissed her hand and I have kissed her once on the cheek. But she is watchful, not like she was in the cathedral. There she was a tourist and I was just a man in the crowd. On her own ground she is also more on her guard.'

'I have nothing to fear then? At least pas pour l'instant. You are not intoxicated with the firmness of the flesh and the innocence of the prize? You still appreciate the benefits of experience?'

'My love, we both understand appreciation. It comes with the years of seeing and longing and tossing and turning when the mood takes us. We are secret people of the night, we two. Our bodies have learned the language of the dark, and that will always be true.'

'I always call you my little Roman holiday, you know. It makes me laugh. And, my Romy, Romy, Romy, it's good to know that mother comes first.'

Sammy Wittman stood shivering in the doorway of a Floral Street boutique. Ten past eleven. There was – what? – a quarter of an hour to go before the curtain came down and the stalls emptied, chattering and gasping with relief. Four and a half hours of Mussorgsky, not counting the curtain calls. Ferris, his snapper, had gone to find the bog in the wine bar round the corner. Only the rain was keeping the temperature over freezing point. And it was all a fool's errand probably. Some grumpy Opera apparatchik muttering down the phone about trysts at the back of the Royal Box and mystery nights out. He hadn't seen anyone worth a spit going in. How could two lines of copy come out, for Christ's sake? And then, from the wetness of the night, a black Daimler appeared by the stage door.

'Ferris!' he howled. 'Get the fuck back!'

Nothing. The useless soak had stopped for another drink.

A light in the offices over the boutique went on suddenly, and he could see the stage door opening.

Two coppers, one smooth gent in a tuxedo, and Her.

'Good evening, Ma'am,' he shouted, running across the street. 'And how did you enjoy the show?'

She turned for a second and he thought she smiled.

'We found it a little long,' she said, and was gone in a shriek of tyres.

He stood panting, remembering. He could have sworn – when she looked at him – that there was recognition in her eyes.

Fountain was getting confused. He could leave the press to Baron, but he still had to try to recall which tale was being peddled that week, and why, and whether it was true. But then he also had to handle the Queen; and the weeks before April were running out. 'I want an engagement,' Millward kept telling him. 'I'll settle for a defined romance if that's all you can do. We can pack them off to Paris or somewhere. But she's got to begin to choose.'

'Well, Prime Minister,' Fountain protested, 'it was your idea to give her the smorgasbord. It's hardly my fault that she seems to be enjoying herself too much to decide. And how am I supposed to steer her anyway, when I don't have proper instructions? I mean, which one do you want?'

Millward looked at Robin Leckie, who began rummaging in his briefcase. 'They're all OK,' he said, 'otherwise we wouldn't have fielded them in the first place. But we have been able to use the delay and the dribble of publicity to get some focus groups organized.'

Leckie opened a thick purple folder. 'Here are the

headlines,' he said. 'Belcher's the candidate who loses his deposit first. A bit of a weed. Perceived as servant class. The Army is a turn-off, especially because he's a Captain. Folks with long memories don't like the vibes. C2s and below, under twenty-five, think Lieutenant would be more romantic. ABC1s over forty wonder why he's not a Major or above. And the Chetwode is a double-barrel-load in both feet. I'm not saying he's impossible. We could probably sell him if we had to. But he's not common enough for a proper commoner and his blue blood turns to water when you hold it up to the light.

'After that, though, it's a stand-off. People like Spain and they've heard about its Royal family. Number nine on the word-association count, just below Sangria and above chicken and chips. They have a fair-to-average score when they start identifying Jaime. *Hello* readers are a real backbone here. We'd be able to use the gossip mags as the heart of any campaign. But the banking is boring and the hair-loss factor doesn't help. He's suitable. He has the "status" and the "connections" people expect. Well over half think that "any religious difficulties could be overcome" and that "liaisons with EU partner members can put Britain at the heart of Europe", but he's not a shoo-in.'

Millward leaned back in his chair and sighed loudly. 'If it was all bloody easy we wouldn't need you,' he said. 'What about the one with the snow on his boots?'

'Alexandrovich. Poor name. Majorities in all groups had difficulty remembering it. Confusion level with Romanian football team ran dangerously high – and of course the Roman name just makes it worse. But the Romanov links *per se* are good. High glamour factor; and the Prince bit is accepted with less chuntering than you'd expect. Women particularly are deep into Tsarist body-rippers. By and large, they know their history. Only one in five thought Rasputin was a restaurant in the Fulham Road.

'Problems: he's almost too old. Where has he been all this time? Import-export. What does that mean? "Is it something to do with the Mafya?" people kept asking. And he looks "too louche" in his photographs. Again, it's not exactly made in heaven.'

Fountain coughed. 'You see our problems, Prime Minister. Dickie Baron and I can play Cupid for all we're worth, but we've got to know where to aim the darts.'

'Counter-suggestibility,' Millward said slowly. 'Eliminate by making the negative positive. Let's spend a week pushing Belcher at her. Brief Cross and Swayne for the boudoir lectures. Tee up Selene as the Captain's biggest fan, and then – when he's out of the frame – we can get weaving.'

It was, Baron explained, a recriprocal visit. 'Her Majesty recently enjoyed a brief holiday in Spain with the Infanta Elena. They are the same age and, of course, distantly related. They have become friends, and it makes perfect sense that the Princess should be asked back to Windsor and Rose Cottage for a few days of shopping and theatre and the things young people enjoy.'

'What about the brother?' asked the *Mirror*.

'Yeah. Is Jaime coming along for the ride?' said the *Sun*.

Baron read, a trifle ostentatiously, from the briefing sheet. 'Prince Jaime is already in London organizing funding for an anniversary production of the *Phantom of the Opera* which will open in Madrid this autumn before touring to Bilbao, Malaga, Mexico City and Caracas. He is not a part of the Infanta's visit which, in any case, is purely private. But no one, of course, can rule out the possibility that he may wish to see his sister while she is here. That, again, will be a purely private matter.'

The *Mirror* and the *Sun*, brothers under the thickest of skins, laughed out loud. Will Wittman, leaning laconically on the wall by the press-room door, smiled with them. This was simple stuff. It wrote itself. But that was the trouble. Baron and Fountain and the lurking smirk of Millward, just off stage, weren't simple at all. Beware honest men bearing straightforward gifts because there were just too many of them swilling around. He had to find an alternative route in somehow. Maybe, if he sat Sammy down over a bottle of Moët, something would bubble up.

'What a nice young man,' Selene said. 'So polite and attentive and suitable. Sir Edgar was telling me only the other day what a tower of strength he was turning out to be. I know he's not much to look at, darling, but he's absolutely devoted to you. He'd be a lovely special friend.'

And the trouble with that, Bess thought, is that it's

just too clumpingly obvious. My bloody mother hasn't somehow just noticed poor little Belchie. He's been drawn to her attention. She's been instructed to sell him on. Why? She is such a lousy actress that it's bound to come out hint-hint nudge-nudge. Fountain is cute enough to know that. But is he pulling her strings because I'm supposed to do what she says, or do precisely the opposite? Actually, she quite liked Chetwode-Belcher, with his spaniel eagerness and collie devotion. He was a nice dog to have around your house. But he was not, and never could be, anybody she fancied. Better, for safety's sake, tell him that quickly. Call off the hounds. Send them, ever so nicely, back to the kennel. And anyway, Alexandrovich was taking her to the ballet next week when he got back from Kiev. To her surprise, when she thought of that, she felt a small shiver of excitement.

Emma was sitting in a brasserie just off the Fulham Road eating breakfast. Two croissants, a brioche, pain au chocolat, a double pot of milky coffee. It was almost twelve-thirty. Another triumph for her patent diet. If you got up late enough, you didn't need lunch. You could potter home, make a cup of tea, and get on with the vacation book list.

The man at the next-door table – the one with his back turned to her on the left – had ordered a BLT baguette. It arrived, scattering small flakes of crisp bacon on the floor as the waitress brushed past her. One dropped on the table and she wet her index finger and dabbed it on to her tongue. Great. The juices flowed. Maybe if she had a baguette too she could skip tea? She raised a hand suddenly and a knife, coated in raspberry jam, clattered on to the tiling. The man at the table looked round.

He was young, with dark hair which curled over the collar of his leather jacket. He peered for a second, then swung back to his food. And then he swung back again. 'It's Emma, isn't it?' he said. 'Caroline's friend from Oxford? Nice to see you again. Still chugging away in the salt mines?'

She stared at him blankly.

'Oh sorry. I guess I've changed since I came down. I'm Sammy Wittman. I used to work for *Cherwell* and things. Would you like another coffee and maybe a baguette? Highly recommended.'

Well, why not? The wastes of Prussian history (1724–1809) were strewn unappetisingly across her desk. They were not going anywhere. Bobby and Clive were in Crans for a late week of skiing. Caroline had stayed in Oxford to keep the Bodleian busy.

'What are you doing now, then?'

'What comes naturally, I guess. I always wanted to be a reporter and the *Express* have given me a chance. It can be quite entertaining.'

He told her the tales the diary didn't publish. The teenage pop star and the High Court judge. The actress who'd married an elderly gynaecologist because he gave her abortions for free. The Cabinet Minister who was thinking about a sex-change op. She giggled helplessly and her eyes began to shine.

'Sorry,' he said, looking at his watch. 'I've got to go. We're staking out a lesbian priest's love nest in the Old Brompton Road and I'm on shift in five minutes. But it's been great to see you again.' Pause. 'Maybe if you're in town for the rest of the week we could have a dinner or something.'

She tore the corner from her paper napkin, borrowed his pen, and wrote down her telephone number.

For the first time that year, there was a hint of spring to the morning. They had left Windsor at six and the sun was still frail when they reached Rose Cottage. The grass lay grey from the frosts and the walnut tree by the pond stood gaunt and stripped of life; but there were crocuses where the lawn touched the granite wall at the roadside. Bess could sense a fresh beginning and her spirits lifted.

Elena chattered incessantly. She had loved Windsor. 'It is so vast, like the Escorial. But it is more part of the town so that the crowds who wind up to your Castle are like ribbons which tie you to the people. There is more history that way. It is like a huge stage where the curtain never falls. It is Disneyland with plastic which does not peel.'

Bess scratched her nose. No wonder Elena wanted to get into marketing.

'But this cottage, it is different. So cosy and secret. So intimate. I know Jaime will love it here.'

He was arriving separately, by car from Edinburgh. He was late. The lunch was cold, a salad and baked ham. He came in with a stamp and a scowl. 'Your English roads are the worst thing about this country. Always, always there are holes and a narrowing of lanes and queues waiting without end. I can never understand why you can never take it in hand. It is not very difficult if the will is there.'

He's lecturing me, Bess thought. Talking at me as though they're my holes and my roads. She grinned. 'Sorry. Constitutional monarchs just use the motorways. They don't run them. But please don't worry, because we've been sitting and chatting. The Hunt don't expect us till two anyway.'

It was his special request. She didn't care for horses much, hated the clobber and the ritual. She'd been force fed on Badminton and Burleigh. The endless afternoons at Ascot, long ago, had finished the job. 'If I want to ride,' she said once to her nanny, 'I'll call for a taxi.' The Infanta and the Prince, though, loved riding. They knew they were in hunting country and they wanted their turn.

The Quorn Hunt sounded grand, a name with resonance wherever foxes cowered under hedgerows. Campaigners had been trying to put it down for half a century, but it flourished still as Parliament drew back from the kill. The reality, to be sure, was not imposing: a low red sprawl of Edwardian brickwork perched on a bare slope east of Barrow-on-Soar. Bricks and mortar, though, signified nothing. It was the service that counted. The Palace had called and the hounds were ready, yapping in the grass enclosure by the road. Bellamy, the Master of the Hounds, was waiting in his full, scarlet plumage. There was ten minutes of bowing and scraping while the Bourbons scrambled into their kit.

'It's a fine day for it,' Bellamy said. 'Is Your Majesty certain she doesn't fancy a ride?'

Bess was absolutely certain. She sat in the front of the Land Rover with Saturday's *Guardian* on her knees and watched Elena and Jaime. The Infanta was perched, like a pretty pygmy, on top of a huge chestnut mare. She rode it with a natural grace, hands light on the reins as the horn sounded and the hunt turned west out of the far gates. But the Prince, mouth set tight, rode a black stallion with flecks of white at the mouth. His hands were taut, the reins pulled tight, and the stallion bucked and kicked as he tried to turn it.

She wound down the window.

'Bastard,' he was crying. There was a torrent of Spanish she did not understand. He had reached for the whip with his left hand and began flaying the side of the stallion so that it squealed and reared, then galloped off after the pack.

Bess shuddered and glanced behind her. The two policemen from her security detail were standing impassively, frozen faced, but she thought she saw a curl to their lips. She knew, without pausing to ask the question, what she felt.

Robin Leckie did not care much for ballet, but his wife had grown grim and restless. Through the long sessions of Parliament he barely had time to come home. At one or two in the morning, after the first editions of the nationals had been scanned and the instant rebuttals organized, he would crawl back to her and slump exhausted at her side. And in the early morning, while he slept, she would rise and primp herself and depart to the catering school she ran on the north side of Holland Park. They did not co-habit, they co-existed. 'If I wanted a divorce, I'd have to make an appointment to ask you for it,' Pam Leckie said bitterly. His shoulders went down. He didn't love her and she had probably never loved him. Their liaison, eight years before, had always been just a coincidence. He was a young researcher at Millbank, down in the smoke from Sheffield, homeless and hungry. She was a trainee chef at the Mirepoix in Queensway, struggling to forget the sommelier from Strasbourg who had loved her and left her with an abortion. They had fallen across each other's paths and settled for what was convenient. He glanced at her, squeezed into an old pink dress a size too small now, mouth open as she gazed around the red velvet sweeps of Covent Garden, and he felt only guilt. Their first night out for weeks. And even now he was on business, doing his master's duty. The tickets were part of his watching brief. His life was a constant plot. He shivered for a second as an inchoate shame lapped round him.

Three minutes. He thought he heard the bell ring in the bars. He clambered to his feet to let a fat Progressive Conservative MP squeeze past him, glowering malevolently, and looked up once more towards the darkness of the Royal Box. Bingo! This time they were there in plain view, not skulking in the shadows. There was a shimmer of breath through the stalls and a buzz of speculation. Bess looked down, leaning into the light, and she was smiling again. She half raised a hand in acknowledgement. Alexandrovich stood up deliberately and positioned himself behind her chair. Robin squeezed Pam's knee and pointed upwards. 'Look,' he said, 'they've gone public.'

Leckie went to the lavatory at the first interval and bent in the furthest stall from the door, whispering into his mobile.

'Simon. We have our love match. We have lift-off.'

'I know. Baron has started fielding calls already. It's a trifle tight, but the timing could be perfect. Do they look happy?'

The man next door pressed the flush button and there was a roar of water. He paused, and the glee abruptly began to drain from him. 'Yes, they look fine. Very open and adoring.' Had he and Pam ever been like that? When would the girl Queen's adoration turn rancid? A year, a decade of disappointment on?

'Anyway,' Leckie said, 'just as long as you know. I must get back to my wife. She thinks this is her treat. I suppose you'll want me to call back at Downing Street after I've taken her home?'

Of course. He pulled his own chain and walked slowly back to Row J. She was shovelling chocolates into her mouth, scattering the wrappings on the carpet in the greedy haste of depression. She scowled when she saw him. He shivered again.

'I don't think he'd have been my first choice,' Fountain said as the Courvoisier circulated. 'Seventeen years is an uncomfortable age gap, even if the records are right. There'll be too many bloody features in the tabloids about the trouble with older men. And they're bound to rake over the ashes and find a few of his old flames. God knows what they'll have to say. You only have to look at him to tell he's put himself about a bit.'

Baron cut in impatiently. 'Does that matter? This is Spring and Summer. People loved it when her grandfather netted the virgin teenager.'

There was a heavy silence. 'I don't think that's a parallel we ought to be majoring on,' Millward said sourly. 'Check how old Victoria was when she got Albert – and Nicholas when he married Alexandra. Even Rainier and Grace. We'll need some precedents which fit our bill if the buggers start grinding away, but we ought to be able to head them off at the pass. This guy is her choice. She's a strong, determined, intelligent young lady. She knows her mind and we must all respect that. And he is pretty dishy in a brooding sort of way, I'm informed. The housewives in their semis with their squalling brats are bound to fall for him. No, we shall only have problems if we let them creep up on us.'

'But can we trust him? Is he reliable? Will he do as he's told?' Fountain was flushing puce with anxiety.

'Oh yes,' Millward said, his voice dropping so that they had to crane forward to hear the end of the sentence. 'Oh yes. I've got his files from the boys at Six. Davidson reckons there's no risk and no wriggling. He will do exactly as he's told.'

Robin Leckie leaned back in his chair, away from the light, and lowered his outstretched left arm with an involuntary flourish. Pulling the chain of life one more time.

Chapter Thirteen

The Prime Minister was talking to the nation again, hands held shyly in front of him as though on the brink of prayer, the breeze from Green Park lending a youthful tousle to his hair.

'I know we all – all of us in this great country – feel a spring in our step and a lift in our hearts. We all join in the joy that our Queen and her fiancé, Prince Roman Alexandrovich, feel today. We look forward to the celebration of their marriage and the happiness of their family life together. Here, in a way we can recognize, is the renewal of a Britain which is precious to us.

'But I have to say that there are other traditions we also hold dear, foremost among them our Parliamentary democracy and the certain continuity it requires to give us the Government we need. So even today, as I transmit our warmest congratulations to the Palace, there is the business of the nation to be done. My administration's life is reaching its appointed end within a few, short months. There is a damaging uncertainty which, if left unresolved, could harm the economic achievements we have set in place. Our minority partners, as is natural, are jockeying for position. The maintenance of good governance is bound to become a harder task.

'I have decided that this damage must be avoided by resolute action. Just as our young Queen knows her mind and prepares to say "I do," so I now know mine. And I say "I will." I will put an end to the speculation. I will do what I feel is necessary and right. That is why I journeyed to the Palace this morning to offer more than the love and respect and good wishes Her Majesty deserves. I went, in tradition bound, to seek the dissolution of this Parliament. That consent was given. There will be a general election on April 27th.'

There was a howl from behind the frosted door to the editor's office and a sudden smashing of glass. Bradshaw's secretary, Miss Pym, jumped to her feet and rushed inside, then rushed out again. 'He's only thrown his ashtray through the screen again,' she said to the new chief sub, who was queueing apprehensively with the centre-spread lay-out. 'He does that sometimes, but don't worry. He'll soon calm down.'

'Alice, Alice,' the editor howled again. 'Bring me the bloody sick bag, Alice.'

They had gone to Sandringham for the weekend. 'I might as well give you the tour, just in case you want to change your mind,' she had said. 'It isn't exactly the Winter Palace.' They had walked the estates together and chatted to the workers in the fields and stood silent in the densest glade along the Woodland Walk as a great grey shrike settled on a lilac bush twenty yards away. And then, in the panelled dining room of York Cottage, they had had supper alone. Leek soup scattered with chives; a pie of pheasant and pigeon laced with chanterelles; a bottle of Vacqueras, all pungent fruit.

'I have a small present for you,' Roman said. 'Just a keepsake to remember our first evening when you were not ashamed to be seen with me. Tchaikovsky, played by Russians.' So they sat by the fire and sipped cognac and let the music swill over them.

She knew something was wrong. There was no butler pacing in the hallway, no policeman by the door chewing gum or whistling through his teeth. Fat Clemmy had not even called in to say goodnight. A pall of tact – unaccustomed, weighty, almost eerie in its unexpectedness – hung over her.

'We've an early start,' she said, kissing him lightly on the lips. 'And I've got a wretched week of factory openings in Cumberland and Cornwall. I'll see you at breakfast.'

But he followed her to her room and, as she turned to kiss him again, swept her inside and closed the door.

'The place is full of people . . .' she began feebly.

'People. Who needs people?'

He undressed her on the silken yellow bedspread, his hands exploring her so that, suddenly, she could feel nothing else. They took control and drove her upwards in a spiral of the senses which seemed to have no ending. It was beyond her imaginings. The fumblings with Tom, the drunken pawing at the parties, the lurid tales that Emma told; all dropped away. There was a dominating professionalism to his kneadings and probings. Too professional, too calculated? She thought for a second of the awful hotel bedroom far away, of Nicky's face frozen in terror, of her mother piloting another orgasm home with every practised squirm and cry. It was the last thought she had before she abandoned thought.

Dear Lilibet,
Did I teach you the facts of life, my love? I know I
was going to, but your mother and I had an
argument about it and I think I may have got rather
plastered. I just hope somebody taught you the facts
of life . . .

The lights in Millbank burned through the night. There was an election coming. The team was reassembling for battle. Special advisers to ministers took their leave and tossed away their suits and sombre ties. Old hands from the lobbyists' diaspora pulled on sweaters and jeans and headed up the back staircase to the open-plan stretch of the war room. Ad men camped amid the video cameras and TV sets on the left of the long window overlooking the Thames. Television directors clustered to the right, furiously debating whether the Prime Minister was Urban Man or Rural Man. Should the first party political come from Paternoster Square or Hadrian's Wall? The pollsters and the spinners clustered at the back, feet on desks, weary eyes glued to terminals and flow charts.

They worked in shifts. They could not afford to stop now. The Party lists of nominated candidates were forty-eight hours off deadline. Every old

Member, every new would-be candidate needed a final computer check. Had they taken orders through the last five years without making waves? When you matched the manifesto point by point with their stated positions, was there a perfect fit? 'On message, on the list.' Leckie had had his simple motto scrawled on a banner. It hung from the ceiling over the chattering printer of the IBM.

A black girl in a tight red T-shirt, breasts unnaturally wakeful for six in the morning, thrust a plastic cup of coffee into Millward's hand as he walked out of the lift. Radnor, the Party Finance Director, was having his first seizure of the day outside the Gents, hissing obscenities at a weeping middle-aged woman. 'It's the wrong column, you stupid bitch. The money came from the Caymans through Luxembourg to Jersey, and then to Account XZ – and now you've sent it bloody back again down that whole loop line. Two frigging million euros gone walkabout somewhere in the Caribbean because you can't tell an Enter button from a Send. I don't care if you did use to work for Lambeth, dearie. You're out on your ear unless I get every fucking penny back where it should be by noon.'

Millward sipped his coffee quickly, holding the cup to his lips for a second to hide the grin. Show business! He loved it. Some of the creeps in his Cabinet, he knew, trembled when elections came round, when the voters had their say. But Millward loved it. You didn't have to pretend any longer, poncing around in the Commons posing as some bloody bishop of a statesman. You could say anything, claim anything, lie about anything – and fit steel caps to your bovver boots. He'd got the system and the machine behind him. He wouldn't be chucked out when the fateful Thursday came round. The question from the polls was whether he'd be able to ditch the bits of the coalition who got on his wick. It looked, as of now, a pretty good bet. The cash was pouring in. Boardrooms didn't waste money on losers. And the small things were falling into place as well; the luck was with him.

'You look cheerful,' Leckie said as he came out of the other lift. He had cut himself shaving. The knot in his tie was twisted. His eyes were bloodshot with fatigue.

'Every little helps,' Millward said, steering him over to the corner with the water cooler. 'Our Virgin Queen isn't any longer, even if she was to start with. They were at it all night, I'm told. The Family itch is there in the genes, just as we thought it would be. So there won't be any messing or second thoughts or falters at the altar. She's pinned down and she's loving it. We can get on with the main event and not worry a scrap. Always remember the old saying, young Robin: get the heart right and the wallets open of their own accord.'

Caroline wanted to like him. She loved Bess, so naturally she wanted to love the man she loved. But how could you tell anything from the formal gavottes of a Palace engagement party? The weather, in one of those spasms of spring they put down to global warming, was balmy: almost hot. They had opened the doors to the garden and watched the dinner suits and the diamond tiaras pant their way on to the terrace. Millward stood at the top of the steps, champagne glass in hand and eyes flitting constantly back and forth. He was in charge. The country gang of royal aunts and uncles and cousins was hammering the Bollinger knowing that, tomorrow, they would be back to scraping their own living from the elderflower wine and honey pots on the National Trust stall. Selene's crowd, waists straining at velvet cummerbunds, bosoms pouting from cups of reinforced satin, were drunk already. Nicky stood a few yards away from them, unexpectedly animated, deep in conversation with a thin youth with ginger hair wearing a suit two sizes too large for him. Bess and Roman had been touring their guests for over an hour, letting an equerry call people to their side one at a time and allowing four minutes, give or take thirty seconds, for chat and embraces.

Caroline didn't want to be part of that circus. Come over and meet your best friend, Madam? Ridiculous. But as the string quartet turned to Debussy and the first of the throng were steered towards the buffet in the Chinese Dining Room, she saw Alexandrovich detach himself from Bess's side and wander down the steps to the lawn.

Millward paused for a moment in mid-sentence as he passed. Perhaps their eyes met. She could not be sure. She, too, strolled on to the grass for a dozen or so yards, to where the shadows deepened.

'Good evening, Sir,' she said, her voice suddenly too loud against the buzz of the background.

He swung round at the sound and came towards her. 'I'm Caroline Northcott. A friend of Bess from school. We met briefly at the Opera once.'

He bowed and took her hand and kissed it. 'Indeed. There is you and somebody else we have already met. A large, jolly girl. Hannah?'

'Emma. They used to call us the three musketeers at Roedean. But that was just the hockey team and it seems such a long time ago.'

She found him difficult to talk to. He was so perfect and contained. The white dinner jacket hung without crease over the powerful body. His brown hair curled naturally back, hovering a millimetre above his ears. The eyes were wide and dark. When you looked into them, you felt you could see straight into his soul. When he had held her hand he was lithe, a boy with a touch of coltish gallantry. But in repose, as they talked, she could glimpse the lines around his mouth etched more clearly: there was an artifice to him, the simulation of a youth left behind. And it was consciously done, acted in every movement, every inflection.

He talked a little about St Petersburg. How his great-great-great-grandmother had heard the shells from the river thud into the walls of the Winter Palace and cried out in an instant, 'Kerensky is finished and the Tsars are finished with him.' How they had fled to the Crimea, crouching in the bottom of boats through the maze of rivers and canals, to where the Empress Marie Feodorovna waited in the Villa Ai Todor, gathering the frightened remnants of family around her. And how, at last, through the maelstrom, they had found the battleship *Ulysses*, which George V had sent them to bring them to a new home.

'So, you see, without this Palace, without the King who remembered us and finally told your Lloyd George what must be done, there would have been no today for me. No love and no marriage. What comes around goes around in the strangest of ways.'

She started suddenly, as though stumbling from a hypnotic trance. He had talked with such passion she had lost track of time. The terrace was almost empty, the clink of plates far in the recesses of the hall.

'I am sorry,' he said. 'We must be friends, you and I. And you must stop me boring you with ancient history.'

As they hurried up the steps she thought she saw a white face, fringed with a crop of gold, peer from the furthest doorway, then draw back in a trice. She thought she saw Selene, but she could not be sure.

Bess was streaming with sweat beneath the brocade and ermine. Time to be ludicrous again. Black Rod was decrepit and panting. He might die before the ritual was over. His breath came in rancid pants. When the great door of the Commons slammed in his face, he seemed to stagger, the rod turned to crutch. But he still swung his stick three times and the show tottered once more along the road. There was no escape.

What a bloody joke, she thought balefully. A House still stuffed with Lords that the Government plucked from the ranks of its old faithfuls and hacks and cash donors (pending another Royal Commission). There might not be many stupid titles left, no Portcullis Pursuivants here or in the Palace. But titles weren't the end of anything. The great and the ga-ga were still strutting their stuff, walking backwards in front of her as she neared the throne. There'd been that stupid song her grandfather had sung at birthday parties. 'I'm Walking Backwards for Christmas'.

She turned to look across the red benches of the Chamber, a sea of faces churning with the elation of victory or dejection of defeat. Millward beaming. His enemies and his erstwhile partners scattered in pockets of impotence. She cleared her throat and clenched a fist below the robe.

'My Government intends to govern wisely and well in the interests of all our people. It will spend extra resources on the care of the needy and provide the benefits those who are sick deserve. It will defend the peace with resolution in the face of any threat. It will work, with partner countries, for the good of all . . . It will introduce measures to secure enhanced participation in the National Lottery . . . and to standardize health requirements for the importation of tropical fruits to these shores.'

God Save the Queen! Millward was still beaming.

'Sometimes I think I'd be better living in the Abbey and going home for the holidays,' Bess said. 'When I wake up in the night, I dream the Archbishop is there at the end of the bed, issuing his wretched little instructions and soaking me in spit.'

Caroline giggled. 'He is a bit of a holy watering can.' Emma began to writhe in laughter. Nicky glowered.

The bridesmaids had finished their third rehearsal. They had dropped the train twice. The best man had not merely lost the ring, but left it in his bathroom at Clarence House. Bess was feeling edgy. The wedding itself, a week on Saturday, would be a big production number, of course. Two dozen trumpeters in full fig even before they got to the gate. But, after the Coronation, she didn't feel daunted. If you'd carried *Carousel*, you weren't worried by *The King and I*. More showbusiness. And this time she had a leading man. Roman had done the first couple of rehearsals perfectly and ducked out of this one. 'I still have a business to run, my love. There's a problem on the samovar line at Swindon and they want my opinion. It may mean sacking the manager, a rather disgusting Pole with a thirst for vodka. Back on Wednesday evening, I hope.'

Why, then, did her headache come and go, and her limbs ache when she woke in the morning? 'Pressure,' said Dr Badger briskly. 'Emotional pressure. You're a young woman facing the biggest day of your life, so of course you feel strain. I'm not going to prescribe anything for that. Take plenty of exercise, swim a lot, and nature will find its own way of setting you back on track.'

She supposed he was right. When Roman was there, beside her, his body eased away the tension. When he was gone, though, the unease came swiftly back. Did she love him? Well, she thought of him, all the time. But she was beginning to wonder how he related to the Firm and to her friends. When she talked of him to Caroline there would be a flicker of silence before the same bromide adjectives. Though nothing was said, she knew Caroline didn't approve. And Alexandrovich wasn't her champion when Fountain or Montgomery or Baron came round laying their trails and issuing their orders. He deferred to them. His eyes seemed to wait for their cue. It was almost as though he was one of them. Perhaps he just wanted his seat on the board, too, to be there when the decisions were taken: but did he need to fawn after his prize?

Bess shivered. There was nothing she could do. There was nobody to talk to who could reassure or – or help, if reassurance was futile. She could not call it off. There was no understudy. Anyway, she had no real reason to call it off. When his hands touched her again, she knew, her mind would change with the whisper of his fingers. A word with Millward, Fountain? An impossible joke. Her mother? Selene kept telling her how romantic he was, how lucky she had been. More gush from the Fount of all Folly. Perhaps that was what was gnawing at her confidence most of all.

Leckie saw the car carry her back to the Palace as he walked across Parliament Square. The face at the window. 'She looks tired,' he said to Millward late that night, as the Scotch came out of the wastepaper basket at last. 'Can we depend on him?'

Millward's voice dropped to a mutter. 'Of course we can depend on him. Haven't you guessed? He's our man, hand-picked to keep the lid on her. Our cardboard Tsar knows where his noodles are buttered in any case, but if he doesn't then all we have to do is call for good old Davidson with his bag of little persuaders. Import/export. He imports a few powdery things that turn a profit inside those darling little nests of dolls – and some girls from the Ukraine who'll do anything for a square meal in Mayfair. He exports a few phoney secrets to the KGB when Six wants to test the waters. There was a suicide in Minsk, a ballerina with an open sixth-floor window and a bun in her oven. Not to mention some trapeze artiste from St Petersburg with the State Circus he knocked off her perch rather more recently. Davidson could keep the tabloids going forever if he opened his safe.'

Leckie was bolt upright now, clutching the glass of whisky with both hands. He felt some terror and, yes, disgust. The terror came first. 'But that's too much to keep under wraps,' he said. 'Too many people will know. Somebody will sell him out, and then there'll be more shit than anyone can handle. We'll all be blown away.'

Millward smiled. 'Relax. The hounds have been snuffling all over for months and they haven't come close. Davidson's a hundred per cent certain. Princey is our boy. We recruited him a dozen years back. We've run him and tidied up after him. The women are dead or buried somewhere in Siberia. The profits are spent. The girls never knew who was pulling their strings. And remember, he was defending our national security: a hero of the Official Secrets Act. He's clean and we're clear. There isn't a code left to crack.'

Leckie decided not to think about disgust. There was beginning to be too much of it around, filling his dreams at night, looking out from his shaving mirror each morning. He poured himself another finger of malt.

'Where's the *Daily Mail*?' she asked. The other mornings were neatly stacked as usual on the breakfast table to the right of the coffee pot and the toast rack.

Plummer looked surprised. 'Isn't it there, Ma'am? Perhaps it hasn't arrived.'

'I'd be very grateful if you'd inquire. Twenty-four hours to go, you know. I need to make sure I've seen everything.'

When he came back he seemed strangely flustered. He put the *Mail* at the far end of table, as though by accident, and began clearing away the egg cups and the pots of jam. She waited till he was gone and leaned over. They wanted to hide something. Of course. 'All My Love to My First Royal Love. The Romeo She Left Behind Opens His Heart to Lydia Lawson-Grant. Even on Her Greatest Day, the Memory of My Juliet Lives with Me.' Tom's mini-series had flopped, she read. He was living in a dingy loft off Sunset Boulevard. The *Mail* had found him waiting tables at the Tower of Tacos. 'But whatever I do and wherever I go, I have lived in the shadow of a wonderful woman. I wish her, and her Prince, a reign to remember; and I hope that, sometimes, she too thinks of me.'

It was labelled 'Exclusive'. Paid for exclusively with dollars. She felt suddenly soiled and despondent.

Dear Lilibet,
The worst thing, day after day, is The Papers. Not because they follow you, though they do – but

because they never forgive and never forget.
Sensitive souls like my father could never come to
terms with that. Every débâcle, every telephone call
out of place had its own Bloody Anniversary,
endlessly recycled. Those awful tapes in full! And
every time I took a new girl out, of course, there'd
be endless spreads of the Loves I Lost. You'll make
mistakes. We all make mistakes. The hard thing is
never to be allowed to put them behind you . . .

They came down the steps of the Abbey into a wall
of sound: a high, squealing wall. The crowd had ten
women to every man. Old women with floral hats
waving flags against the sun that filled the Square.
Mothers with toddlers perched on their shoulders.
And girls: fat girls, thin girls, British girls, girls of the
world.

'She has come, I think, to embody the hopes of
her generation,' said the BBC commentator. He was
fifty-eight and he found the din vaguely unseemly.

Alexandrovich held Bess's hand on the bottom step
and twirled her round into his arms. He kissed her
again and gave his tenderest smile. The squeals rose
orgasmically.

He turned me to the left deliberately, she thought.
Did he mean to kiss me with his best profile towards
the cameras?

Chapter Fourteen

To suffer woes which Hope thinks infinite;
To forgive wrongs darker than death or night;
To defy Power, which seems omnipotent;
To love, and bear; to hope till Hope creates
The thing from its own wreck it contemplates;
Neither to change, nor falter, nor repent;
This, like thy Glory, Titan, is to be
Good, great and joyous, beautiful and free;
This is alone Life, Joy, Empire, and Victory.

Shelley, *Queen Mab*

The smooth grey man from Harley Street the tabloids had dubbed the Gynaecologist Royal pushed Her Majesty's naked legs back together and gave an avuncular shrug. 'Every test confirms it, Ma'am,' he said. 'There is nothing wrong. You're a healthy twenty-three-year-old. An ideal age for childbearing. Your tubes are tip top, almost a collector's item on the scans. Your husband's sperm teems with life for a man of his age. We can try a little IVF and that would obviously increase your chances substantially. But, with patience, I don't believe that necessary. On balance I'd recommend just relaxing and trying again. There is no reason in the world to doubt eventual success.'

She had pulled the green cloth over her knees and sat upright on the bed. He noticed she did not look him in the eyes. 'Thank you,' she said dully. 'I know two years isn't long to wait by most standards. But the Family has always been able to deliver on demand if you read the books, and every month that goes by just seems to build up the looks people give you, and the pressure. I keep getting anxious about it.'

He could have taken her up on the history. Windsor women, to be sure, were usually fertile. They had German hips and procreation written on their genes. They knew their duty. But the men were a bit of a rum collection, some full of the juices, some introspective and confused and prone to impotence. The lineage, on occasion, had needed more than divine intervention to help it along: and the trouble there, of course, was mostly in the mind. He picked the thick pad from his desk and began, rather too floridly, to make detailed notes. There was no physical reason for the months of fretting failure but, in his old-fashioned way, he always reckoned that psychology had an effect somewhere in the mystery of the mix. Some of his patients, he believed, could want a baby too much. And some, in spite of everything they said, did not want a baby at all. He had seen HM and Prince Roman together the last time, three months back. Frankly, close up, he'd found the Russian a touch oily for his taste. The accent was unctuous plum, fruit of the public-school crop, but the sentence structures were too elaborate, and the attention he paid to his wife too confected. 'Bit of a creep,' he wrote on his pad. He noticed that when Roman brushed accidentally against Bess's arm as she was getting dressed after the examination, she appeared to shrink from him, as though the skin recoiled instinctively.

'Is everything else in order, Ma'am?' he said as she reached for her jacket.

'Absolutely,' she said. 'Sometimes, you know, I just feel my life flashing by every year as though I were on a roundabout. Another tour, another gloom.' She laughed. 'But what have I possibly got to be miserable about? I'm the girl who's got everything.'

They had begun to spend more time than she liked at Windsor. 'It makes me feel properly royal, a king in his castle,' Roman said. 'And it is so convenient for Swindon. I can be there to check on things and see my friends in an hour.' He did that increasingly frequently. He had his circle and his little supper club in London: bankers in striped shirts, lawyers from the richest City firms, orchestra conductors, film directors, a Syrian called Ali who ran small arms supermarkets all over the Gulf. Most of them had stone cottages in Wiltshire or mansions in Somerset: the weekend circuit, roses and champagne cocktails. She could not complain. She relied more and more on her own friends, Caroline and Emma, to keep her balance. He didn't care for them, she guessed. Why was she supposed to like his chums?

He had gone west again early that morning. Back around nine unless he phoned. It was July hot, the heat building along the valley of the Thames, then gathering the smell of fried onions and damp armpits as it drifted up from the town. She prowled. She walked alone in the private gardens below the Clarence Tower where no eyes could follow her. But they were prissily ornamental, hacked into sharp-edged beds and trimmed shrubs. They suffocated her. There was no spontaneity to them.

Her rooms were cool as ever. Thick walls; narrow, leaded windows. Drear in winter, but blessed relief now. They did not share bedrooms any longer. 'We have such different schedules', he had said, 'that it is practical to use the space. Why wait around and miss our sleep like some couple in a semi-detached when there are rooms to be together and rooms that can belong to each of us?' Instead, he came to her almost as though to a rota. First Monday, Wednesday and Saturday, now Tuesday and alternate Fridays. Scheduled performances. For the rest – she had come to realize with an acquiescence which had become the satisfaction of relief – she could depend on being alone. One husband, 1.5 couplings a week. Was that what the books meant when they wrote about the Death of Passion?

Bess perched herself on the chaise longue by the window, feet drawn under her. She had been reading *The Brothers Karamazov* from some vague sense of duty. Perhaps she would be able to talk to Roman about it one evening when the silence grew too oppressive to bear. A 'terrible nightmare of thoughts and feelings were seething in Ivan Fyodorovich's soul'. Again. He was going home to Katerina Ivanovna, wild and insane. Again. She sighed and tossed Dostoevsky to the floor. Again. Was there someone she could talk to? Someone, anyone.

It was a dismal prospect. Fountain and Baron had been there that morning to discuss new marketing lines for the Castle shops. She suspected Roman was trying to get them to take his samovars and dolls on what he called the Counter of the Tsars. 'The Consort Collection, each item stamped with the Romanov seal.' Would they bite? It would all be down to margins again, as usual. The last time she'd heard them discussing it there had been raised voices and red faces.

But Fountain had surely gone by this time. There was no Jaguar in the Quadrangle. Nor Selene's Ferrari either. 'We'll come up for Saturday night and keep you company,' she'd said. But the afternoons would still be reserved for shopping.

So there was only Nicky. There for lunch in his blazer and orange cravat, picking at a grey slab of grilled hake as though it were still alive and must die a horrible death, then announcing that he had 'things to do' and would see them at supper for Scowl Soup and Fricassee of Frown. They barely talked from one year to the next. The hatred, years before, as he sat on the Waterloo Vase still made her shrivel and shrink from contact. But a voice of guilt had joined the voice of loneliness inside her. 'Come the hour, come the reconciliation,' she said out loud, and walked with long, determined stride down the deserted corridors towards his room.

He had, of course, chosen the poorest of the suites, the dingiest sitting room and bedroom in the corner where east and north intersected. It lay squashed against the Prince of Wales Tower, beyond a new conversion of libraries and writing rooms which she had never seen used, except by an Italian Prime Minister in need of a cigarette. Nicky wanted to be alone. He never needed to hang out the flags.

She paused outside the door, almost turned on her heel, knocked lightly three times. The oak door was thick and seemed to absorb the weight of her knuckles. No answer. She knocked again. He must have gone for a walk. She could leave him a note, saying she'd called. It would be a gesture, something to show for the summoning of her resolution. She turned the handle and went inside.

Someone had drawn the brown curtains closed in the sitting room. The only light came from the television set in the corner where, without sound, she could see five horses heaving towards the winning line on some green country course. There was a half-empty bottle of Bell's on the coffee table and a white shirt crumpled across the settee. Another fine mess. Almost without thinking she picked the shirt up and began to fold it . . . and then the noise from the bedroom made her start. A rustling sound, perhaps a crinkling of sheets. There was no thump, thump, thump; there were no squeals or pants. Perhaps the Volnay at lunch and the Scotch had been too much for him. She would just check quietly, make sure he was all right before sliding back to the clutches of the Karamazovs. The second door was ajar. As she pushed it gently open a sudden swell of premonition engulfed her. She had been here before, with the puling, demented Nicky at her side. But she could not draw back; she had to know.

Darkness again behind closed curtains. The stench

of old sweat. And two white, naked bodies stretched across the bed, legs entwined in sleep. This is none of my business, she thought: I'm only happy he's got someone in his miserable life at last.

But, as she turned to go, her foot caught something on the floor, a shoe with a leather heel. It was only the tiniest noise, but it was enough. The thinnest of the white bodies convulsed and sat bolt upright.

'What the hell?'

She was going to say 'Sorry, it's only me, Nicky,' but the other body had moved too and another face was peering at her as she stood transfixed, a wan silhouette in the doorway.

'Get the sod out of here. You're bloody sacked.'

Bess ran, slamming the outer door behind her, gasping for the sanctuary of her own room. She knew that voice. And she had seen that absurdity of a moustache twitching through the gloom, outlined against the flesh. Baron. Director of public, and private, relations.

There was nobody to complain to. Not Fountain or Montgomery or Millward, for they were the rest of the board and they, surely, would move to protect their own. Not Roman, she realized with a shiver. Whose side was he on? Not her mother, for she would only laugh and say how lovely it was to see Nicky getting his rocks off at last. And perhaps she'd be right. But still the foetid alarm of that bedroom haunted her, tugged fresh thoughts from the recesses of her mind. They had always told her the Firm was there to protect the Family from itself, to control and instruct; and she, poor fool, had always accepted that. She had fought their plottings and resented their orders, yet somehow they had never been enemies – just the other side, fighting her, striving to keep her in line. Now she saw more clearly: they were not the upright foes of weakness and corruption, they were a part of it. Poor, poor Nicky, with his nose and his flapping ears and his spots. He needed relationships desperately; his snarling petulance, of course, was a cry for love. From Baron though, thirty years older, the spinner of the webs that enmeshed them all? What did he see in their tumblings apart from domination extended and lusts fulfilled? Of course she had always wondered about her brother. You didn't parade through expensive preps and second-rate public schools and emerge without a few sweaty experimentings. But he was damaged goods, she knew, folded in cynicism. Why could they be doing this to him? What the hell was their game? Down in the forecourt she heard the throaty roar of the engine and the rattle of gravel scattered in a howl of brakes. It was 5.30. The shops had shut on Selene.

Caroline, always Caroline, only Caroline. She was closer now, just over in Kensington inching her way up through publishing. She made coffee, checked proofs, dispatched the motorbike riders with their bulky parcels. One day, very soon, they had promised to try her in marketing. Cerebral blondes were always in demand there. They liked cool women with a cool intelligence. The sort of people who sell our books are the sort of people who buy them. It gave the organization tone.

She and Bess patrolled the lake in the gardens at dusk. Bess could feel eyes from the Palace windows following them as they wove between the willows. Nobody, in the five days since Windsor, had said a word. Nicky and Selene had gone back to Clarence House on Sunday morning. Baron had been in Manchester organizing the Ship Canal refurbishment gala. Fountain had stayed in his office, pothering memos. Perhaps they hadn't guessed who the intruder was and dared not ripple the surface by inquiring. Perhaps nothing would ever be said. But surely they were on their guard?

She had told Caroline everything. About her father. 'If I say a word, Millward will hang him out to dry.' About Nicky. 'I shouldn't have been there and it was wrong to go in. It wasn't my business. I can't forget it, though: there was something evil in the air. What was Baron doing with my brother in the first place? He's Fountain's man: he doesn't move an inch without getting clearance. He wouldn't lay a finger on Nicky if he hadn't got permission in triplicate. I keep tossing and turning and wondering. They're playing out a lousy script I don't understand, and I have to be part of that somehow. Do I just stand here and wait? Is that fair to Nicky anyway, because they're bound to be using him? I have to tell someone, and there's only you.'

Caroline was deep in thought, head down, rubbing her knuckles against the bark of the tree until they flecked raw with blood. 'You know I think this whole thing stinks?' she said. 'That it has always stunk? I'm seeing somebody I love – the best friend I ever had –

chopped up piece by piece by these bastards. I started off not thinking about things. There was a King and that was fine. And then there was you and I felt sad because of your father and then exultant, because you could be a Queen to remember. It was all a great adventure. But not any longer, because it's all about them and their power and their positions, and nothing about you or us. Why can't you tell Roman?'

She turned and gripped Bess by the shoulders and searched for her eyes. They did not lift.

'I can't talk to him any longer – if I ever could. He came, he swept me away, and I was ready for it. I needed to be touched, you know. I couldn't take any more nights with Emma going on about her conquests. And he was there and charming and glamorous. But somehow he's not there any longer.'

'Just so . . . just bloody so. They've cut you off here and packaged you away. If we do nothing, then there's no hope. You'll be a prisoner again, stuck in your tower, and they will have won for ever. Bess, you have to fight back. There's nothing worth saving if you don't.'

The Queen pulled her shoulders back and looked towards the lights in the East Wing. 'Right,' she said. 'But if I'm trapped on the inside, how do we call for help on the outside?'

Sammy Wittman did not love Emma, of course. Their occasional conjunctions were an unstated bargain. Once a fortnight or so, he would call her and they would go to dinner in one of the plush little restaurants off the Fulham Road which he would pay for on his

Express Amex card. To dinner with contact, a tidy sum. Then, after the second bottle of Burgundy and the Armagnac, they would wander together back to the little flat she had rented in Westgate Terrace. He would take off his leather jacket and his pink shirt and they would make love in the way she demanded, the round, white body heaving with sweat, the yelps almost mechanical in their timing. Emma liked the food and the easy familiarity of the routine. No fuss, no strings – and the gossip he brought her to pass on to the other girls in estate management. He found the sex predictably pleasant and her continual effervescence a blessed relief from his other explorations around the office: too many secretaries looking for a chance at reporting, too many reporters bringing their neuroses to bed. This was uncomplicated satisfaction; and one day, perhaps, she might arrive with a story. She was still part of the circle of friends and she still had her ear to the Palace ground closely enough to get the Managing Editor off his back when the monthly tally topped two grand.

'Gosh,' she said, leaning back on the pillows beneath him, 'that was hard work. I know smoked fish is supposed to get the old juices flowing, but it just makes me feel bloated.'

He grunted. He was too far gone for conversation.

She pressed on regardless. 'Still, we mustn't complain, I suppose. At least we're not like Royal Chum Number One with her Russian cold fish of a husband making her miserable. Or Royal Chum's brother, being rogered by the hired help.'

Sammy Wittman was suddenly bolt upright,

panting to a different rhythm. She had always skirted gingerly round Bess before. What was different now? The Armagnac had been good, but not that good. He'd seen her giggly occasionally, but never sloshed.

'I thought we didn't talk about HM? Private lives and all that stuff.'

She pulled herself up on an elbow. 'You're right and we mustn't. Bess doesn't talk to me about old Tsarface anyway, so there wouldn't be what you call a direct evidence. But I do keep my ears open for gossip I can give you back – a sort of fair exchange between consenting adults, not a word to mother and so forth – and the Palace is just buzzing with it. Nicky's in love, seen *in flagrante* by a kitchen maid. And you'll never guess who with? Don't even try. He's been making it with the spin doctor supreme and departed editor of your other great organ.'

'Baron?' She was right. Sammy was stunned. 'I know there were one or two rumours about him when he left the news room. He used to go away and address the delivery boys all over the country. "You're our salesmen for the future, come and have a drink." Some people thought it was a bit odd. But this is amazing. Have you got it on the kosher grapevine? You're not having me on?'

Emma grinned. 'After the time I left you hanging on, it wouldn't be fair. No, I'm sure this is the real dirt – but just for you and nobody else as per usual. I can trust you, can't I?'

Of course he said yes.

*

Fountain bit his nails. He did it, as he did everything, with precision, the teeth nibbling carefully in a perfect arc. 'I don't like the silence,' he said. 'Somebody saw you. A girl in the doorway. Davidson's trawled over all the chambermaids at Windsor and had them watched round the clock. None of them look at all jumpy. It has to be Bess.'

'Maybe,' Baron said thickly. His face was redder than usual and his right eye twitched beneath a livid sty. 'Maybe. But they never so much as acknowledge each other these days. Why on earth should she be stomping round Nicky's room in the middle of the afternoon?'

'Christ, you were a fool to leave the door unlocked.'

The flush deepened. 'I know. But he said he'd done it, the useless little wimp.'

'How's he bearing up?'

'Edgy, but with too much damned bravado for my liking. Says he's got nothing to be ashamed of and that if it all comes out we can be together properly.'

'Shit. Can you keep him damped down?'

'Of course I can. That is the point of the whole thing anyway, isn't it? Turn Nicky into a dummy in case we should ever need to play a King against the Queen.'

Bradshaw had booked his usual table at the Savoy Grill, the last bench on the far wall where he could observe his competitors – the *Mail* and the *Mirror* – chatting up middle-rank Cabinet ministers and laughing hollowly at their jokes. The *Telegraph* in the corner was feeding some clapped-out Tory smoked salmon. God, they must be desperate. He'd been miffed to find his proprietor, Lord Runton, twenty feet away with the new Woman's editor, a lush red-head from Australia who said she had a degree in sex therapy. His lordship, stretching towards her with the Badoit bottle, seemed to be pondering a little night-school refresher course. He glared when Bradshaw waved at him. Well, that was all good info in the bank, for strategic use as necessary.

Baron was ten minutes and two dry Martinis late.

'Sorry. Action stations for Manchester tomorrow. The Lord Mayor's had a heart attack and they were wittering about cancelling.'

'Tell the bugger to take his tablets and stop whingeing,' Bradshaw said in his broadest Yorkshire accent. 'Bloody nancy Lancashire hypochondriacs begin at the Pennines.'

The waiter coughed anxiously and pretended to have heard nothing. 'Tomato soup and fishcakes for you as usual, Mr Bradshaw?'

'No,' said the editor with an exaggerated smirk. 'Two pots of Beluga, two grilled lobsters and a magnum of Moët. My guest and I have something to celebrate.'

Baron smeared the caviare on his toast and beamed. 'So what are we celebrating then? Promotion with a chunk of money attached, or retirement with an even bigger lump? I see Lord R is deep into his Wagga Wagga manoeuvres already. Time to be cheerful.'

'Oh I am, Dickie. Fairly dancing in the streets – because, son, I've got you. Got you bang to rights. Shagging the Duke of Clarence senseless from what I hear, causing a right royal rumpus. They won't buy that in Barnsley, my lad. Out to grass quicker than you can say tripe and onions.'

The flush had turned to a porridge grey. The toast sagged as he squeezed it and a sliding globule of Beluga stained the white of the tablecloth.

'It's a damnable lie. I'll sue you and your bloody snivelling sheet to kingdom come if you touch it.'

'See you in court, sunshine.' Bradshaw was sneering. 'And from what I hear, I'd thought your kingdom had come rather too often already.'

Millward had been working on his Fifth Way speech, and it was not going well. Everybody knew the First and Second Ways, because they hadn't worked, and historians were still locked in dispute over the Third Way. Since no one, even now, could quite define what it had been about, it was naturally impossibile to decide whether it had worked or not. The Fourth Way (as in none of the above) had been Millward's own first-term invention. 'And, my friends, as the building blocks of life help us climb ever higher, then Five, learning from the triumphs of Four, becomes the number of our aspiration and our hope for the future.' He scowled. What the hell did that all mean? The Fourth Dimension, as launched at the Dome's pre-demolition party, had promised more teachers in schools, more doctors in hospitals and more euros in the pocket. In short, it had needed all the lasers and balloons and confetti it could get. 'The Fifth Way will redeem those pledges, hire the teachers, train the doctors, create the necessary resources to spread throughout society.' Shit! They were calling it the Fifth Amendment already.

There was a knock on the door. Fountain was white and tremulous. As he stumbled through the sub-clauses of explanation and apology, Millward began to tremble himself, right hand wedged between knees below desk level.

'You're all bloody imbeciles. I said get your hooks into Clarence, not fall on every sodding sword in sight.' Maybe serial suicide could be the Sixth Way. 'And how, pray, did Bradshaw come to get the dirt dished into his terminal?'

'We're checking again. Baron said he kept talking about Upstairs and Downstairs, hinting that it was all round the servants' quarters. But we've trawled over the girls a second time and there's still no sign.'

'And transvestite footmen?'

Millward was snarling now; Fountain was cowering.

Her Majesty's Prime Minister began pacing the carpet. 'It's got to be a twin-track policy. First, defensive. Damage limitation and deniable responsibility. Poor Dickie Baron is going to have a mental breakdown. I want him out of the Palace and tucked up in some Swiss rest home by close of play. I want his resignation on your desk. Leckie will help you draft any statement that's needed. Fine public servant, terrible pressure, strain of dealing with tabloid wolves, delayed trauma of plane crash. I don't care what it says. Just make sure the fornicating idiot is out of commission and right off the radar.

'Second, attack. We can't shut Bradshaw up direct. He hates us too much. He's enjoying this. But where there's an editor there's always a proprietor. I want the Runton files on my desk pronto. I want every call girl he's ever drawn breath with, every office blouse he's ever leered down, every tax return that we're not quite sure about any longer, every television satellite he might want to dump his stinking channels on. And then I want him here in Downing Street by 7 p.m., way before the first editions.'

'But I thought he was One of Us,' Fountain said. 'Didn't he say he admired you tremendously in one of those interviews he's always giving?'

'What old Hot Rod Runton admires most of all is his bank balance. We can try patriotism and the public interest OK, and I shall. But I reckon Lady Daphne taking him to the cleaners in the Strand is the one that'll make him jump.'

Will Wittman finally found Bradshaw in the executive loo. 'It's all in your computer queue,' he said, panting with exhaustion. Five full pages and a splash turned round in five hours flat. An afternoon to remember. 'The catchline is Roydick.'

The editor was standing in one of the high, beige stalls, back to the door. He did not turn as Will rushed in. He did not turn for sixty seconds. What the hell was he doing? Not pissing. The flies were untouched. No, he was writing in crude black lettering along the stretch of tiles.

'Hot Rod is a Weedy, Greedy, Sleazy Wanker.'

*

It was seven in the morning and Kensington High Street had barely begun to wash away the grime of yesterday. Caroline had not been able to sleep. She sat in a Colombian coffee and bagel joint with the *Express* open in front of her, turning, turning. Where the hell was it? She knew Sammy had bitten. He'd called Emma back to pump her some more, then suddenly cancelled last night's date. This had to be the day that Bess began to get her own back. But there was nothing here, just the normal tat about soap stars copulating and footballers' marriages getting transfer listed. She screwed the paper into a ball and hurled it at a litter bin.

Two miles away, the coffee was cheaper and the toast had been scraped too hard, leaving a black residue of crumbs at the bottom of the rack. The Queen had worked methodically through her stack of papers, not varying her routine for a second. Check the *Financial Times* first, so she could keep up a conversation with Millward. Then the other broad-sheets and the *Mail*, and so on down. She seemed almost bored when she picked up the *Express*. Zilch, sweet F A. The eagle hadn't landed. But Baron was gone. She'd seen him climbing into his Daimler last night, coat collar pulled high to hide his face, and two men in black macs she didn't recognize loading his suitcases into the back. His office had called already to cancel the meeting on the Saudi royal visit. He'd been removed from the board: it was obvious. Why, then, was there not one printed word of explanation? She kept her face impassive.

'I'll have another slice of toast, please. And I'd be

grateful if you could ask the kitchen to make it a two-minute one rather than four.'

She mustn't snap. It betrayed her tension and her creeping despair. She produced the broadest of smiles.

It was their seventh wedding anniversary and Leckie was late. Another day on the tightrope. The Lobby had asked about the Slovenian bank collapse and the next Cabinet reshuffle. Not a word until the end when Branksome from the *Express* asked whether the PM had any comment on Baron's retirement. 'Only concern for the health of a fine, skilled professional,' Leckie said blandly. 'All of us at Number Ten know him well and wish him a speedy recovery.' Branksome put his head to one side and let his lip curl. 'I know what you're hiding,' the lips seemed to say. It will be all round the Street and into the gossip columns in a couple of days, Leckie thought. Much nudging and winking and arch ellipticism. We haven't got away with it yet. He spent a long afternoon drafting formulas for his staff to parrot to the press as necessary. 'It's vile, and it's just wrong. Believe me, the Palace won't take this kind of muttered filth lying down. They're ready to sue the pants off anyone who runs it.'

Pam was sitting on a stool in the kitchen when he came in. Her eyes were red and her chin was slumped forward on her breast so that the jowls gathered in foreboding.

'I'm sorry,' he said. 'It was one of those days.'

'It's always one of those days. I cook and put a bottle of something decent on ice. You come crawling home hours late. The soufflé is leather. The Meursault is corked. I'm not having it any longer. I married someone I thought would be there for me, not a bloody Prime Minister's poodle.'

He could think of nothing fresh to say. She was right, of course. What she meant was that he didn't love her, that only the job turned him on. He did not follow her as she stamped up the stairs. He picked at the crust of the cold soufflé with a knife and poured himself another Scotch. It was almost over. One curt sentence would finish it for good.

Leckie walked over to the sideboard and gazed at himself in the mirror. Red eyes, pasty cheeks, the face of failure. For the first time, he'd failed at something. 'For as long as you both shall live . . .' It had not been enough for his mother and father. They had worked, day and night, at a marriage which had faded into hostility. Now their son, that damned sallow face in the mirror, had worked at nothing which did not fit his narrow little agenda of advancement.

His eyes turned away as the phone in the hall, the frigging sentinel of doom, rang. It was the Downing Street switchboard again. Jeesus, couldn't they leave him alone for a minute?

'Robin, Simon here.' No apologies, no courtesies. 'Look, I've been thinking who we could put into Baron's slot. It's a nightmare. We can't do the usual trick of wheeling over some whizz-kid from the CBI, and any journo is going to be dodgy for months until we get him house-trained. We need somebody who's up to speed and utterly trustworthy and available fast.'

'Yes,' said Leckie wearily. Why call now to recite the obvious?

'Robin, you're a friend as well as a colleague. There is no other answer. Robin, we need you.'

Chapter Fifteen

Leckie spent the morning sorting his computer files. Some – the data banks of quotes and pledges – could be simply bequeathed to his successor. Indeed, Toby Simcox, shunted over at the double from the FO, probably had access to most of them already. The screen began to flash at him. 'Do you want to keep Terrorism, impossibility of compromising with?' Perhaps: he supposed so. 'File pending decision.' But he'd leave the Davidson briefing notes, the Triple X files, for Millward access only until relationships got a little clearer. Simcox was a career civil servant, after all. You could never quite tell when those chaps would get a panic attack of self-righteousness. Should he take a quick copy, though? The dirt on Alexandrovich and Selene and Nicky and the rest of that awful crew? Of course. He didn't want to be stuck over at the Palace having to get clearance from Number Ten every fifteen seconds. He tucked the disc in his briefcase.

Miss Dobson brought him a Cheddar-and-grape sandwich and a cup of tea. 'Don't forget you're due for your first board meeting at two.' She sniffed and blew her nose on a Kleenex. She was always sniffing.

Tomorrow, he thought with a glimmer of glee, she would be sniffing all over Simcox.

A solitary grape rolled from between the cardboard sheets of granary bread and tumbled into the tea, splattering his keyboard with Typhoo. Leckie cursed and began dabbing it with his handkerchief. How, he wondered suddenly, would he cope doing his own washing, clearing up his own messes, going home to his own empty apartment? That was well on the cards.

'Aren't you going to congratulate me?' he'd said to Pam at breakfast as she'd sat silent, wrapped in that foul lilac dressing-gown, picking loganberry pips from the yoghurt out of her teeth and wiping them, one by one, on to the side of her plate.

'What is there to celebrate? More early mornings, more midnight oil – now with added fortnights in Botswana making sure the schoolkids wave their flags for the cameras? Just don't expect me to put out the flags if you ever come home.'

He shrugged to himself, threw the rest of the sandwich in the bin, swept everything left on his desk into the briefcase, and closed his old office door behind him as though he was closing a chapter of his life.

Millward took the chair, as he always did when there was a crisis. Fountain fretted alone on his left. Montgomery, looking round nervously, took the place on the right where Baron had sat. Leckie positioned himself carefully a metre south of Fountain, the semi-detached isolation of the newcomer. He pushed his seat back from the edge of table so that he could cross his legs and lounge a little. Lounging took away the strain.

'Well,' said Millward sourly, 'there's only one item on the agenda. Sir Richard's resignation is in writing at the top of your pack. We need to accept that formally and agree a suitable letter of thanks. Then Robin Leckie here needs appointing in his place and duly minuting. All agreed?'

'A devoted servant of the truth who worked unstintingly for the public good,' said Fountain, staring at his sheet of paper.

'I said agree it, not write a hymn about it.'

Fountain licked his lips and lowered his eyes, seeming to scan the fragment of carpet he could see beneath his knees for alien crumbs.

'Now, not for minuting, Any Other Business. There's been a leak which could have been lethal. We think we've mitigated, though don't start dancing in the streets yet. We're lucky that Robin has volunteered to help us out of a jam. But, gentlemen, there'll be jams today and jams tomorrow unless we can get our security in order. Of course Davidson is on the case. He will plod and bug his way around as usual. No doubt, in the end, we shall have our spy. But I don't need to say that every minute that goes by without a suspect is a minute of vulnerability. Our vulnerability. So, where have the internal inquiries got to?'

Suddenly the door behind him opened.

'I'm sorry,' Bess said. 'I hadn't realized there was a board meeting until I called Sir Edgar's office about something else and they told me it was just starting. I do hope I haven't kept you waiting.'

'Not at all, Ma'am,' Millward said, grinding to his feet. 'We were lamenting the collapse of poor Dickie Baron's health. You may not know that he has been taken gravely ill. The doctors are divided over whether it is some kind of stroke or a virus. In any case, they recommend complete seclusion and rest for up to six months. There is no possibility of him carrying on; but equally it would be quite wrong to make too much display of his departure. He deserves our care and his privacy.'

'Of course,' she said. 'I'm as sad to hear this as you gentlemen must have been. And who shall we turn to now?'

'We're lucky to be able to make an outstanding appointment, Ma'am. You know Mr Leckie already.'

'Only as your man, Prime Minister. Not until now as one of us.'

Leckie had straightened. She had wonderful green eyes, he thought, and they were running over every inch of him. He found himself, from half-remembered instinct, bowing stiffly from the waist. The eyes allowed no lounging.

'It's a privilege to be able to help, Your Majesty.'

She sat, at once triumphant and depressed, in her study, door closed, the music turned high. Wagner, Brünnhilde's Immolation Scene. A celebration and a booming deterrent. She needed to think.

It had worked. Baron was gone overnight. He had vanished without trace, smitten by some undiagnosable malady. No more connivings, no more fornications in the smelly recesses where her brother lived.

That boil was lanced. But it had been done so swiftly and in silence. Not a cheep from the *Express*, or anyone else, for that matter. Not a word on the radio. The *Standard* first edition they always left on her desk might have something. Yes, page two – 'Ill Health Forces Palace Retirement'. Five plain paragraphs, with a line or two at the end saying that a replacement would be found as quickly as possible. No clue yet that the Prime Minister was donating his own Twister-in-Chief to the cause of the hush-up.

Caroline had told Emma. Emma had whispered it in her journo friend's ear. Then why wasn't it in the paper? They must have been nobbled somehow. She scratched her nose in disbelief. Papers like the *Express* *not* printing lousy stories about backstairs antics at the Palace? Might as well ask a monkey to give up nuts.

Bess felt a shiver of unease. She had lost the plot, and its mysteries began to unnerve her. Perhaps they knew that she knew and were planning some retribution. Millward's face had been a picture when she'd come through the door unannounced. But his revenge, as she also knew, could be suffocating. Back to the sin-bin of isolation. If he was certain she'd been behind the bouncing of Baron, there would be a price to pay. Thus the insolent Leckie with his creased jacket and tie hanging loose, leaning back in his chair as though he owned the Palace. Perhaps he was to be the outside enforcer; perhaps he already had his orders.

She needed to talk to Caroline, but she had to be careful. If they were suspicious they'd be watching.

Bess kept her father's little palm-top in the top

drawer of her dresser, thrown there casually with old diaries and handbags and two broken watches. It was supposed to look like just another defunct memento, a sentimental bit of bric-à-brac. The MoD had taken ten months cleaning and losing it after they brought it back from the wreckage of Brazil. She had nagged and nagged them. But it was still working. One of the young electricians at Sandringham had taken it away over a Christmas and returned it with the smile of victory. 'No sweat, Ma'am. It's as good as new.'

To Thornbird@Bookythings. mustard.uk. 'Launching tonight at the garden. Stop by.' Not code, but not giving away too much. Her grandma's everlasting memorial charity had another book coming out that week, *The Best of the Best Remembered*, an anthology of anthologies. They'd been pleading with her to drop in at Kensington Palace and give it her blessing. It would not be much of a coincidence if her old friend in publishing happened to drop by too.

Dusk had arrived with a scud of clouds as her car turned through the wrought-iron gates. The grounds were clear of people now. She saw the tiny memorial garden on her left, the floodlights picking out the single rose tree in the centre plot and the pile of uncleared flowers on the path in front of it, left day after day by the same small old women in headscarves and sensible shoes. 'Not much of an outcome,' her father had once said when they'd visited it for some anniversary or other. 'They were going to make a Hampton Court of it, but then the locals cut up rough and the money ran out as usual, so the Treasury went for a couple of ping-pong tables and a seed catalogue. Dignified and restrained, they said; but they would, wouldn't they? It didn't stop them putting a bust of the Chancellor of the Exchequer in the corner behind the geraniums.'

The road wound through a line of trees to the conservatory they'd eventually built at the back, over the old car park, when the last of the sitting tenants had finally been evicted twenty years before. The Princess Pavilion, available for trade shows, cabaret nights and fund-raising suppers. All proceeds, less necessary expenses, to the charity whose administrators now filled the rest of the Remembrance Centre. As the car door opened, she noticed a burly man in a blue suit standing to one side behind the policemen. She had seen him before walking the corridors of the Palace or waiting in Fountain's outer office. Some kind of caterer, perhaps? But she had never been introduced. She glanced for a second at Lady Margaret, stiff and watchful at her shoulder. Swayne's eyes were on this man.

'Who's the bulky chap by the door?' Bess said. 'I seem to see him everywhere these days.'

'Do you, Ma'am? I really couldn't say. Perhaps he's some kind of additional security detail.'

Too damned casual. She was watched. She was watched continuously. Here was somebody else to keep watching for.

'Ladies and gentlemen, you would not expect me to say anything fresh tonight about the grandmother I never met. In that sense, there is nothing fresh to say. But there are always new generations who need a distillation of what has already been said, and older generations who will wish to be reminded of it. For these reasons, I'm sure this anthology of anthologies will be as popular and well-received as all the previous anthologies, and it gives me great pleasure to be here with you today to turn the first page of this imaginative venture.'

She gave the scrap of paper back to Swayne, who stuffed it in her severe, black handbag. 'More pearly words,' said Bess. 'One day – who knows? – they may even let me write them myself.'

Caroline was at the far end of the room by the yucca tree, alone with a glass of white wine. She raised her left hand and gave the tiniest of waves.

'Great,' said Bess. 'Caroline's here. I haven't seen her for ages. Forgive me for a moment. I must go and catch up.'

She ran over and clutched Caroline in a giggling embrace. 'The spooks are on parade, I think. Keep laughing while I talk. Baron's gone, you know: exploded, kaput. They've brought in a new thought-policeman from Downing Street. They're terribly grim and suspicious. Millward looked as though he'd swallowed a poker this morning. But how did they find out without a word in the papers? Did you pass it along to Emma and did she see her man? I've got to get a fix on what's happening.'

Caroline laughed and, hand rocking, spilt wine down the pink front of her silk dress. Bess began to dab it away with a paper napkin. 'Everything was perfect. Em briefed Sammy and Sammy told his brother. They were both really on heat, she says. All

systems blow and off to see their editor who hates
Baron anyway. And then nothing. Em called Sammy
at lunchtime and he wouldn't talk. He said they'd
been nobbled from on high and that his editor was
going round kicking lumps out of the furniture . . .

'And darling, I really think it's a terrific book. So
glossy and thick. I know we've seen all of the pictures
thousands of times, but it's so lovely to have them all
brought together again.'

Bess turned as the song changed. Swayne was two
feet away, pulling a handkerchief from her bag.

'Allow me to help clear up your friend, Ma'am.
We wouldn't like to make more of a mess, would
we?'

'It's obvious,' Millward said. 'Davidson can't prove
it. The yucca tree blanked out his bug when they were
talking. But the chain is clear enough. We don't know
whether she did it deliberately or just let it out in one
of her sub-schoolgirl chats, but Suspect Number One
is the one with the crown. I don't need to tell you
how serious this is. Always before, she's been bolshy
and independent. But she's never been out to cause
trouble deliberately. We just can't have that. The girl
is the enemy. Either we bring her back under control
or we try something more serious.'

'I don't see how that's possible.' Fountain examined
the scuff on his left instep again. 'If you threaten her
again, she'll just deny it. And even if it happened as
Davidson says, we don't know she meant anything
by it. Baron was a bloody idiot to get caught. You
can see why she was upset.'

'What I don't like', said Robin Leckie, 'is the way her Prince never comes this way. He's always off somewhere, visiting friends in St Petersburg, shooting in Wiltshire, yachting in the Bahamas and fitting a few public appearances in between. It's pretty obvious he's bored to tears with playing second violin, but that's not what we pay him for.'

Millward smiled at last. 'Right on the button. We need her out of circulation for a few months with a cast-iron excuse. Like a difficult pregnancy. The nation understands these things. Get hold of Alexandrovich again pronto, wherever he is . . . Tahiti, Grand Cayman, Omsk. And tell him to get his equipment back here and functioning. If at first you don't succeed and all that stuff . . .'

Selene levered herself up on the pillows and looked down at him. 'Well,' she said, 'how goes the Great Spy Hunt?' Her heavy breasts hung against her chest and a thin stream of sweat trickled between them, down into the fathomless caves beneath the linen sheet drawn around her waist. Two minutes before she had been yelping and twisting as usual, locked in the box of pleasure which always seemed to close round her at the end so that she was an object, an animate object, straddled on top of him, not a partner. But now she was cool again. Her eyes examined him and mocked his frailties.

Fountain was still trying to catch his breath. He felt old and ridiculous. Fifty-four? Certainly ridiculous. He swung his arm over the side of the bed and hunted with blind fingers for the shirt of blue-striped

Sea Island cotton she had torn from him and hurled away in another of her bouts of simulated passion. There it was. A button missing, another buttonhole slightly ripped at the corner. His lips pursed in disapproval. Perhaps Housekeeping could be asked to repair it? He pulled it over his shoulders and hunched forward, hiding the pink flesh around his belly.

'We're almost there,' he said. 'There's still a chambermaid we're not quite certain about, and a butler who keeps calling in sick. But we're pretty damned sure it was Bess. That's the hypothesis anyway, and the necessary steps are being considered.'

Selene brushed the damp hair from her forehead and laughed. 'God, what a fuss you lot make about a little bouncy-bouncy. We should all be sorry for Nicky, poor dear. Ten years solitary in boarding school picking his zits and suddenly he finds what life's all about. Whoobloodypee, I say. So my prissy daughter gets shocked? Zut alors! Somebody should take her to one side and tell her the facts of life. That her screwed-up brother was happy for a while, and now he's not. That happiness is nobody's business but your own.'

She pulled him flat on the bed and tugged the shirt from his fingers. 'Isn't that right, Eddie? You saw the difference in him. For five weeks he was almost human. I tell you what – I'll have a talk with her, the way mothers are supposed to. At times like this, children need a mother's experience.'

He was out of bed before she had finished, wrapping the thin towel around his waist, searching for his voice of authority. 'On no account, Selene, on no account are you to say a word about any of this. I'm mad to even discuss it with you.'

'Oh poo, Eddie. We're all on the same team, aren't we? A problem shared is a problem solved, my love.'

Sammy Wittman was not exactly drunk; but he was not exactly sober either. 'I'm owed weeks of holiday already,' he'd said to Will. 'Can I at least take a couple of days not trying to get stories into the paper?' And his brother, eyes rooted to terminal, mouth set in a sulky slit, had nodded curtly. 'Sod off and get stoned. And if you find another world exclusive in a gutter somewhere, call the *Mail* or the *Mirror*. Tell them your owner's balls need a transplant.'

Sammy had been working his way up the Fulham Road for three hours now, one pub at a time. He could still walk in a straight line. You couldn't do the Royal beat if you started falling apart after a few tequilas; but the furies inside him were beginning to slip their chains. This was a great story and it was his story, his just reward for all those evenings of cautious chat with Tubby Emma. It was he who'd put his expense account on the line, he who'd waited and wheedled for scraps and, more self-denying still, not used them when he could have because he was waiting for the big one. And when the big one dropped? The great god in the sky, the supreme turd on the fifteenth floor who existed only to pay his salary, had turned out to be chicken shit.

He turned into Hollywood Road and paused for a while at one of the wine bars which covered the half block before Cathcart Road. Half a bottle of Chablis, time to stop swigging the hard hooch. He leaned against the chrome sweep of the bar and leered at a blonde Australian waitress. She's got tits like the Great Barrier Reef, Sammy thought, hanging out so far that she has to carry the trays low down near her crotch, bare arms straight and straining, to stop knocking the glasses on the floor. He winked at her, elbow slithering along the bar as the effort of coordination hit him. She raised two fingers. He shrugged and staggered to the door.

Suddenly Sammy Wittman was feeling horny. But Deborah wouldn't want him turning up like this, no warning; and Erys was off on some fashion shoot somewhere; and Karyn always shut the door if he smelled of booze. Westgate Terrace, though, was only a hundred yards away. Emma might or might not be there, but it was no sweat to find out. Maybe they could order an Indian on his Amex card. To dinner with Tarka Dhal, Royal contact.

Two of the street lights were off as he swung round the corner, but he could see the lamp in the window of the flat glowing behind the purple curtain. He stepped back in a tiny jig of anticipation and the low, white wall of Number 4 hit the back of his knees. Sammy slumped first on to the wall and then, struggling to find his balance, collapsed backwards into the darkness of the small shrubbery. His head struck the side of a tub of herbs as he fell and, smelling of sage and thyme and white wine, he marinated in unconsciousness.

There was no telling what the time was when he woke up. Ten minutes or two hours later? The Terrace was still black and deserted. Except, as he peered from the shrubbery, a car – an anonymous saloon – slid into the parking spot in front of him. A man in a short coat got out. Sammy was about to haul himself up on to the wall and call for help; his forehead was cut and his right knee ached fiercely. But there was something about the exaggerated stealth of the man that made him pause. And then another man, this one with a hat and a longer mackintosh, appeared from the doorway of a house two or three down.

'Any movement?' said Shorty.

'No. She's in there all right. You can see her moving around against the lamp every so often. I think there were a couple of phone calls, but we've got those anyway. It's just a question of logging the visitors, if any, as and when. Remember to buzz the George if you get a bite. We can be back in thirty seconds if there's somebody worth tailing.

'And Rutherford: keep lively. It could be a man or a woman. If she's young and blonde, buzz at once. If it's a man it may be one of the journo links, so keep your head down.'

Sammy wiped the blood from his eyes and cowered, barely daring to breathe, behind the parapet. Easing himself on to his side and pulling at his flies, he urinated gently into the flower bed. It might be a long night and he was beginning to feel sober again.

It was as though the Palace had yawned. Its mouth was open wide, jaws locked in pain, as the multitude poured unceasingly through.

Bess looked gloomily from her bedroom window.

'Only five minutes, I think,' she said. 'The west tent looks pretty full already. Every year they turn up earlier and earlier. As my father used to say, "There's no such thing as a free cucumber sandwich."'

Alexandrovich leaned into the mirror and gave his tie a final, irritable fiddle. 'Your garden parties are a pain, the worst kind of petit bourgeois confection. Either you hold parties to show how grand you are, as the tsars believed. Caviare and champagne at Peterhof with the fountains running and the great barges bringing their guests across the Gulf of Finland. What are strawberries and long-life cream in plastic bowls to do with that? Or your parties are for friends, people you enjoy meeting, people on your level. But what is this, down below? Postmen with aching feet and district nurses with unpleasant hair and secretaries of Rotary Clubs: people you would cross the street to avoid if you saw them coming. I never quite understand you Windsors. If you are grand, be grand. If you are ordinary, be ordinary.'

'You're pretty sour,' she said. 'Two weeks away in the Monaco dacha hasn't done much for your temper.'

He straightened and his eyes, as she knew they would, became soft again. 'I'm sorry, my love. My Great Aunt Tatyana has always meant a lot to me. She was like a mother through the early years. Her heart will fail soon. There is nothing more they can do for her. She cannot travel, and you of course cannot be with her. But I have my duty, what I feel must be done.'

She bit her lip. What was the point of mentioning the *Sun*'s long-lens photographs of the yacht with its deck of brown bodies and drinks and laughter? Or the night at the Casino the *Mail* diary had chronicled so archly? Who is the Consort consorting with next? If she loved him, she would feel rage at the humiliation. But she knew, with increasing certainty, that she did not love him. He was an alien being, the simulator of a love which had soon turned to disdain and then to a kind of loathing. She had felt sick at the news of his return.

'Come along,' she said. 'The perfect couple have another perfect afternoon performance. You don't have to stay with me after the first twenty minutes. There are hundreds of little chats and smiles waiting for us out there and we'll do better if we split up.'

Gilbert and Sullivan. Rodgers and Hammerstein. Henderson, Brown and De Sylva. Music from the time capsule which enclosed her. The King, she remembered, had once asked a pop group to play on a floating platform in the middle of the lake. Bringing Monarchy into the Modern Age, they'd called it. But the power lines had fouled on a punt, snapped and electrocuted a swan. 'RSPCA Flays Royal Rocker Shocker.' They had retreated, cravenly, to sounding brass and Andrew Lloyd-Webber.

Two hours later, Bess's jaw ached and her face seemed frozen in a smile. She had tried to be interested. No, she was interested. Duty was meeting people, and people were interesting: tons better than cooped claustrophobia. But this meeting wasn't proper meeting, just greeting. You couldn't begin a conversation because Chetwode-Belcher would cough and point out the next hundred pleasantries which needed passing by

3.57. 'Lovely to see you. Thank you for coming. Yes, we're gloriously happy. He is handsome, isn't he? Please don't send me any bootees yet. Have a wonderful day.'

There was a quarter of an hour's permitted respite in the Pavilion marquee where the family could exit for sanctuary, pursued by bores. Roman was nowhere to be seen, last glimpsed with a bouquet of floral-dressed debs near the summer house. Selene was deep into her second bottle of cheap white wine from the Pays d'Oc and calling too loudly for ice. The Deputy Prime Minister, a fat Welshman called Griffiths who'd lugubriously recaptured the traditional Transport portfolio reform in the last reshuffle, stood red and puffing, prodding the lemon slice in his tea. 'I'm so sorry I was late, Your Majesty.' 'Affairs of State?' 'No, traffic.'

She broke free for a while and was surprised, glancing round, to find Nicky at her elbow. He was flushed and his eyes gleamed at her. His chest seemed somehow puffed forward as though in search of dignity.

'Hello,' she said.

'It was you, wasn't it?' His voice was a squeak of fury. 'You were the snitch. You got him sent away. You're ruining my life all over again.'

Bess clenched her fists and let the sharpness of her fingernails dig deep into her palms. 'Who on earth told you that?'

'Who do you think? The only person who ever talks to me, ever tells me anything. Mother knows all about your evil little games.'

She managed to smile. 'This is ridiculous. We both

know Selene. She drinks too much and she gossips with anybody who'll tell her she's beautiful and buy her another round. You can't go round making accusations because of one of her stories.'

'Oh, she's into more than stories.' He was shouting now and the hubbub in the tent was beginning to die.

'Be quiet, Nicky, be quiet. What do you mean, more than stories?'

'I mean your precious, precious new husband, Smarm. I mean the place where people tell each other everything – just like Dickie and me did before you ruined it. She's known your bloody Prince for ages. There used to be a picture of him in the flat in Antibes, not that you were ever there to see it. And now she's always slipping off to visit her chums and go shopping, but when I check her credit cards there isn't anything on them for the day and she comes home looking all puffed and happy. Mum's like she always is: on the circuit. And she knows everything. When I asked her who'd done Dickie in she just giggled and said, "Ask your big sister."'

He was hissing at her now, triumphant and gloating. She walked away from him, head down, into the millings of the lawn. The band struck up again at the sight of her.

'The moon belongs to everyone, the best things in life are free.'

Chapter Sixteen

She took the little palm-top from the drawer and eased it from its leather case.

Dear Daddy,
I've hunted through everything you ever wrote to me – all those millions of words – but I can't find the answer. You told me to be strong. It hasn't been easy. I knew so pitifully little and there was so much to learn. But I think I have found a strength. You told me to be independent. 'My own woman,' you said. Well, you can be independent if people will give you the space, somewhere to stand alone. I'm not allowed any space, though. I am watched every moment. I can't write my own words or voice my own thoughts. I am the person things happen to. And when some of the things that happen are just awful – like the degradation of my brother – there is nothing I can do. Millward and Fountain and the others have me as the enemy. My husband, God help me, is the enemy. My mother is beyond help. Duty, you said. Where's the duty in this? Do I pretend and spread my legs and hope that the seed will grow? That's my first duty, I know. Keep the

*old circle of life revolving, as you used to say. But
the seed will be his seed. When I look at my baby, I
shall see Roman in his eyes and in the twist of his
mouth. I shall be making that bastard a king.*

*But there's the other duty: the duty to keep silent,
the duty not to complain. I can't tell what I know.
It would be the end of everything, even if anybody
believed me. I tried to expose the Baron thing, but
they have ways of covering up I don't understand.
They'd never let me breathe a word about Roman
or about that drunken bitch I call my mother. They
could ruin your memory, Daddy, but maybe you'd
tell me not to care about that. Yet I do care, and I
know that you'd care too. You would tell me to
keep smiling and do what I thought was right, come
what may. I've tossed and turned and cried in the
night. And there is no right way. There is no way.
Please, if you're there somewhere, if this is anything
more than a bad dream, send me a sign or someone
who can help.*

Your loving Bess.

She pressed the Send button and the screen quivered
for a second. Then the box in the corner flashed to
message as expected.

'Not connected.'

They had found Leckie a room with some Chinese
pots and a bed at the end of the west wing. He rarely
went home these days. He had nothing he could call
home to go to. Another endless day and another flask
of Scotch to end it. He sat on the end of the bed looking

out towards the lights of Victoria and wondered what had become of the student who went into politics because he believed in all the usual student things – making a better world, ending poverty. Oh, over in Downing Street, with Millward dropping in for another of his little chats, the excitement had swept him along. His not to reason why, his but to lie and lie. But the Palace was somehow different. When he went for his early morning jog, panting back through the Privy Purse door and driving himself up the stair-case, the whole building and the people in it seemed to demand something of him he could not give. What was it? Loyalty? Perhaps. Whatever it was, its lack made him feel uneasy, soiled. 'Careful, old son,' he said out loud. 'You'll soon be your own credibility gap.'

Alexandrovich tapped lightly on the door. 10.37 p.m., fifteen minutes after they had retired to their separate rooms. Thursday, one of the regular days – and appro-priately spaced, forty-eight hours after his return from Monte Carlo. He liked his routine. It made availability for other relevant interests easier to organize. You didn't have to scrabble round in diaries to find a night.

No immediate answer. He tapped again.

'Yes,' Bess said.

'But it's not open. You have bolted it.'

'Yes.'

'What is this about? Let me in so we can talk.'

'No.'

He thrust the palm of his hand hard against the oak so that it rattled and resounded. 'Whatever else you are, you are my wife. You promised to obey. Will you let me in?'

She pulled the bolt back abruptly and the green of her eyes glared at him. His face had turned from anger to one of the familiar, lop-sided grins. His eyes seem to melt before hers.

'Bess, my love. You were expecting me; this is part of our schedule. I have said nothing and done nothing. I do not understand.'

It was the point she had rehearsed over and over in her mind. Did she throw Selene back in his face and tell him how his skin made her shrink in a disgust which was also self-disgust? Did she scream with the rage she felt, a rage to match her brother's, the rage of a trapped animal? It was not, she had decided, the way queens behaved.

'You don't need to understand,' she said. 'I met you, by design I think, and I was desperate for love – someone to replace my father, someone to be there for, to be my defender as well as my lover, and I thought that was you, with your smiles and your wonderful fingers. But it was all an act, wasn't it? A mechanical exercise? Now, I can't stand the sight or the touch of you. I want you nowhere near me. Please, go and spend more time with your aunts and your friends at their house parties and your business part-ners. You have a separate life you can live. Just lead it. In public, some of the time, we're stuck with each other. They will expect you to put on a show and I shall be part of it. But in private, Roman, I expect nothing and want nothing.'

He shrugged like a boy caught stealing a sweet from

a supermarket counter. 'Very well. But you are mad.'

'I am perfectly calm,' she said.

'No, mad – as in raving mad. You have lost your mind. The pressure has been too much for you. So much death, so much sorrow. There has always been madness in your family, but they have had the sense to see it early and to stow it away in some hospital or home where nobody goes or knows. But now there is no escaping. We have a tragedy on our hands, Your Majesty, and it is your tragedy.'

She could think of nothing to say. She heard the crisp leather of his shoes beating down the corridor and the door at the end of it slamming shut.

Millward had flown back from Brussels that morning, temper shredding with every bumpy mile of the holding pattern over Heathrow. He hated European Councils, with their interminable compromises. Life at home was an endless compromise and life in Europe was just the same. Eighteen hours in search of an agreed text and then seven courses of foie gras, turbot and dead little pigeons gazing at him reproachfully from the middle of the plate. Come back Lord Palmerston, all is forgiven. At least, two hundred years before, prime ministers could send a bloody gunboat. Now all they sent was a negotiating document.

'And Leckie called from the Palace,' his Private Secretary said with a sniff. 'He wouldn't say what it was, but he said it was urgent.' The sniff was disapproving. The Private Secretary had never liked the departed Press Secretary. Too damned chummy with the PM, sitting around through the evenings drinking and hatching schemes the true Civil Service never got wind of until it was too late.

Millward stifled a groan. 'He's a sensible operator,' he said sharply. 'He wouldn't say it was urgent if it wasn't. Get him on the secure line.' The sniff died away.

'It's trouble, Simon. Fountain and I had Alexandrovich in before breakfast, all white and foot-stamping. He went round for the connubials last night as usual. An important one, he said, because this is prime ovulation time on the computer. But she just shut the door in his face. She told him it was finished. She won't let him near her again. No co-habitation, no confinement, no heir, no nothing.'

Millward had forgotten the flight and the foie gras and the drained ache in his stomach. 'Did she say why? Has that devious bastard been playing away?'

'I don't know. Davidson's been too busy on leaks to cover all the bases, but some of that Monaco reporting was getting a bit fruity. Maybe she's jumped to an obvious conclusion. But our second-class Tsar says she didn't make accusations or anything. One minute they were set for coupling as normal, the next she was giving him the bird. He thinks she's gone mad.'

'That', Millward said, 'is the Doomsday option from Scenario Seven. Let's hope we haven't lost the file.'

The Palace had its lists of general practitioners and gynaecologists and consultants on heart, lungs and backs. It had surgeons on tap and life-support systems permanently rigged at the clinic near Vauxhall Bridge. But it did not, officially, have a psychiatrist. Unofficially, though, it had Sir Lawrie Spens, called in when they had wanted to run a surreptitious check on sex addictions during one of Selene's more lurid excursions a decade ago. He was not ideal, Millward thought, thumbing through the dossier. Too high profile. Always rabbiting away on the BBC or knocking off a quick, glib piece for the *Daily Mail*: 'How Fifty Years of Breast Implants Have Made Britain the Silicon Society'; 'Why Working Mothers Should Leave the Quality Time to the Nanny'; 'Has Global Warming Boiled Our Psyches?' But he could also keep his mouth shut when it was necessary, and his pet theories were particularly apposite. He had written a paper for the *New England Journal of Psychiatry* called 'Post-Marital Mood Variations in Developed Society' which the press had, pretty predictably, dubbed the Honeymoon Blues. Four out of ten couples, apparently, moved from feelings of intense satisfaction shortly before the wedding ceremony into a state of suspended belief and growing uncertainty through the honeymoon period.

Typically, then, the next stage is one of lost confidence and even what we may term bereavement before the potential crisis is addressed and the opportunity for a new beginning occurs. Normally this process may be contained within seven to fifteen months, but in exceptional cases – particularly those where other, unrelated stresses have an impact – it can take three or more years. Halversrein, in his study of Hollywood marriages

(Yale University Press) found one possible example of extreme simulated bereavement syndrome which extended over seven years, though his results are inevitably made more complex by the decision of his studied couple to embark on second marriages with different partners before the first cycle could be deemed complete.

That looked promising, a cure or a kill. Millward made a note on his pad. 'Get Davidson to fix holding consultation with Spens re. Wayward Niece situation.'

Leckie felt uncomfortable in her presence. He was there ostensibly to serve her, but in fact to watch and manipulate her every step. And of course she knew that, and let him know that she knew. Nothing was ever said. She was polite and alert and businesslike. 'I'd like, if I may, to begin writing some of my own speeches. Oh, you can vet them of course, make sure I don't step out of line. But I'm not a girl any longer. I'm a married woman who's learned a bit from the last few years. I think I can be trusted to open my mouth in public without falling into some great hole.' Yes, Ma'am, naturally, Ma'am. Perhaps that was just her UDI after Baron, but in the cast of her body it seemed much more. Her shoulders straightened when she confronted him and her face had become gaunter and more defiant, the cheekbones defined and the merest of shadows under the eyes lending a melancholy to the clear green of her gaze. He was tired and unhappy and sleeping badly: and now he was being tested.

'We could try the book fair opening on the fifteenth,'

he said. 'That needs about five minutes' worth with some attempt to say why reading is important to you, so there is the need for some personal input.'

'Can I say why I prefer books to people, Mr Leckie?'

He pretended not to hear. 'We thought it might be a good opportunity to talk about your and Prince Roman's tastes in literature, Your Majesty. We would recommend that the Prince accompanies you. You have not been seen together in public for ten days now, and there is beginning to be a little press speculation we don't find helpful.'

'I thought the press never speculated without your permission, Mr Leckie.'

'Perhaps if I could have your draft script by the twelfth, Ma'am, then we could go over it together? That would give us forty-eight hours to iron out any little kinks before releasing the text.'

'I'll do it tonight,' she said. 'I have nothing else to do.'

He turned abruptly and almost ran for the shelter of his office. He needed clearer orders. Millward would have to make up his mind. The Queen was hostile. The marriage was over. You only needed to read the body language when they came within a dozen metres of each other. There would be no heir and no *rapprochement*, but there could be no divorce either. That was the ultimate balloon waiting to go up, the Firm's last fairy tale exploding. He felt another night without sleep rolling towards him.

'She knows, you know.'

'Knows what?'

'About us. I think Nicky guessed somehow. He is

not always as stupid as he looks. We were talking about Baron and I said it was nothing to do with me or anyone. What I did in my bedroom was my business and nobody else's. And he began to boil over as he does, turning red and then that ghastly white when you think he's going to have a heart attack or something. "Quite," he kept saying. "Quite, mother dearest." He didn't spell it out, but he knew. It would be just like him to go off and blurt it all out to Bess. He hates her so much it's frightening.'

'You bloody idiots, you and your reptile son. What am I supposed to tell Fountain? Agent Alexandrovich, disqualified for active service?'

'Too much active service, if you ask me.'

His arm swung blindly. The blow threw her flat on the bed. 'You are a fool, Selene, and I am a fool too. One word of this to Millward and I'm finished. This is it for us. The end of everything.'

'I don't see why,' she said. 'I mean, what can they do to you? You're their man. You could cause quite as much trouble for them as they could cause you. Oh, of course we can't go around broadcasting it and of course we can cool things for a few months if you really want. One door closes, another door opens. But I'm not giving up without a fight, Alex. I never give up without a fight.'

'Shut the fuck up, you silly bitch.'

'Hit me again, mon amour. It was rather nice.'

Dear Lilibet,
You sounded a bit down when we talked. Don't let the bastards get you down. My great motto from a

life in the trenches. Honestly, you know, I could
have had the glooms before I got into short
trousers, and never recovered. There was my
mother, endlessly on the phone with the door closed
– and Father going round banging his forehead
against the wall. Not to mention Grandpa, barking
away like a singing dog. If I'd wanted to sink into
the slime, there'd have been nothing easier. But
that's when the tough get etcetera. It's your life,
love, and nobody else's. You only have one of them,
whatever the Archbishop says. Always, always fight
your corner . . .

'Ladies and gentlemen. It gives me great pleasure
to be here with you today and to open the Tenth
International Chelsea Book Fair and Literary Festival.
Even in this age of advanced technology, when words
can flash around the world in an instant, when we are
all part of the giant Net of communication, books
have an honoured place in our lives . . .'

Leckie was standing at the side of the town-hall
stage. She looks different, he thought. She wore a
black silk shift. Her arms were bare and her hair was
loose. No suit, no bag; nothing of the matron who
had seemed to grow in the months of her marriage.
She was a girl again.

'Somebody suggested that I talk to you a little about
what books mean to Prince Roman and myself. An
interesting suggestion. He tells me he loves Russian
literature, Turgenev in particular. But I have to confess
that I find that a little melancholy. He, as you may
have noticed, is often away on business of one kind

of another. I'm not much for moping alone if I can help it . . .'

This isn't the script! Leckie thumbed back to page two and began to sweat. Christ, she's vamping it. Except she isn't. She's word perfect.

'Books can make you laugh when you need it. Sometimes when I look around the Palace I think of P. G. Wodehouse and laugh out loud. Books can spark instant recognition. Are my advisers playing Uriah Heap or Valmont this morning? Has the Prime Minister read Trollope or Machiavelli? Am I Jane Eyre or Tess of the D'Urbervilles? Does my dear mother somehow remind me of Chaucer?

'It isn't easy, ladies and gentlemen, to be your Queen. I sometimes feel very isolated. Of course there's the family. But no family, as we all know, is always quite what it seems or would have us believe of it. The plays of Eugene O'Neill are on my shelf too.

'All these words, when you think of it, are part of the existence that shapes us. That gives experience and consolation, and the beginning of wisdom. So to the business of the day. It gives me, again, great pleasure . . .'

The press had gathered in a buzz, checking quotes. 'How do you spell Machiavelli?' 'Didn't Valmont have dangerous liaisons?' They had their code, and they were cracking it already.

Bess stood for a minute, acknowledging the applause. And then, seemingly by accident, she swung to look at Leckie. She smiled, the lips set in a brief, defiant grin.

He did not wait for her. Let the bloody maids do the waiting. This was it, the declaration of war. He paused on the steps and called Millward.

Chapter Seventeen

Sammy Wittman sat in the window of the café, making his second pot of tea last. Five-fifty. The world around Kensington High Street was beginning to pack its bags and head for home. At Benstead and Crane, just across the lane, you could see the secretaries and the sales reps tugging their coats on as they came through the swing doors and felt the chill of the wind. Where was she? He'd been there for nearly two hours already, knees clamped ever firmer together, afraid to take a pee in case he missed her. She might, of course, be working late. That would be a real bore. The waitresses were beginning to clear away even now. There was the clatter of thick china from the kitchen and the thump of heavy yellow scones as they were tossed, one by one, into the plastic bin behind the counter. Damn! Ten more minutes and he'd have to find a doorway to huddle in.

The girl in the black raincoat was carrying a fat leather bag. It bumped against her legs as the door revolved, almost wedging her against the glass. She staggered as she reached the steps and the knotted scarf slipped back from her head. There was a vivid shimmer of gold.

As he scrambled to his feet the edge of his jacket swept the pile of change he'd lugubriously counted on to the floor. The sourest of the two waitresses blocked his way. He scrabbled around for the coins, cursing under his breath. She took them and counted them one at a time. 'Six euros ten, twenty, thirty.'

Bloody, bloody hell! She had turned left out of the building, heading away from the crowds and down through the narrow canyons of Edwardian red-brick apartments that led to the Cromwell Road. He could see her a hundred or so metres on, walking slowly, holding the bag with both hands clasped in front of her. He couldn't run. This had to be a casual coincidence of a meeting. 'I say, aren't you Caroline? Emma's friend?' He began to walk fast, head down into the wind.

And then he saw the young man in the donkey jacket walking ahead of him. There was something oddly familiar about him. The way the coat hung from his narrow shoulders so that, at any moment, it threatened to fall around his waist. Got it. The first man, the man in the car outside Emma's, had looked like that.

Sammy slowed and hung back.

In the distance, Caroline turned and hailed a taxi. As she heaved the bag into the back, Sammy saw donkey jacket pause and look round. A black saloon had pulled out of a parking space; he slid into the passenger seat. The procession headed south, round one more corner, swinging left out of sight.

They're watching everyone and everything, he

thought. This isn't a random check; this is an operation.

Millward had left it to one of the scheduled meetings: Windsor on Saturday morning. She had meant to provoke him. There was no point in giving her the satisfaction of knowing she'd succeeded.

'And apart from the Sudan, Ma'am, which is appalling but no worse than usual, I think that's your list taken care of. There is just one other thing.'

Bess was tense. He was going to say something after all.

'I can't disguise from you how seriously I, and my advisers, take the speech you made at the book fair. It was frankly inflammatory. Yet again you make commitments of silence and discretion to us and then tear them to pieces. I want to know why, and I must have guarantees of your future conduct, otherwise you put the loyalty of those around you in pawn.'

The nail of her index finger bit into the flesh of her thigh. 'And what loyalty is that, Prime Minister? What discretion are we talking about?'

'It's the discretion that has kept the news of your father's role in the crash so silent for so long. It is all our loyalty to the tradition of the Crown.'

She pressed the nail down again hard, through the folds of her dress. I must be cool. He'll preach and he'll patronize and he'll threaten. He will only know how serious I am if I keep calm.

'My father was an honourable man. I loved him and I love his memory. But his honour is part of that memory. He wouldn't want me to make my entire

281

life a lie to protect it, Mr Millward. If we are going to discuss these things, we should do it cleanly, on their merits. What the Brazilian Government decides to do with its Salvador report is its own business.' She paused. 'Though I would have thought that issuing something so different so many years later might . . . well, might raise awkward questions.'

Millward scowled. Whatever else she was, she was smart. She had learned about politics.

'Very well,' he said, 'let us stick to the roles and the duties you have – because you have them. Your father, for Heaven's sake, knew all about that. He was a part of the Family, and that Family's greatest role is to make sure there's a new generation waiting who can pick up the baton. Not just someone with the right father and mother – someone who understands and accepts the responsibilities, someone who is prepared to be guided by those who know better. Your grandfather came too late to that understanding. Your uncle realized it just in time. But you, Ma'am, show no sign of comprehending what is necessary.'

His voice, as she expected, was growing softer again. The words came slowly with exaggerated emphasis.

'You cannot take your own decisions. They are too big. You cannot say the first thing that comes into your head. Everything has to be weighed and considered. You cannot gossip to friends if they blab to the press. You have made your marriage vows and you must stick to them. The Family, amongst other things, needs a generation beyond you. Providing that is the first, most serious business you have.'

The nail snapped back and broke. She got to her feet and looked down at him.

'So, Prime Minister, those are my responsibilities. What about your responsibilities to treat me as an equal? What about Sir Richard Baron's responsibilities? The Palace grapevine groans with stories about him. What about my dear husband's responsibilities? Keep thee only unto her. I think not. The world seems to think he's playing the field. The papers are full of it, leering and winking. Am I just to sit back and open my legs and think of England's future when he comes knocking? You lecture me, but the lecture isn't for me, it's for the people you chose and you control. Go and tell them how to behave.'

She had gone further than she intended, but probably not too far. At least he was on the back foot now, spluttering and pulling his face into a semblance of sincerity.

'Ma'am, you must not believe rumours. Sir Richard was a fine man. His collapse is tragic and any talk about it is vile. As for Prince Roman, the press will print anything that sells a few copies. Have you asked him yourself?'

'There are things, Prime Minister, that a woman senses without asking. Why don't you call him in for one of your fireside chats? Your people are always watching, but maybe they look in the wrong direction.'

'I'll talk to him if you wish,' he said. 'And will you do one thing for me in return?'

'That depends.'

'There are those in the Palace who confide in me who worry about your health, Ma'am. They see the pressures you are under – the strains of marriage, the difficulty they perceive in having a child. You have lost weight and begin, frankly, to look ill. If you care so much about the papers, you know that the gossip columns are speculating already. Poor Bess, Sad Bess.

'I think you should talk this through with someone who can help. Sir Lawrence Spens is an admirable man. He helped the late Queen with her post-natal depression and your mother with some of her earlier telephone problems. I would send my own wife and my children to him if I thought it was needed. Please, let me make an appointment with him for you. You need only talk to him. And perhaps you have too few people you can talk to.'

He thinks I'm a fruit cake, Bess thought. He genuinely thinks I've lost it. There was only one way to put that to rest.

'Right,' she said. 'There is no crisis and I feel fine. But if you need some super-shrink to tell you so, that would obviously be best. Fix me a time with him if you think that's helpful, and then we can all read the Spens Report.'

Davina Fincham-Scott was marrying Otto Reibnitz-Straub. Small romantic earthquake in SE21, not many excited. They had, after all, been living together for over three years now. Her connections to the Harewoods were three times removed, his links with the House of Battenberg more tenuous still. She ran a computer temping agency in Bishopsgate, he handled European securities for Grenfell and Sachs. She was twelve stone, he had a curiously long neck which he

284

was able to swivel without moving his shoulders (and said, cheerfully enough, gave him two seconds' advantage on the trading floor). Neither had access to a sufficiently stately home, so the reception was in an eighteenth-century pile that the London Borough of Southwark reserved for such occasions in a park beside the railway tracks.

A great inflatable marquee embraced the terrace and stretched out across the grass into the night. The chauffeurs stood by their cars in the sweep of the drive and chatted about traffic and football and holidays in Indonesia. A few bored stringers from the gossip columns sat on the front steps of the house and glared at the policemen who hovered above them. Another Daimler deposited another couple at the front door.

'Who's that?' said the *Mirror*, wiping his glasses.

'As I live and wonder,' said the *Mail*, 'it's young Nicky, your Duke of Clarence, out on the razzle for once in his miserable life.'

'And who's that with him?' said the *Standard*, scrambling to his feet and beginning to shout for his photographer.

'It's a woman,' said the *Mirror*. 'He's out with a woman.'

And not just any woman, thought Sammy Wittman, sidling into the laurel bushes and reaching for his mobile phone. The sparrow of a girl in the blue dress holding Nicky's hand – holding it and looking up at him – was the Infanta Elena. Serious royalty, serious stuff. His news desk answered on the second ring.

*

Toby Hunter usually stopped in London a couple of nights a week. There were economics seminars, book launches and television discussion shows requiring his attention. The Michnik Professor of Neo-Keynesian Studies at the University of Oxford was always in demand. He'd wear his brown cord jacket and one of his frayed pink shirts and run his fingers through the distraught mop of hair. 'The Japanese production figures aren't just worrying – they are potentially calamitous. This could be the Crash of 2004 all over again, but worse. Shanghai could be a wipe-out by Friday.' But, by Friday, Toby was usually back in his cottage in Studley, looking down on the spires snoozing far below and calculating his VAT returns.

Today, though, was Wednesday. The taping session for his new BBC series – *Hunter's Ten Great Global Calamities* – had overrun by a couple of hours. He'd have to stop at his club again, in one of the chaste garrets the Reform reserved for country members; and maybe he'd just catch the end of dinner.

But the kitchens had closed at ten, bequeathing only cold cuts in the Non-Smoking Room. He sat, the cuffs of his shirt trailing in the mayonnaise, on the front edge of a scuffed leather armchair, balancing a plate of tongue and wizened lettuce on his knee. The bulky man in a loud check waistcoat on the sofa opposite was silent and intent, peeling open his sandwiches and pulling away the fat from the ham with his fingers.

As Hunter reached for his carafe of Burgundy on the idiotically minute side-table, the salad slid on to the floor. 'Sod it,' he said, too loudly, and began mopping the carpet with his handkerchief. 'I should have had sandwiches too.'

'Not unless you're a cardboard-and-slime addict,' said the waistcoat man, licking mustard from the tips of his fingers. 'Better never than late here, if this is the best they can do.'

Hunter piled the debris together and shoved it in the shadow beneath the table.

'They're still doing coffee and biscuits in the hall,' he said. 'Can I offer you some? And maybe an Armagnac.'

The twenty-four-hour news screen in the corner by the bust of Asquith flicked silently from picture to picture as they walked out together into the great atrium. There was Nicky Windsor and his mother; and then Bess.

'I used to teach her for a couple of terms,' said Hunter, pausing for a second.

'You taught the Queen?'

'Economics at Oxford. It's what I do. Toby Hunter. You may have heard of me.'

'Are you the one the *Sunday Telegraph* calls Professor Catastrophe?' The grey man did not mention his own name. 'How did you find HM? They say she's a bundle of neuroses.'

'Not at all,' Hunter said. 'She's very bright. Did a terrific essay on the legacy of Milton Friedman and concluded there wasn't one. I gave her alpha triple-plus. She'd have got a first if they'd let her stay. A funny, intelligent girl, with eyes to knock your socks off.'

'There was that awful love tangle, wasn't there?

That must have shaken her up – on top of all the deaths in the family, I mean.'

'Of course. But she's very strong.'

Sir Lawrence Spens flicked a granule of brown sugar from his waistcoat and watched it fall among the umbrellas in the elephant's foot by the door.

Davidson and Swayne sat in the staff cafeteria. They had met, as if by accident, beside the woven basket of tea bags. He had chosen the Prince's Breakfast Blend; she had chosen Fine Assam. They were sharing a packet of Camilla's Crunchy Shortcake.

'As I understand it, the remit has widened,' he said, letting the biscuit dissolve on his tongue and swallowing lugubriously. 'We're asked to become more directly interventionist. Action not surveillance under Chapter Seven of the Code.'

'Not to authorized force?'

'Hardly. Category 3, sub-section E. Small physical contrivances designed to create specified psychological impressions and conclusions.'

'Can I get you some more hot water?'

The eggs floating on a swamp of spinach were hard and globular. She cut them in half and prodded disconsolately at the twin hillocks with a fork, then pushed the tray to the side of the desk. She felt hungry, but not hungry enough for such slop. The Palace kitchens had cost too much, Montgomery insisted. There had to be real financial efficiencies. But why had that meant sacking four of the six duty chefs? Those who remained cooked only the inedible and the indigest-

288

ible. She was too thin, she knew. She had only to examine the way her collar bones stood sharp against her shoulders to see how the flesh had shrunk. Her face had grown tight and angular, so that her eyes seemed to bulge from their sockets. But either she did not feel like food or, as this evening, the food appeared designed to repel any appetite. Eggs Florentine. Who needed the poisons of the Medicis when the dish of the day tasted so malignant?

There was a knock. Lady Margaret Swayne was not stopping. She stood in the doorway, coat draped over her left arm, right hand poised against the lintel.

'I'm sorry to disturb you, Ma'am. I saw your husband as I was leaving. He asked me whether you could join him in the Sculpture Gallery.'

'He didn't say why? No, never mind. Thank you, I'll go down in a second.'

She had not seen Roman for two days. He was always away in Swindon on business. His consortium's latest project, she'd read somewhere in the *Standard*, was the purchase and renovation of High-grove and the opening of its gardens. 'The house is redolent with romance,' he'd said. 'The public deserves the chance to savour its mysteries and to wander through the acres of vegetables in silence and remembrance, talking to the cabbages as those who once lived there did. We shall call it the Highgrove Experience.'

Why was he back? Why was she summoned to the presence? Never mind. The rain was beating against the windows of the room. The walk – any walk – would do her good. And the galleries were her favourite part of the Palace, linked by the thing she loved most, the great Nash Entrée Staircase, curling in a sweep of gold against the whiteness of the walls and the deep red of the carpeting. Hack colourings in a way. Where would the State Rooms have been without their endless white and gold? But this was different. If you stood at the bottom of the staircase and looked into the Sculpture Gallery, its pillars like teeth, the carpet a stretching tongue, then the gold of the balustrade was a giant's mouth opened wide, a cavern of excitements.

There was no one in sight. Overtime and dusk had swept the corridors and the halls clean.

She walked to the end of the Sculpture Gallery, searching amid the alcoves and the chill marble heads. 'Roman?' Perhaps he'd gone upstairs to the Picture Gallery. She climbed the flight on the left, calling out softly for him. Just as she reached the grey Grecian urn, six steps from the top, she heard a sound below and turned to look. He was there, standing in the shadows, hands clasped behind his back.

'Where were you? I've been looking everywhere.'

And then she staggered suddenly. Her foot seemed to catch the edge of the carpet and she found herself stumbling forward, head thumping against the gilded bronze as she fell, body rolling over and over, legs flailing. She knew nothing more.

'Bess! Bess!'

She sat suddenly straight. Alexandrovich had put a cushion at her back. Two off-duty footmen in mackintoshes, caught as they had unlocked their bikes from the rack in the side yard, hovered nervously.

'I'm all right,' she said. 'Only dizzy. Please give me a hand up.' But as she tried to stand there was a burn of pain in her right leg, just below the knee, and she sank back, wincing.

'I'd just lie there, Ma'am,' said the older footman, pulling at his ear. 'I reckon you've broken something. Giles, call the doctor and get an ambulance standing by.'

Alexandrovich pushed another cushion under her head. 'He's right, Bess. Don't move. Help will come.'

There was somebody standing on the stairs behind her. She could see his outline, but the leg was throbbing too viciously for concentration. She could feel the skin of the knee stretching as the swelling grew.

'No need,' said the voice on the stairs. 'I've made the calls already. The ambulance will be two minutes maximum.'

He came down and stood beside Alexandrovich. Massive body, narrow-set eyes. What was his name? She'd heard Fountain mention it once or twice. Donaldson? No, Davidson. She lost consciousness again.

Will Wittman had sworn violently when the call from the office came through. He'd been working all day on a colour mag piece. The Curse of the Romanovs. An inordinately extended caption of an article, a morass of dates and adjectives; not something you could toss off in five minutes. The screens made his head ache. The snatched sandwich five hours before was a distant memory. His stomach ached too. Luigi was actually, finally, physically heading his way with his signature starter – emu carpaccio, quails' eggs and diced mango – when the throb of the mobile in Wittman's pocket demanded his return.

'Why do you need me?' he'd snarled at the Night News Editor. 'It's a perfectly simple tale. Queen falls over on stairs. Queen breaks leg. Queen faces four weeks confined to barracks. No fears for life. No mounting anxiety. No lead story. It's a stick on page one and a pile of the usual crap from *Express* Doctor Michael on page seven. I can't offer anything extra but my by-line.'

'That's not what Bradshaw thinks,' said the nocturnal king of news dourly. 'He says clear down Ten and Eleven for fourth edition. He wants you and 1,200 words with pictures on The Unlucky Windsors. You know, death, disaster through the ages, and now this. Maybe we could call it The Curse of the House of Windsor?'

Will shuddered. But he began to write and, as the words came, so did a notion he was suddenly pleased with.

Have we been here before? Is history, in its savage way, repeating itself? That was the question which haunted Royal insiders last night as Young Queen Bess lay in agony, her leg snapped brutally in two after a supposedly accidental Palace tumble. For consider the elements of this new tragedy. A beautiful girl caught in a marriage to an older man who seems to see her less and less. A marked loss of weight through the past weeks that is the talk of Palace circles. And now a wounding and mysterious fall down a flight of stairs which, but for Samuel Parker's legendary gold balustrade, might have been far worse. Even, perhaps, fatal.

Those are the factors the Royal inner circle were weighing last night. It is, of course, too early to draw any conclusions – and everyone wishes Her Majesty the Godspeed of an early recovery. But, as one Windsor expert told me anxiously: 'We have been here before. Those of us with long memories are praying that this is mere coincidence.'

'Which expert is saying that, then?' said Sammy, throwing his coat on the floor and peering over his brother's shoulder.

'Why you, dear boy, if you want to be useful. After that, you can make the coffee.'

The clatter of tea cups on the trolley outside the door woke her. A weak sun peered through a gap in the thick yellow curtains. Bess moved and felt the fibreglass of the splint dig into her hip. Time? It was ten to eight. Place? Where the hell was she? The jigsaw puzzle of the night before reassembled in her mind. The Princess Stephanie Clinic on Millbank. They'd prodded and probed her for hours. Set the leg. Bathed the head. Scanned the brain. Doped the patient so that she drifted in a haze of aching anxiety.

She reached out and fumbled for a light switch. The room was large. Blue ceiling, grey walls, a long stretch of teak sideboard, a couple of Hockney prints, a small refrigerator set over the washbasin. Hospital? It was like any plush hotel room anywhere in the world. She smiled to herself. Queen rushed to Inter-continental suite in concussion drama: Room Service fails orange-juice test. Christ, her tongue felt worst of the lot, thick and sore and immobile. Had they put a splint on that, too? There was a small mirror on the table by the bed. Her right eyebrow had caught an edge on the balustrade. It was a livid mix of orange and green and black, beginning to drain down into her cheeks. The bridge of her nose was cut and plas-tered. The rest of her face was a sunken, oppressive white. She looked at the leg, hanging from a slim frame at the foot of the bed. Shambles! How on earth had she been so bloody stupid, so bloody clumsy? She'd just swung round when Roman called and looked down. And then, what? What, what, what?

'How are we today then, Your Majesty? Alive and kicking and starving, I shouldn't wonder.' The nurse was red-faced and stout, bosom pillowed in the pink linen of her uniform, the short body seeming to propel itself in hops from foot to foot. The plastic tag at her waist said 'Sheila'. The accent was broadest Aus-tralian.

'Now let's make you respectable for visitors, Your Highness. Get that hair cleaned up and that bruising sponged down, plus all the little toiletries we girls need. Do you want a pan first? Doctor will be here in twenty minutes.'

'Coffee,' Bess said desperately. 'I need coffee and juice.'

'Only spring water till further notice, I'm afraid, Ma'am. We've had no clearance on blood tests yet. We can't get the old jungle juices mixed up yet.'

Bess was pummelled and dabbed and heaved open like a drawer. Sheila talked constantly with every tug and push. She came from Perth. She was seeing the world. She had a sister in Vancouver and a brother in Manchester. 'But he's in jail, so I don't reckon he counts.' Still, there was a symmetry to life. She had to admit it. 'My family left the Old Country two hundred years back on a prison ship. Nice to see one of us repaying that debt, I always say. What goes around, comes around. And who'd have thought that one of us would get to look after the Queen one day? Have you used that bed pan or shall I bring it back later?'

Bess felt herself sinking into the sheets. She could request nothing that was granted. Her protests went unheard. She was an object to be tossed, turned, ignored. She could only lie there and let things happen. She had ceased, for the moment, to feel human. Her eyes closed to shut out the room, but the light shone irresistibly through the lids and seemed to turn the recesses of her mind a virulent yellow.

Dear Lilibet,
Mrs Bowler said you were in the Sick Bay with
mumps when I called. Flowers follow soonest.
Meanwhile, my love, keep taking the tablets. I'm
the world's worst patient. I went mad at Eton when
I did my ankle in at that wretched Wall Game. But
at least you get a little thinking time that way – a
chance to get the grey cells buzzing again. Would
you like a crossword? . . .

Leckie called Millward as a matter of routine. 'We've got the second bulletin. Do you want to clear it first?'

'Of course.'

'The consultants attending the Queen at the Princess Stephanie Clinic in London issued the following statement this morning. "Her Majesty spent a comfortable night after emergency treatment for a broken fibula in the right leg and possible concussion sustained in her fall. The leg has been re-set satisfactorily and there is no current reason why the Queen should not be mobile again in two to three weeks. A full recovery is anticipated. No initial evidence of any lasting effect from the head injuries has as yet been discovered. Nevertheless, the Queen's consultants consider it sensible for Her Majesty to remain in hospital for a few days whilst careful monitoring continues. Further bulletins will be issued in due course. At the moment, the Queen needs both rest and quiet. She may be visited tomorrow by close members of her family."'

Leckie could hear the suck of Millward's teeth down the line.

'Fine,' he said. 'But check with the hospital if we can add a few words to that last sentence.'

'Like?'

'Like "close members of her family and such other medical specialists as may be considered necessary".'

'OK. But what does that mean?'

'It means that Lawrie Spens might drop by for a low-key chat. And that perhaps the gentlemen of the press might be allowed to get wind of it somehow.'

*

Sheila from Perth had a best friend, Shona from Auckland. Shona was six feet tall, with a fuzz of ginger hair cut close to her scalp. Sheila did days, Shona did nights. Both of them, it seemed to Bess, were united in noisy bustle. She felt so damned tired as the bruises all over her body blossomed and flourished. She needed sleep; but sleep, amidst their banging entries and stock patter, was seldom allowed its turn. She would lie awake, apprehensive, waiting for the next flurry to burst through the door. Meanwhile the visitors had begun to trickle in, sitting on the Regency chairs at the foot of the bed and mouthing the same ritual inquiries.

'How are you, darling?' asked her mother, wriggling on the chair in a devout simulation of concern, the hem of her skirt twisting higher up the thigh with every squirm. 'Look, I've been shopping for you. The loveliest white nightie in Ghent lace that Night Owls could supply. When the world is your bedroom, I always say, then dress the way the world understands.'

Her husband, for reasons he did not explain, came with Fountain, who did not remove the tight coat of black lambswool which appeared to have been moulded to his body.

'My dear,' said Roman with an exaggerated sweep of his left hand. 'We have all been so worried about you.'

'Yes,' said Fountain. 'The whole of the Household sends its best wishes.'

Alexandrovich, as though before witnesses, planted an elaborate kiss on her forehead. Bess sank still deeper into the pillows. 'I see the roses came,' he said. They filled the corner of the room.

'Thank you,' she said.

But it was Nicky, the following morning, who made her freeze into rigidity so that the broken leg flapped from its ropes and pulleys, caught in a wind of change.

'Your brother, Ma'am,' said Sheila, redder than ever, hopping backwards as he came through the door. 'And the Princess Elena.'

He was wearing bottle-green cords and a thick blue sweater with shoulder pads, which dipped where his body ended, then spurted outwards again in a display of triumphant artifice. He was somehow different, hands thrust into pockets, hair slightly yellowed and swept back from his face. She gazed in amazement. He looked like a man of action. Indeed, he looked manly. He clasped an arm around the sparrow by his side and walked, almost swaggered, across the room.

'Hi sis,' he said. 'My fiancée and I thought it would be good to drop by.'

Bess sat up straight and clasped her hands beneath her breasts. 'Well, congratulations,' she said. It wasn't real. He kept hugging Elena, the fingers massaging her flesh. 'This is all very sudden.'

He perched on the bed and began to chatter away. To a script, she thought. He'd memorized the entire spiel: to be delivered *fortissimo*.

'Well, you know how good relations with Elena's family are. They go back generations. With a different stroke of luck it could have been you. But I felt, and Mother felt, that it wasn't good for me to be the odd one out playing the bachelor prince for ever. We've had enough of those in the family and it tends to attract a lot of stupid talk. And Elena was over here on a language course in Eaton Square and, one way or another, we met at a friend's house, and things sort of developed from there. Didn't they, love?'

He squeezed her again so that the breath hissed from her.

'Si,' she said cautiously. 'Things they developed.'

Bess caught Elena's eyes for a second. They were dark and, in the recesses, deeply sad. Her lips were drawn into a bubbling smile, but a string from far away was tugging at the corners of them. The eyes were a cry for help.

'I'm sorry,' Bess said. 'I was just going to call for a nurse to get me to the loo. But Elena will only need to pass things over. Would you mind just giving us a moment, Nicky?'

'A what? Oh, right.'

'Forget that,' she said as the door closed. 'Lena, you do know, don't you? I love my brother, but he's not the marrying kind. What on earth is this all about?'

The sparrow took her hand. 'It is about what it is about, Bess. Please don't ask me any more questions. It is all settled by those who settle these things. It is all arranged.'

There was a single easy chair by the window over-looking the Embankment and a low, round coffee table with magazines scattered over it. Spens sat down and crossed his legs. Bess propped herself on a single crutch and stood watching him extract a bewilderment of coloured files from his briefcase. He chose the red, white and blue ones.

'Needless to say, your colleagues at the Palace are greatly perturbed, Ma'am.'

'Why? I don't see why. I fell. I broke something. I'm fine now. It happens.'

'Ma'am, nothing just happens. There is always a reason. Not, maybe, for the accident itself, but for your state of mind at the time. You were distracted. You fell. What I want to get to the bottom of is the reason for that distraction. You're sleeping?'

'When I can. Nurses are always barging in, as though it was their job to keep me awake.'

'So you're not sleeping. How was it before the fall?'

'Much the same, I suppose. I'd go to bed feeling pretty exhausted, then wake about three and lie there wondering.'

Spens drew a question mark in the air with his pencil.

'Sorry. Wondering how I can survive in this job. Wondering where my husband is and who he's with. Wondering what our dear Prime Minister has planned for me next.'

She was going too far. She wasn't on home ground, able to retreat behind her desk and ring for Swayne or Cross. She was in hospital, trapped against the edge of the bed, unable to run or hide.

'I don't understand what you mean. Your husband loves you. The Prime Minister is there to protect you. They are both devoted to your success. Why should you think otherwise?'

Her leg was aching again and the blood was gathering in her foot so that it was suddenly tingling. She slumped backwards on the desk. 'This is between us, isn't it? I mean, you're bound by oaths and things?'

'Naturally.'

And so it began to pour out. The way her father still seemed to be there, part of her life. The misery of Oxford and the fear of the newspapers. How Millward bullied and threatened her. How Nicky and Selene and Roman were . . . but no, that was too much. She was burbling, letting it all spill out in a river of relief that there was somebody here to listen. No, she had to keep something back.

'I see.' Spens looked at his watch. 'They said no more than half an hour. This isn't a proper session and we mustn't tire you out. I'll get them to prescribe something stronger for the nights and I'd allow no more visitors for a while. You're not altogether well, Your Majesty. Of course we can all understand why. Too many physical shocks, too many emotional shocks. Anyone in the world might fall prey to delusions after that. But you do need rest, complete rest. And you will need intensive counselling.'

She lay there when he had gone, staring at the ceiling. The madness of Queen Elizabeth the Third? Shona brought her supper. A slop of grey mince and cabbage with a charred vol-au-vent floating on the surface. Bess pushed it slowly to one side and picked up the tablets Spens had had delivered. Suck one, swallow one. Then wait for the night to come.

*

'We called the desk,' Caroline said. 'No visitors until further notice. The Day Sister wouldn't add much. She thought we might be press people trying it on. But I think, in the end, she knew that wasn't true. Bess needs continual monitoring for concussion. Her face is a mass of bruising, so she isn't fit to be seen anywhere. She is, not surprisingly, pretty shocked and tired. They're keeping her in hospital for a few more days so she gets total rest. That's all we or anyone else needs to know. If we send her cards or books, the Sister will make sure she gets them.'

'I still think she'd like to see us,' said Emma, swirling a moody spoon in the mug of coffee. 'If brothers and husbands and mothers get a piece of the action, people who love her ought to have at least five minutes to cheer her up. And what was that Spens man doing in there for half an hour with all the hacks hopping up and down in the street? So he's a shrink. So what? Bess is the toughest, most sensible nut I've ever met. She needs examining like a hole in the head.'

'Good line. Watch for it in print any time soon.' Sammy was sitting cross-legged on the carpet in Emma's flat. They were his best chance of an exclusive out of all this. He had to keep dropping in. They probably didn't trust him, and they were probably right, but he was becoming part of the furniture. 'The word on the street is that there's more to this than a simple fall. Did she jump or was she pushed? Put Spens into that equation and the jumpers have it. It's only a matter of time before somebody writes that. Moffatt from the *Mail* says he knows it for a fact. His lobby man asked the question directly this morning and got fobbed off with a pile of waffle about tests and anxieties. Millward isn't exactly going out of his way to choke it off.

'And meanwhile, of course, there's Nicky. I mean, what a shitty time to come out with the good news. Your sister's lying in hospital with the curtains drawn and suddenly the Prince of Poofs has whipped six stone of Bourbon princess out of the closet and is parading his miraculously altered state for every camera in town. What the hell is that little melodrama about?'

Emma opened a new packet of chocolate biscuits. 'They were cheering him on television. There was a line of old ducks on the pavement outside the clinic waving flags when they came out. Did you see his jaw? It dropped so far it got tangled in his shirt collar. Sweet twenty-two and never been cheered before.'

Sammy walked over to the window and looked out at the night and the silent street and the white houses bathed in moonlight. The lights at the corner were still broken. The black car from last time was still parked beneath it. He thought he saw the glow of a cigarette from the front seat.

'Put your weight on the left crutch, your M, and swing your leg. Beautiful. Take it slow. Now right and pause and lean and swing. That's great. It's just technique. You'll be beetling off down the corridors in no time.'

Bess felt no pain, only the continuing tingle in her feet of being upright again as Sheila and Shona propelled her round the room. But she was weak. She looked down at the arm that hung loose as she grappled with the crutch. It was thin, the bones of the elbow defined. She paused by the mirror on the wall as she edged past and saw a face she barely recognized, yellow and distended as the bruisings staged their last stand. Whatever became of me? she thought. Where have I gone to?

The light on Millward's desk had a small green shade which left his face in shadow. He was flicking his finger across a console of computer keys, eyes down, mouth silently reciting the words from the screen on the right. 'Unemployment, 1.6 per cent below the OECD average. Growth, 2.4 per cent, 0.2 above average. Investment, back to the record levels of ten years ago. How, my friends, do you define success except by the statistics which prove it real and lasting?'

Leckie sat silently in the beige armchair by the fireplace, waiting his turn.

Millward gave a short sigh of satisfaction and hit Execute. 'Sorry,' he said, 'I was running late anyway and Washington wanted another jaw about the summit. Is the President sure about Congress? Are pigs sure about flying?

'So. We just need ten minutes to make sure our tackle's in order. This is complicated business, Robin, and we can't leave it to Fountain and the flakes. She can't stay in the clinic much longer. No problem. We'll cart her off to Sandringham again and pull down the blinds. But we have got to get the message right. Concern, but not alarm. Care, but not intensive. Rest, but nothing more for the moment. She's got to be still in play, yet just beginning to slip towards the edges.

Absolutely no appearances and no sightings. Gone and very slowly forgotten while Nicky plays the smitten prince and gallantly steps into the breach. There mustn't be anything sudden about this. We need people to get bored about Bess, without any spurts of headlines. Slow and steady while he who may have to be King gets his profile tuned and we see whether he's biddable. It isn't necessary to decide things now. This whole scenario's about options, not decisions.'

Leckie perched on the arm of the chair and looked at the man in the shadows. 'That's what's so tricky,' he said. 'We've a game and plan, but we don't know how we want it to end. Is there a King or a Queen at last knockings? You've improvised brilliantly so far. Bess can't be trusted. She doesn't obey orders. She's a disaster waiting to happen. There has to be an alternative and he hates her, so that's easy. When she falls over, opportunity knocks. You believe she's not quite stable. Spens comes back with a report stuffed with her delusions. But she is the Queen and we can't just wipe her away, shouting the magic word Abdication. This is the most serious gambit we've ever been involved with. It's people's lives. We need to know how we want it to come out.'

'Robin, Robin, Robin.' Millward's voice had that trickle of treacle to the vowels which Leckie had come to know too well. The thicker the treacle, the deeper the calculations. 'Robin, we both recognize what all this is about. We've been through it together. I'm here to help the Royal Family survive. The only way to do that is to keep them under our control. They have to take orders: instantly, silently, without questions.

They are objects in the Prime Minister's Department. They put their trust in us. We save them. That is the essential bargain through nearly four decades. Remember when they were taking their own decisions and saying the first things that came into their heads? Then, they were always heading straight for the cliff. They talked about fuzzy-wuzzies on Commonwealth tours. They lectured us on caring societies while they treated each other like dirt. They swapped beds before breakfast. They were a disaster actually happening.

'Downing Street didn't get involved because we wanted to, Robin. We found ourselves dragged into the mire. We had to take over their budgets and write their speeches. They couldn't cope any longer, so we had to cope for them. It was our duty; and, my God, it was one we could have done without. And when the King went phut on my watch, Robin, it was my duty, our duty. You and I, doing our duty. Will Bess ever take orders? I hope so, naturally. But she is reckless and Spens thinks she can probably only get worse; in which case we have to find another way. Our chum the Duke of Clarence is the alternative from hell and his bloody mother lights the fires down below: but they have reason to take orders because they can see what's in their interest. Perhaps they know that we're only doing it for the good of the nation.'

The vowels came served on a runcible spoon. Leckie was being spun himself; it took one to know one, he thought. There was a hidden agenda beyond the hidden agenda, floating down there somewhere just out of sight. But did that matter? It was beginning to matter through his long, wakeful nights. Sidelining Colonel Baxter or pushing the lemmings of the Lobby over the wrong edge was one thing; this was something else.

'Got it,' he said slowly, standing up. 'I'll push on with arranging a schedule for Young Love that will make Cupid weep. Charity balls, maternity wards, hands held behind the laurel bushes. Let the trumpets of joy sound forth, and all that crap. And meanwhile we'll store the girl in a deep freeze somewhere and see what comes around. What do you think? Weekly policy reviews? Fortnightly? The board will need to keep on top of this one.'

'Weekly until she's safely stowed away,' said Millward. 'Then monthly will do.'

The vowels had flattened again.

The final press conference at the clinic was set for noon. The doctors would say that the Queen could go home to continue her progress. Leckie would say that, for the moment, Sandringham was home. He'd plead for the peace and quiet Her Majesty needed after her traumatic ordeal. 'Those who wish her well again, gentlemen, will do well to leave her alone.' No pictures. She would be loaded into an ambulance at the back. No quotes. Except that perhaps, Leckie thought, there ought to be a few words he could throw to the hounds. You could wrap up this stuff so tight that the suicide theories might break cover at last: and that was not part of the script yet.

It was what, 11.15? Chill, but with clear blue skies. He had been at his desk from six, the ritual call at the gym forgone in the greater cause of fixing Nicky's weekend at Cowes. He'd stroll down to the hospital and maybe see if he could get thirty seconds with Bess to get a quote organized.

Leckie turned the collar of his worsted up high round his face as he ducked out of the side of the Palace and slipped through the line of coaches into the anonymity of Buckingham Palace Road. He walked faster than he'd intended, head bent forward, weaving through the side streets of Victoria into Pimlico. There was a wind which seemed to come straight down the Thames, then buffet against the tower blocks of Millbank and turn north in a swirl where the buildings grew too close for the sun to shine. The gusts pursued him, pummelling his back, and he hunched lower. At least the cold was clearing his head. He had lain awake through the night again, replaying the Millward meeting, wondering whether things had not gone too far. What was it the old Labour General Secretary had said to his troops years before, the month Leckie arrived in London and the Party coffers ran temporarily dry? 'I'm afraid we'll have to let twenty of you go. Pack your bags, clear your desks, and leave in an orderly fashion. No cash, no pay, no jobs. It's best to be on your way quickly rather than prolonging the agony. That way, brothers, you stand the best chance of moving on. And I believe that, in a year, you'll thank me.'

Thanks, but no thanks. Would anybody, a year on, thank Leckie for the lies piled upon lies? Would anybody, a year ago, have seen the Queen ferried out of harm's way while rumours of her mental breakdown buzzed? There was one answer to that, of course. Millward would thank him. He was there to do Millward's bidding, for reasons clearly explained and always accepted.

He was near the end of Horseferry Road now, weaving round the back of MI5 and glancing into the windows of the sandwich bars where the spooks took their elevenses. Was that Davidson sitting behind the coffee machine, mouth clamped on an innocent doughnut? A young woman in a maroon coat pushing a pram veered across Leckie's path and he stopped for a second on the kerb. Why was Millward not telling him everything? He knew the signs; he had seen them used on others. The finagling of Parliament; the steering of the Cabinet; the sweetness that swilled when donors and cheque books arrived. He'd always rather savoured the spectacle of deceit, because he was in on the sport. But now he wasn't so sure. Was he still in, or somehow on the way out?

'I'm authorized.' He showed his security cards at the desk. 'I called ahead. Dr Vengkatorani said I could have a few minutes with her.'

The Nigerian nurse with the imposing backside nodded curtly and pressed a bell. 'Sheila will come down and take you in. She'll stay with you while you talk. We're under instructions not to let Her Majesty get excited and we think she needs constant reassurance. Sheila is always there when she wakes up.'

She must be worse than he'd thought.

'Is she sedated?'

'Only painkillers. But they make her a little drowsy.' The red-faced Australian battle tank brooked no arguments. 'The Queen's a little darling. Very quiet and modest and polite. Not at all regal, if you understand me. We'll all be sorry to see her go, but it's for the best now. She just seems to have got so low the last couple of days. She hasn't seen anybody but Mr Spens, and he says to make sure nothing disturbs her – especially not that family of hers and that husband. Her blood pressure was right up after they'd visited.'

'I won't take a second,' Leckie said. 'She doesn't really need to say anything, just nod.'

Still, he wasn't prepared when the door opened. The curtains were half drawn so that the lamp by the bed caught her head in a halo of light. She was sitting upright, pushed forward by a pile of pillows. She had somehow shrunk since he'd seen her last, her body lost in a smock of white linen knotted at the shoulder. The hair was tied back and the expanse of the forehead made the eyes seem to protrude in a perplexed, anxious stare.

'Mr Leckie,' she said. 'This is an unexpected honour.'

'I'm terribly sorry to disturb you, Ma'am. It's only very brief. As you know, they'll be taking you to Sandringham this evening. We'll be holding a brief press conference downstairs in half an hour. I just wanted to be able to say that I'd seen you and to be able to give some sort of direct quote you agreed with. Perhaps that you're recovering steadily and are very grateful for all the public concern and messages? It can be quite short.'

A pillow slipped from behind her with a soft plop and she leaned back a little so that he could see all her face. The green of her eyes was suddenly almost translucent, and he thought – who could say? but he thought – that the lips curled briefly into a smile.

'I'd like to be a bit more interesting than that. Say I took a stupid tumble, and it's not just the leg that hurts but that I'm covered in bruises. Say I look a real fright and that no one in their right mind would want to see me like this. But say thanks to everyone who deserves to be thanked, and that I intend to write to them all personally while I'm locked up in Norfolk. And say that I'm thinking of those who are thinking of me.'

Leckie had taken notes. 'Of course I'll do all that, Ma'am. I'm glad that you're stronger than . . . well, stronger than the bulletins say.'

'I'm all right,' she said. 'The body is mending OK. You should have seen the bruises forty-eight hours ago. I can hobble round and I'll soon be skipping. No, the trouble, Mr Leckie, is that grave men with grave faces keep telling me I'm losing my mind. Do you think that's true? Is that what you'll be whispering when you get out of here?'

He found himself stammering. 'No, of course not. No, of course, no.'

Sheila coughed and heaved herself out of the chair. 'That's enough, Sir. She has got to be calm.'

Bess's eyes followed him in retreat. 'If you don't think it, then, say that too. Say I'm laughing and reading – and that I want to see my friends. Say I'm perfectly normal.'

He was muttering. 'I will. Naturally I will.'

Naturally, though, he knew that he wouldn't. It

wasn't part of the scenario. But what did he think in his heart?

That was the damnable thing. He thought she was battered and drugged and lonely. But he thought she was normal too.

Chapter Eighteen

'When is it official, though? Poor Nicky's never been exactly patient. He's enjoying himself for the moment, I know, being the centre of attraction and all. But he's my son, and he'll soon get bored if there's no progress on the big things like the Spanish State visit. I mean, is Bess going to take a back seat, or isn't she? She's been up at Sandringham for weeks now with Spens and the quacks digging a trench to her door, but you never hear whether she's better or worse. The last time I went up to see her, she was perfectly frightful to me. Just like always, so I thought she must be improving. But, when I told Nicky that, he got into one of his usual rages. Breaking things, swearing. He kept saying he'd made all the sacrifices and now he wanted his reward. Sod Fountain, he said. Sod them all. If I'm going to be King and get married and keep on acting for the rest of my life, then I want to begin the rest of my life.'

'Can't you give him some pills or something? The powers that be won't be rushed. Millward says it's got to be at least six months. The public mustn't get the feeling it's being force fed. Tell him we have to fade Bess out so gradually that there's a point where suddenly he's the man and nobody asks awkward questions.'

'But there are so many awkward questions. When is he supposed to marry that little Spaniard? She keeps going back to Madrid most weeks and you can tell, absolutely tell, that she can't stand the sight of him. And vice versa, of course. They'll only keep it going if they're sure that there's a payback time.'

'Look. I'll get Number Ten to have a word with the Zarzuela Palace. Maybe we could confirm a visit a couple of notches down – for Wimbledon and things – which Nicky can play host at. We could scrap the State stuff for a while and have another go at the romance. The Spanish will understand that. They've had their own troubles down the years. Leckie's got this new line about the Infanta as his bird of paradise.'

'He used to have a bird once when he was tiny, a budgie we called Fergie.'

'So what's that got to do with anything?'

'Nothing, except it died. He stuffed its head into a pillow, then pulled all its feathers out one by one. I had to simply feed the maids cash to keep it quiet.'

'Oh.'

'Are we going to get together then? I've got to be in Bond Street by three, and you feel terribly limp, my love. Shall I get you a magic tablet from the bathroom cupboard?'

'I think I'd rather have a cup of tea.'

Dear Lilibet,
Do you get enough time to yourself? It's a difficult old balance. Sometimes, as this week, I'm chasing

*my tail from Cranley to Gib, with a side flip to
Majorca thrown in. Never a moment alone, and
that's vital. Otherwise you just feel battered. But,
all the same, too much solitude can shiver your
timbers. I remember my father, long ago, walking
the Highlands on his own, kilt flapping, head down.
He said he needed the peace of it all, but somehow
he seemed spaced out when he came down the
corrie. Little and often, my dear: that's the magic
ticket . . .*

They had wanted to move her on to Balmoral. It was
further away and the screens of spruce and pine were
thicker; out of sight, out of mind. But she had come
to hate the grim hulk with its mountain of marbled
memories and she pleaded with Spens to change
their minds. 'Why can't I go to Wymeswold for a
week or two? It's small and it's private and it's
full of happy times.' He had his Wimpole Street practice to think of, and Scotland was going to be a drag
anyway. 'Right,' he said, 'but just books and music
and total rest. Swayne will make sure you get it. I
shall be free over the weekend. Perhaps a Saturday
and a Sunday session? We need to talk more about
your mother.'

Her face clouded, as he knew it would. When they
talked of her father, there was a growing animation.
Once the sadness diffused she would smile and laugh
to herself: the bond was as strong as any he could
remember. But the rest of them – the mother, the
brother – were a total pain. She shrank into silence.
It was as though he could pull a wire merely by

mentioning them, and tip her back into despair. Saturday would be desperation day.

'What do you want me to find?' he'd asked Millward the evening before. 'How is this supposed to play out? I am not a free man. I have my obligations. I can't find things that I don't believe are there.'

'Or possibly there?'

'Psychiatry is the art of the possibly.'

'Look, the girl is distraught. She's skinny and sleepless. She doesn't eat. She may have made a stupid attempt to do away with herself. When you talk to her, she tells you that her father appears to her in constant hallucinations. She rejects her mother, hates her brother and makes all kinds of wild allegations about her husband. As for the rest of us, the people with real obligations, she treats us as enemies. Your reports are inches thick already. The Queen is a basket case. She needs sedation and isolation. It's the best for all of us.'

'Well, possibly,' Spens said, rising to his feet. 'But the more we talk, the more I question that judgement. Selene and Nicky are pretty odd, too. The cuttings on Alexandrovich aren't exactly flattering. There may be a good case for changing the whole approach to this treatment. Even getting a second opinion.'

Abruptly, Millward swung on his heel. 'There is no call for any of that. Your client here isn't some scatty actress who thinks she needs a nose job after another flimsy marriage, so that you pass her round your chums in a blizzard of cheques. Your client is the State and your patient is the Queen. The Queen needs your help and the State needs your unquestion-

316

ing loyalty. We both know what has to be done. Do it, or . . .'

He didn't trouble to finish the sentence. Spens had not always been great and good. Who recalled the time, a quarter of a century ago in Exeter, when the fourteen-year-old daughter of the Labour agent had made all those allegations against him? The touchings and the fondlings and the tear-stained shriekings? A terrible misunderstanding, of course. Nothing to get the authorities involved with. His word against a hysterical child. But such matters, he knew, were never completely forgotten. There was always a note, always a file. Who remembered? The State, as Millward would say, has ways of remembering.

'I'll just drive up for the day and check,' Leckie had said. 'The press keep asking about her. They say their readers are interested, the postbags keep pouring in. Either I stonewall, in which case they camp on her doorstep, or I give them some first-hand fodder.'

Fountain had merely grunted. 'Do what you think is necessary. But if you ask me, I'd just tell the hounds to bugger off. We don't want stories about her. We want nothing said and nothing written.'

'Well, it's always a balance. At the moment we're turning her into a mystery woman with a mystery illness.'

He had phoned Swayne to say he was coming. Ten minutes later she called back. The Queen says, could you bring up the things in the second drawer of her dressing table? Postcards and rings and presents her father gave her? She says she misses them.

He cleared the drawer in a moment and shovelled the contents into his briefcase.

The drive lifted his spirits. He began at six, half an hour before the worst of the rush, and was crossing Charnwood Forest by eight, watching the sun touch the outcrops of granite and the sheep in the fields below trot by the hedges. He stopped at a pub in Woodhouse Eaves and ordered the biggest breakfast they had, wiping the last of the egg from the thick white plate with the third round of fried bread and shouting for a second mug of milky coffee. This wasn't the Royal territory he was used to: the manicured acres, the lushness of fortunes spent and the drifting stench of decay. This was a smaller, human place. Since his marriage had folded, since the move into the tiny service apartment in the East Wing, there had been nothing human to his day. Rise, wash, work, eat, wash, sleep; then wake at three and lie staring at the high ceiling and listening to the buzz of traffic around Hyde Park Corner. He had not loved Pam, but she had been a presence for him, a warmth of flesh to hold in the night. Now it was his life, a cold life, on hold through the board meetings and the press conferences.

Leckie began singing to himself as he wove through the narrow lanes of the Wolds. He smiled when the two policemen patrolling the village street pulled him over and jabbed his identity cards into the computers that dangled from their belts.

'Just park beside the pub, Sir. It's all arranged and it causes less talk. Then the gate is the blue one, second on the left.'

Swayne was leaning against the open door of the

cottage, arms folded in front of her, jaw set in its familiar jut. 'She's in her room. Up the stairs and it's the one at the back of the house with the windows looking over the farm. I don't need to do all the doctor's instructions again, do I? She's been unnaturally cheerful since she got here. I wouldn't like it to disappear.'

He knocked. Bess was wearing a white shirt buttoned high at the neck and a pair of scarlet slacks in some kind of sail-cloth. Her hair had grown and it fell lushly to her shoulders. She was still bone thin, but the gauntness was gone. A tray of coffee and rolls lay on the small table beside her desk. The plate was scattered with crumbs and a knife smeared with raspberry jam had dropped beside the milk jug. She was smiling.

'Good morning, Mr Leckie. Any visitor is better than no visitor.'

Hostile? Mocking? He had no idea.

'Do you want to go for a walk? There's a back way into the fields and a footpath along the stream in that little valley. I'm not allowed out without a bodyguard, but I'm sure you'll do.'

She wrapped a blue cotton sweater around her shoulders and, with the lightest touch of her fingers, steered him down the stairs and out through the kitchen. The crutch was gone. She carried a slim cane which she barely leant on.

'You're looking better, Ma'am.'

Was he supposed to be pleased about that? Would Millward beam when he reported back?

'I am better,' she said. 'It's being here, away from

the weight of everything. And I've decided I'm not going mad.'

He walked slowly beside her, trying not to hurry.

'Are you here for another of your famous bulletins? Her Majesty spent a peaceful night and took her pink pills as ordered?'

'That sort of thing. We can decide what to say before I leave.'

They reached the bank of the stream and he looked into the water. To his amazement, it was teeming with tiny fish; he caught hold of a tree with his hand and lowered himself close to the surface, peering. 'I used to do a lot of fishing when I was a lad. It was what my dad did to get away from my mum. "Six hours on the river if you want, my boy, and don't say a bloody word or you'll scare them off." I used to call it the Bonds of Silence.'

She laughed, the sound gurgling from her throat. 'I'm afraid we did more of the hunting and shooting. Bang bang you're another dead grouse being slobbered over by some smelly labrador. I liked the walks, but I couldn't stand the sport. Or the company. Maybe if they'd had your Bond of Silence it might have been bearable.'

She leant over the water beside him. 'What are they? Minnows, tiddlers? A lifetime in Harrods Food Hall hasn't equipped me for this.'

'That sort of thing,' he said, taking her arm so that she could crouch beside him. 'If we were somewhere a bit more exotic, like one of the Swiss lakes, they'd be scooping all this stuff up in a net and chucking it into the deep fryer for breakfast.'

'I don't believe you,' she said severely. 'You can spin me any yarn you like about your Ribble or your Ouse, but we used to spend holidays in Switzerland. My mother had an aunt with a house at Vevey which she kindly donated from time to time to keep the old coffers stocked. Sort of Guildford Sur Lac. We'd go there a lot if my father was overseas again on some duty tour, which he usually was. Nicky and I would wander down through the vines to the water's edge and sit there while Selene . . . while Selene did whatever she did with the friends who came to stay. But I never, ever saw anyone frying minnows on the jetty where the steamers came in. We never had anything smaller than kilos of perch.'

He glanced at her, trying to make it seem like an accident. She was prattling like – well, like what she was, a girl with a life to live. Take away the marble halls and the miles of carpeting and the bloody military bands, and she was something quite different.

'Tell me more about yourself,' she said.

They walked a little further, beyond the clump of willows and reeds where the first field ended, and he chatted about his family: the father who'd started to drink when the computer-chip factory went bust in the last recession but three and died much too soon when his car hit a lorry on the Pontefract road; the mother who'd never got over it and almost willed her own death three years later. 'I'm not sure she could stand living with him, but she couldn't stand living without him.' The sister with two children and a husband in accountancy who lived in Altrincham and voted Tory. 'We're not what you'd call a nuclear family. Or at least, if we are, the bomb's gone off.'

There was a muddy puddle by the stile into the next field. She picked her way gingerly around it, but the slope up the bank was steep and she put her weight on the cane. It slid on the slime and she staggered back three paces, wincing as her leg took the strain. 'Damn. Almost a disaster.'

'I think that's enough,' he said. 'I don't want to go back telling the hacks that Her Majesty was last seen face-down in the mud clutching her knee.'

She pulled a metre or so away from him as they walked back and her eyes, when he caught them, had become watchful again. 'Bulletins,' she said. 'I almost forgot for a while that you're Millward's man on official business. If I ask you now what his game is, what he proposes to do about me, you'll just turn blank and formal and I'll see you taking notes in your head. Tell me, Mr Leckie, what am I supposed to do? Am I fit to return to civilized society and take orders? Or am I parked here for ever until I'm just a distant memory and the show has moved on? I am a prisoner, you know. I can't phone out or talk to my friends. Mr Spens arrives twice a week and looks solemn and tells me he'll try and go deeper next time. Mostly I feel like shit. When I wake in the night, I wonder whether I'm really lost, another of the Windsors who vanish from the history books and aren't heard from again. Poor Bess. Isn't she living in a home somewhere? But then I hear your boss's voice and the way his vowels turn to honey when he's talking to me, and I think I'm sane enough considering, and that I'm part of something so big that I can't understand.'

'Treacle,' said Leckie, without thinking. 'Treacle, not honey.'

Swayne was sitting on the bench under the apple tree when they returned. 'That was over thirty minutes,' she said. 'Too long for Your Majesty to be on her feet yet.'

'Sorry,' said Leckie in his softest burr. 'We weren't hurrying because we thought the exercise was doing her good.'

Swayne scowled. 'Mr Spens and Dr Badger let me be the judge of that. Little and not too often, they say.'

Bess had had enough of their sparrings. 'Mr Leckie is here on duty, Lady Margaret. Could we have some coffee in the living room and then we can do our draftings and let him be on his way. Any man who serves Sir Edgar Fountain and Mr Millward won't have time to sit around with us all morning.'

The room was chintz wall to wall, a suffocation of pinks and whites and elaborate floral patterns. Leckie's nose wrinkled instinctively.

'I know,' she said. 'It's like your Auntie Irene's or something. Absolutely terrible, and I'm going to change it the moment I can. But when you're stuck with so much bloody good taste everywhere else, at least it makes a change.'

The bulletin took two minutes. HM was making excellent progress. The leg was almost as good as new. No permanent impediment expected. Holiday and rest doing immense good.

'Won't they think that much too cheery?' she asked.

'The next question will be when I'm coming back to London, and I'm not sure that's on anyone's preferred agenda.'

'Well, of course I'll have to check with the stethoscopes. And my masters, I suppose. But the point of coming is really to have a few direct bits of observation to pad out the briefings with — and you are much, much better.'

'Did you bring the things I asked for?'

His bag was in the hall by the front door. He fetched it and emptied a pile of letters and cards and boxes on to the table behind the coffee tray. 'All present and correct, Ma'am. There was nothing left in the drawer when I'd finished.'

She picked her way through the debris. 'I was sorry to bother you. It looks an awful old pile of junk, but I hate being separated from it. Things my father gave me.'

She showed him the last letters from Brazil and the diamond ring he'd given her when she passed her A-levels and the card with kisses he'd left on her dressing table backstage at Roedean after *The Lark*. 'To the Maid who lights my way.'

Bess's eyes seemed to water for a moment. 'He was awfully sentimental sometimes. So soppy I had to keep it from my gang. But you can see he cared.'

'And what's this?' said Leckie, picking up the slim box of red leather.

'His palm-top. The one he carried everywhere and sent me messages on when there was no other way. Poor Daddy wasn't much of a hand when it came to using it. All fingers and thumbs. He liked pen and paper best. But they picked it out of the wreckage and sent it home to me.'

'Is it broken?'

'Stopped short, never to go again.' She opened the keyboard and showed him the lifeless screen. 'Just a relic.'

He was on his way in two minutes, pausing at the gate and seeing her and Swayne standing side by side. For no reason he could precisely pin down he sang to himself on the road back to London. He thought that he might sleep tonight.

Bess went back to her room and sat for a while in the window, looking out over the meadow and the stream. Then she rummaged in the lining of the suitcase under the bed. Got them. The two tiny batteries she'd found in the kitchen cupboard. Were they live? The screen on the palm-top came up clear and strong. She was back in touch again. She could talk to the world.

'Her Majesty had improved a little?'

Fountain pursed his lips. It was as though Wall Street had finished ten points higher after a lethargic day of trading.

'Yes, pretty bubbly and maybe a kilo heavier,' Leckie said. 'She'll be wanting her throne back next.'

Fountain growled under his breath. 'You better talk to the chairman. I don't think gold coaches down the Mall are exactly top of his hit list.'

Robin Leckie, of course, knew what the message had to be. Thirty minutes on, he was delivering to the

Palace press corps in the best monotone he could contrive.

'I saw her this morning. She is in reasonable spirits but she still needs recovery time, and her doctors are reluctant to set any dates at this stage. She has thrown away the crutches, though. We are probably talking weeks rather than months, but months it could still be.'

Will Wittman leaned back in his chair. 'What about the Spanish visit, Robin? Our readers are pretty excited about that, seeing the Infanta and her dad in their full kit. Will Nicky be the one still doing the honours then? It's a decent angle if he is. Prospective son-in-law shows fiancée's dad round his stately piles. My readers could identify with that.'

Leckie had his text in his pocket. 'The King and Queen of Spain, together with their daughter, Elena, have decided that a full State visit at this juncture may not be wholly appropriate, given Her Majesty's indisposition. But they do intend to arrive on the dates announced and conduct a programme of engagements involving the Spanish community here in London.'

'And the one on the Centre Court too?'

'Undoubtedly. The royal host for their stay will be HRH The Duke of Clarence, assisted by his mother. It is possible, but not anticipated, that the Queen will be able to travel back to meet them during their stay.'

'Does Bess want to be there, Robin? Does she approve of this match? And will they be announcing a time and place while they're here? People are already saying Nicky will never go through with it, you know.'

'Gentlemen, ladies.' Leckie wished he was back in

Downing Street. At least the Lobby never asked such crass questions. They fed him second serves far short of a length – and he dispatched them in a blur of muscle. 'Gentlemen. The Queen is a personal acquaintance of the Infanta Elena. They have stayed together on holiday in Spain. She is, without question, wholly supportive of this match. She would be the first to welcome the Infanta into our own Royal Family. But what she cannot tell, and nor can I, is whether she will be fit enough to carry the exceptional burdens of her office on this occasion. Only time and her doctors can tell. But she is in better heart. I saw her this morning. She sends her regards to you all.'

Millward phoned while he was in the shower, the steam from the panting tank of hot water misting the windows of his poky, brown flat.

'Robin. Damn you, Robin. Where were you? I thought you were out.'

'Just in, Simon. Getting into a bath robe.'

'I read the transcript of your briefing. Bloody upbeat. People will be expecting her back any minute – and we both know that's not possible. What the hell are you playing at?'

'Simon, she is getting better. Swayne and the other creeps must have told you. There'll be glimpses of her walking and riding again soon unless you're going to lock her in and chuck away the key. I've seen her for myself. My credibility matters to me, and to you. I have – broadly – to reflect the truth, otherwise I'm shot. And she can always have a relapse if that's necessary.'

There was a hollow chuckle. 'OK, I suppose. It's your business.'

'But,' Leckie said doggedly, 'remember I'm still flying blind. Until you say if she's ever coming back, really, then I have to keep the options balanced. It's an unsteady state, and it's tough to organize.'

He could hear the intake of breath. 'This isn't the time for that conversation. But you're right. The time is coming. I'll see what Mr Spens recommends and put it to the Cabinet as a discussion paper. If we move, we'll have to do it with due process. There'll be every journalist in the world banging down our doors if we don't.'

'So you think she's unfit to reign, and you think we can establish that?' Leckie could feel his voice rising too querulously. He fought to get it under control.

Millward didn't respond. 'I'm in Brussels all day tomorrow and Wednesday, back Thursday morning unless the Danes and the Romanians start waving their vetoes again. The board meeting is ten on Thursday. If I come at nine-thirty, we could put a little sand on the tables – then maybe in a few eyes.'

Robin Leckie held the receiver three inches high and dropped it with a thud. They had made up their minds. 'I'm not mad,' she'd said, with a glow of green. But somehow they would find a way to bring madness upon her.

Bess's last words on the cottage steps came back in their nagging simplicity.

'Oh, I know what I was going to ask you,' she'd said. 'Who is Davidson?'

*

'Long time no get it together, darling. Where the fuck have you been? Apart from Swindon and Omsk – and bloody Tomsk?'

'I sailed. Hamburg to Stavanger and back. It took me eight days. Eight days of peace and solitude, away from this hell hole of a Palace with its poncing servants and its endless meetings. I only think clearly at sea these days.'

'Heavens, you are getting a profound old thing. And what, great Tsar of the higher wisdom, did you think this time? Mostly of the next girl in the next ruddy port, if I know you. Brigitte in Bergen, Greta in Gothenburg. No wonder you haven't managed a decent shag all evening.'

'You are a crude and distressing woman, my pet. Your breasts have fallen, your stomach is becoming a round little pot, and your thighs – to be blunt – are too fat. But you have a wicked tongue, so I still find you interesting. And your maturity brings – what shall I say? – knowledge of how to please. Not like your daughter. She was eager to please only herself for the first few weeks. She did not know what pleased me. Alas, by the time she began to find out, she no longer had any interest in my pleasure.'

'What are we going to do about her, Romy? I keep telling Fountain she can't come back. Nicky would be utterly destroyed if he didn't get his chance now, and so, frankly, would I. With Bess, I'm an appendage. She hates me and tries to cut my credit cards off. I have no influence with her of any sort. I just hang on. But Nicky needs me, and that little slice of tortilla will need me too once they're married. Someone will have to find ways of keeping her interested. There's probably so much she doesn't know.'

'You are an evil bitch, my dear. You ask what we must do about your daughter, the fruit of your loins, and fifteen seconds later she's locked away for good while you find somebody new to pervert. As for your question, I think it an easy one. I have no future with Bess. If she stays as Queen, what is there for me? No warmth, no kindness: she has shut me out of her life. But if she were somehow to be declared unfit and hidden away, then I am the grieving husband who must carry on, and who your State must pay to carry on. Nobody will begrudge such a tragic figure his small entertainments.'

'Fountain says we may both need to testify when more doctors get involved. She'll say her mother and her husband are having it away. We'll swear she's as mad as a rat. We win.'

'You and I, the lovers she screams about, throws herself down staircases about? What a ridiculous idea. Show me how we could possibly do it.'

'There. Yes, there.'

Caroline was making coffee when she noticed the small yellow light on her terminal flashing. You have a message, you have a message. She sighed. Publishing taught you the hard way that technology was king, there to be obeyed without question or delay. Now she was editing, her life was all deadlines, days spent sweating over a hot computer. Be sure to get me to the printers on time.

Actually, there were three messages. The first one

from the Deputy Distribution Manager (South of England), wittering on about dinner some time at the Solent Literary Festival. Thanks, but no thanks. The second from Em, who'd read in the paper that Bess was supposed to be on the mend. Tentatively, possibly, don't break out the champagne just yet. And the third from an address she suddenly remembered. Granduke@travelling.love.uk.com.

Back in the land of the living with a way, at last, of getting through to you. But Swayne could find it at any time, so don't bank on continuing. Leg better, head better: just need help now. They're trying to ease me right out of the action, and probably make Nicky the King. I know too much about him and Alex and Millward and the rest of them. I'm a loose cannon. They've got a pond full of quacks telling me I've lost it. But I haven't, Carrie. And I'm damned well going to fight them. I must break out. Can you and Em find a way of coming to Wymeswold on Sunday a.m. just as the church bells start ringing and find your way by the stream in the field at the back? I'll try and give Swayne the slip and see you there. At least, if we meet, you'll know I'm still the Bess you remember. And maybe we can all think of something. Love, B.

Caroline copied the message and stored it in the middle of a book about twentieth-century novelists she was plodding through with increasing desperation. Chapter Ten: The Essential Humanity of Martin Amis. Nobody would look for it there.

She reached for the phone. 'Em, I've got the coffee on. Yes, and something harder in the cupboard

if you want. Sammy's coming round, you say . . .'
She paused. It was decision time. 'Sod it. Bring him
along.'

They sat, as arranged, in Leckie's office next to the
boardroom.

'I haven't slept,' said Millward plaintively. His
black suit was crumpled, his white shirt stained at
the cuff: he had shaved so badly that a thicket of
hair nestled, untouched, just below his left nostril,
and a globule of dried blood waved at the end of his
chin.

'The Romanians did their thing as per prediction.
It took us seven hours to buy them off, and even that
means drinking lakes more of their filthy wine.'

Leckie nodded. 'Simon, remember I know what it's
like. Been there, done that, issued the communiqués.
What I need now is a fix on Bess before we start the
board strategy bit.'

'Fine. It's as you'd expect, but I've had to spend
time talking to more shrinks and the creeps who call
themselves Constitutional Experts. Put them together
and we have lift-off.

'Spens will go up for another of his sessions
tomorrow morning. He'll suggest, closer to the end,
that she ought to be seen by a wider team. I have Ellen
Cloris from the Home Office lined up – and panting
for the Benson job, Chief Government Psychiatrist,
when he retires at the end of the year. She is eager to
please. And so, of course, is Badger. No relevant
qualification, I know, but what a reputation. He
delivered Bess twenty-four years ago and now he'll

put her away again. QED. We've a stack of witnesses who'll back up Selene and Alexandrovich. Swayne, Cross, even Davidson if it gets tricky. I don't anticipate any bother.'

'So one minute she's Queen and the next she's sitting in some tower playing a harp?'

'Not quite. The experts are pretty firm about that. Unless the shrinks can certify that she's beyond treatment – which they won't because no treatment means no fees – we'll have to go in stages. Temporary warrants making Nicky the Regent and so on. Once she's out of the game, though, I don't think we need worry. It is a tragedy. We shall all be duly mortified. But life must go on, Robin. There will have been a problem that needed addressing and we shall have addressed it, not for ourselves alone but firmly in the wider public interest.'

Leckie remembered the girl in the white shirt with the honey hair tossing in the breeze from across the meadow. He remembered the way she rested her hands on her hips and twirled her cane for glee at his jokes. Not mad, not bad: just 'a problem'.

Spens crossed his legs and clasped his hands together on his knees. 'So you went into your brother's bedroom and saw them together, naked and grappling? What did you feel?'

'I felt sick.'

'Did you tell anyone? Your ladies-in-waiting or your mother or your husband?'

'No, not immediately. Later I told my friends.'

'And they believed you?'

'Yes, of course.'

'And found a way of leaking your story to the newspapers?'

'Yes.'

'But not a word of it was printed. Why do you suppose that was?'

'I don't know. I suppose Millward got at them.'

'The Prime Minister intervened and the papers did as they were told. Isn't that a trifle unlikely?'

'I don't know. It happened anyway. And Baron left immediately.'

'What would you say if I gave you a report from Sir Richard's doctors utterly repudiating these fantasies? He was suffering from acute overwork. He lives peacefully in the north of Cyprus now and is fully recovered. He denies your story, of course; and so does the woman he intends to marry. A Serbian sculptress. She will be his third wife.'

'I don't see that proves anything.'

'This isn't a court of law, Your Majesty. I'm here to help you, to help you recover. Let's return to that hotel in your childhood when you say you found your mother with a man and your brother was traumatized. I have talked to the Duke of Clarence. Would you be surprised if he disclaimed any knowledge of this supposed incident?'

'I'd be amazed.'

'And of his telling you about your mother and Roman?'

'He's lying. They are all lying.'

'Just so. I have some colleagues who would like to see you, Ma'am: back in London in a more formal setting. Perhaps, with their assistance, we may come to a better understanding.'

Dear Lilibet,
The one thing that won't get you down, love, is the
waiting. Most of my father's life was waiting on the
subs' bench of history. Most of my brother's was
waiting upon the waiting, seeing the line form along
Generation Gap. Most of my life, when I think
about it, has been filling in time, hovering, being
around just in case. Rather like going to the
dentist's and finding a queue. There's nothing you
can do but eat painkillers and hope he'll get back
from lunch some time soon: life as a void with
attendant pain. At least you're clear of that. You
won't have to wait for anyone or anything.

Up beyond the stream, over the narrow pasture where four bored cows chomped at the spring grass, there was an old barn with a stunted oak tree by its side. Sammy Wittman and Alton Krantz, the photographer he usually worked with on stake-outs, stood behind the barn, breathing heavily. Krantz had carried his heavy video camera – the one which took stills simultaneously when he wanted – across a mile of potato fields. Sammy had trudged in his wake with the sound equipment. Neither was trained for the country life. Krantz had torn his leather jacket on the barbed wire across the gate which led from the Burton Road. Sammy's leather boots were plastered in mud. They cursed and checked their watches and waited. It had been a real sweat to get Bradshaw's permission to come at all. He'd groaned, hunting round in his files. 'We all signed up to something with the ruddy Press Commission. No harassing Her Majesty during her ordeal, etc. Here it is. See, my name on the bottom line.'

'But look at the small print,' Sammy had said brightly. '"I undertake that none of my staff, nor any freelance operatives under my instruction, will trespass, either physically or by photographic intrusion, upon the premises or immediate curtilage where Her Majesty may be convalescing." That means we're in the clear. She's not going to be in the cottage or anywhere on the curtilage, whatever that is. She's going to be a hundred yards away in absolutely plain view.'

'If you're a cow,' Bradshaw had grunted. But the house lawyer, swiftly summoned, confirmed Mr Justice Wittman's learned opinion. 'It's a bit legalistic,' he said. 'But then I'm a lawyer – and so, more important, is the chairman of the Commission. I reckon you're in the clear.'

Sammy looked at his watch again. Five to ten. The church bell in the village began to ring. And there, winding their way up the stream, were the stalking horses. Emma was puffing along in a lime-green anorak and pink-striped tights, a red scarf wound around her head like a turban. She looked rather more conspicuous than a combine harvester. Caroline, slim and silent in a blue denim jacket, walked behind her, the sun catching the cropped gold of her hair. They seemed two ordinary girls, perhaps from a shoe shop or sock factory in Leicester, out for a stroll.

'Action stations,' Sammy said. 'Any moment now.'

336

And then the gate in the high hedge at the back of Rose Cottage swung open. Bess did not hurry. She sauntered over the meadow which led to the stream, stopping for an agonizing moment to examine a clump of grass thirty metres down the slope tufted by three isolated daffodils, then walking on again. She stood out even at that distance. Blue jeans, a cotton sweater in dazzling white, her left hand pushing the hair back from her face.

Krantz had edged in front of the oak tree and was filming continuously. Sammy had the long-range mike pointed towards the spot, twenty seconds on, where the girls would meet.

'Gosh,' said Emma. 'Fancy seeing you. And how totally fabulous you look. Fit as a flea and twice as beautiful.'

Caroline kissed her on the cheek then hugged her. 'Em's right,' she said loudly. 'You look amazingly well. Surely they can't keep you cooped up like this much longer?'

Bess tossed back her hair and smiled for the cameras far away. 'I'm raring to get back to London,' she said, her lips moving with exaggerated precision. 'I'm Queen and I want to be with my people and do my job. I've put on kilos and rested till I'm sick of books and television. They don't pay me to take endless holidays. They pay me to work and serve and be a Windsor – and I keep telling the doctors they're being absurdly cautious.'

There was a cry from the gate of the cottage, and two men ran into the field. The fat policeman was wearing his uniform and purpling with exertion. The thin plain-clothes man had been on the lavatory when the alarm sounded; his hands clutched at his trousers and his shirt tails flapped in the wind.

'Ma'am, Ma'am, you're not supposed to be out here,' said the fat policeman. 'Please come back with us this minute.'

'But I've just met my oldest friends, sergeant,' Bess said. 'Why can't we all go inside and have some breakfast and a proper chat? Where's the harm in that?'

Swayne had arrived by now, stepping between them, taking charge. 'You,' she said, glaring at Emma and Caroline. 'You are trespassing. You are jeopardizing the Queen's health. Go now, or I'll have you arrested.' The detective had buttoned his trousers by now and moved to her side.

'Oh don't be such a drag, Lady Margaret,' Bess said, head still turned to the barn. 'You know this is all ridiculous.'

Swayne seized her by the arm and propelled her back towards the gate. The two policemen stood astride the path by the stream as the friends retreated. Emma turned by the willow and blew them a kiss.

'Great pictures,' said Krantz. 'Great sound too. But what the hell was all that about?'

Millward was just going to bed, stirring his hot chocolate, pulling on his black silk pyjamas, thinking wistfully of the wife who preferred to stay with her children in Lichfield, when the first editions arrived. Natalie, the number five in the Press Office, was a decorative rather than intelligent presence. Increasingly, they left her to do the evening shift and, maybe, share a Scotch or a glass of Vouvray with the Prime Minister. Not the service that Robin Leckie had given him in the good old days of brain engaged, but a service none the less.

She wore a tight grey skirt, ridged over the bulge of her rump so that the fabric lifted a couple of centimetres higher up her thigh. Her blue linen blouse was losing crispness with the hours, wrinkling and straining against her formidable jut of a bosom. Millward regarded her laconically. Had she been put there to tempt or divert him? There was always a second agenda in Whitehall. Visions of healthy, jiggling flesh did not arrive randomly in the Prime Minister's dressing room at five to midnight.

This one, though, on closer inspection, was biting her lip. 'The *Express* first, Sir,' she said. 'We think you ought to see the *Express* first.'

He heaved the red dressing-gown from the back of the sofa and drew its belt tight round his waist. The papers were spread as usual over the mahogany card-table he kept by the bookshelf.

'What's this?' The voice rose with an edge of fury. 'What the hell's this?'

Her chin trembled, seeming to send secondary tremors down her body. The breasts wobbled. The knees below the untugged skirt turned inward on each other, as if for mutual support.

'It's the *Express*, Sir. It's what we thought you ought to see first.'

'Get Leckie,' said Millward. 'Wherever he is, whoever he's with, get him and get him over here now, this minute. If not five minutes ago.'

She scuttled; he sat at the table and, once she was gone, jabbed his glasses on his nose.

There were four, five, six, seven pages of it. 'The Smile that Says: I'm Fine Again!' (page one). 'Buoyant Bess Tells Chums She's Fit and Raring to Return to Palace' (page two). 'Spring in the Air and a New Spring in her Step' (page three). 'Top Docs Absurdly Cautious, Says Radiant Queen' (page four). 'Who Told Police to Keep Her a Virtual Prisoner?' (page five). 'Curvy Monarch Shows a Great Way with Jeans' (*Express* Fashion Special, page six). 'We Tell the Nervous Ninnies of Authority: Give Us Back Our Bess' (*Express* Opinion, page seven – from the paper that's white and blue and read all over).

He called Swayne, then Davidson. He shouted at both of them. How could the wretched girl have been allowed to wander out of the cottage? Hadn't they smelled a set-up? Why hadn't he been warned? Cock-up; cock-up; cock-up.

Leckie was wearing a pair of old cords and the first sweater out of the cupboard. His hair was a tangle and his chin a field of stubble.

'I'll have Lord Runt of Runton on toast for this,' Millward said. 'I'll have that crud editor of his cut into pieces and strewn all over the steps of the Press Commission. I'll introduce laws to have them both flayed in a public place. This is gross, unforgivable intrusion which will repel honest journalists everywhere.'

Leckie knew, of course, that he was rehearsing as usual. It was Question Time in the House that afternoon. There was no point in letting him get too wound up.

'I doubt many people will go that way, Simon. The quotes are absolutely explicit and the pictures are great from her point of view. She looks 100 per cent and nobody's going to get too worked up about that. Runty won't sack Bradshaw for letting the people see their Queen grinning her head off. And anyone who knows anything about it will also reckon that Bess was posing for the cameras. See the way she's always in focus, always turned with the sun on her face. It may be a set-up, but it isn't one we can do anything about.'

Millward was silent, thinking again. 'I'll get you a car and driver,' he said. 'Be in Wymeswold by five before the full corps of creeps has time to gather. Bring her to the Palace so we've got her under our noses. And try and think of a decent tale to tell on the way. I'll see you back here by ten.'

Leckie took five minutes longer than the waiting driver expected to shave and arrange his hair. He wore meticulously creased slacks and an Italian jacket of wool and mohair. He had taken care. There was a smell of exotic aftershave in the air.

'Would you like the window open a little, Sir?'

They roared pensively into the night.

'So, what now?' she asked. 'Is it hanging or flogging, or just another life sentence?'

She shifted on the leather of the seat and looked at the first flickers of sun appearing over the granite teeth at the mouth of the forest.

'Both the Palace and Downing Street were pleased to see you looking so restored,' Leckie said carefully.

'That news inevitably means more journalists shouting for quotes and pictures. It means that Rose Cottage isn't viable for you any longer. The chairman and the board think it best, in the circumstances, to have you in London so that the speediest judgements can be made as necessary. In your own best interests.'

She was laughing at him again. 'How can someone as nice as you sound such a total prat?' she said.

He put his hands in his pockets and hunched lower in the seat. Behind on the road he could see the car with Swayne and the man from Special Branch coming closer. Their driver was confirming positions on the radio, shouting a little as a refuse lorry roared out of a turning on the right.

Leckie looked at her and searched again for the green in her eyes. 'I just want you to think of me as a friend like your other friends,' he said quietly. 'I don't expect you to believe that, but it happens to be true.'

She said nothing. Ninety minutes later, when the car swerved a little round Hyde Park Corner, she slipped towards him and her hand brushed his. He could not tell whether it was deliberate, but the touch of her lingered with him.

Fountain, pacing in short, tense steps, stood waiting in the Palace courtyard, just as he had waited for her years before.

Chapter Nineteen

————

Detch, the plodding MP for Worcester South, once a Parliamentary Under-Secretary for Social Security (Secondary Disbursements and Subsidiary Pensions), but now anxious to be remembered for anything, however oleaginous, was second on his feet at four minutes past three. 'Will the Prime Minister join with me in extending the good wishes of the whole House to Her Majesty the Queen on the occasion of her return amongst us after her distressing period of sickness, or sicknesses, and will he take the earliest opportunity to offer his personal congratulations on her reported return to full and glowing health?'

Millward sipped a glass of water and licked his lips in instinctive distaste.

'I thank my Honourable Friend for his sentiments, which I am sure reflect the feelings of us all, and will indeed convey them to Her Majesty, of whom I hope to seek audience at her earliest convenience. I'm sure we all share the sense of relief he speaks of.

'I would not, however, be doing my duty as the chairman of the board of the Royal Household and thus as your most honoured representative in Royal affairs, if I did not sound a small note of caution over the events of the last thirty-six hours. It is true that the Queen's condition is much improved. Her leg has healed. Her doctors regard her general spirits as partially restored. But they ask me to beware any thought of euphoria.

'It is too early, much too early, for her to resume the full ordeal of her State duties. Appearances can be deceptive, especially when they disguise a fragility which has given great concern in the past. When we see a butterfly struggling in a strong wind, we instinctively wish to protect it – not to expose it to crueller blasts. In particular, we wish that an intrusive and often callous press does not see this as its cue to resume its harassings and persecutions. The Queen has recovered as well as she has because of the privacy she has enjoyed. I know everyone will join with me in stressing the need for that essential privacy to be continued over the coming months and years.'

There was the familiar chuntering of assent he'd been toiling to awake. Kick the tabloids hard enough and it always came. Too many of the Hon. Members knew who their real enemies were.

'And one final point, if I may, Mr Speaker. I have the privilege, the privilege our people extend to me, to stand very close to the Royal Family which has served us so devotedly for centuries. There are times, hard times, when I consider myself almost *in loco parentis* on behalf of the nation. So I wish, this afternoon, to pay tribute not just to Her Majesty's fortitude, but to the strength of her mother and her husband – and, of course, her brother, who has stepped into the breach to such effect. We are all – all of us – a team. We will all – all of us – serve the greater good as best we can.'

The sketch writer from *The Times* leaned over to the sketch writer from the *Telegraph*. 'Simple Simon does it again,' he said. 'When the pie was opened, the birds began to sing.'

The boxes were back. A tentative signal of victory, she thought. She was being permitted to resume the scanning of her Government's business, delivered *en masse* without aid or explanation of the impenetrable code of the Civil Service. There was trouble in Patagonia, where the Buenos Aires regime had declared Welsh a prohibited language. The new Israeli Prime Minister was planning to build a sports complex on the Golan Heights. The Sultan of Brunei had lost his last $5 billion on the roulette tables in Macau and was offering to buy two dozen British Vulture jet bombers if we could offer an extended line of credit. Trials of the latest computerized hospitals – the ones which needed no nurses – were progressing favourably in the Bristol area. There was hope of a joint study with the Weston-super-Mare hospital which needed no doctors.

When Millward came it was as though nothing had happened. He told her about the borrowing requirement and the expectations of interest-rate reductions by the Federal Reserve. He spent fifteen minutes on the twenty-year timetable for the refurbishment of the Channel Tunnel. 'You may be required to cut some ribbons in Ashford next spring. I'm sure you'll wish to have the details at your fingertips.'

'Well, Mr Millward,' she said at last. 'And what about us?'

'Us, Your Majesty? We go on, as I told the Commons. Carefully, prudently, taking every effort to avoid undue exertion. Sharing responsibilities with those strong enough to help us bear them.'

'You mean I'm back on sufferance? You'll put up with me for a while, because that's politics, but you'll always be looking for a chance to get me put away if I give it you?'

The vowels grew plummy. 'No, Ma'am. Not for a second. Think of yourself as I think of you. As that butterfly in the wind. Think of the delusions that have clouded your mind in the past few months. Let us just see. Let us see how you greet your family now – and whether the husband who loves you can be at your side. Let us take it gently, and see; for there are so many watching.'

There is no victory, Bess thought. There is only another game on the same sad board until the Queen is finally in check. I can't sit here and wait for that. I have to attack.

'Would you consider a proposition?' she asked. 'What you politicians call a deal.'

'Usually I am the one who makes the deals.'

'For one reason or another, Mr Millward, we do not trust each other. You don't consider me suitable. You may even think me slightly crazed, though not as crazed as you pretend. For my part, I have no reason to trust or admire you. You want to control every part of my existence, in effect to be an uncrowned King.

'Perhaps that is the modern way. It is certainly the way prime ministers have tried to operate for four decades, since they realized that somebody sentient had to take responsibility as the genes of self-preservation deserted my family.'

'I call it saving the Monarchy,' said Millward thickly.

'Yes, so here is the bargain. I never thought to be Queen, and maybe I can never do it the way you want. I hate the people you've surrounded me with. I hate my family and they hate me. My husband was my mistake; though not, I sometimes think, all mine. I have to find my own way and make my own friends.

'Give me two years. I'll pose for the photographs you want and shake the hands and make the speeches. I will play the happy families you want, too. But, for the rest, we'll have a bargain, and I can try to be myself.

'If I succeed, you'll accept that. If I fail, then there will be no question of bringing in Spens and the rest again. I will go of my own accord, saying the words you write for me, eating whatever humble pie is necessary. Now, do we have an arrangement of convenience?'

He rose abruptly. 'I've told you, I do the deals. Make it a year and we're probably in business.'

She nodded. It was as she had expected. The coalitions were getting rocky again and there'd have to be an election some time in the next fifteen months. Millward always put his own flexibilities first.

They drove to Sandringham in three separate cars and posed on the lawn in front of the house. There were thirty-two photographers, running as a pack through the gates by the church and on to the grass. They shouted and jostled and barged. 'Big smile now then, Mum!' 'Over here, Mum, over here!' 'Give her a kiss please, Your Worship!'

Bess and Alexandrovich posed for a while together. He put his arms around her shoulders and hugged. She fought to keep her body language neutral. He planted a kiss in the centre of her forehead. She smiled adoringly. He bent to kiss her on the lips. She pecked like a constipated hen and turned away. 'One more time, Mum! One more time!'

Nicky and Elena had second billing. She seemed to be shrinking by the minute, Bess thought, as though repelled by his touch. Nicky bent in search of her, lips puckering and a winsome smirk transfusing his features. He can't kiss; he can't love; he's an emotional cripple who's mugged it all up, Bess thought. Caught between pity and fear, she looked again at the tiny, dutiful Spanish girl. 'Say Manchega please, Infanta! And another one, *por favor*!'

It was time for Selene's entrance. She had been making entrances all her life. This one involved a dramatic swing of the French windows and a wobble of high-heels and décolletage down the three steps to join them. Her chin was flexed to hide the plumpness of its first cousin just below. Her stomach was sucked inwards. Bess watched in familiar awe. The cameras were still Selene's life. 'This way now, Your Highness. Bend a little forward, if you please. Turn into the wind.' The bob of gold began to blow in Selene's face. Her hand, from long practice, went to her temple so that the long, supple fingers could tease it back into place.

They stood together in a line at the last. Bess in the middle, the supposed heart of attention, her cherished family around her. 'Over here now, Mum!' She glanced too far to her right and, in an instant, saw Alexandrovich's hand run down Selene's back as though programmed for automatic action. Sod it! Who cared?

'Was that what you wanted?' she asked Leckie when the circus had left town in a squeal of gears. 'Did I keep my bargain?'

He bowed extravagantly and clapped his hands in mime. 'Another great piece of our national theatre,' he said.

They were in his office discussing the Spanish visit.

'They still think Nicky should have the leading role,' Leckie said. 'After all, this is meet the in-laws time. Of course, now you're feeling better, you're bound to be there, and they suggest that you and the Prince together might take them to the tennis on the Saturday. But Millward cancelled all the State stuff when we didn't think you could make it, and the board hasn't reinstated it. There wasn't time to rustle up the pipes and drums – and anyway, the informality goes with the softer image we're trying to create.'

She giggled helpessly. 'Do you know how ridiculous you sound? New Sweeter Regals with the taste that melts in the mouth. Don't you and your lot ever get tired of the endless remakes?'

'What do you mean, Ma'am?' He seemed to be

bridling, his professionalism suddenly in question, but there was a matching smile on his lips.

'I mean it's an endless game for you, isn't it? And I'm not a stupid little girl any longer. I've read the books. I've read my father's letters. You're programmed to see us as just another product, aren't you? First we're starchy and out of touch, so we have to wear casual sweaters and joke with pop stars and open supermarkets. Then some focus group somewhere decides that we aren't being properly Royal, so out come the robes and the carriages again. I wasn't asleep all that time Baron was lecturing me. Because I was straight from school, not knowing a thing, the powers that be thought I needed the majestic treatment, so they made me a bit distant and starchy. I was rationed and I got more of the big, formal dinners so I could wear the kit. They didn't want me chatting in the check-out line in case people thought I was working the counter.

'But now, I guess, another bloody group has decreed that that's gone too far. Bring out the sweaters. Get the jeans out of the cupboard. I'm supposed to be everybody's favourite daughter again. Except, of course, that this time it's a supporting part, isn't it?'

Leckie blushed and floridly buried his head in his hands.

'Except that I'm to be kept on the fringes, not doing too much in case I go off the rails, while Nicky gets his turn in the sun. Make her ordinary so she can be written out of the script when it suits.

'I don't mind that, you know. It's my idea, the agreement with Millward. But you mustn't manipulate me, Mr Leckie, and kid yourself that I don't know what's happening. Because I do.'

She had begun by mocking him, then let the words run out of control, turn fierce and biting.

He shut the folder on his desk and suddenly got to his feet, standing before her with arms folded, eyes downcast. 'You're right, of course. You might have read the research and gone to the briefings. You could do my job, and do it better. And now, as I'm sure you realize, I have to make some kind of choice.'

The green of her stare caught him.

'I owe everything to Simon Millward. Without him, I'd be stuck in some marketing job stuffing envelopes. He's clever and shrewd and, most of the time, he's trying to do his best for everyone. Oh, sure, some of that involves putting Millward first, but it's only practical.

'One thing has led to another. I don't know everything that's gone on, but I know enough. I know how desperate Simon has been to keep you under wraps and the lengths he's gone to. I understand that, because I understand him. But believe me: I don't feel proud about it. We were out of control and, perhaps, we will be again. Maybe we've lost our bearings. Millward truly believes we have to take the kings and queens chance throws up and turn them into puppets if they're going to survive. And once, I believed that, too.'

She had never heard him make a speech like this before. He stood straight before her and, for a moment, she thought he was going to put his hands on her shoulders.

'Bess,' he said, and the use of her name made him pause for a moment. 'I'm sorry. I'm not turning traitor or switching sides, but I reckon I ought to start doing the job I'm paid for – which is helping you more. I'll try to give you the advice that's best for you, and I won't play every end against the middle. Think of me as a kind of double agent, but your double agent.'

She had somehow planned for this moment and felt sure it would come. They had been together too much, natural colleagues: and she'd come to look forward to the diary meetings and the rehearsals. There was a bond.

'Thank you, Mr Leckie,' she said, lingering for a second over his name, rolling it on her tongue. 'I hope we can make a fresh start.'

The deal, carefully tabulated, allowed excursions as well as visitors. She could go to Caroline's and to Emma's, and sit with them on the carpet drinking wine and gossiping about their lives and hers. The car to take her back waited below. Beyond it, twenty metres down the street, was the second car that her friends always pointed out. But it was a kind of freedom.

This time there was no point holding back. She had nothing to lose. With a second glass, it all poured out. The betrayals, the fornications, the whole damned thing.

'Sammy would kill for a story like that,' said Emma.

'It's more like a book,' said Caroline.

*

The Spanish Number Three was losing, slowly and rather gracelessly, in five long sets. He could lob and retrieve all afternoon. It was what he did. But the ape of a blond American always seemed to find a service ace when hopes of recovery rose. It was a dogfight of a semi-final carried over from Friday, when the clouds had opened at three. It was consuming the better part of Saturday in decelerating tedium.

Bess looked at the skies and saw more clouds piling high over Sutton and Richmond. The King of Spain, slumped back in his chair, hands thrust into a thick woollen overcoat, was snoring gently. Late starts for rain equalled long lunches. His second wife, a sallow Croatian heiress he'd met in Chamonix seven winters before, the sorrowing widower seeking solace, clung to his arm for warmth. Elena had gone to the loo six games before and not returned. Nicky was the only one sitting up and taking notice, but it was the ball boys who seemed to excite him.

Bess stood up and wandered down the green tunnelling of the President's box. Two bulky men in blazers hovered by the entrance chatting to a young lieutenant from the Royal Marines. They stiffened when they saw her.

'I just came for another cup of tea,' she said, nodding into the long, low lounge of the All England Club. The lieutenant saluted her with an elaborate clicking of heels.

Leckie was sitting in one of the orange armchairs tapping intently on his portable computer. He seemed not to notice her as she stood beside him, then, looking up, scrambled to his feet. 'Your Majesty,' he said very loudly so that the white-haired couple by the window put their strawberry tarts back on the plate and peered at him.

The bar on the right had a television screen bringing the drab news from the Centre Court. It was six-all in the final set and the yellow gorilla from Tuscaloosa was just serving for the match. Double fault. He hurled his racket dimly at the grass, duly collected his fine from the umpire and sat glum on his stool, abusing himself furiously beneath a pink towel. The screen cut away to scores from other courts.

'Hey,' said Bess, 'Clare Baldring's a set up in the Plate on Number 17. She was two years below me at Roedean, but pretty amazing even then. Do you think I could go over and give her a cheer?'

Leckie stowed his computer away and had a word with the blazers. 'I don't see why not,' he said. 'Let's wander for a bit.'

It was the fag end of the fortnight and the crowds had gone. Elderly couples in raincoats sat on the wooden benches down the central gangway chewing sandwiches and pouring soup from flasks. And there, just beyond Court Eleven, stood a solitary infant in a blue dress and red wellington boots, beginning to wail a pitiful dirge. 'Mummy. I want my mummy.'

She couldn't have been more than two. Her hair was a mass of ginger curls. Her nose was covered in freckles. She had wept silently for minutes, but now distress had seized her. 'Mummy. I want my mummy.'

Bess stopped and looked around. Nobody was paying the slightest attention. She bent over and picked the child up. 'Tell them there's a lost toddler near

Eleven,' she said to the blazer, then sat on an empty bench and hugged the picture of ginger misery until it fell silent.

'We're finding your mummy,' she said, and began wiping away the tear stains. Leaning over the barrier on the far side of the court, Krantz shot happily away. Two reels in three minutes, until a large ginger woman clutching a green umbrella ran down the gangway and began shouting at the child.

Bess eased herself away and joined Leckie. Clare Baldring had lost the second set. And the *Express*, yet again, had game and match. 'Angel of Mercy Queen comforts terrified toddler'; 'Wimbledon hugs from the Monarch of Love'; 'The Cry of a Child, the Compassion of the Mighty'. Exclusive pictures. Exclusive story. 'If only I'd known, I'd have thanked her ever so warmly,' said Big Ginger, holding her own photo-call.

'And exclusively useful image-building,' Leckie said to himself when the papers dropped. Bess had the touch the tabloids responded to. She was also a natural actress. They were on their way.

Leckie read restlessly, insatiably. Her school magazine was lying in the sitting room while he waited for her to come back from the gym.

'What was the name of your economics teacher?' he said when she arrived, still drenched in sweat.

'Bowler. Mrs Bowler.'

'You see here she's in hospital. They don't say, but it sounds like cancer.'

He never had to prompt Bess. 'I must go to visit her,' she said. 'She wrote to me when I was in hospital.

She's a kind, good person, and she feels worse about what happened than I do now.'

Leckie did not ask for publicity. Indeed, he seemed to go out of his way to avoid it. The managers at the Royal Sussex were warned about the press. 'The Queen wants a few minutes of peace with a cherished old friend, not a scrum,' he said sternly. The car used the entrance at the side where the ambulances came.

Margaret Bowler was thinner, her face more pinched, her hair a stark white. But she was getting stronger, she said. 'They caught it just in time, they think. And how are you, my dear?'

Bess talked of palaces and kings. She joked. She repeated what Millward had told her last week about economics. 'He says the money supply is getting out of control again.' Mrs Bowler moaned for her pension.

And, at the last: 'How is Tom?'

He was well, she thought. She had heard from him at Christmas, playing understudy in some Eugene O'Neill revival at the back of Greenwich Village. A Long Day's Journey into Pay-Days. He'd been hoping for a part in a daily soap called *Ferry* about a crew who kept going to Staten Island and back looking for love. 'But he hasn't let me know what happened. I suppose he would have, if he'd got it.'

She was wan and defeated. 'You know how long I cried over what he did?' she said. 'It was as if you were my daughter, and the man who betrayed you was a stranger – not my son. He knows that, I think. He never comes to see me. He seems too ashamed.'

Bess held her hand for a while, then arranged her flowers on the locker next to the bed. 'I'll keep in touch,' she said, and left by the same side door, the collar of her coat turned straight against her cheeks.

Billy Hoggett from the *Mail* was standing behind an ambulance with his camera ready. Roger Crumby, holding another bunch of flowers and a tape recorder, drifted in to interview an ecstatic Mrs Bowler ten minutes later. The Angel of Mercy was flying again; but, more important, showing sympathy and concern for the mother of someone who had treated her despicably. A nation of women would clasp her to their bosoms.

This was not, Leckie knew, his finest hour. She had not realized what he intended this time. She would probably be mortified if she did. But now this was spinning for real and he'd promised to do his best. The *Mail* opt-in provided suitable camouflage. Fainthearts needn't turn up for the later rounds.

They were united in a single question, to which Leckie had two answers.

'Hospitals,' Bess said. 'Why I am doing so many hospitals this week? Children's hospitals, old folks' hospitals, hospices, emergency wards, recovery wards. It feels like the whole of Britain has suddenly gone to bed and asked me to come and visit.'

Leckie grinned. 'There were always hospitals asking for you,' he said. 'But there was a limited-response policy in operation then. Your masters were running you on what we call the B1 schedule – mostly short formal events with some civic dimension. You dressed up; you arrived; you pulled a piece of string and left. Contact and coverage: restrained. Public-affection quotient: small. Actually it's quite a sophisticated programme. The old Queen's sister developed it sixty-odd years ago to fill in the blanks between holidays. They used to call it M25 then because it always meant a quick getaway, but it's a damned sight more refined these days. Fitting events to images is like doing a dinner menu. Choose your guests, select the desired impact, then go and rootle round in the Food Hall. Back-loaded, if you see what I mean.'

She shook her head slowly. 'I haven't the least idea what you're talking about.'

'OK, I'll take it from the top. But I'm amazed nobody has been through this with you – at least, not even the basics.

'Once upon a distant time, monarchs ruled and the rest of us touched our forelocks. Your bog-standard command/control system. They didn't need to be popular or loved or any of that pap. They needed to be able to give orders and have them obeyed. Right?'

'Right.'

'But then things changed and nobody took the orders any longer. Oh, they bowed and scraped as heretofore, because it was extremely convenient. They didn't want to abolish anything; they wanted to preserve it after a fashion. But that created another sort of problem. There wasn't enough for kings to do – and, worse, they had to be loved for not doing very much. So the politicians invented a new purpose for them: charity. I once wrote a monograph about it for the Institute of Perception Orchestration. I called it the Good King Wenceslas Syndrome; but Disraeli probably called it something else.'

She smiled. 'You mean, we're the first great spin?' she said. 'None of the histories put it quite that way.'

'That's because they're all written by historians. But where did your name come from? Windsor. Not Saxe-Coburg-Gotha or Mecklenberg-Strelitz or Hesse or Wettin. The ultimate re-branding exercise. For Battenberg read Mountbatten – long before Horlicks became Vitanut. Even before Archie Leach became Cary Grant. Who saved the children and cleared the battlefields and sat stony-faced through God-awful variety shows because they raised a few bob? Your family did, because they had to find something to do. Defining purpose.'

'But what makes hospitals so important?'

'It's all in my monograph. I call it Related Nightingale System. The saintly Florence was one of the original old bags. A bully, a blusterer, disorganized as Hell. She didn't learn a new thing after the Crimea. She bawled around holding everybody else back. But none of that mattered, because she'd become the Ultimate Nurse. She was beyond criticism. Give her a lamp and a ward of chaps without legs and a little night music and she was totally impregnable. Why else do you think all your Georges and Edwards went round naming hospitals after themselves? They were buying into the Nightingale brand.'

'And me?'

'They kept you away from that for the first years because they were nervous of you. They thought you might be too good at it. They were majoring on making you a bit starchier, a bit more regal. Now we've got to put the boot on the other foot. Your charity begins at home.'

Later, when Millward asked the question, he did it with a snarl. 'Why all these bloody hospitals, Robin? Every day she's out somewhere cuddling kids or juggling bedpans. You'd think we'd signed her up for NHS recruitment. Our Queen isn't supposed to be loved, remember. She's there pending further developments. You're letting her get away from us.'

Leckie shrugged expansively. 'There's not much I can do about it, you know. You should see the waiting lists. Half of your own backbenchers are lined up, begging her to save some cottage hospital in their constituencies before the election. I'm only going with the flow, and frankly I doubt I could turn off the tap now if I wanted to.'

He had had sight of the latest Party internal polling which gave Bess a 76 per cent 'favourable impression' rating and Millward only 52 per cent. 'Perhaps you might like to tag along with her when she does the maternity wing at King's on Friday?' he said brightly.

Millward reached for his diary.

Chapter Twenty

'I'd like a sabbatical.'

Sammy Wittman had not been looking forward to this moment. Sabbaticals sounded too gentlemanly for the *Express*. If you wanted time off, you called in sick and hoped your desk hadn't been cleared when you got back.

'A what?' said Bradshaw viciously. 'Mr Arty-Farty wants an extra holiday to lie around stroking his ego. We don't have any of those in stock here. Lord Runton takes all our ration with him to his villa in Thailand.'

'I know. But I want to write a book.'

'Son, my reporters write stories. Seven hundred words maximum, with two hundred of them optional cuts. They don't write books. Authors write books. Son, you're no author.'

Spare me the folk wisdom and the Yorkshire Pud, Sammy thought. Bradshaw wasn't quite the dour demon he made out. He had even (one girl researcher in the library had once discovered amid whoops of glee) written poetry when he was nowt but a lad, nursing his sensitivity and sending it in long-hand to the *Keighley and Bingley Chronicle*. But maybe this wasn't the moment to start trading rhyming couplets.

'This isn't any book,' Sammy said doggedly. 'This is a definitive look at our modern Royal Family with unparalleled access to top Palace sources. And that's just the blurb. What was the secret truth of the Queen's alleged illness? Persecution; harassment; the grim facts of a loveless marriage. I shall call it *The Tragedy of the Virgin Queen*.'

Bradshaw snorted. 'Vergin' on the unbelievable, more like.' But his eyes were thoughtful. 'So all right, for the sake of argument. You get eight weeks off the diary to put some words on paper. I look at them first. If they're halfway as good as you make out, you can have another month on full pay. Lord R has publishers hopping whenever he crooks his finger, because he owns them. We offer the manuscript to one of them – and you keep half of the advance. The rest goes into my Special Projects budget and I use it to get the serial rights, guaranteed. That way there's something in it for both of us.'

Sammy had seen most of this coming. 'If we're just talking hardback rights and I hang on to everything in paperback?' he said.

'Done.'

'And it gives me great pleasure . . .'

Fountain folded his hands behind his back. Selene fiddled for a scrap of lace in her handbag. There was a genteel round of applause. The Duke of Clarence had spotted this one early, lying in the Palace post tray. The new Ward Seven at Great Ormond Street (Post Natal Emergencies). 'That's mine,' he'd cried. 'My turn.'

So there, at two in the afternoon, he stood, the cameras poised, his double-breasted charcoal suit buttoned tight across his pigeon chest, his crinkles of hair scraped back.

'Please hold a baby for us, Sir,' called Billy Hoggett.

'Give us all a great big smile,' shouted Alton Krantz.

HRH delved into the nearest cot and tugged out a swaddled object which began to howl shrilly. His arms straightened in alarm, holding it far from his body, its contorted face turned square towards the flash bulbs. Its face began to turn puce with the effort, and then a vivid yellow.

'Take it away,' said the grand Duke in a thin squeak of desperation. 'Somebody take the little wretch. It's being sick on my suit.'

Selene shut her bag with a savage click. The counter-offensive had stalled at the first puke.

Alexandrovich made no effort to hide his irritation. 'This could have waited until tomorrow,' he said. 'The plane from Kiev was four hours late. I have been working all week promoting our British exports, touring, touring without rest. I have sung for our suppers in every town in the Ukraine. I'm tired – but you say you must see me now, this minute, as though I were one of your secretaries. It is really too much.'

Fountain waved his hand dismissively. 'Spare me the full ordeal,' he said. 'Most of the stuff you're promoting so gallantly comes from your own factories. Most of the deals you're trying to make wouldn't survive a Department of Trade inspection. You exist here for a purpose, Prince. The question is whether that purpose gives the Firm and the board good value any longer.'

'What the hell does that mean? You recruited me as the most suitable consort, remember? The chosen one. It's not my fault the bitch has changed her mind, that I'm left in this useless limbo. But I try to give value for money. When you say come, I come. When you say smile, I smile. And for the rest, I get on with my life.'

'You go away too much and stay away too long.' There were tiny flushes at the corners of Fountain's mouth. 'While you drink with your friends and peddle your trinkets, the world is changing too. See the papers this morning? Twenty million euros raised in a night for the orphans of the Bangladesh flood. Who did that? She did. One begging letter from the High Commissioner equals one plate of chicken khorma with the Queen at 100,000 euros a time. Lots of pictures of her cuddling Bengali toddlers with eyes bigger than her own.

'She is beginning to have a sort of power, my Prince. And meanwhile you're dropping off the bottom of the polls. Two out of five on Gallup this week had forgotten your marriage. Only 6 per cent thought you were doing a good job – and 40 per cent of those didn't remember what the job was. You are too expensive and too damned invisible. Now, how do we put that right? A baby was part of Plan A, remember, but where is the baby?'

'She will not let me touch her. When there is no audience, she turns and leaves. Her door is locked against me. What am I supposed to do?'

'Have you thought of begging? My board has to adapt to market forces as best it can. We did not want this headstrong, untrustworthy girl. We pursued other options. But there is no point pretending that the forces are as they were, or that our calculations are unaffected. Mr Millward does not like what is happening. Like me, he prefers known quantities, biddable players. What he cannot stand is a costly arrangement which yields no benefits. Which neither progresses nor changes. You are becoming an impediment, Sir, a vulnerable impediment. Such things, unattended, have a way of becoming insupportable.'

She had sat late into the night for three nights now, long after the rest of the Palace slept, tapping her notes into the computer. The beginnings of the book. It had begun as a simple narrative of events: death, isolation, the whole damned plot. But it was impossible to put everything in. How could she strip Nicky's sexuality bare, even at second hand? He was her flesh and blood.

Selene? She was still her mother. There were ties that couldn't be bundled up and thrown away. And she had promised to love and honour Alexandrovich before 225 million witnesses. The pair could perhaps – gently, elliptically – be described as the adulterers they were; but mists of vagueness descended on the tiny keyboard as she tried to make the words flow. The point of the book, as endlessly discussed with Caroline, was not the copulation or the conniving; it was the charade of the life that they – the board, the company – had tried to inflict on her. The story of the prisoner in the East Wing. And how is your wife today, Mr Rochester?

That was best told in episodes, with only a few names and dates attached. So she was settling for notes, and patches of description. Wittman would make something different of it anyway. It was best to let him get on with it.

There was a sudden sharp rapping at her door. Ten past one? What on earth . . . ?

'It's me. The husband you never see. I must speak to you.'

'Wait.'

She buried the palm-top under the silk of the pillow and pulled the cord of her dressing-gown tight. 'It's very late. Won't it do in the morning?'

The rapping changed to a heavy, insistent banging, his fist smashing against the panels. She could hear him swearing in Russian under his breath.

Bess slid back the bolt. His hair was a sodden tangle. His forehead dripped with sweat. The shirt was stained and held by a single button. The brandy on his breath enveloped her like a poison cloud.

'You never come to visit me, my wife, so I must visit you. I must ask you why you are always so cold when we are together? Such a frigid, stuck-up little witch, dreaming your dreams and smiling your secret smiles when the door is locked. They say you are beautiful, but you give none of it to me. I sit like a fool in my room as if it were a cell and I had done something to deserve your contempt. But I have done nothing.'

He lurched towards her, lunging with his left arm

and catching her a swinging blow to the shoulder. She fell backwards on the bed and cried out, more in alarm than pain. Now he was astride her, slobbering, tearing the gown away from her body. She fought with her elbows pummelling against him, driving into his rib cage until he drew back and looked down at her.

'Why do I revolt you? What have I done? Do not say other women. With Russians there are always other women. They come and go like vodka on long evenings of boredom. But they mean nothing – and you are my wife.'

She leaned towards him, the green of the eyes lit with scorn. 'Yes, I am your wife. But would even Russians expect me to lie back, smiling, parting my legs, when you get back from another afternoon of fucking my mother?' And she spat in his face.

Left arm pinning her flat to the bed, he began to hit her with his right fist. Cursing, shouting, the knuckles already raw. She could feel herself reeling into unconsciousness. She made one final twist at escape. Her hand, scrabbling below the pillow, found the palm-top sealed in its wooden box, and she swung it in an arc of despair. It caught him hard on the bridge of the nose – and suddenly there was a gush of blood on to the sheets around her. He staggered back across the carpet, spraying scarlet, clutching her torn dress-ing-gown to his face.

His eyes were dazed and he gasped with pain. The nose seemed to flap loose with every movement.

She levered herself to her feet. Covered in blood, naked to the waist, relentlessly calm. 'Get out,' she said slowly, clearly. 'Get out of my home, my marriage, my life.'

The eyes above the bundle of the gown were hunted and fearful. He turned; and was gone.

Usually Bess would come down to Leckie's office after breakfast and sit with him going through the diary. Since she had learned to trust him, since she felt he was working for her, she liked the feeling of security and, increasingly, the gossip and the banter. She had a friend on the inside now as well as those beyond the walls.

But today it was already nine o'clock and there was no sign of her. He called Fat Clemmy. 'Is she stirring? Do you know her movements?'

'The Queen is resting in her room. She had her coffee sent up and says she doesn't wish to be disturbed.'

That was awkward. He had a heavy week fixed for her and some things – like the keynote speech at the World Congress of Health Service Executives – couldn't wait. He had a board meeting at ten and a speech of his own to the Worshipful Company of Stationers at six.

'I'll have to call her direct,' he said. 'If she's ill, she's ill – but my whole day disintegrates if I'm not sure.'

The voice at the end of the line was soft. 'Oh fine. I'm sorry. Just come up.' She didn't say what was wrong, but he could sense the strain. He ran up the stairs and along the corridors.

Her room was dark and gloomy, the curtains barely parted. She was dressed in jeans and a loose-fitting olive cotton blouse. She sat at her desk, with her back to the door. She did not turn as he came in.

'What's the matter?' he said. 'Bess, what's the matter?'

Her shoulders straightened and she pulled the curtains apart, then swung to face him. Her right eye was hidden in a livid bruise which spread down her cheek. Her jaw was bruised and swollen. Silently she tossed her hair back so that he could see the weals and scratches on her neck.

'Alexandrovich,' she said. 'Alexandrovich is the matter. He tried to rape me last night and made a terrible mess of it. But don't worry. If you think I look bad, you should see him.' And, wincing with pain, she smiled. 'The trouble is what I say and what I do now. I can't go out like this, but I can't stay in either. I need lots of ice and lots of advice.'

This, when Leckie thought about it much later, was the moment everything changed for him. One second he was standing looking at her – the face he saw constantly, the gallant grin, sunk in weals of destruction. The next, almost instinctively, he had put his arms round her and kissed her on the slit of the eye, his lips hardly daring to brush her skin.

'The bastard. The mad, evil bastard.' Her head touched his shoulder, seeking comfort, and she said nothing. Then it was over.

'They aren't going to get away with this,' Leckie said. He stepped back, his brain churning. There'd been a moment coming for months, ever since the walk in the fields near Wymeswold. And this was the moment.

'It's finished for me,' he said. 'They have got to be

stopped. I said I'd do what I could to help you. Forget that. I'll do everything and anything. This is war and I have to choose – and it has become my war too.'

The board were toying with their Bourbon biscuits and pondering great questions of one lump or two. Millward had arrived fifteen minutes early, wanting a quick word with Leckie; but Leckie, his secretary said brightly, was out of the office with his bleeper turned off. So they sat and waited. Montgomery's report in transport costs lay on the table. Fountain fiddled with his pen. The Prime Minister looked at his watch and wondered distractedly whether the new President of Serbia would make small talk over lunch. Leckie came in five seconds before the carriage clock on the mantelpiece hit ten and nodded affably, burying his nose in a green folder of press clippings.

'The minutes were circulated,' Millward said tonelessly. 'Any points that aren't covered later in the agenda?'

She didn't knock. The door was suddenly open and there she stood, with Fountain's pair of secretaries twittering behind her. Headscarf, sunglasses.

'Since I'm always on the agenda,' she said, 'I thought we might take any other business first. I have some damaged goods to report.'

She pulled the scarf back and took off the glasses, twirling them in her fingers, then looked at them squarely.

'Good God,' said Millward. Fountain's mouth was open. Montgomery's hands crumpled the edge of the transport assessment. Leckie held the green folder steady. She swung to let Miss Cunliffe and Miss Drake inspect the damage. Witnesses. They squeaked alarm and scuttled back into the outer office.

'Good God, Ma'am. How did you do that?'

She peered at him through the slits of bloated pain, the green still glinting. 'We all know about Ivan the Terrible, Prime Minister. Welcome to the court of Alexandrovich the Appalling.'

'There's nowhere to go,' she said. 'I can't go out like this. The gardens will be full of tourists in fifteen minutes. But I'm sick of the rooms and the offices and the everlasting miles of corridor.'

'I'll take you to Windsor,' Leckie said. 'At least there's a little private space there. Fountain will see the point of getting you out of town, and we can talk in the car.'

'Where's Alexandrovich?'

'Gone. Just gone – on another world-export tour until they make up their minds what to do about him. They might have tried to hush it up still, but too many people saw you. And heard you. He can't stay after that.'

The Daimler with the darkened windows edged slowly along the Embankment. She had a scarf knotted around her head and the biggest pair of sunglasses she could find. She huddled in the corner of the back seat. 'What did you mean when you said "They're not going to get away with it"?'

'I meant I know too much that sickens me. And I haven't told you everything.'

So, for the first time, silent in a traffic jam in

Hammersmith, he began to tell her what he knew. Why Millward was so desperate to keep her on the tightest reins. How he had used her to keep the coalition whole and to swing the last election. He told her about Nicky and the reason for Baron's seduction. 'Your brother's such a fool. Millward thought that, that way, we could keep him in the waiting tray, ready as needed.' Selene? 'She's a pathetic bitch. She's greedy for anything they can give her, and there's so much on her she has no choices left.' And Alexandrovich? 'The same. He did a little freelance work for MI6. They found him for us and we let you choose him. It was a risk. He's got form stretching back to the Steppes, but they thought the Romanov tag was worth it.'

Bess took off her glasses and looked at him squarely. 'So tell me about Davidson,' she said.

'I don't know everything. He used to be 6, but now he's seconded to 5, a little unit called the M team. I think it's M for Monarchy. He's Millward's man. Simon clicks his fingers and Davidson does what's necessary.'

'Like pushing me down the staircase? Like trying to make everyone think I was suicidal?'

Leckie's eyes were wide. 'I never knew that,' he said.

'He was there on the stairs behind me when I fell. I've kept playing it over and over in my mind. When Roman called from below and I turned, something hard caught me in the small of my back. What was it? Perhaps a stick of some kind. Perhaps an umbrella. Davidson was carrying an umbrella.'

'Bess, I swear I didn't know. Millward had Spens

on parade and I thought – well, we all thought – you might be ill. You'd gone through so much.'

She laughed bitterly. 'Gone through? Been put through? And all because I wouldn't salute when the bugle sounded. It's deformed, you know. The whole bloody thing has just become a monster nobody can control. I think my father saw that coming. We're puppets now, he'd say. Simple damned puppets when the politicians pull the strings. Once they'd decided we couldn't be allowed to choose anything for ourselves, we became the messenger boys and girls for their message. The old Queen didn't realize it, but when she got into trouble she gave the whole game away. They didn't want the drama of tipping us out, but we had to take orders, their orders. Tools of the trade, by Downing Street appointment. And see where it's got us, he'd say. At least before we were only a messy charade, not an utter bloody sham. Oh, he was playing along. He knew the form and he knew his duty. But he knew what we'd become, too. Professional whores to the greater glory of whoever could find a use for us.'

'It didn't always seem that way to us,' Leckie muttered. 'We thought we were helping.'

'Helping? Helping to cut us off from any form of life? Helping to bug our friends and push us into bed with the slime of your choice? Helping to run us off to the funny farm if we rebelled? Helping us turn into androids? Is that what you meant by helping?'

The car was picking up speed now. She could hear the howl of the great jets low overhead. 'You're right,' he said miserably. 'I know that now. It's just that, on

373

the inside, you don't always see things so clearly. You tell yourself that there are institutions which need preserving and fixed points in people's lives that are part of being our sort of nation. And you tell yourself that this is big business now, making profits, employing thousands. That we owe them something, too.'

'Spare me,' she said. 'The Chief Executive Officer and the Prince Consort are banging the Queen Mother to keep our exports buoyant?'

'Christ,' he said. 'That's something else I didn't know.' As they walked together through the clipped hedges and plucked lawns of the private garden, they began to lay their plans. 'We're a team,' he said. 'I've tried to make you safe by making you popular. If you're loved, they can't move against you. And you are loved.' They were looking at each other intently. Look, but do not touch.

'Yes,' she said.

'And now we must work carefully for something more than that.'

'Yes,' she said.

Sammy Wittman showed his visa and his press pass for the fourth time, winding down the car window and making small talk to the Turkish troops in their bottle-green fatigues. And this, he thought, is supposed to be one country again, one confederation. If this is one country, I'm a Turkish Cypriot. But the drive was still worth it, climbing steeply into the mountain ranges north of Nicosia. A deserted road with only boulders and the occasional military post for company. And then there was the view they had told him about. Suddenly the car stood at the foot of the pass and the slopes, green, covered in olive trees, rolled down to the sea. You could see for ever. No wonder the Greeks he'd been drinking with last night in the Hilton had grown mournful when they talked about it. The lost land, never reclaimed. There was peace in the Balkans; peace even in the Middle East now that the Israelis were sharing their water again. Only this benighted paradise bucked the trend. At least they'd given the villages back their old names. Reluctant marketing Turkish-style. He looked at his map. There was Kyrenia, white cottages, a gaggle of hotels to the left, the red walls of the old Crusader castle to the right. And there, winding off beyond, was the narrow road to Bellapais. The Villa Marisa was what? – the seventh on the right, pink stucco shrouded in a clump of lemon trees. There was a small, dusty car in the drive.

'Anyone at home?'

Sammy clumped back and forth along the patio, making as much noise as possible.

The man who came to the door was wearing dirty khaki shorts and an open cotton shirt. His face was red and his bald head was blistered from the sun. The hair on his chest, like the hair of his moustache, had turned a grizzled white. 'Don't I know you?' asked Baron blearily. 'Anyway, come in and have a drink.'

It was only eleven, but already his mouth was slack and the words were slurred. There was an arch of vines at the end of the patio, a table, two plastic chairs, a half-empty bottle of Keo brandy.

'I'm Wittman from London, Sir, from your old paper. Just on holiday, but they told me where you lived and I thought it would be good to drop by. You're very much remembered, of course. Quite a legend. Is your wife at home?'

Baron poured himself a tumblerful of brandy and sipped it noisily. His hand shook and the drink tipped down the hair of his chest, streams bifurcating over the pot of his belly. 'Fuck. No, my wife is not home. My wife is in Istanbul with some bloody carpet salesman. But I am here and bored out of my skull and looking for a little company. How is that crud Bradshaw? Have they sacked him yet?'

It was twelve-thirty before Sammy thought the time was right. He fiddled in the canvas bag he'd brought, turning on the tape recorder, then triumphantly produced another bottle. 'Do you know this one? They said it was orange and the best thing they make here.'

'Filfar,' said Baron. 'Sweet muck, only tolerable with a pile of ice.' He tottered into the house. A toilet flushed. He returned with new glasses and a tray straight from the freezer.

'Do you miss the Palace life?'

'How can you miss a load of wankers?'

'There are a lot of people on the Street who think you were treated pretty badly. They say you were under orders to help the Prince grow up and people jumped to the wrong conclusion.'

'Wrong conclusion? Right conclusion? But orders were orders. Get your claws into the snotty bastard. Keep him on the straight and narrow as per Fountain orders. I didn't like it. Who would? Like rolling in a field of zits. But I was doing my duty, and precious little thanks I got for it, packed off to obscurity on a pension with a wife who told me she bent both ways until Mustapha showed her his flying carpet.'

Sammy clucked his tongue in simulated sympathy. 'I don't blame you for being angry,' he said. 'After all, the Prime Minister was in on the entire thing and you could really say this was an affair of State. You were doing what was necessary. Most people would reckon you got a lousy deal.'

'Don't talk to me about frigging Millward. He sits on top of the Palace, jerking us around. You can see Fountain jump to attention when he coughs. What you don't see is him fading into the scenery when things turn sour. Of course he bloody knew. It was his bloody idea. Fountain just posted the notices.'

'I'll get some more ice,' said Sammy eagerly. Twenty minutes later Baron was asleep in his chair, snoring helplessly. A column of ants marched over the table and along his arm, gathering on his heaving belly where the last of the Filfar had fallen. Enough was more than enough. 'Recorded Bellapais, October 7,' said Sammy into the recorder, and switched it off. A lemon had fallen from the tree near his car and lodged on the bonnet. He tossed it in the air for a second, then hurled it into the depths of the shrubbery.

'Strike one,' he said.

'I don't like it,' Millward said. 'She's behaving, and it isn't natural. She's plotting something.'

Leckie looked surprised. 'That's what I thought a few weeks ago, but I've changed my mind. She likes being useful. All the hospitals have made her feel wanted, and I think the reaction to the children is genuine enough. And not having Alex around is a blessing and a half. That was our biggest cock-up. If we'd stuck Belcher on her, at least he'd have kissed the babies and kept the home fires burning. Not much stimulation, I grant you, but a decent enough cove. Which reminds me, what news of our wandering Tsar?'

Millward scowled. 'Last sighted in Sarawak. The Malaysians owe us a favour or two. He's got the PM's yacht for the duration. Sabah, Penang, a week in Brunei shelling monkey nuts with the indigent Sultan. Our High Commission is doing its best. Whenever he's in port they toddle him down to the local computer emporium and let him wave a bit of Swindon software for the cameras, but it's so boring that even the Malaysian press aren't carrying pictures any longer. Somewhere between Java and Sumatra we'll just let him slink away for a few weeks and see whether anyone notices.'

'It's not an answer, Simon.'

'I know it's not a ruddy answer. But he's off the park while we look for one. And maybe you're right about Bess, maybe she has buckled down at last. Watch her like a hawk though, young Robin. She may have learned, but she may be getting ready to stir the pot again.'

'Yes, Prime Minister. Naturally, Prime Minister. But I still think you're too nervous. When she got beaten up she felt she'd got a hold over us at last, and perhaps she has. She needed to win one some time.'

Millward scowled again. Leckie smiled his most expansively sincere smile – the one the Lobby, at moments of high stress, had dubbed his Lockjaw Grin.

'He's raging inside, Edgar, and I can't seem to keep him calm. They promised me, he keeps saying; they promised me that if I did what they said and got married like a good boy and behaved like a King, then I could be King. But now she's still there and crowds cheer her and nothing happens and where am I? Where the hell am I? he keeps saying. And it's a good question, Eddie. We thought we had a deal, but now, every time I mention it, you just grunt and change the subject. She's getting more powerful day by day and she thinks she can treat me like dirt – but I'm her mother, her own bloody mother, and I won't be talked to like that. And what I also want to know is, where's Alex-androvich? He wouldn't have put up with her airs and graces, but he's gone and when I ask Travel when he's due back they just smile at me and say his trip is open-ended on present schedules. So he hit her, Eddie. So what? Most of the men I've known have hit me from time to time, but I never bore any grudges. You could hit me, Eddie, and I wouldn't say a word. Pas un mot. I just want to know what's going on now and why your lord in Downing Street doesn't have a thing to say for himself. When's Roman coming home? Nicky and I miss Roman terribly.'

He sat on the side of the bed and pulled a towel around him. In the mirror he could see the limp white flesh and the droop of his neck. Perhaps he could also see the anxiety in his eyes. She was there in the reflection, too. Naked, with a streak of scarlet on her shoulder where his nails had caught her, a tangle of sheet half tugged across her groin. The blonde hair was tousled and matted at the fringe. Her mouth turned down at the edges in an endless trickle of complaint. She exhausted him, and he knew more clearly than ever how she was using him. It had been one of her virtuoso performances this afternoon, a symphony of strokings and pummellings and boun-cings rising to the familiar climax as her body panted above him. But it had been the act again as usual, the familiar rousings to the call of duty. The eyes he saw in the mirror below the golden fringe were cold and scornful.

'Shut up, you stupid bitch,' he said. 'Alexandrovich isn't coming back. Nicky will have to bide his time, and so shall we all. Meanwhile, the marriage to Elena is going ahead as planned. Your damned daughter is playing her hand. We've no option but to keep on playing ours.'

There was the chug of an engine in the mews out-side and the bang of a door. Someone rang the bell. Cursing, Fountain pulled a bath towel around him and opened the window. 'Yes,' he said, leaning out.

'Berry Brothers and Rudd delivery, Sir. The three crates of Lanson you wanted delivered on Friday.'

'Oh honestly . . . Didn't they tell you I called on Monday to cancel?'

'No record of that here, Sir.'

'Well there is now. Just take it away.'

*

Sammy Wittman had been in St Petersburg for five days and the chill and the gloom of the place in late October was beginning to depress his spirits. It wasn't snowing yet. They said it didn't often snow. But the wind from the east, howling up the expanse of the Neva, branching voraciously down the maze of canals, was a savage enemy after the balm of Cyprus. He had Trigorin, hired from MTV research, and Trigorin had a couple of sidekicks who existed in the half world between the Mafya and the Government where stones, unofficially of course, had to be turned over and actions taken. Yet, at root, it was all down to Sammy. He'd had the tip from Emma. It was his last ten thousand dollars, the nest egg for the holiday he never took, which had hired this gang for the week. Only two more days and he'd have to call it quits. The book would go on and the Baron stuff – first hand, on the record, not wrapped up in the generalities of the anonymous notes Em kept passing over – was gold dust. He'd get the money back in the end. There would be more though, much more, if this other angle came up.

'We know her name was Sheliapin,' Trigorin said as they ate their scrambled eggs and drank their coffee in the basement of the Architect's Club, buried beyond the reach of the wind in a shell of oak panelling and stained gingham tablecloths. Why did they always meet here, underground, in this deserted place patrolled single-handed by the bored waiter with the itchy backside? 'Vera Sheliapin. There are seven V. Sheliapins known in St Petersburg, collating every information source. She is none of them. If she is married, then of course we have nothing. We do not know her name. My men have checked the registry. She did not marry here, but Russia is such chaos that she could have married elsewhere – perhaps Belarus, perhaps even Finland – and there would be nothing to show. So we have what you call a brick wall. We know that she is thirty-five or thirty-six, with blonde hair, and that she was one of the great stars of the State Circus. Madame Vera of the triple somersaults and the flashing eyes. But that was eight years ago, before she broke her back in Beijing and vanished from sight. None of her old friends have heard a word from her. She might be dead or in some hospital. It is only your sources, Mr Wittman, that tell us something different.'

Sammy sighed. 'Usually reliable sources,' he said. 'What do you suggest? I'm paying you by the day. Do I go home early and save my money?'

Trigorin scraped the last of the egg from the thick plate and spread it slowly across a slice of black bread. 'No, my friend, no. What is it you English say? If at first you don't succeed, ask for another girl? Today we plod the streets trying again. My boys will trawl the private clinics asking after women with problems in the backs. I shall call on the three V. Sheliapins we find listed. Sometimes when people change their names they do not do so very much, just enough to confuse the computer.'

'And me?' Sammy asked. 'What shall I do?'

'Keep warm in your hotel, my friend. You are ill with the cold, you shiver. Let those of us who are paid to look do the work we are paid for.'

But Sammy had not stayed long in the room with

382

the frayed carpet and the television snowing early for Christmas. The shouts of the cleaning maids, pushing their squealing trolleys, repelled sleep. He read his notes again and leafed listlessly through the circus programmes he'd gathered from the man with the tiny shop near Clapham Common.

If she could change her name a little, then perhaps she could change it a lot. He'd loaded the whole of the St Petersburg telephone directory on to his lap-top. Were there any other names, Circus names, he could try? Popov, the great clown? No, nothing with a 'V'. Durov, Zapashny, the families whose memories filled the programmes? No. He was bored when he came to the last name on his list. Golovko, Lena Golovko. Forty years before she'd been the slim blonde on the trapeze, one of the wonderful Flying Cranes. And her love life seemed to have flown too – from Vilen who pushed the trapeze and left her for another woman to Mikhail, the other man in the act who caught her, and married her. Golovko: that would be an alias with a touch of bite to it.

There were three V. Golovkos on his laptop screen. One specialized in computer graphics. One – out near the airport somewhere – didn't answer. But the third answered on the first ring.

'Vera Golovko?'

'Da.'

'Do you speak English?'

'A leetle, but it ees long time. Who are you?'

'I'm a journalist.' He paused and crossed his fingers. 'I'm writing a history feature about the State Circus. I thought you might be able to help me.'

'Oh yes,' said the voice from afar. 'I love the Circus. Those were my greatest days. What is it you want to know?'

'Just your address,' said Sammy, scrambling for a pencil. 'I can come straight round if you're free.'

The street, when he found it, was by the side of yet another canal a few blocks back from Nevsky Prospect. As he walked away from the main roads, the straggle of shops and pizza bars ran out and the buildings were bare and grey, with dingy tunnels of entrances opening into courtyards where feeble strands of grass plastered the earth in the middle like hair across some balding head. He found the right courtyard at last. There was a rusting motorbike, without wheels, on the edge of the grass. Four desultory chickens had pecked the grass clean. She lived two storeys up the open staircase behind a door with boards nailed over the bottom where somebody, no doubt filled with vodka, had tried to kick it in.

'Madame Golovko?'

She leaned on a thin silver stick and her body seemed bent a little forward. But it was still a strong body. The shoulders were muscular and square and the breasts high. Her hair was pulled back in a band so that her full face turned to him in the hallway. A striking face – a sweep of cheekbones, a full, mobile mouth. There were lines around the eyes and the pallor of fatigue touched her cheeks, but she was still beautiful. God, she must have been fantastic.

'I'm Sammy Wittman. We talked on the phone.'

'Come in.'

There was a small living room down the hall with a window looking out over the bare wall of the block next door. Two easy chairs covered in faded red velvet, a small settee with a Kazak rug thrown over it, a small oak table, a sideboard strewn with photographs in leather frames.

'You wanted to talk about the Circus in the old days? Of course I was only a very humble person, one of the assistants then, but I am happy to help you. I remember much.'

'Ah,' said Sammy carefully, closing his pad, 'there must be some mistake. I thought you were one of the great stars, Vera Sheliapin, the one they called the Empress of the trapeze. See, I have some pictures in my bag. Is that really somebody else? It might be your twin sister, Madame Golovko.'

She shrugged. 'So what of it? I live here quietly in peace, with my memories and my child. Who cares about trapezes now? I must hobble up the stairs and keep my – what is it you call it? – my privacy. If you want me to help you with your article, you must keep my secrets.'

'It isn't your secrets I'm interested in,' he said. 'It is the secrets of Roman Alexandrovich that concern me. You were lovers. Your daughter, maybe, is his daughter. You could, perhaps, use some money.' He looked out at the grey wall.

'I have money.' She levered herself to her feet and paced angrily. 'No, no money. If he knows I have talked to you he will cut off what I have, this flat, the food that feeds my child, and maybe his friends will come again, kicking at our door.'

'No one knows I am here,' Sammy said carefully. 'There are people with me, but they are elsewhere following other leads. You can be my source and I will protect your confidence. It is one of the things I believe in.' Why not? he thought. He'd only quote her direct if what she said would blow Alexandrovich out of the water. It would have to be a damned good story. Correction: it was a damned good story. 'And he doesn't seem to keep you very well, does he? He lives in a Palace with servants and tables filled with food. You are kept in this place and your face tells me you often go hungry.'

There was a rustle of clothes down the hall and a thin whimper of pain. 'Excuse me,' Vera Sheliapin said, 'it is my little Irina. She has another of her fevers. This place is so damp. I must change her sheets and give her the medicine.' She was ten minutes. When she returned, her shoulders seemed somehow straighter and there was a light in her eyes. 'Very well, Mr Wittman,' she said. 'What have I got to lose? Once he used to come many times to see us and to tell us he would look after us, but now we hear nothing from him. He is away, always away, in some place where we cannot go, and he leaves me nothing but memories. I will be your source for a thousand dollars. What is it that you wish this source to tell you about Yevgeny Roman Alexandrovich?'

'How you met. How you came to be lovers. How Irina happened.'

She threw her stick on the settee and laughed. 'The usual things happened, Mr Wittman. A meeting at a party when the Circus was in Moscow. Much drink.

Many nights. But we were more than just lovers, we were together, joined in vows.'

Sammy glanced down to make sure the tape was still running. 'You were married?'

'Not were married. Are married. We are discussing my husband.'

Elena, as had become her custom, called to see when Bess was free. No problem. Tea at four? She arrived in jeans and a shirt of sky-blue linen, clutching a bulging shopping bag. 'What else is there to do? In Spain, I am allowed to be useful, to have a career. But here I am merely the fiancée of Nicholas. I must stop with my aunt, for propriety, but the press allow me no peace. When I tried language school, they were always there at the door, embarrassing the other students. So somehow I must keep myself amused and organize for the wedding.'

'It should help you to have the time to get to know Nicky better,' Bess said, letting sympathy coat her irony.

'Yes, I suppose so.' She was a sad little bird, barely bothering to hide her broken wing. 'But he has other friends and he says he likes his solitude. We have all our lives to be together, I think.' Their wedding was set for March and nothing, not the sneers in the gossip columns, not the smirking tattle of cocktail parties, brought any delay. What was arranged must be done. Bess passed the Bourbon biscuits and, for a second, let her hand grip Elena's tiny fingers. They were curiously cold.

'Don't worry,' she said with as much meaning as

she could contrive. 'Things that are dark have a habit of getting brighter. I have a feeling that a lot will happen before you get near an altar.' And then she talked of private, silly things – memories of childhood, friends, the days with her father. Elena was a victim, walking head down to the scaffold. She needed all the warmth Bess could give her.

Sammy had to tell someone. He had the story of a lifetime and the clinching bits – the Baron testimony, the full dirt on Alexandrovich – were his alone. He needn't have followed the vague leads that flowed through Emma. He could have sat on his backside and let the notes she passed to him do the bulk of the work. He could have added the adjectives and pocketed the boodle and nobody would have raised an eyebrow. But that wasn't Supersleuth Wittman. He was made of sterner stuff. He'd deserve the awards that were heading his way. He was bursting to tell someone.

Emma? Not much of a kick there. Like feeding cough pastilles to Deep Throat. His publishers? They were a cog in the Runton machine. They would report his triumphs straight back to Bradshaw so that the rush into print would suddenly take hold before he'd written a story to be proud of. He needed a professional friend he could trust. Caroline, with her own publishing cool. Of course, Caroline.

She sat wide-eyed in the Criterion bar as he spilled out his victories.

'We haven't just got them on toast. We can hang the bastards out to dry. They must have known

Alexandrovich was married – or else they were bloody incompetent fools. And Sir Dickie was using his dick on a set menu, seducing the Duke of Clarence because that's what they wanted at the top. This isn't just another mound of Royal ordure. This is the works.'

She was thinking in overdrive. 'You're about to be seriously rich and seriously famous,' she said. 'This goes way beyond the routine stuff your contract will cover. Why don't you give me a copy and I'll let one of my lawyer mates hold it up to the light for you? There's no sense in selling yourself short when you've got so much more to sell.'

Buy a little time, she thought, keep it under wraps. And now let me get back to Bess. Sammy walked down Piccadilly whistling. Not only was she fantastic to look at – blonde and slim and delicate where Em was brown and tubby and galumphing – but she was such a razor intelligence too. Totally, absolutely, stupendously cool. A suitable object of desire for any . . . well, any crack investigator about to fall into a canyon of gold.

Since she had cried on his shoulder, Leckie had never touched Bess again. He longed to touch her, of course. He knew now, for a certainty, that pity and remorse weren't part of this equation. He loved her and sometimes, waking in the night, lying eyes open, brain racing, he dared to hope that she could love him. But there were bleak impossibilities to it all. He was Millward's agent (retired, turned). She was the Queen and, whatever else Alexandrovich was, he was still her husband. He had to be desperately careful. When he went to her room, he left the door ajar. When they walked together, he kept in plain sight. Their serious moments were in his office, covered by piles of diary dates and paperwork. That was where she told him what Sammy had found. He put his feet on the desk for a minute and laughed, then he opened the drinks cabinet behind the picture of Mrs Simpson he'd bought in a jumble sale ten years before and brought here as a defiant joke to make Fountain's eyebrows twitch.

'Champagne,' he said. 'I've a half bottle of Moët I nicked from the Paraguay State dinner in case we ever really had something to celebrate. This is our moment, Ma'am. Cheers.'

Chapter Twenty-One

Dear Daddy,
It's such a small word. Duty. You knew what it
means. You told me about it constantly. I have had
to try to learn what it means and to see it for
myself, as you would have me see it. Please, tell me
if you can, help me if there's a way: is duty merely
accepting a role and a way of life, or can it
sometimes mean not accepting anything at all?
Must doing my duty be a passive thing? Or can my
duty be active?

The years had their own punctuation marks for Bess.
The opening of Parliament, her birthdays real and
ceremonial, the garden parties and the flower shows.
They were there, in their appointed place, to signal
her world turning slowly through 365 days, another
year gone, and another, until her reign was done. But
the greatest punctuation mark of all, dismal in its
ceremony, heavy in its festivity, was Christmas at
Sandringham. This would be her sixth.

She motored there with only Fat Clemmy and a
policeman for company, across the frozen tundra of
West Norfolk covered in a frost so deep and a fog so

freezing that the bare fields were white with frost at three in the afternoon. She had a play centre in Sheringham to open and wide-eyed infants to hug for the cameras. The rest of the Family – Selene, Nicky, his bedraggled fiancée, some minor Gloucesters and junior Kents – would make their way direct. 'And this year,' she'd said in a spasm of unexpected gaiety, 'let's make it a sort of works outing. Are you free to join us, Sir Edgar? And perhaps Mr Montgomery and Mr Leckie, too? I'll even ask our chairman if you think that's right.'

The chairman, in his own flowing hand, on Number Ten notepaper, much regretted that he would have to decline Her Majesty's kind invitation. Too many children home for the holidays and his houseproud mouse of a wife too afraid to upset them. But perhaps he might drive up on Boxing Day afternoon and pay his respects and take a glass of mulled claret with the board? Would Mr Leckie be so kind as to arrange one of his photo-opportunities?

She stayed longer in Sheringham than she'd intended and night came early. The roads were unrelentingly icy and the winding trek along the coast route through Cley and Blakeney, their cottages of grey stone suddenly looming out of the fog, seemed to take for ever. At six the mobile phone in the front rang anxiously.

'It's the BBC, Ma'am', said Sergeant Coxridge. 'They can't wait beyond seven without authorizing triple time for the technicians.'

Damn! 'I'd forgotten all about it.' Every Christmas needed a Christmas message. This year, as in occasional years before, the BBC had opted for a change of venue. 'Our viewers always appreciate seeing you relaxed inside your own home, Your Majesty.' There was even a bit of pre-ordained business in which she'd hang silver bells on the Christmas tree. But the recording was this afternoon and, on current progress, they didn't stand a prayer of getting there. 'Let me speak to them,' she said. The voice at the other end was young and perplexingly matey. 'Hello, Bess, I'm sorry about this mess.'

'Sorry, who's this?'

'It's Adrian. Adrian Pryce. You know, from wherefore art you and all that stuff at Oxford. Didn't the men from Auntie tell you I was your duty director this year? And is it still all right to call you Bess?'

She laughed so loudly that Coxridge glanced round at her. 'No, they didn't. And yes, of course. But my timings are a terrible pig's ear in this weather. We're just crawling. Would it be OK tomorrow morning early? Before I go to church? We can feed the crew mince pies if that helps.' She chattered away about old times for five minutes and gave the phone back to Coxridge with a smile. 'Well, I think I've talked my way out of that. You don't need to rush. He says that now Australia and Canada and most of the rest don't take it any longer, we can be pretty flexible on timings.' It was eight before she crawled the final mile and found the Family assembled uneasily in the white of the Drawing Room, sipping sherry and shuffling restlessly beneath the Edward Hughes portrait of Queen Alexandra, tranquil in her airbrushed majesty.

*

'So for me, as perhaps for you, Christmas is the time for children. I've met so many children this year. All of them bright-eyed and looking out at a world which perhaps they don't understand but which they do see as full of hope and full of promise. They have an innocence which sustains them and from which I, too, draw sustenance. It tells me that beyond one generation there is always another, beyond one set of dreams there is always a new age of young people with the capacity to make dreams of their own. That is why Christmas means so much to me and to my family. It is the festival of continuity, but of renewal too. A time to look back and a time to look forward. God bless you at this special time, and a very happy Christmas to you all.'

Adrian panned slowly up from Bess, wriggling on one of the arms of the Sheraton sofa, and lingered for ten seconds on the chandelier of Dresden porcelain while the last of the credits rolled. 'Well,' he said, 'it wasn't exactly Shakespeare, but you did your best.'

'It's one thing I can't seem to shift. Every year the script arrives direct from Downing Street. I think Mr Millward writes it himself. Even Sarah Bernhardt would have had trouble with it. Gosh! I'm late. I must get to church.'

She was on her feet and heading for the door when the sound recordist uttered a dismal wail. 'There's just too much background at the end when she brushed against the tree and it set the bells ringing. I can't fade it because the mikes on her and on the tree were almost touching. We'll have to do it again.'

'Now it's my turn to grovel,' said Adrian. He was

394

wearing a Glastonbury T-shirt and cord jeans. He grinned ruefully.

'No,' Bess said. 'I've absolutely had it on time. If we can't fix it, we'll have to do it straight after lunch, live.'

'Fine. Let's build our own balcony and live dangerously again.' And he blew her a kiss.

'Eat first, work later,' she said. 'Join the party.'

She had set out to make it a rather grand occasion. The leaves on the mahogany table were pulled out to their fullest. Twenty-two at the trough. She'd decided to use the turquoise-and-gold Minton for a change. Nicky was always breaking the Mecklenburg-Strelitz and they were running short of side plates. She sat at the heart of the table, looking out towards the garden, and put Elena opposite. 'You get the best of the Spanish tapestries there.' She patted the chair on her left. 'Adrian, here. So we can chatter.' There were no place settings. Selene swept grandly to her right hand. Nicky followed, then doubled back as an afterthought to lower himself into the cell beside his fiancée. The Gloucesters and the Kents began ravenously consuming bread rolls. Leckie sat silently at an extremity below the Goya tapestry. The white glow from the lawns seemed to give the Braemar green of the room a fluorescence of its own. The revellers themselves were palest green and ethereal. Perhaps we need one more tapestry, she thought with a grin. Did Velázquez do a Last Supper?

'How's Caroline these days?'

'Blooming. She says she's got the blockbuster of all

time coming next spring. Very hush-hush and exciting. And on your old front? Julia?'

'Married to a stockbroker with two kids and a pile in Virginia Water, I'm afraid. A loss to the profession, but she's stopped drinking, so we can't complain.'

'And Tom?'

He winced and looked at her eyes glowing green with amusement.

'It's all right. I've learned that not everyone in life lets you down.'

'He's getting married too, I think. The widow of some filthy-rich semi-conductor chairman from Buffalo. Another loss to the profession.'

They pushed the food over in heated trolleys from the conference centre these days. It did not travel well. The turkey, already sliced, wore a thin patina of age, the potatoes dripped fat, the sprouts might have been cooked by the European Commission. She toyed with it for five minutes then pushed the plate away. Nicky was far into his second bottle of Margaux. The Gloucesters had finished the Puligny-Montrachet and were beginning to colour and simper. She hadn't touched a drop. 'Well,' she said, glancing at her watch and getting up suddenly, 'duty and my audience call. On air in thirty minutes.'

Adrian loosened the old World Wildlife tie he'd found in a cupboard. Selene complained about the champagne. 'A brute of a brut.' Bess and her director walked in to the Little Drawing Room and locked the door behind them. 'Better get on with the pud and the crackers,' Leckie said to Fountain, 'then we can all hit the port in the Saloon and watch the show.'

Fountain had indigestion. He looked sourly at Leckie and there was the merest puff of a belch as he stretched for a napkin.

'Hello, and my Christmas greetings to you all. This is the sixth of these broadcasts to you at this time. And today I want to do something very different. I want to explain why I think it will be the last.'

Fountain's hand began to shake abruptly, spattering the vintage Dow across the pearl grey of his waistcoat. He leaned towards Leckie, growling. 'What's she doing? What the hell's going on?'

'UDI,' said the Director of Corporate Affairs.

'When the King, the Queen, the Prince and the father that I loved were wiped out so tragically, I knew instinctively what I must do. I must take a throne I'd never expected or wanted. I must carry on. I didn't have many illusions about myself or the job. My father, in his wisdom, had made me see this Family and this role for what it was. But I knew he would have wanted me to try my best.

'Well, I did try. And I learned much more. I learned that a young girl with a Crown can never make the mistake of falling in love. That the pressures of the fame, the press, the life, can blow love away in an instant and leave only betrayal and sadness in their wake. That I was not allowed to be myself but, more difficult still, that I had become not a Queen but a political totem pole. Once upon a time, you may remember, my family was allowed to make its own mistakes – and we made plenty. We were supposed to be an example. We were hopeless at that. We couldn't adjust. We were chilly and heartless or wild and reckless. Then we were flaky. Sometimes, it seemed, we did little but drift from one bout of casual sex to another. It was what we did in our tight little circle, because there wasn't much else to do.'

The blood had drained from Fountain's face. 'She's gone mad. She's utterly mad.'

'You wouldn't stand for that, and you let us know clearly. We were required to clean up our act. But how was that possible? We were what we were. Ordinary extraordinary people. Not very bright, not very self-aware. So we called in the only people we could: the politicians with their polls and messages and image makers. We asked them to save us and, in their fashion, they tried – the only way that they could. They turned us into a corporation. They told those who were too chill and starchy to become relaxed and informal and to smile a lot as though in some supermarket queue. They took rebel spirits and made them conform in ways that drained the life from us. We were not allowed our own friends or own thoughts. We read their scripts. The script I was supposed to read today came straight from Downing Street. We took orders from their advisers, like lowly backbenchers in thrall to the whips. We had become figments of political imagination.'

Far away in Lichfield, Millward sat by the television, hunched and silent. 'Daddy, Daddy, can we open the rest of the presents now?'

'Bugger off.'

'We were not even allowed to marry the man or the woman of our choice. Not for three generations now. Our partners were provided for us – no, inflicted on us – to a pattern of other devising. In the twenty-first century, these were arranged marriages – arranged by our masters to keep us subservient and to please the focus groups that rule our existence.

'I want to talk frankly about my own marriage. It is over. You may not know that. The man who calls himself my husband, a man who betrayed me and beat me physically, is on another of the world tours the politicians invent for him when there is nothing else to do. But I know now that I was deceived into marrying him, manipulated like a magician's assistant. And I know much more. He was already married, with a wife and child. He is married to this day, to someone else. He is a bigamist. The bigamist of their choice and their providing.'

There was a shriek from the white armchair by the fireplace. Selene had fainted. Leckie took the winter roses from the Wedgwood urn by the television and emptied the water gently over her.

'Please, at this point, note that I have proof – full proof – of what I say. I'll make sure the press has the documentation the moment I finish. And I'm naturally sorry to give you all this heartache at such a time. But there is one final, unshakeable thing you should know. I've seen the institution we call the Monarchy on the inside for six years now. I know it to be a sham and a charade, because I've been there at the heart, part of the deception, the political pawn of no choice. And I think this country deserves better than that. The people I'm privileged to meet – the young, the children in need – are too good and too strong and too hopeful for this cynical pantomime. It is time that we all grew up. So today I'm not merely announcing my resolve to abdicate and lead a life where I can be useful again, where I can look myself in the mirror clear-eyed. I'm announcing what I hope will be the end of the throne. For you see, there is no easy succession. My brother, my heir, the Duke of Clarence, agrees with me. He does not want to be King. And my mother agrees, too. They will tell you so themselves soon. The Family is resigning. We're over. Please let us go and find a new and a better way to serve you. Please let us go so that we can all move on.

'Thank you so much for listening. And may next Christmas be a joyous one for us all.'

There was a hammering on the drawing-room door. 'Fabulous,' said Adrian. 'I've never seen you so good. And the script, amazing.'

'I wrote it myself,' she said, and turned the key of the door into the Saloon.

Robin Leckie had been sitting on the arm of a chair by the fireplace. A non-combatant, an observer of human nature falling apart. But now he was on his feet in the middle of the room. 'Ladies and gentlemen . . .' He clapped his hands. Crisp, resounding blows. 'I think Bess . . . I think that the Queen will want to talk to her immediate family and business colleagues first. Would the rest of you wait next door please?' The simperers and the snorters, the also-rans, filed slowly away.

And then she was there, framed in the central arch, still a girl, still loose and lithe, in a blue smock of a dress. She reached behind her head and pulled out the clip that had bound her hair back. It fell forward and she ran her fingers through it. 'Well,' she said softly, 'thank you for listening. Now I hope you will learn your lines too.'

Nicky rose to meet her. His face was brick red and he spluttered obscenities. 'So you're finally going, my stupid little sister. So, great. But don't suppose that I'm just going to walk away with you. I shall be what I always ought to have been. King.'

She stepped by him and into the centre of the carpet. 'I imagine you're all thinking much the same thing,' she said. 'But let me, with my able assistant, review the situation more carefully.'

Leckie pulled a tiny tape recorder from his pocket and laid it on the mantelpiece beside the Swiss bracket clock.

'Let's hear from our old friend, Sir Richard Baron.'

The slurred voice was loud. It seemed to echo from the minstrels' gallery. It told of orders from on high, of seduction and control. There was a deathly silence.

'And now, perhaps, from the first and only Mrs Alexandrovich.'

Leckie loved the bit where Vera's voice ceased to quaver and flared into vehemence. 'Not were married. Are married. We are discussing my husband.'

Fountain was interrogating his brogues. Montgomery's mouth had not closed for ten minutes. Selene gripped Nicky's hand. Elena sat alone in the corner between the Gilis D. Brier tapestries, a handkerchief twisted to rope between her fingers.

'Consider, then,' said Bess. 'This is just the beginning of the evidence. I can, and will, cite much more if it's needed. You asked me a few weeks ago why you saw so little of your fiancée, Elena. Perhaps we should call in my brother's new footman, Forster, and ask him about Tuesdays and Thursdays at Clarence House.'

The brick red had turned to a phosphorescent yellow. Selene put her arms around him. Elena raised her eyes and spat once, viciously, into the log basket.

'Then there is you and my darling mother, Sir Edgar. My friend Mr Leckie knew about you two, because I told him. I told him what Nicky said. But he wished for proof and he needed pictures.' She tossed them on the carpet in front of him. He saw himself, white breasts pendulous, towel held to waist, leaning out of his mews window. He saw Selene replenishing her lipstick on his front doorstep. He saw her blowing a kiss. 'Date stamped and timed in sequence,' she said. 'Perhaps you should have taken the champagne after all.

'And as for you, mother, dear sweet mother. Did you tell darling Eddie you were making love with Alexandrovich before, during and after, too? Not so much a bedroom. More a railway station.' For once Selene did not squeak. Fountain looked at her and buried his head in his hands.

'So you see, you all have something to lose. Something you can never live down, never recover from. Good news. Robin and I have a proposition for you.'

There was the merest shuffle at her back and she caught the look in Leckie's eyes. 'Ah, welcome Lady Margaret,' she said, spinning on her heel. 'Join the party. I assume you've been on the phone to your old friend Mr Davidson. The intelligence king who pushed me downstairs, but pushed, I'm afraid, rather too hard. No, I didn't see him. But Forster did and I think we can rely on his testifying. Shall we need to, though, I wonder? It was Davidson who found Alexandrovich for Mr Millward, wasn't it? It was Davidson who ran the checks and believed his lies. Intelligence? Just another bungle from the home of awful bungles. They thought I was the enemy. There's been nothing so stupid since the Mr Burgess and Mr Maclean your lot are always going on about. I assume the Prime Minister will soon be asking a few questions of his own.'

Swayne's face closed in a trap.

'So. It's Christmas. Let us talk turkey. Alexandrovich is the named villain of this piece. He can't hide; he can only run. And we all need a villain. You, brother; you, mother . . . do what I said you'd do. Sign the statement Robin has ready. It says you agree with me, that there's no question for you of this farce going any further. Then we'll find you a nice pension, enough to buy two love nests for whoever you want in decent obscurity. And as for you, Sir Edgar, and the silent Mr Montgomery, it can be business almost as usual. I won't denounce you. I'll leave Mr Millward to take the heat and find his own scapegoats. As far as I'm concerned, you can run Enterprise Monarchy just as before – without the bother and expense of running an actual Monarch. Heritage Inc. Extra bonuses all round. I bet half the drawing room would bite your hand off for bit parts if you fed them enough loot.'

'I must take instructions,' said Fountain in an aching monotone.

'Just so. I think I'll let Mr Leckie talk to his old chum first and then, by all means, get your orders. But don't take more than thirty minutes. I wouldn't want to keep the press waiting longer than that. They're dangerous when hungry. They might eat any other scraps I feed them.'

She smiled one last time, and was gone.

Chapter Twenty-Two

_____

'You twisting little shit . . .'

'Maybe, Simon, but I said you were going too far.'

'Never to harm her, though. I always believed I was acting in her own best interests – and the country's. One more disaster and they'd have been done for.'

'Very well. Let's not argue every toss. The question is what you're going to do next.'

'I'm coming to Sandringham anyway to see her. I'll begin to make my judgements then.'

'Simon, that isn't good enough. You can play the concerned statesman if you like – but what about Selene and Nicky? Either they sign up now or I take the rest of the dossier to the hacks. We told them half an hour. That was twenty-nine minutes ago.'

'It is up to the Duke and the Duchess. I'm not their keeper. But I should quite understand if, on reflection, they found it convenient to fall in with your wishes. I could not possibly seek to change their minds.'

'Great. I'll put Fountain straight on. And Simon . . . Happy Christmas.'

Bess was waiting in the corridor, walking distractedly between the polished pistols in their cases and the silver racehorses frozen in time a century after their last stakes were run. 'Well?'

'He's cut them adrift. He's letting them sign. No, he's telling them to sign in his own convoluted way. We've won. Won, won, won. And you were terrific.'

'I just played the part as prescribed. Maximum surprise, maximum certainty, minimum time to wriggle off the hook. I couldn't have done it without you, Mr Leckie.'

She extended her left palm towards him. Half acknowledgement, half surrender. His right palm came flat against it for a second and their fingers touched.

'Just one more play,' he said, 'and then we can start to celebrate.'

Sammy Wittman lay naked on the bed examining the ceiling of her flat. It was stained and old with flaking plaster motifs of Cupid at the four corners. The head of the one to his right was missing. Caroline untangled herself from the chaos of sheets and leaned across him, her small, sharp breasts rubbing themselves slowly across his chest.

'You're a hero,' she said. 'You had your chance to be part of history and you helped us make history instead. Greater love hath no man than he will give away his own story to help a damsel in distress.' Her short bob of hair glinted gold, framed in the light of the bedside lamp. Her grey eyes were luminous.

'I've still got a hell of a book,' he said. 'The misery, the last Tsar, my part in his downfall. Perhaps, a few years on, I'll be able to do the rest. So I'm a bloody idiot? I know. But you asked me nicely.'

He could hear his own words echoing as he uttered them. They seemed to come from somewhere outside his body, to belong to a Sammy he did not know and had never met till this moment. Caroline, too, felt herself drift beyond reality. She had been desperate when she'd talked to Leckie. 'For God's sake,' he'd said, 'this is the jackpot. Seduce him, appeal to his better nature, anything, but get him onside with the stuff.' She had done both and found, to her intense amazement, that he did have a better nature – as well as all the normal animal instincts.

'You mean we had this story in our hands and you let it get away?' Lord Runton was often bad-tempered. Today he was Vesuvius.

Even Bradshaw quailed. 'I don't know that for a fact,' he said. 'Young Wittman has just dropped off the end of the earth. But his brother and I are hopping.'

'I suggest', said his Lordship, 'that that may be the best for both of you. Hop off. And don't think of hopping back.'

Millward had driven straight back to Downing Street. How could he open presents and repair the usual pile of digital crap the kids would break in fifteen minutes when he needed to be alone to think?

'But you can't go . . . it's Christmas,' his wife had wailed.

'Crisis at bloody Christmas,' he said, slamming the door behind him.

The holding statement was fine in the circumstances. Custodians of the national interest needed time and gravitas. The fact that the Royal Family seemed to have abdicated *en masse* needed due deliberation, or at least the appearance of it. The Cabinet appeared to have gone drunk or AWOL. Simcox – poor, wet, windy Toby – was a lettuce leaf in a plague of rabbits. 'I can't hold them, Sir. The Lobby are demanding a meeting. But I've nothing to meet them with.'

'What's new? Play them Land of Hope and Glory and give them a drink.'

It was seven when Colonel Baxter called. Urgent, imperative, breathing portent and Pomeroy. 'I thought you should know, Prime Minister, that I have spent the last three hours consulting my Traditional Liberal colleagues in detail as well as making contact with both wings of the Conservative Party. And we have joined in common cause. The Monarchy isn't some optional extra of our British heritage, Mr Millward. It is the binding definition of our nationhood – a gift too precious to be thrown away on the whim of a girl, or of her inadequate brother. There are others in the line of succession. We jointly insist that you ask them individually, in order, whether they are prepared to serve. There must be continuity and you, Sir, must not bow to this emotional blackmail. For if you do, and I must warn you solemnly, we shall not serve under your leadership again.'

'Thank you, Colonel,' Millward said, the voice swelling into orotundity with every passing word. 'That's the most useful advice I've had all day. Thank you so much, and goodnight.'

Simcox could not vouch for the first polling figures when they arrived at five to midnight. 'Most of the telephones were engaged and none of the focus groups seemed particularly focused.'

'Never mind, Toby. Sometimes, I find, principle has to come first.'

'Your Majesty . . . if I may still call you that?'

She looked at Millward bemusedly. Leckie lounged on the arm of the drawing-room sofa, his head cocked to one side.

'I think my friend, Robin, will have told you of my deep concern and regret over this chapter of unfortunate incidents and misunderstandings. There are things I shall regret till my dying day – not because I was wrong but because over-zealous employees clearly went too far. I thought I would just say that briefly, and sincerely, before I go outside and read a prepared statement of my own to the press.'

'What statement?' said Bess.

'Wait,' said Leckie. 'I think we can all wait a few minutes to find out.'

There was still a thin crust of snow on the lawns and icicles hung from the urns which flanked the steps from the terrace. The press were chill and miserable – and hungry for the word.

'Gentlemen, ladies. Forgive me for detaining you. I have a few words to read, and I regret that I will take no questions.' Regret? The *Mail* and the *Mirror* were swapping hip flasks. 'As I am obliged to, I have followed the Royal decisions of the last twenty-four hours with care and with natural perturbation. Some of the things the Queen revealed in her broadcast yesterday are profoundly troubling. I have, this morning, asked Lord Justice Harcourt of the Court of Appeal to inquire into the conduct of our security services in the positive vetting of Prince Roman Alexandrovich. Those who are found to have lapsed in conduct and in the punctilious execution of their roles can expect no quarter from him, I am sure. Equally, I shall be asking Sir Edgar Fountain, the relevant Chief Executive, to conduct his own inquiry into the way that junior members of his staff may have treated Her Majesty and her immediate family. These are heavy matters and I believe Sir Edgar will give them due weight.

'But, ladies and gentlemen, such urgent steps do not address the nub of the decision I must take on behalf of all our people. The Queen, a young woman of beauty, intelligence and compassion, another true Queen of Hearts, has made her own decision. She carries her family with her. I have resolved that it is right to respect that decision. The hallowed roots of the Labour Party from which I come, whose blood still flows in my veins, have always been republican, as you may realize. As the elected leader of our country, a leader for all, I naturally tried to put aside such instincts. It was not for me to disinter them for reasons of narrow ideology. But now, my friends, they are disinterred. Now, in clear conscience, I can follow the dictates of my inner voices. I do not resist Her Majesty's decision, I endorse it; and I shall summon every sinew of my being to pass it through the Houses of Parliament and, if needs be, through the ultimate test of a general election.'

It seemed, momentarily, that it was over. And then he lifted the text again. 'One final thing. If we are to make this transition, after so many centuries, we shall need a first elected President who commands our respect, trust and love, a person of conviction beyond Party and wisdom beyond years. It is my intention, gentlemen, to ask the Queen herself to fulfil that role. It is the British way to manage our great transition. I hope, on consideration, that you will agree with me that it is also the only way.'

The man from the *Mail* had dropped his hip flask. It rolled down the slope of the lawn spilling Martell V S O P on the snow, and when he looked at it, it had seemed to form a giant question mark.

'You didn't tell me.'

He had found her at last, alone in the Ballroom, standing square beneath the marble bust of Victoria with its bulbous cheeks and grimace of irritation. She was angry, the green eyes blazing.

'I couldn't tell whether he'd bite. I only mentioned it as a thought. If I'd asked you, you'd have said no. But it's the clincher, Bess. The Monarchy in Britain comes back and back whatever you throw at it. Mad Kings, serial fornicators, abdicators? They roll with the punch and put on a new face. What was sour is suddenly smiling, what was casual gets covered in pomp. And there are always people – the people out there, the little grey ladies waving their flags; the newspaper editors who need something to write about

– who'll resurrect it given a tenth of a chance. No, my love, we had to drive a stake through its heart. It was the only way. Walk out and take the rest with you, get the PM lined up – then succeed yourself while the ferment dies. The box is locked shut and you've thrown away the key. The only way it was ever going to happen.'

She let her right arm, swinging loose, brush against his hand, and then seize it tightly.

'What's wrong?'

'Nothing,' she said, 'there's nothing more to say. Can I have this dance?'

There was the old pump-action gramophone on the side, as presented by the King of Swaziland to George V, and a stack of ancient records in their yellowed paper covers. She found some Strauss at the third attempt. He cranked the handle. Gold and silver, gold and silver . . . He took her tight by the waist, pressed her against him, and swept her away.

Afterthoughts

Robin James Leckie and Elizabeth Margaret Windsor were married in a quiet, private ceremony at Marylebone Registry Office. The Archbishop of Canterbury was not invited. The new Mrs Leckie left immediately after the ceremony for a presidential visit to Germany. The couple hope to take a honeymoon when circumstances permit.

The Right Honorable Simon Millward, four times elected Prime Minister of Great Britain, is to join the board of the Hong Kong and Shanghai Bank as non-executive chairman. Mr Millward already holds seventeen other non-executive positions on City boards. His autobiography, *The Diadem of Democracy*, has been published in 122 languages. Mr Millward is the current Chichele Lecturer in Applied Ethics and Modern Morality at the University of Oxford.

Sammy and Caroline Wittman invite you to a launch party for their new publishing house, the Pixie Press, at the Old Ship, St Ives. Please bring a bottle.

Emma Lacey met Rodney Chetwode-Belcher at the Leckie marriage ceremony. They took a drink or two together afterwards and then some surprising substances the Captain had brought back from Bahrain. They are expecting to marry quietly some time next spring.

Ben Bradshaw presents the morning show on Talk Radio, writes a regular political column for the *Yorkshire Evening Post*, and occasionally appears in Test Match coverage describing the prospective state of the pitch. 'Flat, dead and bluudy rubbish.'

Angus Davidson is a village postmaster in Knowstone, North Devon. The Post Office intend to declare him redundant next year.

Nicholas Windsor, the Duke of Clarence, spends much of his time with friends in his villa on the island of Kowpat Flong, Southern Thailand. His mother, Selene, has married again, to Count Oskar Liebernitz, a Palm Beach couturier and hotel owner. Her own memoirs, *The Quest for Contentment*, are to be filmed next year as a TV mini-series. Her column in the *Palm Beach Courier* is syndicated to 2,124 papers around the world and she was voted America's Most Loved Talkshow Guest at last year's Emmy awards. When her Count is away, she is sometimes visited by a bearded painter and artist from Arizona who has been heard to swear fluently in Russian.

Sir Edgar Fountain has retired to Northampton where

he will shortly take up a part-time appointment as auditor general of the Althorp Trust.

On completion of her term of office, President Elizabeth Leckie will join the United Nations as senior promotions manager for Unicef, the children's fund. Her husband, Mr Robin Leckie, is already executive director of the World Children Rescue special appeal.

And Even More After . . .

He was away in Geneva for more meetings and her weekend was suddenly free. The Sudan delegation had missed their plane. 'Take a couple of days off,' she told Anna, the apple-cheeked Swedish nanny. 'It's a chance for Tom and me to spend a little enhanced time together.' Thomas, the boy who might have been King, was nearly three, with a mass of golden curls and a mind of his own.

'It's a lovely day, darling,' she said. 'Let's go out.' Crisis, of course. 'Want to play pooter, need to play pooter.' She sighed and switched off the computer and bundled him, squealing, into the back of the car. 'Whether you like it or not, you're going out to enjoy yourself.' She had no plans, but suddenly – as though on auto-pilot – found herself turning down the M4. 'I know, we'll go to Windsor, where Mummy used to live, and you can go round a real castle.'

'Want pooter.'

She was wearing the old red jacket from M&S she used for shopping and a headscarf. She put on her sunglasses and plonked Tom, still yowling, in his pushchair. They joined the long queue of tourists winding slowly up the hill.

'How much is it?' she said at the desk.

'Can't you read? Twenty euros – and five for the child if he's under three. But the pushchair is two euros extra.'

They wandered through the crowds, and she believed that at last she was invisible. She could be nobody again. St George's Chapel was being cleared for some service or other and she melted behind the far pillar at the back until silence came. Even Tom lay in his chair, eyes finally closing. She knew what she had come for: to do, one last time, the thing she remembered most from her own childhood. There, just out of the shadows, lay George V and his Mary together, joined for ever in death and cold, white marble. She licked her index finger and placed it, as before, on the bridge of Queen Mary's nose, trailing it up to the forehead, then flattening her hand across the brow and feeling the chill of stone.

'Goodbye,' she said gently. 'Goodbye to all that. You did your duty, and I hope I did mine.'